Gabrielle Kimm teaches English at secondary school level. She is the author of one previous novel, *His Last Duchess*.

Also by Gabrielle Kimm

His Last Duchess

The Courtesan's Lover

GABRIELLE KIMM

sphere

SPHERE

First published in Great Britain as a paperback original in 2011 by Sphere

Copyright © Gabrielle Kimm 2011

The moral right of the author has been asserted.

A CIP catalogue record for this book
is available from the British Library.

ISBN 978-0-7515-4455-8

Typeset in Fournier by M Rules
Printed and bound in Great Britain by
Clays Ltd, St Ives plc

Papers used by Sphere are from well-managed forests
and other responsible sources.

MIX
Paper from
responsible sources
FSC® C104740

Sphere
An imprint of
Little, Brown Book Group
100 Victoria Embankment
London EC4Y 0DY

An Hachette UK Company
www.hachette.co.uk

www.littlebrown.co.uk

For Cathy Mosely
and
for Sahra Gott

Troppo infelice cosa e troppa contrario al senso umano è l'obligar il corpo e l'industria di una tal servità che rischio d'esser dispogliata, d'esser rubbata, d'esser uccisa, ch'un solo un di ti toglie quanto con molti in molto tempo hai acquistato, con tant'altri pericoli d'ingiuria e d'infermita contagioso e spaventose: mangiar con l'altri bocca, dormir con gli occhi altrui, muoversi secondo l'altrui desiderio, correndo in manifesto naufragio sempre delle facoltà e della vita: qual maggiore miseria? Quai richezze, quai commodità, quai delizie posson acquistar un tanto peso? Credete a me – tra tutte le scigure mundane questa è l'estrema: ma poi, se s'aggiungeranno ai rispetti del mondo quai dell' anima, che perdizioni e che certezza di dannazioni è questa?

It is too miserable, and contrary to human reason, to force your body and energy into such slavery: terrifying even to think about. To expose yourself as prey to so many men, with the constant risk of being despoiled, robbed or killed; with the chance that one man, one day, may take from you everything you have acquired with many, over a long time; to say nothing of the other dangers – of insult and contagious, frightful disease. To eat with another's mouth, to sleep with another's eyes, to move according to another's will, endlessly rushing towards the inevitable shipwreck of your abilities and life: what greater misery can there be? Believe me, of all the world's misfortunes, this is the worst, and then, if you consider the needs of the soul as well as those of the world, what perdition and certainty of damnation is this?

VERONICA FRANCO – *Venetian courtesan (1546–1591)*

She would go to Napoli, she thought as she crossed an empty, cobbled piazza. That would be far enough away from Ferrara.

His Last Duchess

Napoli
1564

One

The dress I'm going to wear to meet my new Spanish patron has just been delivered – and it is simply gorgeous. I hold the skirts up against me and gaze at myself in the glass. It's truly one of Bianca's best. She chose the brocade for me – crimson and gold, straight in from Venice, she said, and she has given the dress the most glorious deep-red underskirt. At least nine yards of fabric in each piece, apparently. It feels thick and heavy and smooth and sumptuous, and it smells of warm spices.

I think I'm looking forward to this evening.

Crossing to my chamber door in my shift, with the skirts bundled in my arms, I call down to my manservant. 'Modesto, can you come up and help me put all this on? Cristo said he'd be here before the Angelus strikes, to take me to meet this . . . what's his name? Vasquez.'

His voice sounds from the kitchen. 'I'm just preparing your lime.'

I had almost forgotten. 'Thank you, *caro*. I'll come down and get it,' I call back. I lay the heavy skirts carefully across my bed.

Standing at the big table in the kitchen, Modesto has a knife in one hand and a lime in the other. I watch as he inserts the point of the knife just under its skin, about a third of the way down. He scores right around the fruit, then slicing through the rest of the flesh, he separates the two sections. He squeezes most of the juice from the smaller half into a bowl, and finally flicks out a couple of stray pips with the tip of the knife. 'There you are, Signora,' he says, handing me the little cup he has made and sucking the lime juice from his fingers. 'That should do. Go and put that in.'

I run back upstairs to my bedchamber, pull my shift up and out of the way, and, with practised ease, tuck the lime-skin up inside my body. Modesto seems to know just the most comfortable shape to cut it – I can hardly feel that it's there.

I hear his footsteps on the stairs, and then he knocks at my chamber door. 'You done, Signora?' he says from outside.

'I am,' I say, shaking my shift back down over my legs again. 'You can come in. It's all done. Everything in place. No unwanted offspring. Hopefully.' I smile at him. 'Thank you, *caro*.'

'Come on then, let's get you ready, Signora. Bum first,' he says, picking up a crescent-shaped, stuffed linen roll. I obediently put my arms up and, standing so close in front of me that I can feel his breath on my cheek, Modesto reaches around my waist and lays the roll in place on my hips, shifting it so that it sits where it should, projecting out behind to give me a suitably voluptuous arse. He ties the ribbons neatly in front.

Over my head, then, go the underskirt and the beautiful brocade overskirt, trailing on the ground round my feet and looking exquisite. I reach for my bodice, and hand it to him. 'Can you lace me in?'

'Turn around then, Signora,' he says, 'and arms up again.'

The bodice is already loose-laced and the sleeves have been attached. Modesto lifts it up over my arms and head and pulls it down. I wriggle it into place, putting my fingers down inside the top edge to shift my breasts into a more comfortable position. I want them sitting up as high as possible for this dress – and for this occasion. Modesto pulls the laces in tightly and fastens them in a secure bow. My chemise has crumpled inside all the boning – the lawn is so fine that that happens easily – and the folds feel irritating. 'Can you pull my shift down for me, *caro*?' I ask him. 'It's all rucked up.' He obliges, crouching down in front of me, lifting my hem and reaching up into the impossible folds of the skirts, searching for and finding the bottom edge of my chemise. His fingers brush against my thighs. He tugs gently downwards and I can feel the rucks unfolding.

I straighten the V-shaped front of the stomacher and pat it flat, and we are almost there.

Looking down at my chest, and then across at my reflection in my huge glass, I bite down a smile. I asked Bianca to cut this one low – and she has taken me at my word. The neckline is wide – out to the points of my shoulders on each side – it's been cut deep and she has lace trimmed it. In fact it's only the lace that is covering my nipples. They are virtually on display. I let out a soft breath and touch them with the tips of my fingers.

'He should be suitably impressed, Signora,' says Modesto, smirking slightly.

'Is it too much, do you think, *caro*?'

'Absolutely not – you look wonderful.' He pauses. 'Let's do your hair.'

Between us we concoct a web of complicated braids, leaving a fair amount of hair down, and then I wind a string of red Murano glass beads through the web. Garnet ear-drops and a heavy gold ring on my little finger, and I think my preparations are complete.

'Stand back, then, and let's see,' Modesto says.

I stand back and preen, as Modesto frowns in appraisal, his thumbnail caught between his teeth. He stares for a full minute, as I turn this way and that, pushing my chest out and arching my back, arms held out sideways like a dancer, so that he can have a full and uninterrupted view of the package I intend to present to my new patron in an hour or so's time.

Finally, he draws in a long breath and says gravely, 'Well, if this doesn't impress him, he's either blind or stupid, or would rather be fiddling with some grubby little *bardassa*'s ill-fitting codpiece.' He smiles at me and his black eyes crinkle. 'You look like a queen, Signora. Go and sit down in your chair and keep yourself clean, and I'll fetch you some grapes.'

'Thank you.' A thought occurs to me as Modesto turns to leave the room. '*Caro*, could you run round to the other house after we've gone, and let Ilaria and the twins know that I won't be back till the morning? I believe they think I'm coming home tonight.'

He nods a brusque assent.

I'm so glad I didn't know about limes before I had the girls. I don't know what I would do without them.

I have a cloth over my lap as I eat my grapes, and Modesto has given me a bowl into which I have been told to spit the pips. Cristoforo – the Conte di Benevento, *Capitano di Cavallo* in the King's Regiment – is a little late, and while I am waiting, I am entertaining myself by holding the bowl out at arm's length and trying to spit my pips from increasing distances to test the accuracy of my aim. Cristoforo knocks and enters my chamber just as I am leaning forward and holding the bowl out at full stretch. I have just let fly with one of my pips, and it has just plipped into the bowl, when his face appears around the door. My smile of satisfaction vanishes at his obvious amusement.

'So, this is what the more eminent courtesans do when they're alone, is it?' he says, grinning.

'Don't make fun of me!'

6

'I wouldn't dare!'

I pretend to scowl. 'I was bored and you were late.'

Cristoforo bows low in apology and I stand up, letting my cloth drop to the floor. His gaze rakes me from head to foot and, much to my satisfaction, it is clear that he approves of what he sees. 'You look particularly lovely, if you will allow me to say so,' he says. 'My Spanish friend is going to be . . . *overwhelmed*, I think.'

'And shall you be jealous of his spending time in my company while you're away, readying yourself for battle, Cristo?' I say, looking at him. Stocky, crop-haired, heavily muscled, he is struggling to keep his face straight.

'Of course. I shall be devastated – how could I not be?' He puts on a stricken expression, but beneath this, the smile he seems unable to prevent is open and happy, and I don't believe him for a moment: I doubt he'll pine for me when he is away. I understand that he will be preoccupied – of course he will, he's an important soldier – and I know that he is introducing me to this man, Vasquez, out of concern for my well-being while he's away, but his lack of involvement feels almost insulting. He has, after all, been one of my most regular patrons since I first arrived in Napoli.

'So, are you ready, *cara*? Shall we go?' he says.

I nod, and together we go down to my front door. Modesto watches us leave the house.

Despite the fact that Vasquez's apartment is well within walking distance, Cristo has come to collect me in a little covered carriage. Inside, it's very small and smells of warm leather, and my skirts fill the space between the two red velvet bench seats; they billow up in front of me, puffing up much higher than my knees. No floor space can be seen at all, and when Cristo climbs in from the other side and sits down on the seat opposite, he has to push the brocade out of the way to make room for his legs. He taps the roof of the carriage with the hilt of his sword and, with a rumbling lurch and a scrunch of pebbles, we are off.

'Now, listen again,' he says. 'I want to make sure you remember exactly what's going to happen. This needs to go well.'

Feeling a little frisson of excitement – I've always enjoyed the moment of introduction to a new patron – I lean forwards to hear what he has to say.

'*Maestre* Vasquez can't wait to meet you,' Cristo says. 'He's had a meal prepared for the two of you, I believe, so I hope you have an appetite. His is prodigious.'

'I haven't eaten anything other than a small bunch of grapes since this morning.' I'm starving, if the truth be told.

'Modesto and I have sorted out the financial side of the affair—'

'Yes, he told me.'

'And you'll be pleased to hear that your new friend will be paying handsomely! More than I do, at any rate. So you'll be financially secure while I'm away, at least. All you have to worry about now is looking beautiful and doing what you do best.'

I smile at him, pleased at his confidence in me. But I am still a little hurt that he seems so happy to be handing me over to another man.

'When we arrive, I'll leave you in the care of *Maestre* Vasquez's servants, who will help you set up the surprise. They've been paid well to keep the details from their master and they'll make sure everything runs smoothly.'

And Cristo runs through the exact details of what I am to do, one more time.

Cristoforo raises a hand in a final farewell salute as the door closes, leaving me inside with the *Maestre*'s servants. This is not the front door to the big house in the Via dei Tribunali, but an unimpressive side door that we only reached by stumbling down a cobbled alley-way so narrow that I had to hold my skirts bundled up in front of me, to stop them brushing against the walls and getting stained.

Inside, even in these servants' quarters, this house is opulent. Cristo was right – my new patron is clearly wealthy. The three young men who are to prepare the 'surprise' hustle me down a long covered walkway, one behind me, one on either side, press-ing in close, moving fast. They are dressed in old-fashioned, stiff black fustian doublets with starched ruffs, and they all seem intrigued and excited by their task. They are grinning, and chat-tering to each other in Spanish. All three keep glancing around them. It feels clandestine and furtive. I smother a laugh.

'Quick, this way, Señora!' the tallest of the three whispers, in heavily accented Italian this time, pointing to an iron-studded door to our right. He reaches out in front of me and opens the door, whereupon, feeling these men's hands on my shoulders and in the small of my back, I am shuffled through and out of sight. The men close and latch the door, then whistle out their relief at having suc-ceeded in their covert operation so far.

Just inside this door is a spiral staircase – wooden, narrow, winding up and out of sight. My new friends urge me to begin climbing and, with one man in front and two behind, I have little choice in the matter. We soon reach another door, which proves to lead into a beautiful upstairs room: huge and bright, with four great floor-to-ceiling windows, through which the evening sun is blazing in thick, downward-sloping diagonal shafts of yellow light.

At the far end of the room, a table has been laid for two; it is positively glittering with glass and silver and I can see a spray of some brightly coloured flowers in a bowl in the middle. Several dishes, covered by gleaming silver domes, have been placed on a nearby *credenza*.

I wonder what we shall be eating.

Between each of the windows, facing into the room, stands an ornately carved, cross-framed chair, upholstered in gold-coloured silk. And at this end of the room, just near where we are standing, fiercely lit by the sun, is an enormous *lettiera* – a monumental bed. The carving on this great monster matches that of the chairs, and the hangings are of the same silk. It is as though the bed has been swathed in sunshine.

One of the three servants darts forward now and draws back the bed-hangings. The bed within is made up, with the sheets neatly folded back on one side, away from one of several plump pillows. The latent sense of invitation is irresistible.

I feel my hand being taken – the tallest of the servants, who seems to be the only Italian speaker, is pulling me towards the bed, saying, 'Señora, my master arrive very soon. But he not expecting you for another hour. We must get you ready for surprise him.'

I nod. The servant pulls from a pocket in his breeches a roll of a deep red satin ribbon – as wide across as the span of my spread hand. This he flicks out to lie widthways across the bed. Then, from under the bed, he drags a bolt of fabric; pulling the whole length of it off its roll by the armful, he flaps it all out, like shaking out a freshly laundered sheet, across the bed on top of the ribbon. This fabric is sheer and golden – almost transparent – and it shimmers in the low light from the window. It's absolutely beautiful. It is far wider than the bed, though – I watch as the servant leans across and carefully doubles it over, making it two thicknesses deep.

'We could deliver you to Vasquez in a carpet, like Cleopatra,' Cristo had suggested.

He seemed excited by the idea, but I demurred. 'That's a horrible idea, Cristo,' I said. 'It would probably ruin the dress, which cost a fortune, any carpet you might be able to find will probably be filthy and I'll end up covered in dust and cobwebs, and smelling of old wool. Not very attractive. It may have been all very well in ancient Rome, or Egypt or wherever it was, but I don't fancy it in the slightest, here in Napoli.'

Cristo saw my point in the end, and so we discussed for some time how we might adapt Cleopatra's plan to suit the occasion – he was wedded to his idea of concealment and would not be moved from it. 'People like unwrapping gifts,' he said.

'Quick!' the servant says. 'Get up here!' He and the other two men help me to seat myself as near to the middle of the bed as we can manage, without creasing my clothes, rumpling the golden fabric or disturbing the straightness of the ribbon. They almost lift me, in fact. I lie down; both ribbon and gauze stretching out flat on either side of me.

'Ready, Señora?' my new friend asks. His tone is deferential, but his eyes are dancing. He licks his lips, twitching down a smile.

I nod again. 'Quite ready, thank you. Just don't wrap it too tightly. It must be left loose – this dress will be ruined if it's crushed.' I fold my arms across my chest.

'Maestre Vasquez will be here in moments, Señora,' he assures me, leaning across me and taking the far ends of the sheer length of doubled-over fabric. He lifts it back towards himself, letting it fall so that it completely covers me from head to foot. He gently tucks it in under me. Then he takes the other side and folds this back over the first layer, tucking that in on my other side, until all the ends are (so I imagine – I can now see almost nothing) out of sight and I am neatly wrapped like a big parcel inside four layers of cypress gauze. The last thing I feel is the servant's hands tying the ribbon around the level of my belly. Not one part of me remains visible – not a wisp of hair, not even the tip of one shoe.

I feel somewhat confined, and find that I cannot really move my arms properly, but I suppose it *is* still more comfortable and sweet-smelling than a carpet would have been.

'Are you quite comfortable, Señora?' my friend asks.

'Quite, thank you,' I reply politely. My words sound oddly muffled.

'We go downstairs, now, and tell *Maestre* something important is deliver to the upstairs chamber – as soon as he home. He not be long. You wait.'

I hear footsteps, the click of the door closing, and finally a soft and sunlit silence.

As I have been instructed, I wait.

And wait.

And wait.

All I can hear is my own breath, inside my silk cocoon, and the rustling of my skirts as I shift position a fraction.

What will he be like, this Vasquez? Cristoforo has assured me of his wealth, his eminent standing as a senior official in the occupying army, and of his desire for my company. But what sort of man is he? I wonder if I shall enjoy what is about to happen. Will he be gifted in the arts of the bedchamber? Might he even be someone who will turn out to be more to me than a paying patron? Perhaps, in time to come, I shall look back fondly on this evening as the moment something extraordinary began. But then, of course, the converse is just as possible: tonight's tryst could as easily turn out to be that fateful encounter that every courtesan secretly dreads. Because such fateful encounters do happen. It happened to me all those years ago, after all, did it not? I was lucky to survive that night.

I might not be so fortunate another time.

My scar tweaks as I remember.

But . . . Cristo made it all sound so enticing the other day.

'You tell me you need a new patron — well, what would you say to a Spaniard?' he said.

'A Spaniard? An Inquisitor?'

Cristo laughed. 'No, no, no — nothing like that — can't imagine any of them spending a single scudo *on such sinful and wicked activities as a liaison with a courtesan — even one as beautiful as you, Francesca. No, this man's a tremendously wealthy* Maestre de Campo *in the Spanish Army. I've been working with him for months. Now, I could be wrong, but from what I've heard him say, I am given to understand that he's becoming increasingly desperate for the attentions of a beautiful woman. He rarely goes an hour without mentioning the fact, as it happens.'*

I smiled, and Cristo grinned at me. 'He's as rich as Croesus,' he said. I glanced over to where Modesto was standing by the door to my chamber, but my manservant's face was unreadable.

'He's young,' Cristo went on, 'younger than me, a good soldier — not the brightest, perhaps, but clever enough to have been promoted several times. He's a bit particular, I suppose you could say. Others might say pedantic, but—'

'I really meant, shall I find him attractive?'

Cristo laughed. 'That's not for me to say, really, is it, cara? *Come with me the day after tomorrow, though, and I'll present you to him — with a suitably ostentatious flourish, I think — and then you can decide for yourself what you think of our young Miguel Vasquez.'*

I wanted to know what Modesto thought of this idea, before I agreed to anything.

'I think you should do it,' he said after a moment's pause. 'What

with the death of the Conte di Vecchio, and now the news that the Signore here is leaving the city –' he nodded towards Cristo then turned back to me '– you have to think of your financial position. With the likes of Emilia Rosa and that simpering little bitch Alessandra Malacoda rising to such dizzying heights in the city, you're going to have to make sure you keep pace. Old and decrepit he might well have been, but the Conte di Vecchio had status in Napoli, and his patronage was a godsend last year.'

I looked at my feet and pushed the toe of my shoe down into a knot hole in the floor. He was right, I knew, but, wanting to justify myself, I said, 'But I have other patrons. There's Filippo . . .'

Modesto rolled his eyes.

Irritated, I added, 'And I took on Signor di Cicciano a few weeks ago.'

Cristo's eyebrows lifted. 'That young reprobate? I've heard of him. You should be careful, Francesca – I'm surprised you're still in one piece, from what people have said. I'm serious, you must take care.'

The same thought had occurred to me, on a couple of occasions in the company of this new patron. Michele di Cicciano can be very wild. Perhaps Modesto had a point, I thought. I need someone steady. Rich and steady. At least whilst Cristo is away.

A door bangs somewhere below me. Somebody shouts, and then several male voices rumble incomprehensibly. Heavy footsteps thud on a staircase. My pulse quickens. Perhaps this is him. Oh, dear. Cristo said he had a 'prodigious appetite'. . . . What if he is enormous? Shall I end this evening completely flattened? I fiddle my lips between my teeth to redden them, then lick them. I try to lift my arm to pinch colour into my cheeks, but the servant has tied the ribbon too tightly, and I can't reach my face without spoiling the lie of the cloth.

No one comes into the room, however, and within seconds, the sounds from below fade away. My thoughts begin to wander again.

The poor Conte di Vecchio. I feel horribly responsible for his death. I told Cristo about it – I said I'd killed him. Oh, I know I didn't actually do it, but I still feel so guilty about it that it seems to me sometimes that I did. I should never have agreed to see Vicino da Argenta that day – vile man that he is. It was stupid of me. Modesto has always told me I should keep away from him. And if Argenta hadn't been with me that afternoon, the Conte di Vecchio would still be alive, Modesto would be happy with the money I'm earning, and I wouldn't be lying here like an oversized birthday present, unable to move, almost entirely ignorant about the man I am to bed.

Cristo was shocked when I told him about the Conte di Vecchio. He had known that the old man was dead but not how it had happened.

'I hadn't seen him for two or three weeks,' I said. 'He'd been on a trip, I think.' I pictured the old man – Giovanni Battista, the elderly Conte di Vecchio: stooped, stiff and slow in his movements, the wreck of a once debonair adventurer. Lovemaking had cost him dearly every time, I think, but he had enjoyed it – on the days when he was able to manage it – and on those occasions when his bones had ached too fiercely to permit him to rut, he had just liked sitting in my bed with me and listening to me reciting poetry, or reading to him from my diaries. He was a dear old thing, he was the means of my establishment here in Napoli, and I am genuinely sorry he's gone. And not just because of the money, either.

'Go on,' Cristoforo said.

'Well, as I say, he'd been away for ages. So had you.'

'It's an annoying habit of the army, to request one to work from time to time.'

I ignored his sarcasm. 'So, seeing as all my favourites had declined

15

to come and see me, I had to resort to scraping the bottom of the barrel.'
I paused. 'Vicino da Argenta.'

Cristoforo did not need to comment. The expression of disgust on his face was eloquent.

I gave him a wry smile. 'I know – the man's repulsive.'

'Then why?'

Shame glowed warm in my cheeks as I admitted it. 'Because I needed the money.'

Cristoforo shook his head and made a soft 'tut' of disbelief with his tongue. The heat in my face flared now with irritation. 'Don't look at me like that!' I said. 'I have a living to make just as you do. I have two houses to manage and my children to care for. If the men I prefer choose not to come and see me, I have to make do with the ones I would rather avoid.'

He inclined his head in reluctant acceptance of this.

'Anyway,' I said. 'Vicino had come here early on the evening that Giovanni Battista died. He was drunk – which was hardly a surprise – and he was being particularly boring. I had no wish to engage him in conversation, and he seemed incapable of actually doing anything very exciting, so I decided that the best way to deal with the situation was probably just to make sure he couldn't expect me to talk to him.'

Cristoforo raised a quizzical eyebrow.

'My mother always told me it was ill-mannered to speak with your mouth full.'

Cristo tipped back his head and barked out a laugh. I continued my tale. 'And then, the door to my chamber – this chamber – bangs open. Thinking it's Modesto, I take no notice, and just carry on with what I'm doing – Vicino's too drunk to care about the interruption – but it isn't Modesto. It's Giovanni Battista.'

I had glanced over my shoulder from where I was crouched on the floor in front of Argenta. The expression on his poor face – it's still *haunting me. He looked utterly devastated. He said nothing, just stared at me for several seconds, and then blundered blindly out of the door. I made to follow him, but as soon as I started to stand, bloody Vicino caught my wrist and tried to hold me back, and by the time I had pulled myself from his grasp, the front door had slammed and the Conte di Vecchio had gone.*

I explained all this to Cristo, and then finished my story by saying, 'Modesto told me how the poor man had staggered off up the street, and then collapsed when he reached the piazza. Several people – including Modesto – tried to help, but it was no good. He was dead in minutes.'

Cristoforo rubbed a hand around his unshaven jaw, and puffed out a disbelieving sigh. 'Poor old man.'

A dove clatter-flaps past the window, startling me out of my reverie. It's warm here, and the sun is lying across the gauze over my face. I wriggle a little, feeling a prickling tingle in one of my feet.

He has to be here soon.

And then the door opens, banging back against the wall and making me jump.

Oh, *Dio*! I hope it's him – I shall feel decidedly foolish, trussed up here like a goose prepared for the table, if it's anybody else. Several sets of footsteps clack into the room, and I hear men's voices, speaking in Spanish. One of them is my servant friend from before, I think, but the others are unfamiliar. Their indecipherable conversation rumbles for a moment, and then an order is barked out, the various footsteps retreat and the door clicks shut.

Somebody strides across the room. I hold my breath. The new-comer pauses, and then I hear soft male laughter, which ends with a cough. A voice says in Italian, 'Oh, yes! Juan was quite right –

this delivery is indeed "*significant*". Well, well, well, I wonder what it can possibly be. Whatever it is, it must be investigated *immediately*.' This voice, like the servant's, is breathy and heavily accented, though this man speaks more softly, and his grammar is accurate.

A faint tug near my middle pulls me slightly to one side – he's undoing the ribbon. Taking his time, he peels back the fabric, bit by bit, leaning over me to untuck the various layers of gauze. I can hear his breath, soft in his nose. Then, after several seconds, blinking in the light, I am finally able to see who has released me from my wrappings: at first he is silhouetted against the window, but then he moves to one side into the shadow of the damask-hung bedpost, and I can make him out more clearly.

Maestre Vasquez – I presume this to be him – must be some thirty years old; he is neat and slightly built, with short dark hair and a tidy beard. Like a mythological faun, he has pointed tips to his ears. On meeting my gaze, his smile broadens, he runs his tongue over his lips and, holding out a hand, he gestures to me to sit up.

'Señora Felizzi? I was not expecting to see you so soon. Or for you to arrive quite so *covertly*.'

'Signor Vasquez.' I swing my legs around and stand, smoothing out my skirts with my hands. Then, my gaze on his, I drop down into a curtsy, but my would-be patron takes my hand and pulls me back to standing. We are much the same height. He releases my hand, and, stretching out to touch the neckline of my dress, he feels his way softly down from my shoulder, fingering the lace as he goes. His hand moves across the horizontal, then pauses, his eyes widening as he reaches the first of my all-but-exposed nipples. 'Are you hungry?' he says, pinching it for a brief second.

I run my tongue over my lips and smile assent.

'I have had food prepared for us. Come and eat.'

Vasquez lifts the covered platters over onto the table. He seats me in one of the two chairs, pulling the other round so that he is sitting close to me. Filling our glasses with a tawny-coloured wine, he then lifts off the domes. Olives. Some sort of tiny bird's eggs, nestling in a bed of shredded leaves and little flowers. And oysters. Shucked and gleaming and dressed with lemon slices.

Picking up an olive in his fingers, he offers it to me, obviously expecting to put it directly into my mouth. 'Señora?' he asks.

I smile and open my mouth a little. His fingers rest on my lips for a brief second. I turn the fruit over with my tongue, enjoying the briny sharpness, and, having removed the flesh, I push the stone forward so that it protrudes from between my teeth. My new friend grins and takes it from me.

'More?' he asks.

I nod.

He repeats the process. Twice.

I reach forward then and pick up an oyster, holding it up for him to eat. He tilts his head back, and, touching his lip with the edge of the shell, I slide the oyster into his mouth. He flicks his head to throw it to the back of his throat and swallows it. As he sits forward again, a thin line of liquor runs down his chin into his beard, and I lean towards him and run the tip of my tongue up the track of the juice, holding the side of his face with my fingers. He smells of brine and incense and garlic.

Letting out a long, slow breath that shivers as it leaves his mouth, he says, 'Oh, you are going to be worth every *scudo*! Benevento sang your praises to the heavens, but I think now that he failed to do you justice.'

'I always hope to please.'

'Your hopes are being fulfilled as we speak, believe me,' he says, picking up another oyster. He raises his eyebrows questioningly. I nod, and he slithers it into my mouth. Its sea-smelling bulk is thick in my throat for an instant and then it's gone. Vasquez leans forward and runs his tongue along the edge of my lip.

I open my mouth a fraction.

And that, it seems, is invitation enough for him. He stands, takes my hand, and flicks his head towards the great gold-draped edifice on the far side of the chamber. 'Come with me, now, Señora,' he says softly.

And, tracing around inside the curve of his palm with my fingertips as we walk, I follow him across the room.

I suppose in the end it was not an unpleasant evening

As I lay wrapped in silk like a spider's supper last night, waiting for Vasquez to arrive, I passed the time wondering what my new patron would be like. And, now that I've lain with him, I know that he's greedy. Maestre Miguel Vasquez is a greedy man – greedy for me, greedy for food, greedy for life. His appetites for both his fine suppers and my body would appear to be irrepressible. At times last night I felt that he might almost devour me . . . my lips are tingling this morning – they're quite bruised from his attentions – and my poor breasts are almost numb.

He says little, the Maestre. But there's a fervent eagerness about him – an unsettling intensity that seemed not far from desperation at times yesterday. Has he always been like this, I wonder, or is it just that he has been waiting a long time for an encounter such as we had last night?

Perhaps he will relax a little more next time.

I hope so. Appetites like his often lead to trouble.

Two

It's Wednesday evening. Filippo di Laviano is running his tongue over his lips. 'You know you deserve a particularly severe beating, you insolent little slut,' he says, pointing an accusatory finger at me.

'Why?'

Frowning, Filippo pauses to consider. 'Oh . . . because . . . because wicked, unprincipled strumpets like you need to be kept in their place . . . and . . . men such as myself,' he says proudly, one hand on his chest, 'have a responsibility to uphold the morality of the city of Napoli.'

I smother a laugh. It's really rather charming. This quiet and unassuming man was introduced to me a year ago and it didn't take me long to discover that his subdued air of self-deprecation stemmed almost entirely from the fact that for years he had been quite crushed by the suffocating loneliness of a marriage to a frigid woman.

That first time we fucked, he actually wept with guilt-drenched relief and then poured out a tangled explanation of his many frustrations with his wife. So he tells me, on the occasions that he does manage to persuade her to lie with him (and yes, it *is* persuasion – I absolutely believe that he has no stomach for true coercion), she each time submits obediently, he says, but with a prick-deflating expression of martyred resignation on her face as though she were praying for the achievement of sanctity through suffering.

Poor Filippo endured this for years before being introduced to me. He has never felt able simply to go drabbing, as so many in his situation might well have done. Although he now loves to address me as though I was the most disgusting of lewd harlots, he in fact recoils with fastidious horror at the thought of actually associating with genuine street whores. And who can blame him? The mindless vulgarity and diseased bodies of those poor bitches are far too much of an obstacle – even for one in so much need of relief.

So that I could try to assess what sort of man he was, I asked him quite early on how he felt towards his wife each time she showed such antipathy to being bedded. I thought I knew what he might say. He was sitting in the big chair under the window and took some moments to answer my question; he just stared at the floor, muffled in shame. I watched him, saying nothing. Filippo is a big-boned, heavy man – he must be nearly fifty years old – and though his hair is still thick, it is quite grey. But at that moment, despite the bulk and the silver hair, he looked more like a little boy, caught out in a serious misdemeanour.

When he did speak, it was in hardly more than a stammering whisper. 'I know it sounds terrible to say this, but . . . God . . . sometimes I almost feel . . . that I could beat her for what she does to me. But I would never hurt her . . . *never* . . . I couldn't . . . she doesn't mean to . . . it is *I* who—' He broke off and I could see that he was drowning in guilt. He had confirmed my suspicions.

So I offered him a possible solution.

He stared at me. I'll never forget his wide-eyed expression of total astonishment as I raised an eyebrow, smiled at him and said, 'You may do what you please in here, Signore.'

So, Filippo now comes to see me almost every Wednesday

evening; he pays me what he always says is an *exorbitant* fee, so that he can spend a few entertaining hours each week being the 'guardian of the morals of the city of Napoli' – or whatever else has happened to take his fancy. Without guilt or redress, quite shamelessly, and always with the greatest enthusiasm, Filippo returns here again and again, so that he can continue to take out his long-running marital frustrations upon my ever-available backside.

Today, as always, his face is eager, and his gaze is fixed upon mine as he unfastens his doublet with trembling fingers.

'If, as you say, I deserve a beating . . . Signor Guardian . . . well, what do you intend to do about it?' I ask, hands on hips.

Filippo raises an eyebrow and wags an admonitory finger at me. 'Oh, you deserve a lot more than a beating, my girl. It's disgraceful – this city is quite overrun now: absolutely teeming with grubby little trollops, all with a vastly over-inflated opinion of themselves and –' he sucks in a breath and says pompously '– it all needs dealing with! Take off your shift!'

I pull my chemise over my head, and Filippo reaches for my wrists. 'Hold onto that,' he says, taking my hands and placing them onto one of the bedposts. I swallow a yawn. I'm unexpectedly tired today – I've been a great deal busier than usual for the past couple of weeks – and as Filippo runs his big hand over my buttocks, I am suddenly unsure whether I really feel like indulging him for the next few hours. He must see something of my fatigue in my expression, for he pauses for a moment, straightens and then adds in quite a different voice, 'If you are certain you don't object, *cara* . . .'

Oh, dear – this won't do. It won't do at all. Filippo has paid in full for his pleasures this evening, and he must have what he wants. His wife may be able to refuse his advances, but I don't have that luxury. Every courtesan's expensive reputation is easily blighted and, in this business, word spreads as fast as a whore's legs; I cannot ever appear anything less than enthusiastic. I summon a smile, which I then lick with the tip of my tongue. Filippo's eyes move to my mouth. 'I never object, *caro*,' I say. 'You know that. Not to anything.'

Filippo's expression clears, and a pinprick gleam of lasciviousness brightens his eye once more. 'Well, in that case . . .' he says happily. His fingers move to the fastening of his belt and my buttocks clench involuntarily.

I know what to expect of this evening.

Filippo lies on his back with his eyes closed, and an expression of blissful repletion stretches the corners of his mouth. My hips are stiff: I feel like I do after a long day's ride and my arse is flaming as I walk uncomfortably across the room to the table upon which stands a big, deep-blue decanter of red wine, which shines dark purple where the light from a candle glows behind the glass. I fill two goblets and pad back to the bed, really tired now and relieved that the evening is all but over.

'Drink, Lippo?'

'Turn around,' he says. I do so.

Seeing my bottom, his expression changes. 'Oh, dear – I seem to have been rather over-zealous. Are you sure you're . . .' He hesitates, and I smile at his familiar anxiety. It's the same almost every week.

Filippo's needs, though always energetic, are uncomplicated. But I admit I am often tired by the end of his hours with me – though he has nothing of, say, Michele's unpredictable wild energy, Filippo is as demanding a companion in his way. I am often all but *dislocated*, too. In fact, on numerous occasions, flattened like a spatchcocked chicken beneath Filippo di Laviano's oblivious weight, I have wondered if I would ever be able to straighten my legs again. But given all this, it is still less exhausting to be passively on the receiving end of Filippo's 'punishments' than it is to fight with Michele the way I always seem to. It's not nearly as exciting – but it *is* less tiring.

'Yes, I'm quite sure I'm . . .' I mimic his worried expression and his unfinished question and he laughs.

'Well, then yes I would like something, yes – thank you, Francesca.'

I hand him one of the two glasses, and place the other on the table next to the bed. Climbing back a little gingerly under the covers, I take a long draft, and swill it around my mouth for a moment, enjoying the dry, sucking feeling against the back of my teeth.

'I should think you needed that, you trollop. You ought to be exhausted.'

'Your performance was most impressive, Signore,' I agree.

He smiles proudly and speaks again, hutching himself up and back against the pillow. 'Francesca, can I ask of you a considerable favour . . . an enjoyable one?'

'More enjoyable than the one I have just done you?'

'That wasn't a favour. You were well paid for it.'

I incline my head in acceptance of this. 'Tell me, Filippo, what is it?'

'Well, I have been invited to a play – a meal and a play – next month, by a friend who teaches at the university. At the Long Chamber in that beautiful building in the law faculty, just off the Spaccanapoli – near the Piazza San Domenico Maggiore.'

I say nothing, but wait to hear more.

'Maria does not wish to come with me . . .' A fleeting wince as of pain crosses his face. 'I've told you before, that apart from familiar short excursions, she does not care to leave the house very often and she is usually anxious in company – but, oh, Francesca, I really don't want to go alone to such an occasion. If I go alone yet again they will all begin to talk. I wondered if you might think of coming with me.'

'But . . . can you *really* wish to be seen in public with a *courtesan*, Filippo?' I am astonished. He has never asked such a thing before. Unlike some of my previous patrons who have enjoyed flaunting me around town like some sort of prize exhibit, Filippo has always been at pains to keep his relationship with me entirely covert – we have never met outside the confines of this house.

He surprises me again. 'I won't be with a courtesan,' he says with a boyish grin. 'I had thought that you might disguise yourself.'

'What – false whiskers and breeches?'

Filippo throws his head back and laughs. 'Ha! A delightful prospect – but unrealistic. No, I have it in mind to pass you off as a respectable widow. A cousin, I think, newly emerged from mourning . . .'

I swill down another bursting mouthful of wine. 'Will there be other women there?'

'Oh, yes – quite certainly!'

'Do I not run the risk of being recognised?'

Filippo frowns. 'No, I don't think so. Such dedicated academics as Luca and his fellow tutors rarely bother themselves with salacious gossip. No, Francesca, with your hair simply dressed and in, perhaps, some modestly cut frock, I think we could create a believable alias.'

'What will your wife say?'

'I shan't tell her. She is unlikely to ask and I shan't volunteer the information.'

'Oh, I don't know, Lippo . . .'

'Might these tempt you?' Filippo hands me his goblet and then climbs out of the bed. He crosses the room to the untidy pile of his clothes which he discarded some time ago with such haste, and crouches on his heels before it with his back to me. I watch him rummage through pockets, searching for something. His heavy body is pale in the candlelight as he bends forward: prick and balls hang like dark giblets beneath the creamy globes of his buttocks.

'Ha! There we are. Close your eyes.'

He hurries back to the bed and scrambles under the covers.

'Keep your eyes shut and hold out your hands.'

I put the wine glasses down and do as he asks. Something small and soft lands in one palm and I open my eyes. A little leather bag lies in my hand. I finger it and feel beads of some sort within.

'Go on. Tell me what you think.'

I loosen the strings and tip out a rope of pale-pink pearls and two matching earrings. They are beautiful and I am astonished.

'Pearls. Filippo, are these not . . . ?'

'Yes! Your disguise. Forbidden to courtesans, are they not, pearls? They will be perfect. So . . . will you come? I'll pay for it all.'

The laugh that escapes me is short and disbelieving. Almost a snort. But the idea is entertaining and I smile at Filippo and agree. 'Very well, I'll do it. Shall I have a new name?'

Filippo leans across and kisses my cheek, saying, 'I had thought that *Signora Marrone* has a pleasingly anonymous ring to it. Francesca Marrone.'

'Very chaste.'

'And so you must be. Well, until we come back here after the play, that is.'

'What do you want me to wear, then, Lippo?' I ask.

'Dark blue, I think. High-necked and modest. No slashes, no ribbons – just the pearls. Dress your hair like a mourning Madonna.'

'I'll call Modesto – he can take the order around to the seam-stress.' The underhand covertness of Filippo's plan has begun to appeal to me. I climb out of bed and cross to my table. Rummaging through a drawer, I pull out a sheet of paper, quill and ink and scratch a few lines, sketching a rough design for a suitable dress. Feeling another twinge in my hips, I sit back down – care-fully – and show the paper to Filippo.

'Oh, yes, Francesca! Exactly what I had in mind. You will be quite lovely.'

'Not too lovely, presumably. You won't want this friend of yours and all his academics asking awkward questions about your propriety.'

'Luca is such a trusting, unsuspicious soul – it will never cross his mind that you are not what you purport to be.'

'Oh, don't say that – you make me feel deceitful.'

'And so you are, you trollop. If it is honesty you want, then per-haps you should not worry about new dresses and simply go as you are now.'

'Oh, no, Filippo, don't start again! Modesto!' I slide out of reach of Filippo's hand which is once more in search of my bottom.

Modesto opens the door.

Modesto is my secret weapon. His unimpressive size belies his strength – and determination – and more than one of my past patrons has underestimated Modesto's ruthlessness – to his cost. His and my histories intertwine over nearly three years, since the day that I heard him sing for the Duke of Salerno. Now, the Duke was one patron I was *very* glad to see the back of – with his endless drinking and the seemingly constant stream of visiting friends and relations. He never seemed to be able to grasp the fact that I have never been at all fond of entertaining more than one at a time.

Modesto was still singing for a living, then. It's a terrible shame that, since his illness, he only has the vocal stamina to sing occasionally, but Modesto's voice is still hauntingly beautiful – enough to bring tears to the most cynical of dry eyes. Its beauty is deceptive, though: its womanish pitch has fooled many into believing him a weakling, but, to my surprise at first, his condition has not, as I initially believed it would have, sapped him of a man's strength, even if he has been so cruelly denied a man's ability to rut.

'Signora?'

'Modesto, *caro*, can you run this round to Bianca for me? Oh . . . I suppose it's too late now?'

He nods.

'In the morning then.'

His eyes rest for the briefest of moments upon my breasts and then he reaches for the paper I hold out, nods a token bow and backs from the room.

'Why do you not cover yourself up when he comes in,' says Filippo. There is a bite to his voice, which I ignore. He has asked me this too many times. I say, as I always do, 'Oh, he's seen all I have to offer far too many times. You know perfectly well that I can't see the point in dressing and undressing just for him.'

'And do you . . . *entertain* him, too?'

I climb back onto the bed and sit on my heels, one knee on either side of Filippo's legs. I smooth his hair back from his forehead. 'As I've told you before, it doesn't suit you to be jealous, Lippo. When you're here, you know that I'm all yours. And you understand Modesto's circumstances – you must see that that's one of the reasons I want him here to work for me.'

He huffs a reluctant acquiescence.

'Do you wish me to walk you home, Signora?' Modesto asks after Filippo has left. His fingers grip the edge of the door as he peers into my chamber. I am sitting at my table, with my head leaning heavily on one hand. My backside is hot and stinging; the rest of me is beginning to feel cold, but my wrap is hanging on a hook on the far side of the room and I haven't the energy to walk across and fetch it.

'No,' I say. 'I have had far too much wine, it is much too late, and Ilaria and the girls are not expecting me back until tomorrow night. I'll stay here. Michele will be here before noon. Oh, dear . . .' I groan at the thought. 'I must sleep, but I'm hungry. Is there anything to eat?'

'A few slices of yesterday's pigeon breast, a couple of orange-poached sardines and those peaches.' He points to a large wooden bowl half-full of fruit, then adds, 'And a great deal of bread.'

'How horrible. Is that all?'

Modesto glares at me. 'I am afraid so, Signora.'

I take a peach from the bowl and bite into it. The juice runs down my chin and I tip my head back, wiping my face with the heel of my other hand and sucking at the dripping scoop of peach flesh. The wet pulp catches against the end of my nose. 'What have you been doing all evening?'

'There's little food in the house because that great fat lump of a cook hasn't been here for a couple of days – as you know – and, unsurprisingly, *I* have been doing what you pay me to do,

Signora. After what happened the other week with the Conte di Vecchio and that little *stronzo*, da Argenta, I'm surprised you even ask. I've been sitting outside your chamber with my knife in my hand, listening to you shrieking and gasping, ready to come in if the screams start to sound too alarming,' he says drily.

'You know Filippo, *caro*. He would never hurt me.'

'So you say. Stand up for a moment, Signora.'

Somewhat reluctantly, I stand.

'Turn around.'

I turn away from him. He makes an irritable noise with his tongue. 'Have you seen the state of your buttocks? You say he doesn't hurt you? Why do you let him do that?'

I shrug. I feel very tired and rather sick. 'He needs to.'

Modesto rolls his eyes in irritable disbelief and shakes his head, but he none the less crosses the room to a carved table below the window, upon which stand a number of Murano glass bowls and pots. Picking up one of these, he holds it in the palm of one hand, scoops two fingers into the contents and walks back to me. I lean on one arm upon the table and Modesto (none too gently) rubs the mixture onto both buttocks whilst I finish my peach. Despite his lack of finesse, the smarting skin feels cooled. Taking my wine with me, I cross to my bed and lie down on my stomach.

'You let that man go too far, too often, Signora. It is unwise. How do you think you are going to be able to sustain the image of this . . . this . . .' he struggles to find the words '. . . this *termagant* with whom Signor di Cicciano so loves to fight – or the reincarnation of Aphrodite that the *Maestre de Campo* has practically started to *worship*, if every time you turn your back on the pair of them, they see that you have some other man's red stripes

32

across your arse? They won't want you – either of them – if they see you as a victim. And you can't afford to lose either one of them.'

'I won't lose them. I have them too firmly hooked.' My words are muffled from where my cheek is pressed into the pillow, but I am too tired to lift my head. 'Stop being cross with me, will you? Why are you angry?'

'Because you never seem to know when you are well off, that's why. It's just like with Argenta and the Conte di Vecchio – you're risking the patronage of two wealthy new devotees, both of whom are happily paying through the nose for their pleasures, just so that you can indulge some poor creature who can't actually afford you. You forget, I know *exactly* how little he pays.' Modesto jabs an irritable finger in my direction.

Now, I have always regretted telling Modesto why I choose to ask Filippo for such a small fee – he pays little more than half the amount the others give me each time. When I admitted it to him on that one thoughtless occasion, Modesto just stared at me in disbelief.

'*He reminds you of your uncle?*' I remember him saying, shaking his head as though doubting my sanity. '*Your* uncle? *Dear God, Signora, what was this? An incestuous childhood liaison or something?*'

'*Don't be disgusting!*'

'*Well, what then? What is it about your uncle that could possibly make you wish to make a charity case out of Signor di Laviano?*'

I tried to explain it to him. It was not because of any great virtue of my Uncle Bigo's – he was just kinder to me than anyone else was, I suppose. He made me laugh. Before my mother died – before I became the newly preferred target for my father's drink-fuelled ill temper – my big, bulky, silver-haired Uncle Bigo's visits were frequent and eagerly anticipated. After her death, however,

33

he stopped coming. I was never told why. I haven't seen him since I was seventeen.

I glare at Modesto. 'It's my choice what my patrons pay me. I like Filippo,' I say. Modesto does not. 'And he needs me.'

'You are worth far more than this, Signora – you could be greater than all of them: greater than La Rosa, than da Mosca; certainly *far* greater than Alessandra Malacoda, and she's fucked *royalty* – though God alone knows what anyone sees in that stick-thin little trollop. All this misguided charity will do your reputation no good in the end – even if the man does remind you of some long-lost relative.'

'Very well, I'll ask Filippo to wield his belt more gently next time. Happy?' I can feel a scowl crumpling my face as I reach across and pick up my glass with fingers now sticky from the peach juice. I drain the last few mouthfuls and feel my head become woolly. My eyelids begin to close of their own accord and I can feel the room circling slowly around me.

'Oh, go to sleep, Signora,' Modesto says then in a voice much gentler than before. 'Come on, I'll wake you in good time for Signor di Cicciano in the morning. You'll be fit for nothing at this rate.' He crouches down beside the bed, and strokes my hair back away from my face, saying in little more than a whisper, 'I know you're tough, Signora – God knows, you need to be – and I know that you pride yourself on the fact that you never cry, but let's do our best to keep it that way, eh? We don't want any unnecessary cause for tears, do we? Come on, let's both get some sleep and get ourselves ready for tomorrow.'

I feel Modesto's hands underneath me, freeing the blankets from under my body, and then a comforting warmth as he pulls them up and over me. I hear him moving about my chamber. He reaches under the covers, picks up each of my hands, one by one, and wipes the sticky juice from them with a damp cloth. He dries both carefully. I am almost asleep as he leaves the room, but he might have said as he goes, or perhaps I am dreaming it, 'Bloody whores. God – there are times when I'm almost glad I'm a eunuch.'

Three

Shaking his head in amused disbelief, Modesto went down to the kitchen. With the cook away, only cold ash lay in the fireplace and there was a chill in the air. A brightly painted plate, on which lay several slices of cold pigeon, stood next to three large flat loaves of bread on the longest of the shelves, and half a dozen thickly glazed sardines stared mournfully up at the edge of their tin-glazed dish. Amongst the clutter on the table stood several bottles of wine, one uncorked, which Modesto now picked up; he drank straight from the bottle and wiped his chin on his sleeve. Sitting down on a long bench at the side of the table, he put his head in his hands.

He sat lost in thought for some moments, then, the heaviness of his eyelids confirming the lateness of the hour, he stood, stretched and left the room. Climbing the stairs to a long, low room at the top of the house, he put his candle down on the table and crossed to the windows. He closed and fastened the shutters. Heeling off his shoes, he pulled his knife from his belt, and laid it on the table in front of the candle. He unfastened his doublet, pulling the laces through the holes and easing open the stiffened front. Leaving the doublet still laced to his hose, he stepped out of the whole thing in one piece and hung it all over the chest at the end of his bed; the empty legs of the hose lay on the floorboards like flaccid brown snakeskins. Sitting down on the edge of the bed, he cupped a hand around his genitals and rubbed, unsticking where the soft flesh had been crumpled inside his hose, and wondered as he did so if he would ever be able to touch himself without remembering.

When his mother's first scream wakes him, he is upstairs in the cramped and damp-smelling room in which they all sleep. He, Sofia and Giulia are well used to the ineptly smothered creaks and cries of their parents; for a long while Modesto thought his father was hurting his mother every night and he would lie wide-eyed in the dark beside his sisters with cold threads of terror creeping through his head, listening to his mother's guttural groans and his father's grunts. At those moments he hated his father. He knows now, though, what it is that his parents do, and when he hears his mother scream downstairs, he feels no fear, just wonders why it is that they are coupling down there instead of in their bed.

But the second scream is sharper and now Modesto is afraid.

'No! You shan't do it!' Her voice is high and thin.

'Agnese, stop it! The decision has been made and they have come to do it tonight. We need the money.'

'I won't let them — Oh, God, please, Giuseppe, please stop them. They'll kill him . . .'

'We will have to take her away — she will scare the boy. It will be far more difficult if he is frightened,' says a deep voice Modesto does not recognise, and these words are followed by a confusion of scuffling and more panicked protestations from his mother. The door to the street is opened — a blurt of sound from outside — and then closed.

Sofia and Giulia are awake now and the three children listen silently to what is happening below them. Male voices rumble indistinctly. Giulia holds Modesto's hand. Her grip tightens as the chamber door opens. Their father stands in silhouette and says, 'Modesto, get up and put some clothes on. You are needed downstairs — some people have come especially to see you.' His voice is stiff and sounds unfamiliar.

Fear congeals in Modesto's throat as he dresses and follows his father; the cold lump of it swells when he sees three unknown men in long black clothes in the room at the bottom of the stairs. They all turn towards him expectantly, but they do not smile when they see him.

'Is this the boy, Giuseppe?'

Modesto sees his father nod.

'How old?'

'Ten, Father.' One of the men crouches stiffly and speaks to Modesto in a strange accent he does not recognise. 'We have been told what a beautiful voice you have, boy. Do you like singing?'

Modesto nods.

'Yours is the voice of an angel, they tell me. Now, would it not be a shame to lose that divine gift? In a few years' time, your voice will change, will it not? If God has given you a voice like this, should you not do everything you can to make sure you take care of it? It would be a sin to risk its disappearance as you grow up . . .'

Modesto nods.

'We can help you to make sure that you keep your beautiful voice all your life. What we must do is not difficult and it will not take long. Come now.' And the man takes Modesto's hand. He holds it too tightly and Modesto wriggles his fingers to try to free them but the man is too strong; when the man and his two companions leave the house, Modesto has no choice but to go with them.

Modesto shivered and pulled the covers up and over himself, tucking them in snugly around his neck with one hand. Pulling his knees up towards his chest, he pushed his other hand down between his legs and held his empty scrotum protectively. The unwanted pictures poured in as though a dam had ruptured and he pressed his head against the pillow, clamped his thighs around his wrist and let out a soft noise of distress.

There is a huge tub in front of the fire. Made of wood, in slats like a barrel, it has a sheet draped over it and it seems to be almost filled with water. A woman is turning from the fire with a steaming jug in her sacking-wrapped hands. She adds the water to the tub, puts down the jug and leaves the room, staring at Modesto as she goes. He does not like the expression on her face.

'Sit down, child,' says one of the men in black clothes.

Modesto sees a chair near the tub of water. He sits on it.

'Here,' says one of the tall men. 'Drink this.' He holds out a glass to Modesto, who stares up at him and does not move. 'Come on, child, drink it.'

Modesto shakes his head.

'It is part of our plan to help keep your marvellous voice safe for you.'

Another shake of the head.

'I am not offering you a choice, boy – drink it.' The voice is suddenly sharper and more urgent and Modesto is very frightened. The man pushes the glass into the hands of one of the others, takes Modesto by the wrist and pulls him to his feet. In one swift movement he pulls Modesto in towards him so that he is standing with his back pressed against the stranger; the man's arm is holding him in tightly, wrist still held firm. With his other hand, he holds Modesto's hair and pulls it backwards, turning his face up. Modesto sees someone else's fist holding the glass up in front of him, tilting it towards his mouth. He shuts his lips tightly and turns his face away, but the second man reaches out and grips Modesto's chin and he cannot help it – his mouth opens. Liquid pours into it and he chokes. But despite his retching, most of the bitter contents of the glass goes down his throat and then the men sit him back down on the chair.

'We need to wait about ten minutes,' Modesto hears one of them say. They all stand round him. They are very tall in their black clothes and they do not smile.

A strange noise soon begins in Modesto's ears – a soft hissing – and his face prickles. He begins to feel very sick; his eyelids are heavy. His eyes close, but he stretches them open again and rubs them, afraid to sleep in the company of these men. He wants to run from them, but his limbs will not move now and soon he closes his eyes again. This time they stay closed. He leans against the side of the big tub and his head droops: he no longer has the strength to lift it, though his mind is still clear.

Imprisoned now inside his body, he feels himself being lifted from the chair. Fingers fumble with his laces and someone takes off his doublet and shirt. He wants to stop them doing this and shouts at them to leave him alone, but the shout crawls out of his mouth as a mumble, and nobody listens. His shoes and hose are taken off and someone lifts him up – big hands grip under his armpits and knees. Hard fingers dig in.

He is put into the water. It is warm and comes up to his chest. He lies in the water for some time.

'Is he asleep?'

'Yes.'

No I'm not! Modesto screams at them silently through cold lips that will not move and he tries to open his eyes, but the lids are too heavy.

'Be quick, Paolo – the quicker you are, the less likely we are to lose him.'

Another pair of hands pushes his knees apart; he experiences a brief feeling of terrifying, wide exposure and then big fingers grope between his thighs and grip, a white hot pain cuts through the suffocating torpor and Modesto's eyes snap open. The noise he makes is not a scream – he cannot do it; it is more of a groan. And the water in the tub reddens around his legs.

*

It was particularly vivid that night. Although virtually no day passed in which he did not think of what had happened to him that day, it was rarely so painful. He seldom recalled the details with such intensity. He screwed his eyes shut and an animal noise came from him as he remembered once again the howling enormity of his loss. He was unaware of crying out, but moments after the sound had left his mouth, his door opened and Francesca said, 'Dear God, Modesto, whatever is it?' in a voice pitched high with anxiety.

She was untidily bundled in her wrap and wildly tangle-haired. She held the edges of the wrap bunched together in the fingers of one hand and crossed the long room to the bed where Modesto lay curled in a tight bunch of stiffened limbs.

'*Caro*, are you ill?' He turned his face away from her, and felt rather than saw Francesca drop to her knees beside his bed. She stroked his hair and murmured words he could not catch. He began to weep then: hard, reluctant sobs that coughed their way out of him as he stiffened in shame to be seen so by her. She rose from her knees and slid under his bedcovers; pushing him across the bed to make room for herself, she wrapped her arms around him and pulled his head onto her chest. Despite himself, Modesto clung to her and she held him tightly as he wept, one arm around his bulky body, fingers gripping his back, the other hand cupping his head. He could feel her cheek resting on his hair, her own hair fell around his face.

She held him without speaking for a long while; later, they slept.

Modesto opened swollen eyes to find his head still pillowed on his mistress's breast. Her wrap had fallen open and his cheek was pressed against her skin. Her arm was heavy and warmly sticky upon his back; her legs were scissored around his body.

She still smelled of peaches.

He could feel his face moving gently up and down as Francesca breathed, and was struck by a bitter irony: how singular it was, he thought, that he – a mutilated gelding – should be held *gratis* in the arms of this beautiful woman, when other whole men regularly paid a king's ransom for the same privilege.

He could, he knew, have done more than just lie in her arms. She had offered – several times – at the beginning. On hearing his story that first time, she had gazed at him, her lovely mouth part-open in shock. ' Oh, *caro*,' she had said, in a whisper. 'Why? Why would anybody do such a thing? How *could* they?'

He had had no answer.

'What happened, after . . .'

'I was very sick, for some time. Where they had cut me became infected, and I had a fever. For weeks. They thought I would die.'

She said nothing, but a single tear swelled, spilled over and ran down towards the corner of her mouth.

'When I was better, they sent me away. To train my voice. It took nearly eight years. And then I began to sing for a living.'

She had stared at him without speaking for a full minute. 'And then you met me,' she said. 'In Salerno.'

'I did.'

'And . . . have you ever . . .' she paused '. . . ever lain with a woman?'

His face burning with shame, he shook his head. Catching the inside of his cheek between his teeth, he bit it, trying to keep his face steady, and he saw her gaze move to his mouth. 'If . . . if you ever want to . . . to try,' she said, her fingers fiddling absently with the knot of laces at her breast. 'If you ever want to try, *caro*, you have only to ask. Just tell me.' She should have phrased the question differently. He *wanted* to try almost every day, but wanting to and feeling able to, are, he realised, two very different things. The thought of trying, and failing, and . . . of her witnessing his failure, made him feel quite sick.

He lifted his head. She opened her eyes.

'Oh. Oh, *caro*.' Francesca sat up. The soft skin on the inside of her thigh stuck for an instant on Modesto's belly as she pulled back from him.

Modesto said nothing. The corners of his mouth lifted a fraction, but he could not quite complete his smile. Embarrassment, shame, gratitude and flickers of what he realised must be his own pitiful version of desire, buzzed about him and he lowered his eyes in confusion.

'It hasn't been that bad in a long while, has it, *caro*?'

Modesto shook his head.

'What made you remember this time?'

He shrugged.

'Why do you do it?'

Her question startled him into speech. 'Why do I do what?'

'This: live here with me, watching and listening to what goes on here, day after day. God, Modesto, it must be hell for you. Why? Why do you want this?'

'You asked me to come here. When I had to stop singing – after I'd been ill. You know that.' He paused. 'You need me.'

It was Francesca's turn to stare without speaking. After a moment she said, 'You had a choice.' Her voice was low and he heard pity in it, and concern, and her compassion moved him.

'Yes. I made a choice,' Modesto said. 'And I don't regret it.'

'Ever?'

He shrugged again.

Francesca frowned. 'Are you ever . . . ever . . . jealous? Of the others?'

Modesto considered.

At times his jealousy burned like a brand. There were moments when, seated outside Francesca's chamber listening to what was happening within, his fist would clench around the handle of his dagger and his loathing of whichever visitor it happened to be would threaten to erupt into rash action. These men had, in such abundance, what had been taken from him – cut from him – with such callous disregard for his well-being. But then it would strike him, even as he got to his feet, that in fact he possessed something precious that none of these paying patrons had ever had: he *knew* the Signora in ways none of them ever would or could. Private, unspoken ways more intimate than the wildest of those men's purchased couplings.

What he had said to her was true: she needed him.

In his strange, indeterminate position as something between nursemaid, pimp and bodyguard, he had had occasion to comfort her at her most vulnerable – faint with fatigue, flushed with fever – he had washed her, mended her clothes and braided her hair with more care than many maidservants. But then, on other occasions he had – with fierce enjoyment – swung a heavy fist and laid out a rowdy, drunken customer who had begun to frighten the Signora. And once – just once – he had walked a naked and gibbering, sadistic aristocrat backwards out into the street at the point of the man's own rapier, threatening to run him through if he ever – ever – showed his face in the vicinity again. A trembling and terrified Francesca had clung to him on that night, he remembered, gasping out her gratitude for his having quite certainly saved her life.

After a long pause, his eyes fixed on those of his mistress, Modesto shook his head and said with a small, twisted smile, 'No. I am not jealous.'

'I could not do any of this without you.'

'I know, Signora.'

She reached for his hand and squeezed it. And then the absurdity of the situation suddenly struck Modesto and he began to laugh.

'What is it?'

His laugh died away into a sigh. 'Nothing. Just . . . just the thought of us tucked up here together: the seedless and the strumpet. What a bloody pair.'

'She is upstairs, Signor di Cicciano,' Modesto said. 'In her chamber.'

'Thank you. Can you take this?' Michele di Cicciano swung a coat from his shoulders and draped it over Modesto's outstretched arm, crossed the hall in a couple of long-legged strides and took the stairs three at a time. Modesto hung the coat on a hook by the door and followed the visitor up to the first floor. The door to the Signora's chamber was already closed by the time he reached the little landing and Modesto sat down upon the chair which stood just to the left of the door. He hunched and rolled his shoulders, preparing for a long wait. Sometimes – with trusted patrons like Benevento, for instance – she would say that she was happy for him to leave her unattended, but with men like Cicciano, whatever she said, he knew better.

Although he never exactly tried to listen to what went on, on the other side of the chamber wall, it was hard not to hear, and Modesto frequently found he could not prevent lively images forming in his mind to match the sounds he heard. Depending on his mood, he could find himself either entertained or enraged. Today, though, he felt oddly awkward when he thought about last night's intimacy with his mistress – it somehow made the contemplation of her energetic liaisons with her patrons rather harder to endure.

All he could hear at present was an indistinct rumble of

conversation, and he tried not to think of what was to come, distracting himself with thoughts of the covert concert engagement the Signora had told him about some hours before.

But then her voice, sharp with anger, cut through Modesto's musings, and his pulse raced.

'*Cazzo!* I said no! Just get rid of it, Michele! Put it away!'

Modesto stood, his heartbeat thudding in his ears; he put one hand on the handle of the door and reached for the hilt of his dagger.

Signor di Cicciano said something, but Modesto could not distinguish his words, and then the Signora spoke again, her voice cracking.

'No – I know, but not in here, damn you! You *know* why. Just give it here, or—'

There was a moment's pause, and then the sound of a slap, a muttered oath from the Signore and the beginnings of a scuffle.

Modesto pulled the dagger from his belt.

He opened the door.

Neither the Signora nor Cicciano heard him and he stood frozen, knife in hand, watching the two of them from the doorway. His mistress was crouched like a cat above the Signore, who lay on his back on the bed, arms flung up above his head, each of his wrists held tightly in one of the Signora's hands. Her hair hung forward, hiding her face so that Modesto could not see her expression, but even as he was about to step forward and interfere, she laughed. A mirthless little laugh it was, he thought, hard and joyless, but nevertheless, she certainly did not sound frightened, and he began to breathe more easily. He took a step back.

Then the Signore swore. '*Vaffanculo, stronza!*' He pushed upwards against her, trying to shift her weight.

'Ooh, what profanity, *maleducato!*' she said, through her teeth.

'I've told you before never to bring one in here. Haven't I?' She leaned forwards and jerked down on his wrists with each significant word as she spoke. 'Haven't I? Drop it! Go on – let go of it, Michele!' She shook his right arm vigorously: something, that gleamed as it caught the candlelight, fell from his fist to the floor with a clatter. 'You know perfectly well why – and, no, you are not having it back.'

Not having what back? thought Modesto.

'I'll do what I bloody like . . .'

'Oh, you think so, Michele, do you?' Francesca sat back on her heels and released his wrists; she pushed her hair back from her face and flattened her body down onto his chest, her elbows splayed, her fingers gripping his ribcage. A shiver tightened Modesto's scalp and buzzed down through his belly, but, ignoring it, he stepped back out into the corridor as Cicciano grabbed a fistful of Francesca's hair. He pulled the door closed silently behind him, his heartbeat still quick in his throat. There was a moment's pause, another rumble of indistinct voices, more scuffling and then a new sound – a *thunk*, as of metal in wood. He heard the Signora say, 'Ha! There you are – it can just stay there. No – get down! Get your hands off it! I told you, you are not having it back, *bastardo*!' Another slap. A squeal. And a laugh.

Modesto made himself breathe calmly.

After a few moments he sat back down on his chair. The sounds from the chamber became more predictable and Modesto closed his eyes, tipped his head back against the wall and prepared to wait out the duration of Signor di Cicciano's visit.

Four

Filippo di Laviano looked long at his wife. Her head in its crisp linen cap was bent over a small, calf-bound book. One or two tightly curling wisps tendrilled from under the edge of the unadorned linen, but it was obvious that these were rebellious escapees; the severity of Maria's hair and cap was clearly deliberate. This austerity was mirrored, too, in the upright carriage of her spine as she sat reading before the fire. She held the book in the flat of one hand, the forefinger of the other traced beneath the words she read. Her lips moved a little as she mouthed the lines. One might once have thought, mused Filippo, his eyes fixed upon his wife's mouth, that those tiny movements were mute invitations to be kissed. Once. Breathing in a long sigh through his nose, he compressed his own lips briefly and raised his eyebrows in a gesture of frustrated resignation, whilst Maria finished her page. She placed a narrow strip of red vellum down the length of the book and closed it tenderly.

For a time, neither she nor Filippo spoke at all. The room was still and quiet – all that could be heard was the soft crackle of the fire in the hearth. The squares of sky visible in the windows darkened from blue, through indigo to charcoal. Filippo stood for a moment and bent towards a pile of logs which stood to one side of the fireplace; he placed one carefully on the white-burning ghost of a thick branch, which crumbled and fell into the embers under the weight of the new wood. Opening a long silver box, he picked out three beeswax candles which he fitted into a triple candlestick on the mantelshelf. One by one he lit them carefully with a taper. Maria put her book down on the slim-legged table which stood next to her chair.

'What are you reading? Is it still *The Decameron*?' Filippo asked.

'Oh, no – I finished that last week. This is by a woman. Christine de Pizan. It's called *The Book of the City of Ladies*.'

The muscles of Filippo's face felt stiff as he smiled, as though the corners of his mouth were being pushed back down as fast as he tried to lift them.

'It pleases you? As much as the Boccaccio?' he said absent-mindedly, watching the curve of Maria's upper lip.

'Oh, yes. Despite her name, she was born in Venice, did you know?' Maria said.

'Who?' asked Filippo, not listening.

'Christine de Pizan. It is her father who came from Pizzano. She lived in France for most of her life, apparently, and wrote everything in French. I'm very lucky to have found a translation – it would have been such a struggle for me to read it in the original.'

'What is it about?' Filippo tried to arrange his features into a semblance of polite interest.

Maria smiled at him and began to explain. 'It's about the extraordinary achievements of women. She describes having a vision. It is not a vision that ever actually happened to her – at least I don't think so – but she describes three ladies who . . .'

Filippo was still not listening. He saw the light in Maria's eyes as she spoke about this book she quite clearly loved; he watched her slim hands move with unselfconscious grace, and thought uncomfortably of the ease with which he could extinguish that light. With no more than a simple request he could – and too often did – transform this vivid enthusiasm into a stiff and expressionless anxiety. A ripple of guilt clutched at his scalp like a too-tight hat.

The door opened and a thin woman of around thirty-five came in. With her dark hair drawn back from her face in unadorned simplicity, she had the air of a Bellini Madonna, though Filippo had always imagined that the Mother of God would have possessed rather more in the way of animation of feature than his wife's sister ever did. She bobbed a curtsy to Filippo, and sat down next to Maria. Laying a bony hand on her sister's sleeve, she said, 'Maria, I was in the kitchen a moment ago and, do you know, I am not sure that the venison will be ready for tomorrow. Would you be happy with the pork?'

'What's the matter with the venison?'

'I don't think it has hung long enough.'

A flicker of annoyance crossed Maria's face, but vanished almost as fast as it had appeared and she smiled.

'It is not a problem, Emilia. I'm sure the pork will be delicious. We can have the venison on Sunday. Thank you for thinking of it.'

Filippo sat impassively in his chair watching this conversation unroll and pass him by. Neither his wife nor her sister seemed to wish to include him in this trivial domestic hiccup and although he was not in the least interested in the change in the menu, he nonetheless felt the clench of a little fist of resentment in his chest at being thus ignored.

Emilia stood up. 'I think I will go to bed. It's late.' She bent and kissed her sister's cheek; Filippo watched his wife's eyes close momentarily and her mouth push forward in a brief echo of a kiss, as Emilia's lips brushed against her skin. His cock twitched. Even now, after so long, it still twitched.

'Good night, Filippo,' Emilia said then with an unenthusiastic smile as she left the room. Filippo's gaze moved to where his wife sat staring into the embers. 'Maria,' he said.

She glanced across at him, her sudden wariness glaringly obvious.'

'I've told Luca I'll be going to the play on my own. I told him that you haven't been very well.' He paused. 'He says he hopes you will be fully recovered soon. He was very understanding.'

Maria's colour deepened. She nodded, but said nothing, and kept her gaze fixed upon the fire.

'Please don't worry yourself about the matter, Maria,' Filippo said, thinking to himself that it was he who needed to be understanding, rather than Luca.

The next morning, Maria was nowhere to be seen, and Filippo spent a few irritating moments hurrying from room to room searching for her to say goodbye. He did not like to call her. He found her eventually in the downstairs back room, which overlooked the garden, already busy with her book. Today, she had a quill in her hand, and Filippo saw that she was engrossed by what she read. A piece of paper next to the book was already covered with notes, and fresh ink gleamed on the end of the quill as it hovered above the sheet.

'I have to go,' Filippo said.

'Do you know when you will be back?'

Filippo thought about this. It was a Friday, and he was normally at home early on a Friday. It was only on Wednesdays that he was late. But, he began reasoning with himself now, perhaps if he was only ever late on a Wednesday, Maria might become suspicious. Her suspicions would, he was sure, distress her, and he had no wish to do that. So he lied. 'I have a great deal of work to accomplish today, Maria. I might well be late again. Perhaps as late as the other night, though I'll try my hardest to get away before then.'

Maria gave him a tight little smile, nodded, returning to her book, just as Filippo bent to kiss her. She seemed not to see his descending face, and his kiss grazed her temple. Filippo hesitated, then stood upright once more and cleared his throat. 'You might have gone to bed before I return,' he said. 'So I'll perhaps not see you until tomorrow, then, if I am delayed as long as I fear.'

The closing of her eyes as he spoke again was momentary, but Filippo felt chastened. He said no more.

The sun was already high, and though the summer was truly over, the air was mild and no breeze blew. Filippo was grateful that the fiercest heat of August had passed; when the fetid oppressiveness of Napoli's darker streets clung to the skin like sweat-damp sheets, and the black threat of typhoid lurked in every stagnant gutter.

Having decided not to take the little carriage, it took Filippo some half an hour to walk to his destination. He headed east along the street that spanned the very edge of the bay, for half a mile and then turned inland, leaving the sea behind him. As he moved away from the coast, the streets narrowed into a labyrinthine tangle, but Filippo determinedly wound his way through, and he reached the great church of San Pietro a Maiella with ease.

Some two streets further on, the apartments of *Maestre de Campo*, Don Miguel Vasquez, faced onto a dilapidated but obviously once sumptuous piazza, whose peeling stucco and graceful arches were at the same time elegant and shabby, like a fading dowager still clad in the outmoded finery of her youth. The piazza was already crowded: marketeers were setting up their wares, old men were gathering in stiff-legged clusters in the vaulted alleys that led in and out of the sun-filled square; a squealing group of ragged urchins raced the length of the piazza. Filippo stood for a second to let these chattering, tattered starlings pass in front of him, before he set off across the diagonal towards Don Miguel's flaking front door.

Miguel Vasquez ran a finger down his list of activities for the day. Filippo watched him for a second and pondered as he did so on the nature of arrogance. Was arrogance innate in the personality of someone who was prepared to work as part of an alien occupying military force in a foreign country, or did the very nature of the position, *create* arrogance in characters who had not before possessed it? For *Maestre* Vasquez was indeed arrogant, thought Filippo, perhaps even the very personification of the word.

Maestre Vasquez was also, however, slim and graceful. His movements were fluid and quick; he gesticulated frequently in his speech and, though the *Maestre*'s eyes were cold, his hands were as expressive as a dancer's. In his company Filippo was frequently reminded of his own increasing age and lack of agility. Though he could not have been much more than fifteen years the senior, Filippo often felt in Vasquez's presence like an aging, heavy-hoofed hack in the company of an Arab colt.

'Come and see this, Filippo,' said the colt, in Spanish, and Filippo crossed the room to where Vasquez stood frowning at his papers in front of the long window. 'Does the Conte di Ladispoli mean to attend the parade or not?'

Filippo peered at the spidery writing on the small sheet of paper Vasquez then held out to him.

I am, Signore, quite delighted to have been considered amongst your honoured guests, and regret most sincerely that I have not yet replied before but with my travels to Sicily now imminent I have been most sorely pressed and have only just extricated myself from several other less agreeable commitments.

'I think he means to attend, Signore.' Filippo smiled. 'He is always – how shall I say – *tortuoso* in his written communications. Always use ten words when one would suffice, he would say . . .'

Vasquez twitched his shoulders in a dismissive shrug and threw the Conte di Ladispoli's letter down onto a large pile of similar sheets. It took the two men the best part of the following hour to sort out the various replies and by the end, a pile of letters of regret lay to one side of them, they had compiled a list of attendees, and the Spaniard had begun to draw up a plan of the parade ground. It was to be quite an occasion, it seemed to Filippo. A flamboyant exposition of Spanish power – ostensibly for the sake of entertainment, perhaps, but it would nevertheless be meant to be seen as a warning against any future insurrection, he felt sure.

Vasquez then leant across the table and picked up a finger-thick stack of paper. 'Filippo,' he said, 'I need this put into Italian.'

Filippo flipped through the document: close-written in a spiky hand. His heart sank. This was not a task he would enjoy. Spanish had been as familiar to him as Italian since babyhood – his Castilian mother never having managed to master Italian – and Filippo and his superior always spoke together in Spanish, but Filippo found the painstaking business of translating anything this lengthy extremely tedious. He thumbed the sheets and glanced up at his companion.

'By when, Signore?'

Opening a large, calf-bound ledger, the Spaniard ran a slim

forefinger down first one page, then the following. He frowned and the soft tuft of beard just beneath his lower lip lifted as he pouted in concentration. Then, finding what he sought, he tapped the place twice. 'You have ten days. You can have the Long Chamber today, if you like. Nobody is using it.'

'Thank you, Signore – I will do that. May I go and make a start on it right away?'

'Yes. I shall not need you for anything else today.'

Filippo left the room without a word.

He worked hard for several hours. He had had hopes that the document might have contained something titillating: perhaps a whisper of the intransigent Don Pedro de Alfàn's plans for the re-establishment of the tyranny of the Inquisition – news with which Napoli had been buzzing for weeks. The papers, however, revealed nothing at all startling and Filippo was soon bored.

He began to think back to the other evening at Francesca's. Running his tongue over his lips, he pictured the door to her bed-chamber. Ajar. He imagined pulling the door open as he did each week, and he smiled at the thought of the candlelight that always spilled out into the corridor, the warm smell of burning rose-wood – she always had the fire lit – and the headiness of the cut flowers she liked so much. Breathing a little faster, Filippo ran the flat of his hand down over his breeches, rubbed his palm over his cock and shut his eyes. Saw Francesca sitting on the edge of her bed. Saw himself crouching before her, his fingers gripping her knees. He swallowed, wiped his face and returned to his translation. Into his mind came another, less welcome picture: a fleeting glimpse of the sweet curve of Maria's lip. Filippo frowned and began once again to write – with every semblance of enthusiasm.

*

'I worry about you, Maria,' Emilia said.

Maria ignored her scowling sister. She closed her book, replaced the quill in its small iron pot and rubbed at the ink stains on her thumb and first two fingers. Picking up the three small sheets of thick paper she had by now covered with scribbled notes, she read quickly through what she had written. A little crooked line puckered the skin between her brows, but as she finished reading, her expression cleared and she tucked the three leaves inside the green leather-bound *Book of the City of Ladies* with an air of some satisfaction.

Emilia's arms were tightly folded, and her bottom lip pushed forward sulkily as she stood and watched. 'What if it were to become generally known how many hours in a week you devote to your books?' she said. 'And that book in particular. I do not believe I know any other woman who does what you do.'

'It is no secret, *cara*—' Maria began, but Emilia interrupted.

'Well, it ought to be, Maria. It does not seem – I do not know what the word should be . . .'

'Well, perhaps if you read a little more widely yourself, you would be able to find the words you seek with more ease,' Maria said sharply. 'Come, let us go and take the air – and no more criticism of how I choose to spend my time. As we go, I will tell you something of de Pizan . . . perhaps her story will convince you that it is quite proper for women to choose to improve their minds.'

'I doubt very much that Filippo cares for your studies . . .' Emilia muttered.

Maria flushed. 'I think that what passes between a wife and her husband should remain their business alone, do you not agree, Emilia?' And, tucking another curl back under her cap with fingers that shook, she stood and strode past Emilia to the door.

The two sisters walked in silence through the narrow streets.

Maria sensed rather than saw the sideways glances that Emilia threw towards her every few moments, but she made no attempt to talk to her. The stuff of their stiffened skirts whispered as they walked, as though in muffled conversation together, but other than this the two women made no sound at all; each seemed absorbed in her own thoughts.

But now it was no longer her book that occupied Maria's mind: she thought instead of her husband.

She was sure that Filippo believed she did not love him.

The sisters who had raised her so carefully after the death of both her parents had done their work well, she thought. As well as instructing her in the faith, they had taught her to read, to write both in Latin and Italian, to be intelligently curious about the world around her – and to regard the 'will of the flesh' with dark dread, in case it should lure her into irreparable sin. Even now, more than ten years a respectable wife, Sister Annunziata's dire indictments still whined inside her head if ever she sensed Filippo's gaze begin to wander to her mouth or her breasts. Great iron gates would clang down around her and she would feel her face close in upon itself, shutting her away from him behind a carefully practised mask of untroubled elegance.

Wincing, Maria saw herself each time as Filippo must see her: repulsing his advances, turning from his kisses, cold and apparently unaware of his need for her. He still wanted her. Although she was unsure why, after so long with no encouragement, she knew that her husband did still look at her with longing.

And though she never responded it was not because she did not wish to.

He had leant past her at dinner only yesterday, reaching for a wine bottle. They had been sitting together, with Emilia facing them across the table, and Filippo had inadvertently pressed against her side as he had stretched across her. She had sensed his warm bulk, and smelled his comfortable male smell of woodsmoke and sweat. Glancing at his hand gripping the neck of the bottle, Maria had held her breath. How easy it should have been, she thought angrily, to have smiled at him then, to have perhaps reached across under the table, out of sight of her sister, and stroked his thigh for a moment, just to show him that he was loved. That he was desired.

But she had not been able to move.

It is not long after midday prayers, and the sun is fierce. Sister Antonia has closed the shutters in the big room which Maria and Emilia have shared for nearly a year, but little white slivers of light are pushing their way through the gaps between the slats, dappling the walls and sliding over Maria's bed.

The room smells — as it always does — of beeswax and dust, and there's a faint, faint whiff of mould from the stone walls, which to Maria has always seemed somehow more of a taste than a smell.

'I think you two children should stay in for a while now — it is too hot to go out this afternoon,' Sister Antonia says, and it's true — the sun has been baking down all morning. Although it is windy, there is no respite from the heat: the wind is hot, like air pushing out of an unwisely opened oven. Sister's big dough-coloured forehead glitters with glass beadlets of sweat, and the dark hairs on her upper lip are shining. Her face seems too fat for her coif. It bulges, and the stiff, stained, linen edges of the coif dig in all around her face. Maria imagines that when Sister Antonia undresses at night, her coif must leave a deep groove all around her face; as though she were wearing a mask.

'Have a little rest now,' the big nun says, as she leaves the room. 'You can come down later and help prepare the evening meal.'

She bustles out of the room like a pillow in a habit.

Maria lies still for some moments with her knees crooked up, and watches the light playing across her dress, little pools of creamy whiteness that shift and move across the blue linen as the branches of the tree outside rustle uncomfortably in the hot wind; then she shuts her eyes and listens.

Emilia's breathing has slowed: she must already be asleep. Her sister always sleeps easily, Maria thinks with a pang of envy. She herself knows all too well the unnerving mixture of stifling boredom and unpredictable fears that can fill a wakeful night.

Outside, cicadas chirr rhythmically — on and on without pause, a ceaseless accompaniment to the afternoon; though sometimes they do suddenly stop — inexplicably all together — for seconds at a time, leaving a silence like a ripped hole in the noise they have been making. When they start again each time, Maria imagines the sound as grains of sand, trickling back into the hole.

A new noise.

Above the scratchscratch of the cicadas comes a grunt. Scuffling and leaf-rustling.

Maria crosses to the window and puts her eye to one of the gaps in the slats.

The boy from the village is climbing the big tree again. He often spies on her in the gardens when she is outside, and tries to see in through her window when she is indoors. She watches him now: long thin brown legs sticking out of tattered breeches, grease-spiked black hair and a prominent nose like a goose's beak. His skin seems dusty. He both intrigues and repulses her: his eyes are bright and knowing, and his stare often sends a little warm worm of embarrassment down through her guts, but there is something of the mantis about him, she thinks now, as he moves from branch up to branch with slow deliberation, bare toes seeking the next foothold, hands reaching and grasping, craning towards her window to try and see in through the shutters.

She knows that it is probably sinful to think it, but she likes the idea that the boy wants to look at her.

There is a whip-crack of splintering wood.

'No!' Maria gasps and presses her face to the gap in the shutter, feeling her nose flatten against the resin-smelling wood, but the boy is falling away from where she can see. She hears another grunt, several more cracks, and a deadened thud. Then nothing.

Fumbling with the fastening of the shutters, Maria unlocks them and throws them wide. Hot sunlight pushes into the room, making her wince, and for a moment she is quite blinded. But then she sees a crumpled angular shape on the ground. Unmoving.

'What is it? Mia? Why have you opened the—?'

Maria ignores her sister, and, panting, scrabbles her way out of the room.

The sisters say he has broken his neck. Maria and Emilia have not seen the boy – they have been forbidden to go to the sickroom, but they've heard the sisters whispering; have seen them shake their heads and cross themselves; have heard the endless chanted prayers in the chapel. Four days ago, Maria heard Sister Cecilia say he still cannot move at all. Sister said he might die.

Maria wants to see him. A lump of guilt like a cold plum has been lodged uncomfortably in her chest for days.

Emilia says, 'But it's his own fault, Mia, he was being nosy. It's very sad, if he has hurt himself, but—'

'How can you say that?'

'Well, it's true. It's nothing to do with you.'

Maria stares at her sister for a moment, then turns on her heel and makes for the door.

'Where are you going?'

Maria ignores her.

The plum has shifted up into her throat. She has to see the boy.

She walks down two long corridors, out into the sandy square, dimpled all over with footprints, that lies within the cloisters, and in through the door on the far side. The sickroom is around the next corner.

The door is open.

Maria walks up to it, slowly, slowly, heartbeat thick and loud in her ears.

She hesitates. Holds her breath. Peers into the room.

Sister Angelica is standing in front of a table, with her back to the door, ladling soup from a pewter jug into a small bowl. The boy is lying on a truckle bed in the corner of the room: an abandoned marionette, all strings severed. His face is now ashen and slack, and the goose-beak nose stands out, as though it has been stuck on as part of a disguise. His mouth is crooked, his lips loose and too wet. A thin line of dribble has slid from the corner of his mouth, down his jaw towards his ear like a snail's trail. And his eyes are enormous: wide and dark with fear.

He sees her.

Stares at her.

No longer insolent and knowing, his gaze moves jerkily across her face, and up and down her body. Pleading. Maria feels sick. He reminds her of a rabbit she once saw in a trap: wire pulled tight around its throat, it lay still and trembling, passive and unresisting in the torpidity of all-encompassing terror.

Sister Angelica crouches down beside the boy and gently lifts a spoonful of soup to his mouth. His eyes move then from Maria to the elderly nun, and Maria sees them bulge slightly as he tries to take the soup from the bowl of the spoon. A few drops seem to trickle past his teeth, but most of it runs down his chin. He cannot move his head. He cannot even open his mouth.

Maria tries to imagine the suffocating horror of being imprisoned like this, locked silent and frightened into a coffin of flesh. The beseeching expression in the boy's eyes makes her feel light-headed. She can feel her stomach churning.

Glancing across at her sister, Maria said, 'Emilia, do you remember the boy with the broken neck?'

Emilia frowned. 'Which boy?'

'At the convent. The one who couldn't move. The one who died.'

'Oh, yes,' Emilia said with surprise in her voice. 'That poor creature. He fell out of a tree, didn't he? I haven't thought of him for years. What made you remember him?'

'I don't know,' Maria lied. 'What a terrible thing, though, do you not agree? To be trapped like that inside a body that cannot do what you ask of it.' Her voice shook a little, but her sister did not seem to notice Maria's unease.

'What a strange thing for you to be thinking,' Emilia said.

There was a long pause. All Maria could hear were their footfalls on the cobbled path. Her sister's face was, as usual, quite impassive and unreadable, and in an instant Maria was rocked by a sudden need to ask Emilia about her intimacies with her late husband. She felt sick. Had Emilia endured the same suffocating, broken-necked paralysis in the bedchamber as she always did? Or had the sisters' hellfire-scorched injunctions somehow passed her by? When Antonio had died – had there been, somewhere beneath the grief Maria knew her sister had genuinely suffered, a wash of relief? She knew, in a jumble of muddled guilt and self-loathing, that if Emilia had indeed been, for the years of her marriage, as miserably confused as she herself still was, she, Maria, would in some strange way feel less alone. Her instinctively compassionate nature hoped – quite genuinely – that her sister's marriage had been a happy one, but another less forgiving voice at the back of her mind could not help yearning for a companion in her isolation.

Emilia interrupted her thoughts, saying, 'Funny, you remembering that boy. You've made me think of any number of things from our time at San Sebastiano, Maria. Do you remember Sister Cecilia and that lizard?'

In spite of her discomposure, the memory of the incompetent and corpulent Sister Cecilia's inept attempts to capture the errant reptile in the convent chapel made Maria smile. The two sisters spent a few moments sharing memories of their years with the nuns, and then they both fell silent once more as they turned towards home.

Maria thought about the evening ahead and the brief sense of amusement she had felt at her childhood memories trickled away and vanished like water into sand. She had guessed what it was that Filippo did on those occasions when he returned late to the house. She sensed something dishonest in his eye, and there was often a certain familiar slipperiness about his lower lip, when he gave his regular excuses.

She did not blame Filippo, though, and in some confused way found herself even feeling grateful to whoever the woman might be, for thus tending to her husband, and so releasing her, Maria, from the obligations she found so difficult to fulfil. But she also knew a painful, screaming jealousy when she allowed pictures to form in her mind of her husband's hands on another body. Even though the touch of those hands on her own skin froze her into immobility. She could hardly bear to think of how Filippo would be spending his evening and yet, with a trickle of shame, Maria admitted to herself a certain relief that tonight at least, he would not need to ask her the question she dreaded.

She felt hot tears sting the corners of her eyes, and wiped them surreptitiously with the tips of her fingers, turning her head so that Emilia would not see.

She hoped this unknown woman did not love her husband. And hoped rather more desperately that Filippo did not love the woman.

I surprised myself last night. I couldn't sleep, and I found myself thinking about Filippo and the impossibility of his situation, and as I lay there thinking, I realised, much to my astonishment, that I actually envy his wife. How strange that must sound, for a courtesan to admit that she envies a frigid woman. But Filippo's wife has something I have never had – a man who loves her. I'm sure from what Filippo says that that is the case, despite everything. I imagine what would happen if I withheld my favours from my patrons, the way Filippo's wife does from him. Dear God, if I were ever even to suggest it, I should very soon be left with nothing and no one. And I doubt it would take long.

Filippo's wife is truly a lucky woman. She is loved for who she is, and not for what she does or how she looks.

Five

Some eight or nine small tables had been crammed into the front room of the dockside tavern; the place was crowded and airless, and smelled strongly of salt and sweat and cheap tallow, and of wet cloth drying against unwashed skin. A clotted rumble of conversation hung over the tables, whilst a man, seated to one side of an open fireplace, picked out a plaintive tune on a wooden pipe. Several women – painted faces, bleached and braided hair – had clustered together nearby to listen. Candles burned at each table, and the faces of the many drinkers were indistinct and deeply shadowed.

Carlo della Rovere was sitting at the far end of the room. He was being watched. A thin, pigtailed young man in dirty, crumpled shirt and breeches was chewing on a fingernail and staring towards where Carlo was rubbing at the filthy glass of one of the windows with his thumb. He watched as Carlo peered out moodily for several seconds and then scowled back down at his now blackened thumb. Carlo rubbed the dirty thumb on his breeches, and drained the small glass of clear spirit that had been standing on the table in front of him, grimacing open-mouthed and blinking as his eyes watered. Turning towards where the young man stood in the shadows, he raised a hand and called, 'Marco!'

The young man's face burned. He licked his lips, flicked the cloth he was carrying so that it fell across one shoulder, and set off across the crowded tavern. After yesterday, he said to himself as he stood up on his toes to edge sideways through a narrow gap between tables, he thought he might allow himself to hope for a few moments alone with this Signor della Rovere tonight, after the tavern closed. Marco had a good idea what he might do with those moments if he was offered them – Signor della Rovere's preferences had been quite obvious, from the fragment of conversation that had passed between them last night. He was good looking, Marco thought – fairer than most men in Napoli – slight, no taller than he himself. And not that many years older. By the look of the Signore's clearly recently purchased doublet – a decent bit of doeskin by the look of it – and that pretty little silver dagger in his belt, he was not short of money. And Marco rather liked the expression on the Signore's face – he looked bored and arrogant and sulky. A wealthy young man in need of entertainment, Marco thought. The sort of entertainment he was more than happy to provide.

Reaching Carlo's table and leaning in towards him, Marco laid a hand on Carlo's sleeve. 'Would you care for another *grappa*, Signore?' he said.

Carlo looked at Marco's fingers for a moment. Then, raising his gaze to the pigtailed boy's face, he lifted an eyebrow and said, 'Yes. Thank you. Bring the bottle, would you? And another couple of glasses. I'm expecting company.'

'I won't be a moment, Signore,' Marco said, his eyes on Carlo's mouth.

Carlo turned back to peer through the little cleaned patch of glass.

Marco wormed through the jostle of drinkers to where several shelves stood ranked with bottles of *grappa*, brandy, rum, wine and ale. He sidled past the elderly tavern owner, bent down and reached for a full bottle of *grappa* from the lowest shelf. Looking back over to Carlo's table, he paused. Two men had entered the tavern and were pushing through the other drinkers, towards where Carlo sat. With the bottle and the two requested glasses in his hands, Marco followed them, watching critically. One was richly dressed: tall, lean, long-legged, his hair close-cropped and curly, and his nose noticeably once-broken. The other was older: slight, more than a head shorter, dressed in salt-spattered seaman's breeches and boots. He was dark and wiry, with tangled hair and a beard teased into several long, twine-thin plaits.

The taller of the two newcomers called out, 'Carlo!' and Signor della Rovere turned around.

'Cicciano,' he said, nodding at the newcomer. 'Glad you could make it. Do you want a drink?'

'God, yes – and I'm sure Żuba here would too. He's just brought me ashore from his ship in some accursed pisspot of a rowing boat. Not an experience I relished. Yes, I would certainly welcome a *grappa*.'

Carlo smiled. 'Signore,' he said to the little man with the Medusa plaits. 'I've been looking forward to meeting you for some weeks. Michele here has told me much about you and your beautiful little ship – a *sciabecco*, is it not? – and the plans you both have for the next few months.'

'And I have heard much about you, *Sinjur*,' said Żuba. His Maltese accent was lilting and lazy.

'I understand from Michele,' Carlo said, 'that he has had your ship refitted.'

'Indeed, *Sinjur*. My little *Għafrid* is looking as beautiful as she has ever done, I think.'

'And in return he's expecting a tenth of your pickings?'

Żuba pecked a nod.

Michele di Cicciano ran the fingers of both hands up and into his hair; he sat with elbows winged on each side of his head for a second, then laced his fingers together and cracked the knuckles. Smirking, he said, 'The "pickings" look set to be particularly fruitful since Żuba received his Letter of Marque.'

Carlo turned to Żuba. 'A Letter of Marque? From De Valette?'

Both Żuba and Cicciano nodded. Żuba began curling the stringy braids beneath his chin around his index finger. Marco, standing in the shadows a few feet away, saw, with a shudder of revulsion, that the little man had only the first two fingers on that hand – the fourth and fifth were merely stumps.

'It's not just any Letter of Marque, either, Rovere,' Cicciano said, grinning. 'As Governor of Malta, De Valette has assured Żuba that as well as all the privileges of becoming a "privateer", he and his men can keep anything they . . . er . . . "acquire" on a voyage. All of it. Every last *scudo*.'

'All of it? But . . . that's extraordinary.'

'Mmm. Never heard of it before. Usually at least a quarter has to be handed over. But this – it's all the delights of piracy, with a reprieve from hanging if you're caught. Now, thanks to Żuba's capture of a particularly troublesome . . . how shall I put it? . . . "regular visitor" from the Barbary Coast, De Valette has declared that our friend here has the right to keep everything he finds – so long as he ensures that he only sets his sights upon the enemies of Malta.'

Carlo puffed out his surprise.

'Which makes my tenth of whatever they find considerably more attractive,' Michele said cheerfully.

Marco stepped out of the shadows. He thumped the bottle and glasses down on the table in front of the three men and turned away, torn between fascination with the discussion upon which he was eavesdropping, and irritation that his expectations for the end of the evening now seemed likely to be disappointed. He snatched up the coins that Carlo had thrown down onto the table, and turned his back, moving away towards another table.

'What's the matter with the boy?' he heard Michele ask.

Carlo spoke softly, but, little more than feet away, Marco could just hear his words. 'I think he had . . . hopes for an interesting conclusion to the evening. I might just have to go and find him when we have finished. I shouldn't wish to disappoint him. He has been so *very* attentive ever since I arrived.'

Marco's insides lurched. He took the grimy cloth from his shoulder and began to mop up some spilled ale. Then, bunching up his now sodden cloth, and keeping his back to Carlo's table, he edged into the shadows.

Michele di Cicciano said, 'Tell Rovere about the encounter with the *Sforza*, Salvatore.'

Żuba curled his fingers up and through his plaits again. 'It was as simple as picking a bunch of flowers, *Sinjur*,' he said.

Carlo grinned.

'The *Sforza*'s a carrack, as you'll probably know, *Sinjur*,' Żuba went on. 'Lovely ship – but none too easy to board. She carries awnings over her decks as a deterrent to uninvited guests – dirty great spars, close-laid like a roof.' He paused, amused. 'Well, she *usually* carries awnings.'

His two listeners waited.

'Happened to hear she was travelling without them on this voyage. Seemed a good opportunity.' Another long pause whilst Żuba drained his glass, reached for the bottle and refilled it. 'Now, a heavy vessel like a carrack – such as the *Sforza* – draws deep, *Sinjur*. Needs nigh-on four fathoms.'

Michele and Carlo both nodded.

'And being square-rigged, she's at something of a disadvantage sailing into the wind when compared to a lightweight little lateen-rigger like the *Għafrid*. She can't turn quickly, see, like we can. Can't sail so close to the wind.'

'Where did you find her?' Carlo asked.

'Picked up the trail just outside Marsala, and then tracked her from there right down past the island of Pantelleria. She slowed when the wind turned to the east, about thirty miles off the island, but our rig suits windward sailing – so we kept the *Għafrid* close in, and caught up with the *Sforza* heading towards Tunisia. Drew up by her stern and boarded aft over the 'castle.'

Żuba paused and refilled his glass again. He said softly, 'It was quick. Not pretty perhaps, but quick, *Sinjur*. The benefits of the unexpected attack. With a *sciabecco* we sail almost silent.'

'The pickings?'

Żuba's smile broadened again. 'Worth it. Well worth it.' He nodded towards Michele. 'Your tenth would have pleased you well, I reckon, *Sinjur*.'

'What was she carrying?' Carlo asked.

'Gold, luckily, and a fair quantity of alum. One or two of the wealthier passengers had a number of . . . items . . . too, that we were pleased to dispose of for them.'

'I'm sure you found good homes for it all.'

'Of course, *Sinjur* – in the end. And De Valette none the wiser, as it happens on this occasion.'

'Even better,' Michele said.

'Just how often are the "pickings" in the form of coin?' Carlo asked.

'Sometimes. Not always. It's as often stones, silks – other goods . . .'

Carlo glanced around the room to ensure no one was listening to him. Picking at his fingernails, he said, 'Might a *ricettatore* be of any help to you, Signore? Someone to get the . . . goods . . . *translated* into coinage for you? I understand from Michele that you might be in need . . .'

'And might that *ricettatore* be yourself, *Sinjur*?'

A flick of the eyebrows by way of assent.

Żuba frowned down at the scarred stumps of his two missing fingers and ran his thumb slowly over the puckered flesh. Carlo gazed steadily at Żuba and Michele tilted his chair back onto two legs, crooked one leg up and rested the sole of his boot on the edge of the table.

'He's good, Salvatore,' Michele muttered. He let his chair fall back onto four legs with a bang. 'As I told you. He will get good prices for whatever you throw at him. For anything.'

Żuba watched Carlo without speaking for several long seconds, his gaze moving from one of Carlo's eyes to the other, back and forth. One hand fingered the tiny plaits beneath his chin.

'And what exactly would you be wanting to gain from this, *Sinjur*?' he said, after a pause.

'Another tenth.'

'No.' Żuba shook his head. 'Too much.'

'A twelfth, then.'

Żuba considered. 'A twelfth of what is left after Cicciano takes his cut,' he said at last.

Carlo frowned, but, after a pause, nodded once. 'Very well.'

Marco reappeared from his shadowed corner. 'Would you care for more *grappa*, signori?' he said.

Carlo smiled up at him. 'Thank you – no.' Marco held his gaze for a moment, then turned to go, but Carlo caught his arm before he could leave. He felt Carlo's thumb stroking his protruding wrist-bone for a second, then Carlo smiled and said, 'I might perhaps see you before I leave.' Marco nodded, ran his tongue across his lip and left, hoping that Carlo was watching his back.

From a vantage point behind a protruding brick buttress, he saw Michele di Cicciano pick up one of the glasses and raise it to eye level. 'Well, Salvatore . . . does the *Għafrid* have a new crew member?'

Żuba curled one of his plaits around his forefinger again, jutting his chin forward so that his crooked lower teeth overlapped the upper. He stared silently from Michele to Carlo and back for several seconds, and then his eyes crinkled into a smile and he raised his glass to clink it against Michele's. 'Aye, *Sinjur*, I think that we do.'

Carlo's eyes glittered and he joined in the toast.

Behind his buttress, Marco fingered the bone of his wrist and watched the three men drain their glasses.

Six

As well as being 'particular', as Cristo said he would be, my little Spanish soldier has turned out to be a very secretive person. It's strange, but he has consistently refused to come to my house in the Via San Tommaso, preferring, he says, to site our tumbles on that great gold-hung *lettiera* in his apartments in the Via dei Tribunali. Personally, I would have thought that if secrecy was such an overriding preoccupation, then sneaking out to my house would be much easier and safer for him than allowing me to visit him in his apartment. But he doesn't seem to share my opinion.

Each time I come here, it is always through that same servants' entrance, though since that first day, it has almost always been Vasquez himself letting me in. If a servant ever opens the door, Vasquez appears within seconds, and dismisses the servant instantly. I can only imagine that everyone is given strict instructions to keep away, for I never see anyone about; Vasquez has made sure that no one interrupts our hours together, so far, and he has always insisted that I bring none of my own people with me. In fact, since that day when I was bundled into his room by his servants, and turned by them into a gauze-wrapped gift, the palatial apartments at the Via dei Tribunali have apparently been completely deserted, apart from the two of us. We climb the stairs to his rooms together each time, entirely alone, our footsteps echoing in the emptiness. I always feel as if I should be whispering.

This afternoon, some three weeks after our first encounter, I have another invitation to dine with *Maestre* Miguel Vasquez.

We eat like royalty at every meeting, Vasquez and I, that's one thing – so I suppose that, despite appearances, there must be servants somewhere in the building preparing the food. Although he is very slight and slim, Vasquez seems to derive almost as much pleasure from food as from fucking. He positively stuffs himself each time we sit down to a meal, whereas I frequently feel rather sick after consuming less than half the amount he does. It *is* always delicious, but it's often far too rich – sucking pig glazed in honey, tiny liver and pork *tomacelli*, oysters, of course – often oysters – the finest pike and crayfish and numberless beautiful bowls of the most fragrant fruits. It's always delicious, but I frequently struggle to finish what I'm given. Thinking about this, if our relationship is to continue, I shall have to start watching how much of it all I actually eat, or I'll end by becoming horribly fat, and then no one will want to bed me at all, and my life as a courtesan will be at an end.

'I'll be back later to bring you home,' Modesto says, as we arrive at Vasquez's apartments. He regards me critically, then tucks a stray wisp of hair behind my ear, brushes something from my shoulder and runs a thumb gently along one cheekbone. As he usually does, Modesto has accompanied me from the Via San Tommaso, and he will collect me again later on. Although Vasquez does not care for my manservant to stay on the premises, he hasn't objected so far to Modesto seeing me safely to and from the door.

'Thank you, *caro*. I'll pass on any interesting tidbits as soon as I see you, of course.'

'Hmm.' Modesto sounds grumpy.

'What's the matter? Why are you looking at me like that?'

'Well – it's all very well your regaling me with these scandalous nuggets of tittle-tattle that you pick up in all the various beds you inhabit, Signora –'

I look sideways at him, and raise an eyebrow.

' – but you ought to write it down more regularly. You need to keep that book of yours up to date.'

'I always do.'

'Always?' Modesto looks sceptical. He glares at me for a second and then says, 'Well. You make sure you do. It's important – you never know when you might need to draw on that store of tasty little snippets.'

'I promise, *caro*. Everything I tell you, I'll write down as well.' I kiss his cheek as the door is opened by the servant who met me that first time. His name, I have discovered since, is Juan.

To my surprise, rather than wearing his usual smile, Juan looks anxious – almost panicked, in fact. Before I can say a word, he has hustled me inside, nodded farewell to Modesto, and closed the door. 'I so sorry, Señora,' he says. 'I not know where he is. He not here since hours.'

'Please don't worry. I can wait. I'm sure he'll be here as soon as he can. Shall I just go upstairs and wait for him there?'

Juan accompanies me up to the big golden room. The evening light outside is as yellow as the damask hangings – it won't be long till sunset, and the shadows are rapidly lengthening and deepening to a rich violet. I sit myself down in one of the chairs and watch Juan for a moment or two, as he riddles the fire and lights a few more candles, though some two or three dozen are already burning. Then he pours wine into a large glass goblet, holds out a hand towards it by way of inviting me to drink and, assuring me yet again that Vasquez must surely arrive soon, he backs out of the room, closing the door behind him.

I am alone. As I was that first time. Though this time I have rather more freedom to move about, luckily. I pick up my wine and drink. It is sweet and heavy, and feels warm and thick around my teeth.

Along the length of the credenza, the usual silver-domed dishes have been laid out. Putting down my wine and lifting up the first lid, I see crayfish tails, fanned out prettily and dressed with some sort of sauce. I dip a finger into the sauce and suck it.

At the end of the bed is a chest, whose polished surface gleams, reflecting the glow of the many candles. A stack of papers sits neatly at one end of this chest. I bend to look at the topmost sheet. It's in Spanish. I speak only a few words of Spanish – mostly gleaned from Filippo, in fact – and so, after fingering through the pages for a few moments, I quickly become bored and pat the papers back into a neat pile.

I take my glass up to the top of the bed, wondering if I might save myself some time later by just undressing now and getting under the covers. As it happens, I'm not very hungry, and perhaps, if the *Maestre* finds me already between his sheets, he might not bother with the meal and I won't have to eat anything. This dress fastens at the front, so I can take it off by myself quite easily.

Sitting on the bed, I heel off my shoes.

I am just squinting down at my bodice laces, which seem to have become tangled, when the door bangs open, making me jump. I drop the lace-ends and stand up, feeling as if I have been caught out in a misdemeanour, and thanking heaven that I'm not still fingering my way through the *Maestre*'s private papers. I doubt he would take kindly to that sort of intrusion.

Vasquez strides into the room, accompanied by three men. He does not notice me in the shadows of the bed hangings. He sounds furious. Having turned round to face his three companions, he starts shouting at them in Spanish, brandishing in one fist a sheet of paper that has clearly been folded and sealed at some point, but is now open; Vasquez flaps it in the men's direction, his face distorting around his angry words.

I have never seen him like this – in my company he has always been softly spoken, eager and greedily energetic. I can hardly recognise him.

The tirade lasts a few moments, and then, on what is presumably an order of dismissal, the three men leave the room. Vasquez slams the door behind them and kicks it for good measure. He reads what is written on the sheet, then screws it into a ball. Then, pausing for a moment, as though trying to decide what to do, he smooths the paper out and reads it again, crosses to the end of the bed and lays the crumpled sheet on top of the pile of papers, through which I was riffling only seconds ago. Then, apparently changing his mind again, he picks the letter up once more, folds it, over and over, and pushes it down into a pocket in his breeches.

He looks up then, and sees me watching him.

The fury slides off his face like melted wax, leaving his expression quite blank.

My curiosity is wildly aroused, but of course, I say nothing. Anything other than silence at this moment would be inappropriate. After all, I know why I'm here. Holding his gaze, I sit back down on the edge of the mattress, pulling at my laces. The knot, thank goodness, unravels. Still staring at him, I unfasten everything and push the sleeves off my arms. The bodice falls to the floor.

Vasquez remains silent, standing still and staring at me, as though bewitched, as I run my hands over and around my breasts, and then up into my hair. I unhook my skirts and let them fall from me, leaving me standing before him in my shift. With my gaze fixed upon his face, I walk slowly over to the table and pick up a tall, thin red glass jug which I know contains water. I do not look at what I am doing, but, holding my arm up and still staring at Vasquez, I run my tongue over my lips, tilt my chin up, and pour a steady trickle of water from the jug down over the front of my chemise, moving across from shoulder to shoulder. I have to stifle a little gasp – the water is cold, but in fact it's not unpleasant. The lawn of my shift is instantly transparent; it clings to me like a skin and I feel my nipples contract.

Vasquez's mouth opens and his gaze drops to my breasts. He looks like a hungry dog staring at a bone.

I think he has forgotten his anger.

'You poured water all over yourself? Are you still wearing the wet shift? If you are, you'd best get it off quickly,' Modesto says, as he closes the front door and we both go down to my kitchen.

'Yes, I am, but it's almost dry now. But, Modesto – listen to this. I've been saving the best little nugget until we got home. Definitely something to put in my book.'

'What? What is it?'

'Sit down, and I'll tell you.'

'Just a moment. Wait till I'm ready,' Modesto says. I sit at the big kitchen table and lean on my elbows. Having filled a small bowl with water, Modesto puts it down on the table, then, picking up a handful of kitchen knives, he sits opposite me and lays them out neatly in front of him. Reaching out behind him to a shelf – tipping his chair back onto two legs in the process – he unhooks a long leather strop from where it hangs on the wall, puts one end of it under one foot, and pulls the other end taut with his left hand. With an expression of tender determination on his face, he dips the blade of the longest knife into the water, and starts whetting it against the strop, first one way, then the other, back and forth, with long, smooth, deliberate strokes. The blade hisses very softly and a thin lather builds up beneath it as Modesto works. Looking up at me, he pauses in his stropping and says, 'Well? I'm ready now.'

I wait for a second, to give my revelation a suitable impact, and then, like dropping a stone into a pond, I say into the expectant silence, 'Vasquez fathered a child on a nun.'

Modesto stops what he is doing and stares at me. '*What? When?*'

'I'm not sure – over a year ago, I think.'

'How do you know – what did he say?'

I pause, trying to remember exactly what Vasquez had actually said. 'We'd finished, and were lying quietly, side by side. He had his eyes closed, and was looking exhausted, when he suddenly turned to me, caught me hard by the wrist, pulled me in towards him and said, "You cannot have a child. You must not."' I imitated Vasquez's breathy, lisping voice.

'He said that? What did you say?'

'Nothing. I just looked at him.'

'And?'

'He said – I think it was more to himself than to me – "I'd be utterly disgraced if it happens again."' I run my fingers over my hair – my braids are coming loose and the whole edifice is about to come crumbling down.

Modesto puffed out a breath. 'He must trust you – to have admitted such a thing to a courtesan.'

'Hmm. I'm not sure it's trust. I think it's desperation. Anyway,

80

by now, after the shouting and the letter, I was simply bursting with curiosity; I had to know. I asked him – I said, "When did it happen before?"'

Modesto smirks at me, shaking his head. 'You asked him outright? *Merda!* You have no shame, Signora,' he says. 'Not a shred. Did he tell you?'

I shrug, nodding. 'It took him several attempts to manage the admission, but in the end he said it. He didn't give me much detail, but, as I understand him, he was newly arrived in Italy, and had been billeted for a couple of weeks near a convent in Milano. The sisters were providing food and drink, apparently, and this particular novice had been detailed to take care of him, and . . . well, one thing led to another, he said, and she ended up expecting his child.'

Modesto pushes his mouth out in a moue of acceptance of this. 'What happened to her?' he says.

'Vasquez didn't say and I didn't like to ask – you see – I do have *some* shame. I said that obviously one cannot be certain about these things, but assured him that I always take every possible precaution, as such an eventuality would be as unwelcome to me as it would be to him – I didn't mention the twins, of course – and he seemed to calm down about it.' I pause, and then add, 'I wonder if that letter was about this woman and the child – maybe that's what made him think about it tonight. What do you think?'

'Whether it was or not, just write all this down, Signora,' Modesto says. 'Get your pen out and write down every last word.'

'I will, I promise. And now could you come upstairs with me and help me into some dry clothes, *caro* – I *am* still a little damp.'

Seven

The next few weeks pass in a something of a blur. Now that I am juggling three regular patrons, two of whom wish to see me at least twice a week, I have almost no time to myself, and, as well as being tired for much of the time, I am becoming increasingly worried about how seldom it seems to be that I can manage to spend more than snatched moments with the twins.

The money I am making is reassuring though. And I suppose that's the thing – I must just keep putting away safely everything I earn, and storing it up. Because I have to: I cannot for a moment contemplate the thought of my girls whoring – even the idea makes me feel sick. I'd rather die than see them doing what I do. Unlike me (I discovered this life late, compared to most), most courtesans are born to it – born into harlotry – like that little snake, Alessandra Malacoda, who, if I am to believe the Neapolitan gossips, was introduced to the delights of the bedchamber at the age of ten by her pimping whore of a mother. No doubt *La Malacoda* has made her mamma proud of her. And she plans, so I have been told, to be just as proud of her own daughter. Hoping she'll be kept in luxury in her old age, no doubt. The child is four. God! The very thought makes me retch.

Beata and Isabella have no concept of what I do when I am not with them. I have spun them indeterminate yarns about my activities, which seem to satisfy their undemanding, childish curiosity, and both Ilaria and Sebastiano know that I would dismiss the pair of them instantly if they ever breathed a word of the truth to either girl.

What I am to do when the girls reach an age where they will start to ask more demanding questions, or to search for answers for themselves, I don't know. I cannot allow myself to think too hard about it; my fears for them almost suffocate me when I let my mind dwell for too long upon what might become of them in years to come. I shall have to find them husbands, I think, and to do that, I will need money. They'll need dowries. So, whatever I feel about it all and however tired I might become, I must just remember why I am doing it.

And there are recompenses, after all. I have a veritable treat in store this evening – it's been a while since I had the pleasure of bedding a virgin.

Whatever the challenges and rewards of one's more experienced customers, it makes a refreshing change to deflower an innocent. I haven't had the chance very often. There is something quite charming about seeing a boy's clumsy attempts gain in confidence as he follows your instructions, though I suppose there is one thing to consider: it has to be said that it *is* something of a responsibility. More than just ensuring that he enjoys the occasion, there is another, more far-reaching consideration: that the experience he has – literally – *in your hands* may colour the attitude he will bring to any other woman he beds in years to come. With every move you make, you might be setting a standard by which he will judge women for the rest of his life. For myself, I have found that the future happiness of those other, unknown sisters weighs just as heavily on my conscience as the present customer's immediate pleasure. You must simply 'tread carefully', I suppose you might say. Nothing too alarming. Let him glimpse the possibilities, but do nothing to encourage the sort of vices you – or others – might regret in encounters to come.

Those will come later, with or without your help.

It was a most unexpected commission. I had turned away from the market in the Piazza Girolamini, with a length of lawn wrapped in waxed paper in a basket over my arm, intending to give it to Bianca the next day, so that she could make a start on 'Signora Marrone's' chaste chemise. The afternoon was bustling again after the quiet of midday and the streets were already thronging and noisy.

A gaggle of colourfully dressed young men had almost blocked the narrow path at the point at which it joined the piazza, and I had to edge between the group and the rough wall of the corner house to gain access to the street beyond, holding my basket high to keep it from banging against any unwary head or back. One or two of the group broke off from their argument and stared insolently at me as I picked my way across the cobbles. At least some of them appeared to have recognised me, though I am now far beyond the pockets of men such as these. I pretended to ignore them as they nudged each other and jerked their heads in my direction. Even after more than ten years' whoring, though, a group like this makes me nervous and I walked a little faster, aware of a faint twinge in my scar. I wished Modesto was with me. They hurled suggestive comments at me like lewd missiles; the ribald remarks followed me until I was able to turn the corner at the far end of the street – but the men did not move. I made no sign that I had heard them at all, though behind the dignified exterior I was struggling not to turn back towards them, to let loose a volley of insults of my own. I know a choice few.

I walked on for some moments, breathing steadily again and taking my time to balance on the uneven cobbles in my infernally uncomfortable *chopines*. Stupid things – I cannot imagine why such unusable shoes were ever invented, and were it not for the fact that they are so much admired in Venice, I should not be bothering to try to introduce them here.

I never feel at ease when I am wearing them, though.

I can't run in them.

I clutched handfuls of my heavy skirts and stepped up onto one of the ridges created by last summer's quake. The ridge runs right down the length of the street, like a cutlass scar along the forearm of a privateer, reminding me unpleasantly of that terror-soaked day last July when the earth cracked and shook for what seemed like hours.

'Excuse me, Signora . . .'

In contrast to the mocking taunts I had just endured, the voice that cut through the jostling chatter and into my thoughts was polite – cultured even – and I smiled as I turned to see who had spoken.

'Might I speak with you?' The slight edge of awkwardness in the voice of the young man I now saw, and the pucker of anxiety between his dark brows, made me wonder if this might perhaps be potential business.

'Can I help you?'

He hesitated.

'It is . . . Signora Felizzi, isn't it?'

I eyed my new companion curiously. Neither tall nor short, well built and square-jawed, he was dressed in a dark-green doublet and breeches of obviously superior quality. He wore his clothes with a faint air of self-consciousness, as though the items were a very new purchase and thus still unfamiliar. In style, his garments seemed designed for someone rather older: perhaps he needed to impress in his line of work. His dark hair he wore a little longer than is currently fashionable. He looked, in short, as though he might be able to afford me.

'I have been told of your . . . growing reputation . . . Signora . . .'

I raised a quizzical eyebrow. 'Indeed? And just what "reputation" might that be, Signore?'

He held my gaze, but flushed. I waited for a moment, rather enjoying his discomfiture and then helped him out. 'How did you know you had found the right person?'

'I was given a description.'

'Which was?'

The young man's colour deepened still further. He said, 'I was told to watch out for a woman with black hair, brown eyes and the sort of beauty that would make me catch my breath.'

Trying not to look too pleased with this, I ask, 'And who gave you this description?'

'Michele di Cicciano. I had approached him to ask for his help with a small problem, Signora,' my companion continued. 'A problem of a very delicate nature. I have a good friend who has a younger brother, about whom he has been worrying a great deal.'

So this young man was not seeking my favours for himself. A shame. But, whatever the business was, it needed to be discussed. 'Perhaps – before you tell me any more, we should go somewhere a little more discreet.' I suggested.

My new friend agreed. We walked together without speaking for some moments and found a low wall in the shadows of the great Castel Nuovo where we both sat down.

The young man began again. 'Well. This boy is a fine lad, but what is bothering my friend is that his brother seems to have shown no inclination at all to initiate himself into . . . into . . .' He flushed an interesting shade of dark pink and stumbled as he tried to complete his sentence.

'Into . . . the ways of the world?' I suggested.

He grasped the straw gratefully. 'Exactly! And Signor di Cicciano feels that you might be the perfect person to . . . er . . . bring this state of affairs to a satisfactory conclusion . . . without denting the lad's self-esteem . . .' He tailed off.

'And just how old is your friend's brother?' I asked.

'Nearly eighteen, Signora.'

With a disbelieving half-laugh, I said, 'Not so old that his reluctance to perform should be a cause of anxiety, surely?'

'His brother thinks it is, Signora – he has his reasons.'

I paused, wondering what those reasons might be, though I was able to hazard a guess. Perhaps he was afraid his young brother might prefer . . . dallying with his own kind. The penalties for proven sodomy are so terrible nowadays that were this so, the young man's brother's fears would be well-founded. Contemplating the thought that I might have been chosen merely as an extremely expensive way of luring a young man from the perils of perversion, I ask, 'Why do you think I should be interested in this child?'

'Hardly a child, Signora. Gianni is perhaps a head taller than me, and already has regular recourse to a razor.'

Something did not feel right. I wanted to know what the real reason for this commission might be. 'In that case,' I said, frowning, 'why should so impressive a young man need the services of a bedfellow as expensive as myself? Would not a girl of his choice suit him as well, and leave his – or his brother's – pocket considerably better stocked?'

The young man smiled broadly and stood up. He leaned back against the wall. His weight was on one foot, the other he crooked up against the cracked roughcast. 'If we leave it to Gianni, Signora, he'll be a virgin until he's fifty.'

Perhaps my surmise was wrong. Perhaps this was all little more than an elaborate joke being set up at the unfortunate Gianni's expense. (If the young man's brother was a friend of Michele's, this was not inconceivable.)

'He's very shy, Signora,' said the man in the green doublet, by way of explanation.

'Do you set me a challenge then, Signore?'

He laughed. 'If you like.'

I liked both my companion and the idea more and more as the minutes passed. My moment's unease lifted. 'Very well . . .' I named a price for two hours of my time. The young man's eyebrows lifted into his hair and he flinched, sucking in a shocked breath through his teeth and whistling it out again, but rallying, he agreed. I presumed that he must be aware that even if it seemed an exorbitant sum, I am, after all, still considerably less expensive than either of those conceited bitches, Emilia Rosa or Alessandra Malacoda, if not yet as well known. But time may change *that*. We arranged a day and an hour and my companion bade me farewell. As he disappeared into the crowd, though, I realised that I had let him leave without having discovered his name.

My new customer arrives shortly after sunset on the appointed day. I am upstairs; there is a loud knock at the front door below and I hear Modesto come up from the kitchen. He opens it and says something I cannot catch and then there is a burst of unfamiliar male laughter, and the sound of feet on the step. I can hear more than one voice outside. Then, after a pause, the door closes and the sounds of the street are cut off. I come to the top of the stairs. Standing next to Modesto is a long-limbed boy with dark curly hair and wide eyes – eyes which just now seem distinctly anxious and self-conscious. This is perfect. Lack of experience can just as easily show itself as timidity or bluster in these situations . . . and the bluster can be tedious. I don't think it was this boy's laugh I heard just now.

His friend has described him accurately: Gianni is tall and, as with many of his height, he is slightly round-shouldered and stoops a little, as though in apology for his excess of inches. An uneven, downy fluff of beard is doing its very best to make an impression upon his face – which none the less still loudly proclaims both his youth and his inexperience.

I come down to meet him. 'Gianni?' I ask and he nods, blushing furiously. I suppress a smile and decide that I must take this one very gently indeed. I indicate that he should come with me back up the stairs. My young customer edges past me, gazing around him for all the world as though he intends to purchase the place.

Modesto gives me a meaningful stare and pats his doublet over the place where I know he keeps a knife, but I smile and shake my head. There will not be any trouble from this boy. With an almost imperceptible shrug and an excuse for a bow, he disappears through the door to the kitchen.

I follow Gianni up the stairs and as he turns his head, I see that he is still wide-eyed and intently absorbing as much as he can of his surroundings. We enter my upstairs chamber. I close the door behind me. Gianni is studying the ceiling, the paintings on the walls, the window hangings, the rug upon the floor – everything, in fact, except me. He is carefully avoiding looking at me.

And I think he is averting his eyes from the bed.

The temptation to shock – to be outrageous and astonish him – is tremendous, but I don't think I will succeed with him tonight if I do. This will need a delicate touch.

'Please, sit down,' I say politely. He sits on a chair and stares at his hands, each of which is gripping a knee. The white knuckles betray his anxiety most endearingly. I watch him for a moment. He has a fine-boned face and large brown eyes; his hair is almost black and falls in tangled curls. A muscle tenses in his cheek. A lock of hair falls over one eye and he flicks his head sideways to shift it, still regarding his hands upon his knees. He moves his fingers a little, but the bone-coloured wheals of tension remain.

'You don't have to stay, Signore,' I say, and for the first time he lifts his head and his gaze meets mine. His eyes are huge and dark. I smile. 'You seem not to want to be here. No one is making you stay, Gianni. The door is never locked. You can leave whenever you choose.'

He hesitates, then, turning his eyes upwards, he speaks to the flaking stucco cherubs who cavort cheerily around the edges of my ceiling. 'I can't leave,' he says. 'If I do – if I fail – I will have to pay my brother back the money he has given you. And I don't have it to give him.'

I had never thought of myself as an obstacle to be overcome. Gianni's honesty is disarming. 'Well . . .' I pause, thinking. 'If you were here in my chamber for an appropriate length of time, per-haps we could deceive them. We could just sit here and talk.' Why did I say that? I have been looking forward to this encounter for days.

Gianni once more addresses himself to the peeling *putti*. 'No, that's not possible either,' he says in a voice that still has the edgy, raw quality of the recently broken.

'You do know that none but the two of us will ever know, Gianni, don't you? I never speak of what I do in here to anyone at all.' Except Modesto, of course.

He pulls his gaze from the ceiling. 'But they would know – my brother and his friend. They will be watching me for changes: they'll see none in me, and will draw their own conclusions,' he says, very wisely for a boy of his years. 'They don't think I will go through with this. My brother is expecting to be reimbursed.'

Go through with this? Is this what I have become then? An unpleasant experience this boy must endure if he is to avoid ridicule and debt?

He continues to watch me, his expression almost hopeless. His shoulders droop even more and one leg begins to twitch. I breathe in slowly and then say, 'Do you have . . . any particular aversion to women, Gianni? Might that be the cause of your reluctance?'

His astonishment is transparent and answers my question.

'Oh, no, Signora, you're quite wrong! It is just that I've never . . . I don't know . . . I . . . I just . . .' He cannot find the words he seeks. He flaps a hand in frustration, runs his fingers through his hair and drops his gaze to the floor.

'In that case, it would seem that you have no choice. So perhaps we had better begin, Gianni,' I say with a smile. 'You never know, you might even enjoy it. Most people do you know.' I lower my voice to a conspiratorial whisper. 'I am told that I'm very good at it.'

Gianni's face is stricken. 'Oh, Signora, I did not mean to imply that—'

'I know.' I interrupt him and take his hand. It is warm and dry and he allows it to lie in my palm. 'I know you didn't. But if, as you say, you are resolved to see this particular challenge through . . .' I raise an eyebrow. Gianni reddens. 'Perhaps you should begin by inspecting the goods you have purchased at so substantial a price.'

His jaw drops and he shakes his head. 'I didn't—'

'Well – that your brother purchased on your behalf then.' I lick my middle finger and thumb and, walking around my chamber, pinch out the candles that stand in brackets on the walls, until in the end, only one remains alight in a brass candlestick on a small table near my bed. I turn to Gianni. I don't think I have ever had one so nervous before. How should I best begin?

Laces. 'Have you ever undone a lady's laces before, Gianni?'

He shakes his head. He is avoiding my eye again.

'Try it,' I say then. 'Take your time.'

I sit down upon the end of the bed and pat the covers. Looking charmingly confused, he sits next to me.

'Watch, Gianni,' I say and I pull the lace ends of my bodice out from where they sit pushed down between my breasts. The laces are damp with sweat. I undo the knot and pull the lace through the first two holes so that he can see how to do it. He raises trembling hands to take the lace from me, and tries to coax it through the next hole, but it seems stubbornly unwilling to oblige him.

'Loosen it all off all the way down the front first,' I say, tucking my chin down to see what I am doing, and pulling slack across the bodice front. I wriggle the two sections of the bodice apart so that the laces lie looped between the holes, hanging in swags across my chest as I stop pulling. Gianni tries again; this time the lace slides through its hole with ease and I hear him suck in a soft, uneven breath. I lean forward a little – partly to help him with the lace, partly to give him a taste of what he will find inside the bodice when he has finished unfastening it. I talk softly to Gianni as he works, playing with his hair as I do so.

After a few moments he says, 'I think I have finished . . .' in a whisper. He is quite right: the two sides of the bodice are hanging forward to reveal the crumpled lawn of the shift beneath. The long lace hangs from Gianni's fingers, but as I meet his gaze, he drops it.

I think I have him now.

'Thank you, Gianni,' I say. 'Are you ready to begin?'

He swallows untidily and nods.

Standing up and facing my young customer I stroke the side of his face with the back of my hand and say quietly, 'You may not have done this before, Gianni, but I expect you have imagined doing it. If you were imagining it now, what would you . . . imagine . . . doing next?'

His eyes are wide and black in the dusk and he is breathing a little faster than before. He says, 'I think . . . I think I would imagine taking that dress from your shoulders.'

I can hardly bear to wait another moment, but I know I can't rush him. 'That's what you should do then,' I say. 'Always follow your imagination.'

He reaches forward and, with his fingers cupping behind my shoulders, hooks his thumbs under the neckline of my dress. Very gently he opens the bodice outwards.

This seems more promising.

Gianni slides the sleeves down my arms and I step out of the dress as he lowers it for me to do so. I stand before him in my shift and the dress hangs from Gianni's hands in great folds upon the floor. His eyes are round and unblinking and he does not move.

'You can let go of the dress, Gianni,' I say with a smile.

'There are no laces in your shift,' he whispers, his fingers still clutching the green silk.

'How would you – imagine – taking it off then?'

'Perhaps you would do that for me. I should not want to presume . . .'

His sweetness is charming and I feel an unexpected stab of what I realise with a shock is envy – for the girl with whom this boy will one day fall in love.

She will be a lucky woman.

I take the dress from him and throw it to one side, step closer to him and begin to unfasten his doublet and shirt. As I do so, he at last finds the courage to lay hands upon me. Trembling visibly, he runs one hand up one of my arms, pushing up inside the loose sleeve of my shift, round the curve of my shoulder and across my back. The other hand tentatively reaches around my waist and pulls me – very gently – towards him. I lace my fingers into his hair, push forward against his body, and feel hard against my belly the indisputable proof that my pupil is indeed now ready to begin.

'Take off your shoes and hose,' I suggest, and Gianni obeys without once taking his gaze from mine. His breathing is shallow and quick. 'Keep imagining, Gianni,' I say. I do not want to break the spell – it has been carefully spun.

'In my mind,' he says, more firmly, 'I am telling you to pull off your shift now.'

I do what he asks and he sucks in a soft gasp.

'And then, if I were imagining this, you would sit back up there –' he points towards my pillows '– and you would ask me to join you.'

I put myself where he suggests. 'Well, Gianni – come and begin,' I say.

He hesitates.

Dear God – how much longer is he going to keep me waiting?

*

But in the event, it takes very little more to break through Gianni's reserve. I am not sure exactly what it is that releases him from his smothering embarrassment: whether it's the sensation of my hands on his buttocks, the softness of my breasts beneath his fingers, or perhaps it is no more than the taste of the honey I have rubbed onto my nipples. But, whatever it is, as I wrap my legs around his body, and pull my hands up his back and into his hair, his gaze meets mine and I see that his eyes are shining. With a brief *frisson* of pleased satisfaction, I know that the reality of the occasion is indeed living up to his imagined expectations.

Of course, now that he has broken through his barriers, Gianni is as eager to rut as any other boy would be, but I think I shall keep him waiting: I have a number of things I want to teach him before I allow him into my body – and I think I might enjoy the lesson as much as he will. To my great delight, my pupil is indeed instinctively – and wickedly – imaginative; his confidence grows quickly as we play together, and before long, he is making as many suggestions as I am. What I thought, at first, might prove to be a difficult and unsatisfying evening, in fact turns out to be a wild, funny, excitable tumble.

And it might indeed have proved to be no more than this: nothing more than an entertaining and profitable night with an energetic innocent – had it not been for my scar.

It all happens very quickly.

We at last reach the moment that Gianni has been waiting for. He lies on his back, visibly shivering with expectation as I kneel over him and begin to show him exactly what I intend him to do next. He runs his hands down the length of my spine – and then his probing fingertips catch on what I have hoped he wouldn't notice: the lumpy ridge of scarring which lies just below my right-side ribs. He starts, and fingers the hard, puckered flesh curiously.

'What is this?' he asks softly. 'How did you do this?'

He is on his feet in an instant, and he scoops me to standing with an arm around my waist, pulling me in with my back against him, held close to his body.

'And just what the fuck do you think you're doing, stronza*?'*

His arm is so tight – iron-hard muscles across my belly – that I cannot breathe in enough to answer him.

'Planning on helping yourself to more than you're worth, were you?' The iron bar jerks in harder.

'You're good, stronza*, I'll give you that – but you're not that good. Bloody bitch whores – you're all the fucking same!' Bending down to his doublet, folding me in two beneath him, he stands us both upright again and in his clenched fist is something small, needle-pointed, which flashes in the light from the window. 'Wanted a bit more silver, did you?' he says in a whisper.*

He grabs a fistful of my skirts with the hand that holds me, pulls me outwards and punches up under my ribs. Not hard. It doesn't hurt much. No more than a pricking sting and a sudden pressure. But a hissing begins in my ears, that all but drowns the words he says next.

'That much extra silver I can spare. You'll not thieve again, I think.'

I wonder why I can only see him in shades of grey as he leaves the room. His colour has quite gone.

I cannot speak. I sit back on my heels and my heart races, as those pictures I would prefer to forget swirl in front of my eyes, vivid and sickening. I feel suddenly giddy. I grope for the words which will not come, but at last I manage to say it. 'Someone was once not as . . . as pleased with me . . . as you seem to be . . . and . . . he expressed his disappointment . . . very clearly.'

I stop. My dance at death's door is not a memory I cherish. I hate anyone drawing attention to my ugly reminder of that day: I am always afraid it will disgust people. It disgusts me.

Gianni says nothing, but he turns me from him, then bends and kisses my scar with great tenderness, his hands on my hipbones. His mouth rests warm on the little twisted ridge for a second and then he brings me around to face him again.

This is something I have never known. Never. His compassion brings stinging tears to my eyes and I do not know what to say to him. We stare at each other for what seems an age, without speaking. Gianni's moment of consummation has been interrupted and now he is hesitant to touch me again, anxious in the face of my distress as I fight to recover my composure. I should hate him to lose the joy of the occasion, though, and after a short inner struggle, I manage to begin to re-engage my pupil in the lesson he has interrupted. He and I resume our activities. It takes a few moments to bring ourselves back to where we were, but in the event, it is not long until, to his obvious delight, Gianni's explorations into this hitherto undiscovered country are complete and he is a virgin no longer.

When at last, gasping and exhausted, Gianni sinks his full weight onto me with a groan, I laugh, fighting for breath. I am a beetle, trapped under a stone. I put my hands up and under his chest and bend my knees up to try to push him off.

'Among the most sophisticated lovers, it is usually thought best . . . to try not to squash . . . your lady . . . *completely* flat, Gianni,' I manage to gasp.

He slides off me at once and begins to apologise, but I interrupt him. 'Stop! I was not serious, *caro*. Tell me – was that worth all that anxiety and trepidation?'

The look he turns on me in the dying candlelight brings an unexpected lump to my throat. 'Yes. Yes, Signora, it was. I . . .'

I do not usually care to kiss my customers, though I am not always given the choice. But when Gianni interrupts his own sentence and holds my face in his hands to kiss me in thanks, I do not even try to draw back.

After a few moments, though, I pull away from him. 'Gianni,' I say softly, 'it's time for you to go now. I think we've run over our two hours as it is and I must be getting home.'

'Oh,' he says. 'Do you not live here?' He sounds surprised.

'No.' I do not expand. He does not need to know.

He helps me refasten my laces without being asked, which amuses me, and within moments we are both dressed and Gianni is almost ready to leave my chamber. Standing awkwardly once more by the door, one hand on the iron handle, he turns back to where I am sitting on a low chair, one foot crooked up on the other knee, whilst I refasten my garter. 'Thank you again, Signora,' he says. ' My brother and his friend did not intend to, but in the end, they have done me a very great favour. As have you.'

'I am delighted to have launched so intuitive a lover upon the unsuspecting ladies of Napoli, Gianni. None of them know it yet, but one day somebody out there will be very, very lucky to have you.'

He crosses the room once more, bends and kisses my mouth again with a confidence neither he nor I could have imagined two hours ago, and then he leaves, standing straighter and looking rather older than he did when he arrived.

*

A little while later, Modesto and I wind our way through the empty streets back to my other house in the sea-smelling street near Santa Lucia – Modesto is carrying my chopines for me, and I am walking barefoot, my now trailing skirts hitched up and over one arm. Modesto sees me in, and bids me goodnight.

The soft snoring from the downstairs chamber shared by Sebastiano and Ilaria tells me that my two house servants are already asleep, when I pause in my hallway before climbing the stairs to check on my sleeping children.

The rest of the house is silent.

Upstairs, the two identical, beautiful faces lie side by side on the pillow, dark hair tangled about their cheeks. Beata has her thumb in her mouth as usual. As I watch them, Bella grunts and heaves over to one side of the bed, pulling most of the covers with her, leaving Beata with nothing. Her thin arms and legs seem fragile, her pointed little buttocks pale and vulnerable, exposed so suddenly. I reach across, pull the blankets back and tuck them snugly around both little girls without waking either.

I go back downstairs, pour myself a large goblet of red wine and take it up to the roof garden.

I feel strangely detached. Almost bewildered.

It is a vital part of being successful in this line of work – being able to distance yourself from the customer. As a *puttana*, on the streets, you have to shut your true self away – lock it somewhere inaccessible – if you are to have a chance of enduring the demands of those men who choose to pay for pleasure. What they want is usually distasteful – it may be downright dangerous – but, as little more than street scum, you have no choice but to allow yourself to become the object they all perceive you to be.

I remember it well.

Now, after nearly two years as a *cortigiana*, I have devised a very different way of playing the game. My game. All my patrons still believe that they can take from me what they want: they are now paying me a small fortune for the privilege and I make sure that I let them believe this to be the case. If they wish to beat me, I am content to be beaten. If they want mothering I can hold them in my arms and sing them a lullaby as I give suck. And if they need to be in subjugated thrall to a wild she-demon I will kneel over them, hold a knife to their throats and make them beg for their pleasures.

I am to each of them what they most desire.

That, after all, is the lot of the courtesan, is it not?

But what they none of them realise – not one of them – is that I make damned sure right from the first moment, that *I* decide exactly what it is that they want. I create the desire in each one of them, and then fulfil it.

It's *my* choice.

Not theirs.

Just as Modesto was saying the other day, I've made for Michele a wildcat with whom he can fight to his heart's content; Vasquez now thinks himself some sort of demi-god, rutting with Aphrodite – and Filippo? Filippo just needs an arse to spank, to nullify the emasculating effect of his wife's frigidity.

The distance must be kept though – with all of them. Just as it was when I used to walk the streets. Intimacy will inevitably destroy the fortifications I have spent years constructing.

I created a desire in Gianni just now and fulfilled it for him: I made him wish to be thought of as a gentle, caring lover; I allowed him to become one and then watched his pride and satisfaction at having achieved his goal.

It was well done.

But I will not admit the thought that is whispering to me now. I cannot. The prospect is terrifying. This strange feeling of detachment that is so acutely unnerving me as I sit here, is something quite new, quite different: something more akin to a bleak, melancholic sense of homesickness than to my habitual whore's professional distance. In creating this desire within Gianni tonight, I have a needling suspicion that I have unwittingly begun something of the same process within myself. I don't think it's Gianni himself that I want – he's little more than a child – but as I think now of his mouth, warm on the ridged skin of my scar, a nagging voice begins to whine around my head like an August mosquito, telling me, over and over again that I have started something dangerous.

Eight

The great vaulted aisle of San Giacomo degli Spagnoli was cool, but as soon as Father Ippolito pulled the door of the little confessional chamber closed, the sweat began to bead on his forehead. When he sat down, his cassock wilted across his knees. The woollen fabric itched: Father Ippolito often thought he might just as well be performing a permanent penance, given the constant discomfort of his clothing in the warmer weather. He ran a thin, nail-bitten hand through damp hair and pinched the bridge of a beaky nose to try to stave off the beginnings of what seemed set to become a memorable headache.

He thought with longing of his first – brief – appointment as priest in Torino. A beautiful place, Torino: cool, mountainous and dignified.

Torino had been easy, compared with his present situation.

Apart from anything else, he had never had to deal with anything quite as unnerving as a courtesan in Torino.

It cost this earnest young man very dearly to hear the repeated confessions of a woman whose multitudinous sins seemed to him to at once monstrous and shamefully fascinating and he often wondered why it was that she always seemed to appear in the church on the days he was detailed to man the confessional. He peered around the door before he closed it, and saw her in the shadows of the second row of seats, seated near another thin woman in a white cap. She caught his eye and smiled; Father Ippolito's face burned and he drew in his head once more and closed the door.

The courtesan was beautiful, he thought, his heart racing: high-cheekboned, dark-haired and liquid-eyed, like an exquisite painting of the Madonna. But even to think this – in any way to link the mother of God with this shameless woman was a desecration, and Father Ippolito mentally berated himself.

He played out in his mind, as he waited, a familiar scene from the gospel: the story of the woman caught in adultery. He thought of Christ's benevolent and understanding forgiveness as he imagined the scene: Christ sitting on a doorstep in the town square, drawing with his finger in the sandy earth as the howling rabble kicked and pushed the unfortunate woman to her knees before Him.

Perhaps *she* had been beautiful.

Perhaps that was what had so enraged the townsmen.

Father Ippolito imagined the kindness in the eyes of Son of God, and the trembling terror of the woman, who faced an unimaginable death by stoning were He to condemn her as her neighbours condemned her. But – what was one simple act of adultery, mortal sin though it might be, compared to the catalogue of lewdness described so vividly to him each week? How calmly would Christ have reacted to *that*, he wondered?

Was this woman trying to tempt him? She regularly subjected him – a celibate priest – to depictions of activities he could hardly imagine, professing remorse at her shamelessness, though this remorse could hardly be heartfelt, thought Father Ippolito, since she returned weekly to reiterate the same transgressions.

Someone slipped into the tiny room on the other side of the wooden divide and pulled the door shut.

His insides gave a jolt.

Through the gauze-hung window, he could not quite make out the features in the gloom, but a soft voice whispered, '*Perdonatemi, mio Padre . . .*'

It was not her.

He murmured the Latin words, heard the woman's muttered responses, and then waited to hear what she had to say.

When it came, it was slow and halting. 'I . . . I am frequently unable to abide by my marriage vows.'

Father Ippolito's heart sank. He mentally fiddled the sand of the town square with his finger and steeled himself for yet another litany of indecency.

'I . . . I . . .' The voice faltered again.

'Please, child,' said Father Ippolito, feeling little more than a child himself, 'unburden yourself of whatever is distressing you.'

'I do not care to lie with my husband, even though I know he wishes me to,' she said in a voice that was hardly more than a breath.

'And . . . are you in need of confessing to the sin of adultery?'

'Oh, no, Father!' A little stronger. 'No. Quite the opposite. I cannot . . . cannot . . .' She stopped without finishing her sentence, paused, and then muttered. 'I frequently commit the sin of disobedience, and when I do manage to obey, it is with a terrible, resentful reluctance.'

Father Ippolito was not entirely sure he understood, but his relief outweighed his confusion and with great enthusiasm he offered the woman the absolution she so patently craved. She muttered her Act of Contrition and disappeared.

The door opened again and this time he was hit by a buffeting stench of garlic so strong it pushed its way through the gauze partition in seconds. Father Ippolito's eyes watered, and he slid as far back away from the partition as the bench seat allowed. A rough male voice muttered the opening prayers and a litany of trivial, predictable transgressions followed. Father Ippolito advised, absolved and quickly bade farewell to this unwelcome penitent, and a few moments later, the courtesan came in, closed the door and knelt down. In the event, he knew who it was before she spoke.

Father Ippolito wiped his damp forehead with a linen kerchief and ran his tongue over dry lips, tasting salt upon them. He had taken in almost nothing of the troubles of his other parishioners that morning, and had absolved some dozen people of sins he had hardly registered, so entirely had his mind been filled by the teeming images conjured so vividly by the courtesan.

He wondered if he should speak to the Bishop.

Perhaps it would be advisable for some arrangement to be made so that he could be relieved of having to endure this weekly exposition to temptation. But then again, he argued with himself, Christ had endured forty consecutive days in the desert, beleaguered by repeated temptations: temptations besides which these brief confessional moments paled into nothingness. Maybe it was the Will of God that he – Father Ippolito – should continue to suffer these tantalizing glimpses of the forbidden, in order to test his spiritual resolve.

He pushed from his mind the thought that he would miss the courtesan's tales of immodesty far too much to do anything that might precipitate their removal from his life.

Father Ippolito rested sharp elbows upon his knees, put his head in his hands and stared at the dusty floor of the confessional box through his splayed fingers.

*

Maria di Laviano finished her penances and her prayers. She looked up and saw a tall woman with extravagantly braided black hair, stepping from the confessional box. Tucking a stray wisp back under the edge of her cap, she watched as the woman knelt down a few seats away from her, on the same row, and bent her expensive-looking head over clasped hands. Maria noticed several large rings on each of those hands. Her own fingers were bare save for her wedding ring. A string of small red stones around the woman's neck glittered in a shaft of sunshine that sliced diagonally down through the gloom of the nave from an opening in a stained-glass window high above her: tiny pools of colour played across her throat and under her chin, like bloodstains.

A moment later, the woman raised her gaze to the roof, and Maria saw that she had tears in her eyes.

She continued to watch covertly for a moment and then started as the woman turned her head and caught Maria's eye. She ran the tip of one finger along under each line of lower lashes, neatly to remove the hovering tears, and Maria felt herself reddening, embarrassed to be caught in the act of eavesdropping upon a moment's vulnerability. The woman then rose from her knees and sidled along the row to the aisle. She bobbed a brief genuflection, turned, and walked towards the great entrance doors; her slow steps rang clear in the vaulted silence.

Nine

'When are you going to tell me what was it like, Gianni?'

'Shut up, Carlo! I've told you I don't want to discuss it.'

'Why? Why not? I think I have a right to some of the . . . *details*, don't you? I'd like to be sure you're telling the truth, apart from anything else – I want to be quite certain you actually did it.' Carlo della Rovere's eyes widened, and he licked his lips. 'I mean: Michele and I deposited you on her doorstep . . . I know you got there . . . but I only have your word for it, don't I, that you kept your side of the bargain.'

'I said I don't want to talk about it.'

'You bastard, Gianni—'

'You hoped I'd fail, didn't you? I can't imagine that you ever thought I'd go through with it. Well I did, Carlo – I "kept my side of the bargain", but I am not going to tell you anything about it.'

Carlo's voice took on a sharp edge. 'You're right – I didn't think you'd do it. If I'm being honest, I only set it up because I thought I'd be getting my money back.' He paused, and then said, 'But listen, Gian: she came highly recommended, so . . . I'd be interested to know – was she worth it? I'd be bloody disappointed to have paid such an exorbitant amount, if she wasn't.'

Gianni glared at his brother and said nothing.

Carlo laughed. Mouth closed, the laugh came out through his

nose as a snort. 'Well? Was she? Michele thinks so. Michele has told me quite a bit about the Signora, Gian – but I want to hear it from you. He says . . .' Carlo's eyes flicked to the door as if to make sure his father was not about to appear. He dropped his voice and ran his tongue over his lips again before he spoke. 'Michele says she's beautiful. He says her breasts are quite exquisite (if one appreciates such things, of course), like warm peaches, he says, and her cunt is— Ow!'

Gianni's fist cut Carlo short. His knuckles landed on the side of Carlo's nose with a crack; the blow knocked Carlo off balance – he stumbled against the fireplace and sat down hard on the hearthstone, blood running from his nose. He clamped one palm over his face and red trickled through the gaps in his fingers and down the back of his hand.

'You foul-minded little bastard, Carlo,' Gianni said softly. 'Don't you dare discuss her like that.'

Carlo sat where he had fallen. His smirk had quite gone. 'The woman's a whore . . . and deserves . . . no better,' he mumbled.

'Shut your mouth!'

'Oh, dear.' Carlo took his hand away from his nose, looked with distaste at the scarlet mess in his palm and wiped it on his breeches, where it left a long, dark smear. When he raised it again, he replaced it, palm-down this time, underneath where the blood was still dripping. 'Has the little boy . . . fallen in love?' He swallowed awkwardly.

Gianni stared at his brother with disbelief. His knuckles hurt and his fingers felt stiff; he stretched them out like a starfish and re-fisted them, cradled them in the other hand. He paused, trying to decide whether he trusted himself to speak, and when the words finally came, they were little more than a whisper.

'Mamma would have been ashamed to hear you say such things.'

'Mamma would have been ashamed to know Papa's best boy had bedded a whore,' Carlo said with a sneer.

Gianni flushed. 'And you think she would have been proud to know it was my brother who procured her for me?' he said. He glanced down at his fist, still cupped inside the fingers of his left hand, and with a last, tight-lipped glance at Carlo, Gianni left the long dining room and walked towards the head of the stairs.

'Going out?'

Gianni turned to see his father. A tall, dark-haired man of some forty years, he was holding the edge of his study door with one hand, and from the fingers of the other dangled a pair of steel-rimmed spectacles. His expression was mildly curious.

Gianni nodded.

'What was the noise about? Carlo sounded—'

'Nothing, Papa. We had a disagreement.'

His father frowned briefly – more, Gianni thought, from concern than anger – and said, 'Are you going down into the town?'

'No. Not so far. I just need some air.'

'A suffocating sort of disagreement then?'

Gianni closed his eyes for a second and then said, 'You could describe it that way.'

'Come and find me when you get back, Gianni, will you? I need your help in sorting out a couple of things for next week . . .'

Gianni nodded again, turned from his father and took the stairs at a run.

The light outside was low and yellow. Gianni walked with long strides away from the house, down the street towards the small piazza. Carlo's sneering words tumbled over themselves inside his head. *Oh, dear. Has the little boy fallen in love?* Had he? He sat down on a low wall and put both palms over his face; his finger tips pressed against his skull through his hair. After a moment or two, sliding his hands around and locking his fingers behind his neck, Gianni stared across the piazza and allowed himself to recreate in his mind that evening's experiences. The apprehension, the crippling, smothering embarrassment, his fear of failure; and then the revelation as he had laid hands on that extraordinary body and had finally understood *why* – why it was that artists and poets had for so many centuries trumpeted their evocations of physical love so joyously in paint, in marble and in sinuous words. Gianni felt a slither of hunger for Francesca move downwards from his throat and he held his breath – closing his eyes, he allowed it to wash through him. His mouth opened slightly, his breath caught in his throat, and the jumbled sounds of the busy piazza wove a net of warm noise around him as he sat on the wall and remembered.

'Is anything the matter, Gianni?'

A voice pushed its way through the net, but he did not move.

'Gianni? What is it?' Gianni jumped as a hand gripped his shoulder. A neat figure in dark-green doublet and breeches; hair slightly too long. An expression of puzzled concern on a good-natured, open face.

'Niccolò,' Gianni said and his heart jolted as he saw his brother's friend, as if afraid that his thoughts might have danced, visible above his head while he had sat there on the wall.

'Just on my way to your father's house to see Carlo,' said Niccolò. 'You coming?'

'No.'

'I haven't seen you since—' Niccolò began, but Gianni cut him short.

'Don't ask. I told Carlo a few moments ago that I don't wish to talk about it. And just so that you know – he wouldn't listen to me and I've just hit him.'

Niccolò raised his eyebrows and drew in a short breath in surprise. 'You? *You* hit him? God – was it . . . that bad?' he asked.

Gianni saw something quite different to the prurient smirk he had seen on his brother's face: behind Niccolò's curiosity and the faint air of salaciousness – was an anxious pucker of obvious guilt. 'Did you meet her?' he asked.

'Yes. Carlo asked me to go and find her to arrange everything.'

'That's like him. Well then, you saw her. What do you *think* it was like?'

'Ah.'

'Yes – "ah". It was . . . extraordinary.' Gianni paused. 'That's all I am saying, to you or to anyone.' The two young men regarded each other. Niccolò looked away first and as he did so, Gianni spoke. 'Niccolò, why . . . why are you friends with Carlo?'

'What do you mean?'

'It is an easy question, Nicco. Why do you like him?'

'What sort of thing is that to ask about your own brother?'

'A simple one,' said Gianni, shrugging. 'He may be my brother, but he's not a very . . . likeable person, is he? I just wondered what it is about him that attracts you – apart from the obvious, but I did not think you were—'

'I'm not.' Niccolò flushed. 'I think Carlo thought for a time that I was.'

'Hoped, perhaps.'

'Perhaps.'

'So why?'

Niccolò frowned. 'I don't really know. I suppose . . . well, we've known each other so long, haven't we, Carlo and I? Since before your mother died. Seeing each other – it's just something that we do. He makes me laugh—'

Gianni raised an incredulous eyebrow and Niccolò smiled

wryly. 'I know you don't often see that side of him,' he said, 'but he does. And then he presented me with this suggestion of his about the Signora and . . . you . . . and it seemed an entertaining piece of nonsense. He was prepared to pay for it all in the first instance, so I . . .' He tailed off.

'Did you think I would do it?' Gianni asked softly.

There was a long pause. Niccolò swallowed. He shook his head. 'No.'

'How did you imagine I was ever going to be able to pay Carlo back if I didn't?'

Niccolò stared at the ground and said nothing.

'Would *you* have done it?' Gianni asked.

'*Cazzo!* Yes, you're damn right I would have done. Chance like that? You're a lucky bastard, Gianni. You going to see her again?'

A knife twisted in Gianni's guts. He paused. 'No.' He tried to sound unconcerned. 'Can't afford to.'

'No. I suppose not. Still . . .' Niccolò shifted his weight awkwardly from one foot to the other. 'I had better be going. Sure you're not coming with me?'

'Not just yet. If you see Papa, tell him I shall be about an hour.'

There was a moment's silence, and then Niccolò said, 'Gianni?'

'What?'

'I suppose I ought to say I'm sorry. We shouldn't have done it to you . . . but . . . well . . . God, Gianni, what a thing to say you've done, eh? Bedded one of the most sought-after women in Napoli on your first attempt . . .' Seeing Niccolò grin at him through a jumbled mask of embarrassment, camaraderie, guilt and jealousy, Gianni felt his aching right hand clench itself into a fist once more. He said nothing, turned from Niccolò and strode away from him towards the river.

*

' "Extraordinary." That's all he would say,' Niccolò said to Carlo, who was sitting with his elbows on the table, a linen kerchief, spattered with red blotches, bunched loosely in his hands. His head was tipped backwards, his nose was swollen and discoloured; one nostril was blocked with congealed blood.

'He didn't hit *you*, then?'

'No.' Niccolò smirked at him. 'No, he didn't hit me. Just you, *amico*. But . . . for Gianni to do something like that – she's certainly changed him, Carlo. He's aged five years in a week. Now I've spoken to him, I don't think there's any doubt that he actually did it.'

Carlo snorted derisively and then winced, and lifted the scarlet-stained cloth back to his nose. 'Are you busy this week?' he said through the linen.

'Yes. I am right in the middle of this business with Signor Mastalli and his godforsaken right of access to that street near Santa Maria. Why?'

'I have a consignment of spices supposed to be arriving on Wednesday and I can't be there to supervise the unloading, whichever day it finally gets here.' Carlo took the cloth away from his face, examined the contents, and muttered, more to himself than to his friend, 'I'll ask Michele – he's bound to have a few men to spare to make sure those thieving little *stronzi* keep their hands off my property.'

'Where is it from, whatever it is?'

'Spice Islands. Saffron mainly – but some cinnamon and cloves. Should get good prices for them – if I can keep it intact. I'm sending most of it on overland to Rome. Can't send it by sea – some damned problem at Ostia, yet again.'

With a click, the door to the dining hall opened then, and Carlo's father appeared. He started at the sight of his elder son, whose nose and mouth were once more shrouded in crimson-blotched linen. '*Santo cielo!* What happened to you?'

Carlo said nothing.

'Hmm. The suffocating disagreement. What on earth was it about, Carlo?'

Carlo shrugged. Niccolò's gaze moved from father to son and the silence stretched out. He said, 'I saw Gianni in the piazza, Signore. He told me to tell you he would be about an hour – some half hour ago.'

'Thank you, Niccolò,' he said. 'Are you staying to supper with us?'

'If I may – Carlo?'

Carlo shrugged again. His father frowned at him, turned and left the dining hall.

Back in his study, Luca della Rovere sat at his desk and stared unseeingly at his spectacles, turning them over and over in his fingers, as he thought about his sons.

He heard the rattle of the front door, then the thud of feet on the stairs, and, a moment later the door to his study opened and Gianni peered round, leaning on the handle.

'You said you wanted to see me, Papa.'

Luca smiled at him. 'Yes. I was just thinking about you.'

Gianni came into the study, pushed the door to behind him and perched himself on the corner of his father's table.

Luca hesitated, and then said, 'Gian, is there a . . . particular problem between you and Carlo?'

Father and son held each other's gaze some five seconds, then Gianni spoke. 'Yes . . . but we can resolve it ourselves. Please leave it, Papa.'

'Gianni . . . ?'

'No, Papa. What was it you wanted me to do?'

There was a pause. Sensing a lost cause, Luca abandoned his interrogation and said, 'Two things, *caro:* can you run up to Signor Cedro and collect the two candlesticks that he has been mending for me?' Gianni nodded. 'And more importantly, can you drop in at Signora Zigolo's and find out if she'll be ready in time with that doublet – I'll be needing it for the evening with Filippo and the Parisettos at San Domenico Maggiore and I don't want to find out at the last minute that she hasn't been able to finish the alterations. It's the only suitable one I've got to wear. Poor Luigi is being so hopeless at the moment; I really don't want to send him to do it. I'd go myself, but I promised I'd stop by next door and read to old Bartolomeo before it gets dark. Do you mind? Unless you'd rather read to Bartolomeo of course . . .'

Gianni grimaced and shook his head. 'No. I'll run the errands.'

'Thank you, *caro.*'

'I'll go now then. I won't be long. Don't wait if the meal is ready before I get back.' Gianni smiled at his father and disappeared.

Luca sighed. He stared at the door for several moments, then pinched his spectacles onto his nose, picked up a book and riffled through it to where a strip of leather was marking the place at which he had abandoned his reading some moments before.

Ten

The twins are sitting on the floor in the *sala*. Both little girls look up at me as I say, 'Modesto is feeling rather sad at the moment, so I thought you two might like to make him some of those little dolls he showed you once. You could run over and give them to him this morning. It would cheer him a great deal to see you. What do you think?'

'Candle dolls?' Beata asks.

'Yes.' I smile again at the two upturned faces. 'Now . . . remind me how you make them. What do we need?'

'Twigs.'

'Twine.'

'Wool.'

'Candle-wax.'

'Let's find it all, shall we?' And my two little girls begin to scurry around the kitchen; Ilaria sighs irritably as they pull open cupboard doors and ferret in corners. Bella holds onto Ilaria's skirts and jumps up and down, saying, 'Can we have candles, Laria, please, can we have candles?'

She ignores the tugs on her clothes and says to me, 'Only got the best beeswax, I have, Signora – do you really want to . . .'

'I only need one, Ilaria, that will be perfect. Bella, take it will you? Beata, get a bowl and put it in the embers – carefully.' They follow my instructions. I run upstairs and pull a handful of wool from the underside of my mattress, then reach for a bag of leftover dress lengths and pick from it a few scraps of bright silk and linen. As I again enter the kitchen, Beata and Isabella are both squatting in front of the fire, breaking the long beeswax candle into small pieces and sliding each piece off the wick with careful fingers; they put the lumps of wax into an earthenware bowl, which stands among the glowing embers. Ilaria is peeling vegetables and scowling, trying to ignore the irritating disruption to her routine, but on my entrance she turns from her work and wordlessly hands me a short stick wound thickly with twine. I thank her and a brief smile flickers across her face.

'Find some twigs in the log basket, Bella, will you?' I say then, and she crawls across to the basket and began to search.

'Will these do?'

'Just right.'

Each twin takes a twig. I hand them each a soft tuft of wool, which they tease out into a thread between forefinger and thumb and then wind carefully around one end of their twig to make a tight, round, knobbed ball. Then about two fingers' depth down the twig, they each tie a length of twine so that an end protrudes on each side. Each protruding thread has a knot at the end of it.

'Bella first.'

Isabella squats back down in front of the bowl of now melted wax. Carefully she upends her twig and dips the woollen ball into the wax. She lifts and dips once or twice and then shuffles back.

'Beata?' She does the same.

It takes some half hour and several dippings, but before long both twins have a headlike ball of wax at one end of their twig and both dolls have a tiny waxen lump on the end of each twine arm, to represent hands. The girls poke eyes into the soft wax with a pin, and then stand their dolls upright in a pot to harden. While they wait they sort through the scraps of fabric I have brought down and choose stuff for each doll's dress. Beata's will be elegant in rose-pink silk, while Bella's creation will be somewhat more sober in deep-crimson linen. A few scraps of lace will complete the picture – Modesto will be most impressed, both girls assure me gleefully.

With my usual lack of finesse, I help the girls cut and stitch, crimp and pinch; and before long both tiny ladies are – as well as we can manage – complete. A little deformed, perhaps, but resplendent none the less.

'Would you like to drop in and give them to Modesto on the way to . . . Signora Bianca's?' Both girls squeal with delight at the prospect of a visit to their favourite shop, and in a flurry of flustered chattering, they ready themselves for an outing. I – rather more calmly – swing a coat around my shoulders and bid goodbye to a grumpy but relieved Ilaria, who is, I think, very grateful to see us leave, though she does press two dried figs into my hand as we go: one for each girl.

'Why are we going to Signora Bianca's?' Bella asks.

'I have asked her to make me a new dress. She needs to fit it today.'

'Can we watch?'

'Can we see all the cloth?'

'Can we do cutting?'

They both speak at once, both run and jump, back and forth in front of me as I walk. Bianca will find something entrancing for them to do while she fits my dress, I am sure of it: her glittering treasure trove of buttons, ribbons, threads and beads always pleases my two self-centred little voluptuaries and Bianca is generous and inventive with her wares. I cannot help laughing at their eager faces. Perhaps, if I cannot find husbands for my girls, I will apprentice them to Bianca when they are a little older. They would enjoy the work, I think. It's a thought, anyway.

I smile at them and say, 'Yes, I am sure you will do all that. But we'll go to Modesto's house first, and give him the dolls,'

As always, I'm allowing the girls to presume that Modesto owns the house in the Via San Tommaso.

Bella and Beata begin to bicker about who has made the most beautiful doll and which one they think Modesto will prefer, whilst I see again in my mind the image of my manservant as I saw him a few nights ago, sobbing in my arms. I rage inwardly for him; I could weep at the thought of everything that has been taken from him. Years ago, right at the beginning, I offered – several times – to give him what he has never experienced, but he always refused. I think he was frightened of being seen to fail.

'Here we are!' I say as we round the corner, and the two girls run ahead to knock at the door.

Bella has her hand raised, with Beata right behind her, when they stop dead. 'Oh, Mamma . . . listen!' Beata says in an awed whisper.

The kitchen casement is open wide, and through it is streaming a sound so beautiful that it seems that the whole street must hold its breath to hear it. Pure and clear, and heartrending as a perfect boy's soprano voice, though much bigger and more resonant, I can hear in it all Modesto's years of loss and pain and wisdom and compassion. The hair on my neck prickles. Thinking himself unheard, my manservant pours his lovely voice out into the silence, and we all three stand on my doorstep and listen, entranced, for fully five minutes, hardly daring to breathe. Then Bella whispers, 'He sounds like an angel when he sings, doesn't he?'

'I don't think an angel would sound so sad,' Beata says quietly.

'Let's go in and give him your dolls,' I suggest in a whisper. It seems wrong to interrupt, but when I open the door, the singing stops.

'Signora.' Modesto smiles to see us all upon his doorstep, but there is a flicker of wariness in his eyes: I think he's still embarrassed at my having seen him in such distress the other night.

'We made something for you, Desto,' Bella says, pulling at his hand as we all go inside; Beata takes his other hand and looks up at him. 'We hope you'll like them,' she says.

Modesto crouches on his heels and, with a little curtsy, the girls each pass him their doll. He holds one in each hand, taking his time to examine the handiwork with an air of grave consideration. After a moment or two, he says, 'I have never seen such well-made dolls. Did you make them yourselves? Are they really for me?'

'Mamma said you were sad,' Beata says, as they both nod. 'She said these would make you feel happier.'

'We did make them, Desto. Just us. But Mamma helped,' Bella says.

Modesto is squatting, thick-thighed on the floor of the hallway. He smiles again. 'Mamma was right,' he says, his gaze on mine. 'They are a lovely present. Thank you, all of you.'

'We liked your singing, Desto,' Bella says, leaning against him.

He puts down a hand to steady himself, lifts his eyebrows and shrugs. 'Hmm,' he says. 'I didn't think anyone was listening. Well. It's not what it was.'

'It was beautiful, *caro*,' I say.

'But we're going to Signora Bianca's now,' Beata says with a meaningful glance at me.

I laugh. 'Don't worry, we are going there right away – the new blue dress needs fitting,' I say to Modesto, who nods.

'You are going to this concert of the Signore's then, I take it?'

'It's not a concert – it's a play. A meal and a play, apparently.'

'When?'

'Seventh of next month.'

He frowns and calculates. 'That's a Thursday.' Giving me a rather dirty look, he turns to the girls. 'Listen you two, before you set off for Signora Bianca's, run down to the kitchen and get the big blue pot down from the lowest shelf. You can take one each of what you'll find in there.'

The girls scrabble to be the first to the stairs to the kitchen.

As soon as they are out of earshot, Modesto turns to me. 'The seventh? It's a Thursday. What about Signor di Cicciano? You know what I said the other—'

'He won't mind – he will be just getting back from a trip. To Malta, I think he said – with his privateer friend. And I don't see Vasquez that week at all. He's away with his troops until the Sunday.'

Modesto raises his eyebrows and pushes out his bottom lip.

'I'll tell you more when I get back later,' I say, flicking a glance towards the stairs. The girls are on their way back up, each holding a large and sticky comfit.

With a kiss for each girl, Modesto takes his leave of us and returns to the kitchens, and I take my excitable children the remaining quarter mile to the house of the former whore, now an accomplished seamstress, who I think is probably the closest thing I have to a friend of my own sex in Napoli.

'Breathe in,' Bianca says.

I hold my arms in the air and breathe in. Bianca lips a mouthful of pins and mutters grunting instructions through her nose, pushing and pulling me into the position she needs with plump fingers. She pins and tweaks and folds and tucks until the bodice – inside-out at this point – sits snug around my body like a silk skin.

Standing back from me for a moment, Bianca frowns critically at the high, concealing neckline I have requested for this dress. She runs needle-pricked fingertips along the upper edge, takes the remaining pins from her mouth and says, 'I don't understand, Francesca. What is this about?' She flicks a glance down to the girls, then drops her voice and mouths the next few words almost silently. 'Has whoring finally lost its appeal? Are you planning on going into a nunnery?'

I smile at her and explain. She laughs. Head thrown back, pin-less hand on an ample hip, Bianca laughs aloud and then sighs noisily. She speaks through the sigh, 'Oh, dear, I should like to see this, *cara*, I really should – *you*, a demure and retiring widow? How entirely marvellous you'll be – I'll make sure of it. Every inch of flesh that might inflame your poor unsuspecting hosts will be well covered, I promise you. And pearls, you say?'

'Present from Signor di Laviano.'

'And entirely illegal of course.' Her face lights up at the thought.

'Of course.'

'What does illegal mean, Mamma?' Beata says, looking up from her bowlful of glittering glass beads.

'It means . . . "beautiful", *cara*,' Bianca says, quickly. 'Your mamma will be beautiful when she goes out next month.'

'Mamma's always beautiful.'

'She is indeed.'

Bianca spends another few moments pinning and stitching and then carefully takes the half-made shell from me, leaving me in my chemise. She and the twins return to the front room, whilst I change back into my old dress; I am just fastening the last lace, when I hear the shop door open, and a man I cannot see begins speaking to Bianca. I tuck the ends of the laces down between my breasts, wriggle my shoulders until my dress sits comfortably and then re-emerge to go and find the girls; I fiddle as I walk with a wisp of hair that has escaped from its braid.

A tall young man is leaning on Bianca's table, pointing with his forefinger at a line written in her ledger. He pushes untidy hair back from his face with the other hand, and I draw in a breath.

It is Gianni.

I step back into the shadow of the passageway with my heart thudding, experiencing again in my mind that moment when he laid his mouth upon my scar and cracked open my defences. I can feel his fingers on my hipbones again. I press my back against the wall of the corridor and peer sideways at him: I don't want him to see me. My much-loved but loose-mouthed friend Bianca shall not know that I've lain with this boy, nor shall I risk my expression revealing the unnerving disquiet he has begun within me. Her gossip-greedy nature would delight in such a tidbit, and my reputation would surely suffer for her revelations.

As I watch him, Gianni smiles at Bianca; she beams, nodding her agreement with whatever he is saying. She taps her finger smartly on the paper in front of her and he inclines his head.

Beata glances up from her bead-threading, sees Gianni and stares openly. Bella senses her sister's inattention; she raises her eyes too. He smiles down at the two little figures and my heart jolts – it is a sweet, brotherly smile that has both girls immediately making huge doe-eyes at him, gazing up into his face from beneath long lashes and giggling. Bianca says something I cannot catch and Gianni laughs.

He seems to be protecting his right hand for some reason; he is holding it with the other, and a couple of times he stretches and folds his fingers as though they are paining him. I find that I want to talk to him and am on the point of ignoring my instinctive anxiety, stepping into the light and surprising him, when he straightens, thanks Bianca and leaves the shop.

'Mamma, you just missed such a nice man. He said we were pretty,' Beata says smugly as I come back through the door.

'And so you are: he was quite right.'

'And I told him you were a pair of naughty little minxes just like your mother,' Bianca says. The girls giggle.

I half-laugh, but say in protest, 'And there was I thinking you were my friend, Bianca Zigolo.'

She smiles, reaches out and strokes my cheek, chuckling as she speaks 'And so I am, *cara,* so I am. But . . . a young thing like him – *Santo cielo!*' She drops her voice again, and mouths, 'I would not let him anywhere near you! Just as well he left before you came out from the back.'

'What did he want?' I ask.

Speaking normally again, she says, 'His father needs a doublet mending. Oh, now *he* is a lovely man, the Signore. He has had his troubles, mind you. Lost his wife some ten years back and has brought up those boys on his own. A good man, he is . . . and that young lad is just like him.' She smiles and then lifts her eyebrows. Glancing down at the girls, who are absorbed in their threading again, she whispers, 'I'll tell you, Francesca, I would not mind having something like that to play with. I would not mind at all. Ooh, if I were twenty years younger . . .'

She pulls a face of exaggerated lasciviousness and I say nothing, wondering what Bianca would say if I described to her exactly what it had in fact been like . . . playing with Gianni.

We collect all our belongings and leave the shop. I take the children back to Ilaria and leave them happily stringing the bagful of beads Bianca has given them. I make my way alone back to the Via San Tommaso.

As I walk, my thoughts jangle uncomfortably inside my head. Why has this sight of Gianni so discomposed me? I truly do not believe I am – even a little – in love with him. He's just a boy. I would be pleased to lie with him again should he ever ask me to – of course I would – but then . . . perhaps women such as me simply don't deserve men like Gianni. Not *gratis*, in any case.

Will it ever be possible to turn the twins into the sort of women that someone like Gianni might one day agree to marry? If, that is, I can manage to manufacture some sort of artificial respectability for them. Will a generous dowry and a few carefully constructed lies ever be convincing enough to conceal the unpalatable truth?

Eleven

'You had an agreement, Carlo,' Michele repeated. 'You shook hands on it. Walk away from it, if it no longer pleases you.' He turned from Carlo and, lantern held high in one hand, began once more to pick his way down the narrow tunnel, away from the warmth and light of the tavern above them into cold darkness. Carlo followed, and for a while the two men were silent.

The ground began to slope downwards, and keeping their footing in the darkness took careful concentration. Carlo had known since he was a small child of the ancient, labyrinthine web of tunnelling that criss-crossed its way beneath the city like the home of some horrible Neapolitan Minotaur, but until this moment, his natural dislike of confined spaces having been encouraged by his father's vehement injunctions against any proposed boyhood explorations, he had never done more than peer into the various tunnel entrances, wondering at the extent of the pitch-dark maze that had lain for centuries underneath the city streets.

The tufa stone was damp and slippery; it smelt of decay and dust, and the men's breath hung cold before their faces in the shifting light from Michele's guttering lantern. The tunnel bent sharply to the right, and then several steep steps dropped the level of the floor some dozen feet.

'But, we agreed upon one twelfth . . .'

Michele merely shrugged. Without turning round, he said, 'You agreed with Żuba, if you remember, upon one twelfth *after* my portion had been removed from the pile, Carlo.'

'Yes, well. "The pile" would have been a damn sight smaller had I not been able to secure a buyer for the silver and if the silk hadn't sold for twice the amount Żuba predicted.'

Flicking a brief glance behind him, Michele said, 'I accept your connections are second to none and you drive a hard bargain. But, a deal is a deal, Carlo – apart from which, if you want a piece of advice, don't even think of ever trying to cross Salvatore Żuba.'

A couple more almost silent minutes passed; the only sounds were the feet of the two men scuffing against the rock floor, and the muttered oaths from Carlo as he slipped and stumbled and grabbed at the walls to maintain his balance.

'However big or small the pile might be next time,' Michele said, 'we need a safer way to get it from the *Għafrid* up into the city; we need somewhere to store things if necessary and Żuba wants to know if this route is still viable.'

'This tunnel is supposed to go direct from the tavern to the sea?'

'Apparently so.'

'If it does – and I had no idea that any part of the *sottosuolo* actually linked to the water – then I agree, it solves any number of logistical problems, Cicciano.'

Michele nodded. 'Żuba says he can bring the *Għafrid* – or at least the cutter – right up into the crook of the bay behind Posilippo, and if we can take any goods right into the city straight from there, then life will certainly be a very great deal simpler and— *Porca puttana*!'

He broke off, swearing softly as the two men stepped from the cramped tunnel out into an enormous, echoing chamber the size of a church. Vast, slabbed side walls sloped inwards and upwards;

several shallow 'rooms' led off to either side and as Michele held the lantern high, Carlo saw another three tunnel mouths leading out of the cavern at the far end, little more than black slits in the tufa. The two men's shadows stained the rocks behind them like great ink blots.

'It's perfect.' Carlo stared around him. 'We could store anything here. Anything. And you are certain that no one else uses the entrance at the tavern?'

'Not as far as I know. Żuba seems confident, anyway. The landlord has been an ally of his for years – was a privateer himself once, Żuba said. Shall we go on – down to the sea? Żuba says we need to take the central tunnel. Both the others are dead ends. Useful storage areas, perhaps.'

Carlo nodded.

'Wait a moment.' Michele stood the lantern on a ridge of rock, and spent a few minutes collecting small stones, and piling them into a neat, conical cairn at one side of the entrance to the tunnel they were about to leave.

'What in hell's name are you doing, Cicciano?'

'I want to be quite certain of finding my way out . . .' Michele said with a grin.

Carlo said nothing, but his eyes were suddenly blacker.

The two men crossed the great cavern; their steps sounded strangely dead in the unmoving air. The tunnel they entered was narrow and dank, and Carlo felt his heart beat faster as the darkness closed in behind them. 'Let's hope whatever Żuba picks up on his next voyage is not heavy . . .' he said. 'If it's gold, I am paying someone else to collect it.'

'The "pile" gets smaller, Rovere, every time you delegate, don't forget.'

Carlo scowled.

They walked on for several more minutes. Then Michele stopped suddenly and Carlo, still staring moodily at his feet as they picked their way over the uneven ground, bumped into his companion's back. He swore again.

'Look!' Michele said.

Carlo edged past him and together the two men gazed down the last twenty feet of tunnel, to where it widened out and opened onto a view of the Posilippo bay. The sky was a lightless charcoal; the moon visible only as a faint yellowish stain behind shifting, dirty rags of cloud. But below them, the hillside fell away towards the great sweep of black water. They stared out across the bay, unmoving and silent for a moment, save for the faint rasp of Carlo's breath, the enticing possibilities of wealth danced in the heads of both young men.

The eunuch opened the door. Shorter than he by a head, and softly thickset, Modesto always reminded Michele of a pug dog, a resemblance which was heightened just now as Modesto's black eyes widened in mild surprise at the sight of the visitor upon the doorstep.

'Signore,' he said. 'We were not expecting you until next week.'

'Is she here?'

'Yes, Signore, but—'

'Then let me in, damn you. I have just spent two hours clambering over an inhospitable hillside; I am cold and hungry and I could do with a bit of company before I go home.'

'If you would care to wait in here, Signore, I will go and see what she says.'

Michele stood in the doorway of the small anteroom and watched as Modesto slowly climbed the stairs, turned left and knocked upon Francesca's bedchamber door. The stocky figure waited a moment, then opened the door and leaned in, with one hand upon the handle, the other pressed against the jamb. He shook his head and then nodded, apparently in conversation with the occupant of the chamber, though Michele could hear nothing of what was being said. After a moment, Modesto pulled back, closed the door again, and just as slowly as he had climbed them, descended the stairs once more.

'If you could just give her a few moments.' he said. 'Would you care for something to eat, Signore?'

Michele nodded. 'Yes, thank you.'

The eunuch padded away down the short flight of steps that led to the kitchen and returned some moments later with a plate of meat and fruit in one hand, and a large goblet in the other.

'Thank you,' Michele said. Modesto walked past him. He put the plate and the goblet down upon a table, pulled a bone-handled knife from his belt and laid it next to the plate. Michele crossed the room, sat down on a folding chair and began to eat.

'Don't hurry yourself, Signore.' The expression on the eunuch's face as he spoke was difficult to read. 'I'll come and collect you, when my lady is ready,' he said.

Michele ate the meat and the fruit, and drank deeply from the goblet, which proved to contain a very palatable red wine.

'I wasn't expecting you till next week,' Francesca said.

Michele slumped himself down heavily in a carved wooden cross-framed chair. 'That's exactly what your eunuch said. Is it a problem to you?'

'No, it's not a problem. And Modesto is a castrato, not a eunuch – he is very particular. To him the word "eunuch" is an insult – he uses it to describe himself sometimes, but he's furious if anyone else does.'

'Castrato, eunuch – he still has no bollocks, whatever he might care to be called.'

'You're lucky I was here – I wasn't planning to be. You really are in a filthy temper, Michele. What would you like me to do to raise your spirits?'

'It's not my spirits I want you to raise, woman . . .' said Michele.

Francesca laughed. 'Come here, then, *scorbutico,* and I'll try to sweeten you up.'

Michele did not move. She crossed to where he sat scowling near the window and stood in front of him, between his splayed knees. He reached forward and held one of her buttocks in each hand through the silk of her skirts, pulling her in towards his body, so that her bent legs rested upon his thighs. She pushed her fingers into his tight curls, and Michele said, 'Where's my knife?'

'Never you mind . . .' Francesca said, absentmindedly, now unfastening the laces of Michele's doublet.

'What made you so angry, the other week? Why take it away from me?'

'You shouldn't have brought it out. I told you why a long time ago, Michele; I'm not going through it all again. It upsets me to think about it.'

'You should know me well enough to know that I would never—'

'Shh . . . I just don't care to have a knife near me. I've put it out of harm's way. Be quiet.' She was squatting on her heels now, still between Michele's knees, and her fingers had reached his breeches.

'Give it back to me when I leave, then,' he said. 'Oh, God – that feels good, woman . . . you are . . . certainly . . . worth every *scudo.*' His breathing had become shallow and his voice was hoarse.

'*Stai zitto* . . . stop talking, Michele. You talk too much.'

Francesca pushed his knees further apart and bent forwards.

Michele stopped talking.

'How did you meet this man – what did you call him? Żuba?'
Francesca said some while later, hutching herself upright and sitting cross-legged on the rumpled sheet. Arms raised, she began to
wind her hair into an untidy knot on the top of her head.

Michele lay back on the pillows and grinned, watching
Francesca's breasts move as she worked. 'By chance,' he said.
'About a year ago. Down at that filthy little inn at Marechiaro—'

'That squalid old pigsty? What on earth were you doing in a
place like that?'

Michele raised an eyebrow and said nothing. His eyes remained
fixed on Francesca's nipples.

Francesca noticed the direction of his gaze and turned her
shoulders away from him. She said, 'Oh, Michele, no – don't even
think about starting again. I'm tired, my mouth is all stretched and
sore and my poor *tette* already feel as if they've been attacked by
a particularly overzealous baker.'

'Baker?'

'Dough.' Francesca mimed kneading, then cupped her hands
protectively around her breasts and smiled at him. 'Poor things.
They're all bruised.' She turned back towards him and stroked his
cheek with her hand. 'And anyway, *caro,* I doubt you have money
enough for a second attempt so soon.'

Michele's smile vanished. He reached across and caught
Francesca's wrist, twisted her arm around so that she gasped, overbalanced and fell backwards, back onto the pillows. Kneeling up,
he leant over her and took her other wrist, pressing both her hands
back onto the bed. 'Listen,' he said softly. 'If I wanted a "second

attempt" I'd have one, bitch, whatever the expense. Do you understand?'

'Get off me, Michele,' Francesca breathed.

'When I'm ready.' Still holding her arms down, Michele bent
and took one of her nipples into his mouth.

'Get off!' she said through clenched teeth. He could feel her
wrists twisting under his hands, and she squirmed around, trying
to kick him. He sucked hard, once, feeling the soft flesh press up
onto the roof of his mouth, and then, almost in a single movement,
he let go of her arms, moved back from her, stood, and reached
towards where his shirt lay across a small carved chair.

'Get out of my house, Michele!' Francesca's voice was no more
than a hiss. She had a hand pressed against her breast.

'Don't worry, *cara*, I'm going. I'll see you on Thursday,' he
said, pulling on his doublet.

'I don't know that I want to see you again that soon now,'
Francesca said, glaring at him.

'Maybe not, but you will be happy enough to see my money, I'm
sure.'

'I'm thinking of raising my prices.'

Michele grinned. Stamping his heel down into his second boot,
he said, 'Let me know how much I owe you next time,' snatched
up his coat from the cross-framed chair, and strode across the
room.

He turned at the door to see Francesca sprawled on her stomach across the bed, snatching up one of her shoes from the floor.
She scrambled up to sitting and flung the shoe hard at him. Michele
raised an arm to ward off the blow; the shoe caught him across the
wrist and fell to the ground. He bent to pick it up.

'I'll bring this back on Thursday,' he said. He waved the shoe
at Francesca.

'*Vaffanculo*!'

Michele blew her a kiss as he pushed past the eunuch, who was on his feet just outside the bedchamber door. He ran down the stairs, and made his own way out into the street, throwing the shoe up into the air and catching it as he walked.

He was almost home before he remembered the knife.

Twelve

'It came from your father this morning, Signore.'

Michele pulled the front door shut and took the letter from his servant. The shadows of both men slid up the walls of his cramped entrance hall as the single candle flame shivered in the resultant draught.

Michele frowned at the paper and then glanced across to see his servant smothering a yawn; for a moment, the boy's face lengthened and distorted, his eyes watering. He blinked a few times and rubbed his face surreptitiously with his fingers, looking suddenly much younger than his twenty-odd years.

Michele flapped a hand by way of dismissal; Franco bowed briefly and left the room, rubbing his eyes again. Cracking the seal, Michele opened the letter and held it up to the candlelight. His eyes flicked across the contents, then he swore, screwed the paper into a tight ball and threw it across the hallway. '*Cazzo!* Same pile of *merda* as the last one,' he muttered. 'And the one before and the one before that. When is the bloody man going to stop asking?'

He pulled off his boots and kicked them irritably to one side of the room, flung his coat across a small chair and took the stairs three at a time on his way up to his bedchamber.

A fire had been lit: its flickering flames distorted the black shadows of the crimson-hung bed, the wall hangings and two large Moorish shields which hung one on each side of the window.

'More than twenty years,' Michele said aloud, as he unfastened the knot at the neck of his doublet. He was breathing fast, as though he had been running. 'Might he not – even unwillingly, the blinkered bastard! – have resigned himself to the fact that his younger son has never, *ever* had one single fucking *iota* of interest in the damned *priesthood*!' He smacked hard at the carved wooden bedpost with the flat of his palm. His hand stung.

'Why were you not at Mass this morning, Michele?' His father's face is dark with anger and Michele can see the big hands starting to curl into fists. 'It was noticed, Michele, it was noticed. Monsignor Rossi was expecting you – asked me if you were unwell . . .'

Michele shrugs. He will not tell his father the truth – that every time he steps into a church now, the prospect of ordination rises up like a spectre from the dust of the floor of the nave; it, seeps from the shadows of the transept, constricting his breathing and deafening him as it wraps itself silently around his head like the mercy hood of an executioner. Even the smell of candle-wax has now begun to make him feel nauseous simply by association.

And then – an image of the baker's daughter. On her back, bent-kneed, she smiles, hitching flour-whitened skirts up into a bolster around her waist with eager fingers, framing her invitation to him. Her breasts push forward. Her mouth is wet and her eyes promise uninhibited entertainment. Michele's hands slide up the insides of her thighs, his fingers dark against the creamy skin. Her legs crook wide.

His cock swells as he remembers.

'I said why? Michele?' His father will not be ignored.

'I . . . I was tired.' He stares at the ground, unable to think of a

better reply. The baker's daughter's nipples look like cherries and they
taste of yeast, and the black threat of celibacy looms as an infinite,
shrivelling incarceration in a mould-stained cell.

'We all have our place in life, Michele. At some point we must all
shoulder the responsibilities meted out to us by God. And God has
called you most specifically. A second son's privilege, Michele. We
cannot afford to defer responsibility because of . . . of something as
pitiful as fatigue. Antonio has already begun to—'

At the mention of his elder brother, Michele stops listening entirely.
The soft skin on the baker's daughter's thighs is slick with sweat as she
wraps her legs around his waist and her roughened heels catch on his
back. He no longer hears his father.

As Michele threw his doublet down across the chest at the foot of
his bed, a branch shifted in the fireplace and collapsed, throwing
a walnut-sized knot of burning wood out onto the rug. Reaching
forwards, he caught it between thumb and forefinger and flipped
it back into the grate. He wiped his fingers on his breeches and
straightened, crossed the room and picked up a dark-red glass
decanter from where it stood on the deep window ledge. Held it up
to the firelight to see how full it was. Pouring the contents into a
large goblet, he raised it to his lips, emptied the glass without taking
a breath, then refilled the glass.

'A second son's privilege,' he said softly.

Suddenly aware that his bladder was full, he opened the door to
the tiny privy that jutted out from the furthest corner of his bedchamber and aimed down through the hole in the seat; the liquid
pattered softly into the ash pile below.

Antonio frowns at the papers laid out in front of him and then gazes up
at his father, rigid-backed with respectful attention. Michele sits on the

floor in front of the fire, scratching behind the ears of a mangy wolfhound and trying to ignore his sister.

'Will you play something with me, Michele?'

He shakes his head, trying to hear what his father and Antonio are discussing. He has not been invited to join them at the table.

Caterina pulls at his sleeve. 'Will you play Zara, *or* Pluck the Owl? *Please?'*

'I will need you to come with me on the twenty-seventh, Antonio, because it's really time that you met Signor da Maiano — and his daughter. He was most insistent about progressing the betrothal. It is about time you—'

'Please, Micco . . .'

Michele's voice comes out much louder than he had intended. He smacks her hand away from his arm and, in his irritation, he forgets for a moment that his father is in the room. 'Oh — stai zitto, Caterina! Leave me alone! You know I hate bloody "Fuck the Owl"!'

Caterina gasps at his profanity and his father turns around. He says coldly, 'Go to your room, Michele, if you cannot behave like a civilised human being. Caterina — go and find your mother.'

The little girl begins to cry and Michele walks past her and leaves the sala, *without a word. The dog scrambles to its feet and follows him, its nails clickclicking on the wooden floor.*

Michele stretched, then stripped off breeches, hose and shirt and threw them, too, across the chest at the end of his bed. He sat on the edge of his mattress; stared at the fat little flames now licking lazily around the embers; rubbed without enthusiasm or interest at his crotch. The heat pushed out from the fireplace against his feet and shins. His eyelids were stiff and his mouth felt dry and sour.

He must, he presumed, have been a consistently deep source of disappointment to his father since early childhood. Countless scoldings, numberless beatings, an almost constant atmosphere of thunderous disapproval – *when, when,* when, *Michele? When are you ever – ever – going to show any sign of fulfilling family expectations? Think about Antonio . . . Antonio tackles his adult responsibilities with admirable application, and . . .*

Michele turned away from the fire, swung his legs onto the bed and lay back on his pillows. Smug bastard, Antonio – not even the imagination to commit the most unimpressive minor indiscretion. Michele pictured his brother – a head shorter than he, dark, softly fleshy – and tried to imagine something he had never seen: Antonio intoxicated. A soft puff of a laugh pushed its way down his nose. He tried to picture Antonio's ample buttocks bouncing above a splay-limbed whore; attempted to see in his mind his brother's normally humourless face cracked wide with laughter at a vulgar joke. And then, despite his anger, Michele grinned as he thought of an unlikely scenario: Antonio in the master's cabin on the *Għafrid,* trying to engage the taciturn Żuba in polite conversation, innocently unaware of the beady little sailor's . . . *unorthodox* method of earning his gold. *Charming ship, Signore, charming. Fast, I imagine? Yes, I should think it keeps you one step ahead of many of the other merchants. Have you done well this year, Signore? Tell me – exactly what is it you trade in?* Michele laughed aloud at the thought.

He lay awake for an hour or more, curled on his side, blankets hunched over his shoulders, watching the fire slowly die, with gritty eyes that, despite their heavy lassitude, refused to close. He finally slid into sleep as the first soft line of pinkish light appeared along the horizon, Francesca's dark-red silk shoe held loosely in the fingers of one hand.

I cannot see Vasquez now, without imagining him fingering his way beneath that poor girl's habit. Every time he lays hands on me, I think of her. What was she like? Had she wanted to lie with him? Or did he coerce her into her sin? Perhaps she was afraid of him. I wonder what has happened to her. And the child. Were they cast out into the street as soiled goods – or have the sisters taken pity on them?

There was an interesting moment yesterday evening. After our rut, Vasquez disappeared off to the room where his close-stool is kept, as he often does, and he didn't come back for some time. This is not unusual for him – his digestion can be problematical, it seems, which I suppose is not surprising considering the amount he eats and the speed at which he always eats it. He was out of the room for longer than usual yesterday; I became bored waiting for him, and decided I would start dressing.

I wanted to go home.

Now, Vasquez had taken his clothes off after me, on this occasion – he often does, as he likes to watch me undress – so his breeches and doublet were all piled on top of my things. I picked up his breeches, wanting to move them off my skirt and, as I did so, a piece of paper fell out of a pocket. It was folded over and over, and had clearly been crumpled and smoothed out at one time. I recognised it at once. It was that letter. The missive that had so angered Vasquez the other day – I'm quite certain of it.

Of course, with a quick glance at the door, not wanting to be discovered openly reading his private papers, I immediately flattened it out and started to try to decipher it. Most irritatingly, it was in Spanish– I could only understand a few words. It was signed 'Alfàn', though and had an official-looking seal at the bottom – broken, but still attached.

Oh, I so badly wanted to bring the letter home with me – I could have asked Filippo to translate it – but I didn't dare. If its contents had so angered Vasquez the other day, then finding it gone might provoke him to violence! And, of course, I would be the obvious suspect.

I thought it might be entertaining to sow a seed of doubt in Vasquez's mind, though – so I smoothed the letter out flat and tucked it under the pile of clothes. I was dressed and ready to leave before he arrived back from his close-stool, and saw myself out.

Now he'll just have to wonder whether or not I've read it, and if I have, whether or not I've understood what I've seen.

Thirteen

Modesto stood at the end of the Signora's bed, with his weight heavily on one foot. He squinted against the morning sun, which, now he had fully opened the shutters, was pouring in through the casement and effectively bleaching out the colour of everything in the room. Dust motes seethed in the brightness.

Francesca sat at her table, somewhat dishevelled, in her wrap, her cheeks rather flushed and her hair unkempt. Her fingers were ink-stained – he was pleased to see that she had been writing. His earnest recommendation – right from the very beginning of their time together in Napoli – that she record everything she said and did with every patron, had seemed to have been forgotten by her over the past weeks, but she had committed something to paper this morning, at any rate, whatever it was.

'So,' he said, 'how was our *Maestre de Campo* yesterday?'

'I've just been writing it all down. You can read it, if you want.' Francesca stretched, winging her elbows up on either side of her head, her fingers in her hair. She yawned. Closing her eyes, and rolling her neck and shoulders, she said, '*Caro* – is Lorenzo here? I'm starving.'

'Mmm, the fat old bastard's in the kitchen, busy making you something he says will be delicious.'

Francesca flashed him a smile. 'Don't be so horrible. I'll just run downstairs and see what he has for me, and then I'll go back to the girls. I promised them I'd be back by midday. Could you bear to tidy up in here a little?'

Modesto watched her go

On the Signora's table was a painted wooden box, its brightly patterned lid propped open, the key protruding from the lock. Two vellum-bound books lay inside the box, one on top of the other. Modesto picked up the top one. The words *Book of Encounters* were inscribed across the front cover in Francesca's hand. He let it fall open, the spine resting in the palm of his hand. He read quickly through the most recent pages, and then riffled back to the beginning of the book.

God, I ache all over! Michele never seems to know when to stop . . . I've no conception of where his endless energy comes from. I do wonder sometimes about him: about his early life. He never talks about himself, but he often seems to have this big, dark anger, burning away like a smouldering furnace, somewhere inaccessible. Somewhere I don't think I have ever reached. There are moments when Michele frightens me. I'm not sure how to describe it. It's like a blankness. An emptiness. There's a kind of nothingness that sometimes flickers across his eyes . . . as though, just for that moment, he is entirely unaware of what he is doing. Or what he might do next. I don't think I like him very much. So many times I have said to myself that I should finish with him . . . but I never do. Maybe it's this sense of danger. Maybe it's the money. Perhaps I actually like dancing thoughtlessly around the crumbling edges of potential disaster. I've done it before, after all. Or perhaps it's just that his wild, unthinking, explosive abandonment is . . . is intoxicating and, like some pathetic inebriate, I'll keep on and on returning to something I know might well destroy me.

Modesto shivered. He pictured Signor di Cicciano's disdainful arrogance, and felt a familiar wash of antipathy push up through him like a ripple of nausea.

He closed the book, put it back down on the table and reached back down to the painted box. Inside, beside the second notebook was a small ivory-handled mirror and, very much to Modesto's surprise, an intricately tooled dagger, its blade a damascened blue steel. He picked it up, weighed it in his palm, then tested the needle point against a fingertip. He frowned at it. The handle of this knife was unlike anything he had seen – instead of the usual protruding pommel, it rose straight up, no wider than the blade, ending in two round, angled 'ears' of delicately worked silver. It was, Modesto observed with a cold lurch of distaste, slim, beautiful, and quite obviously lethal. He wondered why on earth, with her history, Francesca would want such a thing anywhere near her.

Putting the knife back where he had found it, Modesto turned his attention back to the second book, bound like the first in vellum and fastened shut with thin leather laces. This too was carefully inscribed, *Book of Encounters*, and had been dated some year or so previously.

He flipped open the loose-knotted laces and turned to the first few pages. Reading through a few lines, he clicked his tongue in irritation.

'Was it that long ago? Bloody man – I can't believe he's been coming here this long!'

And then this evening I find myself persuading an anxious new patron that, as far as I am concerned, it is in fact entirely acceptable for him to vent his frustrations with his – so he tells me – frigid wife upon my expensive arse as often and as vigorously as he wishes. So long as he pays me what I ask for. (Which I think in his case will not be too much. He's certainly not rich.) He's a big, sweet-natured man and much to my surprise, he's charmingly reluctant to do anything which might cause me the merest fraction of a second's discomfort. In fact, it takes me much of our time together, on this first occasion, to persuade him to lay hands on me at all, despite his obvious hunger for relief – such is his guilt at his infidelity.

'I've *never* understood why you indulge him the way you do,' Modesto muttered, moodily, shaking his head in disbelief. Turning over several more pages he read;

But sometimes I feel as though I am doing no more than wallowing through my life like a sun-warm sow in a swamp. I watched a big black pig yesterday, deliberately tipping over its water trough and then coating itself in the resultant glistening mud. It lay on its side with its little eyes closed and with a smug smirk of blissful decadence on its face, and as I watched, I saw myself, sweat-damp and bone-weary, basking in the admiration of a satisfied customer and looking, I'm sure, just as complacent as did that sow, lazing in the heat of the afternoon sun. Though perhaps – I hope – a little prettier.

Modesto now puffed his amusement in his nose. He looked up, hearing footsteps on the stairs, and Francesca came back into the room, with a piece of bread and a length of smoked sausage in her hands. Her mouth was full; she chewed and swallowed quickly and clumsily, waving her sausage at him, obviously wanting to speak, and then said, 'What are you reading?'

Modesto raised an eyebrow. 'Your description of yourself as a pig in the mud . . .' he said.

Frowning quizzically, Francesca crossed the room to peer over Modesto's shoulder, and then laughed. 'I don't remember writing that at all. I'm not sure why I keep all those books.'

'Because I tell you to, that's why,' Modesto said, snapping shut the volume he held and holding it up towards her, pointing it at her like an accusatory finger.

Francesca smothered a laugh, and bobbed a curtsy. 'I'm so sorry, Signore,' she said in a servant's wheedling tone of subservience. 'Whatever you say, Signore . . .'

'Oh, go and finish your sausage,' Modesto said. He could feel a smile tugging at the corners of his mouth, but deliberately twitched it to immobility. Then the smile faded, and he said quietly, 'Where does the knife come from, Signora?'

'Knife?'

He pointed into the box.

A pause.

'It's Michele's. I took it away from him the other day. Much to his annoyance, I have to admit.'

'When was that?'

'Couple of weeks ago.'

Modesto remembered with a little lurch of his guts the scuffle he had watched from the doorway, and the glittering object that had clattered to the floor.

'Would you like me to . . . dispose of it for you?' he said.

'No. Thank you, *caro*, but I suppose I should really give it back to Michele. He says he feels naked without a knife and he's too mean to buy a new one. I'll let him have it back next time he's here, but I'll tell him to take it away.'

'Make sure you do.'

Francesca smiled and ducked into another little curtsy. 'Whatever you say, Signore,' she repeated, once more in a husky parody of servility.

Modesto shook his head. 'I mean it.' He paused, then said, 'Did you say you wanted to go back to the Via Santa Lucia this morning, Signora?'

'Yes – I promised Bella and Beata I'd take them down to the docks today. But, oh, dear.' She yawned, and rubbed her eyes with the back of the hand holding the bread. 'Oh, Modesto, it's not that I don't want to – I love taking them out and I know they adore seeing the ships – it's just that – I really am tired today.'

'I'll take them, if you like.'

'Oh, *caro* – would you?'

'I'd be pleased to. I'll tidy up in here, we can go back to Santa Lucia together, then you can sleep for a couple of hours while I walk the girls down to the waterfront. They like going with me, I think.'

Francesca smiled. 'Do you know, I've never stopped being grateful to the Duke of Salerno for having decided to engage a castrato soprano to sing at his thirtieth birthday party.'

She finished her sausage, sucked the tips of her fingers, leaned across and kissed Modesto on the cheek. Then, sitting down in a chair near the window, she tipped her head back so that the sun fell across her face and closed her eyes, heaving in a long sigh and blowing it out again softly. Watching her as he began to collect up her scattered undergarments, Modesto saw her obvious fatigue and frowned. He shook his head. Her heart's not in this game like it used to be, he thought. Not since that boy's visit.

Fourteen

Carlo della Rovere swore, as a thick-set man in filthy, salt-stiff breeches stepped backwards and trod heavily on his foot. 'Mind where you're bloody going, *stronzo!*'

'Beg pardon . . .' the seaman muttered, shifting his clearly heavy armful of rolled canvas more securely up into his arms and moving away from Carlo without turning his head. Carlo scowled at the man's back, and spat onto the dockside. He bent down and rubbed his foot.

Looking about him, he saw some dozen ships of varying sizes – two- and three-masted caravels, a heavy, square-rigged galleon, one very battered old carrack with filthy brown sails, and a pretty little *sciabecco*, very like Żuba's beloved *Għafrid* – had been made fast alongside the many wharves and jetties, whilst several more vessels rode at anchor out in the glittering water of the bay. A stiff breeze had picked up since the morning, and the air was now heavy with the ceaseless slap of rope against wood, with the muffled crumpling of furled canvas and with the screaming oaths of the thousand wheeling gulls that rode the wind in buffeting circles overhead. The dock itself was crowded: flamboyantly dressed merchantmen arm-in-arm with women decked out in peacock-bright finery; nut-brown, bone-thin sailors with white-rimmed breeches and bare torsos, seemingly carved from polished teak;

wide-eyed urchins gazing in envy at the insolent faces of those boys already employed aboard ship; ill-clad women with tousled hair and provocative expressions, on the lookout for work.

Carlo pushed his hair out of his eyes and began to chew one of his fingernails. 'Come on! Come on!' he muttered under his breath, the words distorting around his fingertip. 'Don't keep me bloody waiting too much longer, you bastard!'

Sitting on the butt end of an ancient old gun, embedded in the wharf as a bollard, Carlo searched the crowd for the hundredth time, one leg twitching convulsively, his eyes flickering from face to face, from stranger to stranger. He stopped chewing his nail and began tapping his closed lips with his fingers; exasperation was now clamping his teeth together until they ached.

And then his attention was caught by a man, hand in hand with two little girls in matching dresses. This was not the man he sought, but for some reason the new arrival seemed vaguely familiar. As Carlo watched, the newcomer released the children's hands and pointed up into the web of rigging above him. Both girls stared upwards in the direction indicated, nodding at the miming of what appeared to be the tying of a complicated knot. Then the man smiled, now spreading his arms wide in illustration of some explanation Carlo could not hear, his face alight with pleasure, and the little girls laughed. Carlo could not immediately place him, but he knew he had never seen these children before. He stared at them. They were identical. Absolutely indistinguishable. His gaze flicked from one to the other; momentarily distracted from his irritation, he found himself amused and entertained by the girls' extraordinary likeness.

And then, with a sudden stab of realisation, he knew where he had seen the man before.

*

An evening a few weeks previously. A doorstep in the Via San Tommaso.

'Signore – this is my brother, Gianni. I imagine you are expecting him – he has an engagement here this evening.'

The stocky man with the black eyes nods and steps back, arm outstretched in welcome, but Gianni does not move. He stands with his arms folded and his shoulders up near his ears. Carlo grabs his elbow. 'Now, now fratellino,' he says. 'You wouldn't want to disappoint the lady . . .'

'Get off me, Carlo.'

'A little nervous, Signore, I'm afraid,' Carlo says in amused apology.

The man at the door says nothing. Carlo sees the expression of suppressed terror on his brother's face, and laughs aloud.

It was her pimp – that woman's – that overpriced whore of Michele's, Carlo thought, remembering the money he had lost on that venture.

The 'pimp' caught his eye, and started in recognition. Inclined his head.

'Signore!' Carlo called, and, welcoming the distraction, he stood up, and began to walk towards the three newcomers. 'Signore!' he said again.

Another nod.

'I didn't know you had children, Signore.'

A pause.

'They are not mine.'

The girls' liquid-eyed prettiness made sudden sense to Carlo. 'Ah – they're hers, then?'

'These are Signora Felizzi's daughters, if that's who you mean, yes.'

The two children stared up at him.

'And what brings you to the dock, Signore?' Carlo said.

'The children enjoy seeing the ships.'

'Their mother . . . otherwise engaged, then, is she?' Carlo said, raising his eyebrows and smirking as he imagined the possibilities.

The man with the black eyes smiled, but said nothing.

And then, pounding feet and an anxious shout from behind them. 'Rovere!'

Carlo spun around. A squat figure with a softly wizened face like an ageing apple was elbowing his way through the milling crowd.

'Ramacciotti! About bloody time!'

The little man was panting, and sweat was beading his forehead and upper lip.

'Where the hell have you been?' Carlo said.

Modesto watched as the man called Rovere gripped the newcomer by the upper arm and leaned in close towards him. Both men began to walk away up the wharf towards the brightly painted galleon.

'Who was that man, Desto?' one of the girls asked in a whisper. Her grip on his hand had tightened.

'Someone I met recently.'

'Does he know Mamma?'

'No.' Modesto crouched down between the girls and smiled at each in turn. 'No, he doesn't. Don't let's worry about him. Let's think about food instead. Are you hungry? Would you like to see if we can find some comfits? Or some dried figs? Or perhaps, if you're very lucky a . . . a sugar pig?'

Enthusiastic nods.

'Come on then, see over there – there's somewhere we should be able to buy something, and then, if you like, I'll finish my story on the way home.'

Modesto pointed along the wharf to where a likely stall was attracting a fair amount of attention, and the three of them began to walk towards it. The stabbing pain in his chest occasioned by Rovere's presumption that the girls were his children was subsiding. A needling sense of unease, however, continued to unsettle him, though he could not determine why this should be.

Fifteen

'I shall be home well before sunset, I hope, Maria,' Filippo said as he drained his cup of watered wine, and wiped it out with the last piece of bread. 'I had thought I would be detained again tonight, but Vasquez for some reason seems to have other things than work on his mind for once – I have no idea what those things might be of course, he does not see fit to tell me of his private affairs, but he has been quite distracted for days – and, thank Heavens, he has not mentioned . . . mmn . . . that accursed piece of transhlation since lasht week.' He had taken an apricot from a bowl in the middle of the table as he spoke and bitten it in half: with his mouth thus packed, his last few words were almost incomprehensible. He picked the exposed stone out of the other half of the apricot with one finger and threw it into a nearby bowl.

'Translation?'

Filippo waved the rest of the apricot at her as he swallowed. 'Oh, you know – that infernally tedious document that I have been working on for a couple of weeks. I'll bring it home with me and work on it here.'

Maria said, 'I thought you told me that was finished.'

Filippo frowned. 'I know what I said. I know what I told Vasquez. But, well . . . perhaps "*finished*" was something of an exaggeration . . .'

'Filippo – is there a problem with it?'

He sighed and shook his head. 'No. I must simply apply myself to it a little more diligently. It is not difficult, merely intensely boring.'

Maria looked into her husband's entirely familiar face and, with a pinprick of shock, felt Filippo's gloomy anticipation of tedium as though it were her own – the feeling moved within her as if she had occasioned it herself – and in a buffeting tangle of sensation, for a fractured second she *was* her husband. She saw him from the inside outwards. All Filippo's frustrations, his boredom, his guilt at his lies and deceit, his desire for her, the despairing anger Maria saw in him when he came to her bedchamber on those occasions when he could not contain himself – it all screamed through her mind and her body, passing so swiftly that as fast as she acknowledged the sensation, it was gone. Shuddering in its wake, though, was a new and raw appreciation of Filippo's vulnerability.

And to her intense surprise, at that moment she wanted very much to lean across the table, hold his face in her hands and kiss him.

But she couldn't move.

'I'll expect you in time for a meal tonight then,' she said.

The wind was from the south-west, and a smell of wet ropes and fish from the wharves pricked at Maria's nostrils as she began to walk alone towards San Giacomo degli Spagnoli. Filippo had left the house; Emilia was preparing a meal in the kitchen and now she wanted to spend a few moments alone in the church to try to settle her unquiet thoughts.

There were times when her sister's company became irksome even to her: she knew that Filippo struggled to contain his dislike of Emilia and, whilst Maria loved her sister and was still glad she had been able to offer her a home, she could easily understand why another might find her company difficult. Emilia was intractably conservative in her tastes and, raised as Maria had been by the passion-fearing sisters, found any display of emotion unpleasant and upsetting. Maria wondered again, as she had done the other day, if Emilia was concealing as much turbulence and confusion behind her expressionless face as she herself hid so carefully inside her own dignified exterior. She did not feel close enough to Emilia to ask her.

Maria held in one hand her copy of *The Book of the City of Ladies,* which she hoped to read for a while after she had finished at San Giacomo. She needed to be quite alone for a while. She had little more than a few pages left – the red calfskin strip now lay almost flush with the back cover of the book – and she wanted to find a quiet spot where she could finish the story without fear of interruption.

She reached the church, opened the door and stepped into the gloom. No more than a handful of silent figures sat or stood dotted around the cavernous interior as Maria walked up to a bench towards the front and knelt down. The young priest who normally heard her confession walked across the width of the church; peered down the length of the building and quickened his pace. She placed her book on the seat, clasped her hands and rested her forehead against her knuckles; her elbows pressed painfully into the wood of the pew in front and her crossed thumbs pushed up against the bridge of her nose. Eyes tightly closed, she tried to contain her fragmented thinking and order it all into something resembling a prayer, but the words and images danced before her, mocking her attempts and refusing to be disciplined.

Maria felt tears sting behind her eyes as anger began to seep through her. Anger with Filippo for wanting so frequently what she found so difficult to give him – and then for obtaining it elsewhere. Anger with the sisters for so effectively having bricked her up inside her own body – and anger with herself for suddenly, after so many years, needing to break through those fortifications, but so pitifully lacking the means to do so. Anger with God for playing such thoughtless games with her emotions. It all churned in her chest and up into her throat; she swallowed quickly to suppress a scream. She pressed so hard against her forehead with her clasped thumbs that it hurt and she began to feel sick.

After a moment's acute discomfort, she lifted her head. Several people had seated themselves near her while she had been struggling. With a needling start of recognition, Maria saw that one of them was the beautiful woman with the braided hair whom she had seen last time she had made her confession. The woman's head was bent over her hands: the elaborate decoration around the upper edge of her dress gave to her neck a sense of slender vulnerability.

Her own attempts at prayer quite forgotten, Maria watched the woman again for some moments, fascinated by her air of exotic opulence. She stared at her, awed by the richness of the fabrics the woman wore, fascinated by the brazen glitter of the ornaments adorning her hair, neck, ears and hands, charmed by the voluptuousness of the painted mouth as the woman silently murmured her clearly heartfelt orations. Then, catching the baleful eye of a black-clad old crone across the aisle, Maria felt herself blush, embarrassed to have been caught so openly watching another penitent.

She decided to leave.

Standing, she edged herself out into the aisle, bobbed a hasty genuflection and left the building, *The Book of the City of Ladies* held in one hand. She would, she thought, finish her reading out here, in the cool of the shadow of the church.

A low stone bench stood along a nearby wall, and on this Maria seated herself. She opened the book and counted the pages she had left to finish. Less than a dozen. That would not take her long. Tucking the calfskin strip inside the cover, she leaned back and began to read.

But she had barely completed a page when a flash of vivid red caught her eye and she looked up.

The opulent woman was leaving the church.

She was tall, Maria thought, struck by how slow and careful and elegant the woman's gait seemed; the crimson skirts billowed out behind her as she walked, like the sails of a galleon. Maria stared as the woman turned left and began to make her way towards the top corner of the square. It seemed as though it would be no more than seconds before she was lost from sight, when in an instant she tripped, stumbled, and fell heavily forward, sprawling full-length upon the ground with an audible grunt.

Maria stood up.

The woman sat up awkwardly and pulled at her skirts; she fumbled with the fabric and then took out from under the material a shoe, unlike any shoe Maria had ever seen. Its upper was of scarlet leather – an embroidered slipper – but it was the sole that astonished. Some six or seven inches in depth, the gilded sole was a slim-waisted column, shaped like an elongated hourglass. Maria was astounded that anyone could walk at all in such footwear and wondered why any woman would choose to wear something that so effectively hobbled her movements. She was not surprised that this woman had fallen.

And then she saw her face: there were tears in the dark-rimmed eyes and her mouth was twisted in pain. Several people passed her: some stared, a couple sneered, but none offered assistance. Dropping her book as she ran, Maria hurried across the square and crouched down. 'Are you hurt, Signora? I saw you fall, and . . .'

'It's nothing,' the woman said with her eyes fixed upon her foot. 'I have wrenched my ankle, no more. It's my stupid *chopines* – they are quite impossible to walk in. I hate the damned things – in fact I think I'll throw them away when I get home. But –' She hesitated. 'Thank you for your kindness, Signora.' She gave Maria a damp smile, wiped her eyes and stood clumsily, bending to pick up her discarded shoes. Without the impractical *chopines*, the skirts of the woman's red dress trailed on the ground, and she seemed dramatically diminished by the reduction in her height.

'There. I don't think I have damaged anything too badly,' she said, and took a tentative step. With a gasped-in yelp, however, she stopped quickly, her face pinched into a grimace.

'Oh, Signora—' Maria said, stepping forward again.

'Oh, *merda*! *Cazzo!* I am so sorry . . . do you think you might be able to help me over to where I can sit down?' the woman said.

Maria was startled by the profanity, but nonetheless placed one of the woman's arms around her shoulders, and, putting her own arm around the woman's back, held her by the elbow. She was aware of a faint smell of peaches. Together they walked with difficulty back to the stone bench, the woman limping badly. Maria helped her to sit. As she slid her arm from where it had been around the woman's waist, Maria saw *The Book of the City of Ladies*, spine up on the ground a few yards away across the square. The red calfskin strip lay nearby.

'Oh! Excuse me a moment, Signora – I must rescue my book.' She hurried over and picked it up, tenderly smoothing the ruffled pages. Bending and snatching up the leather strip as she returned, she hurried back to the stone bench and sat next to the voluminous red damask skirts.

'I'm sorry. Is your book badly damaged?'

'No. It is of no consequence – I have almost finished it, anyway.'

'What is its name?'

Maria showed her the book.

'And its subject?'

Maria smiled then, and said with enthusiasm, 'Well . . . it was written by a woman, and amongst other things, she describes the creation of an imaginary city for virtuous women and – oh, it's wonderful, Signora – she praises the many contributions women have made – and make still – to . . . to civilisation. It is a remarkable book and most reassuring – I have nearly finished it.'

'Could I see?' the woman said.

Maria held it out to her. She watched as her companion opened the cover and began to flick through the first few pages, frowning in concentration as her eyes moved across what she read. She nodded a few times, as though she agreed with the sentiments she saw expressed, and then, apparently startled, drew in a sharp breath.

'Signora – is your foot hurting?'

A shake of the head.

Maria said, 'What troubles you?'

The woman did not answer; she continued reading.

Maria stared at her, watching her absorption in the words she read. She looked again at the flamboyant red dress; at the woman's braided hair and painted face. She took in once more the bright stones on fingers, ears and throat. The discarded *chopines* suddenly took on a new significance and something hot slid over itself in Maria's belly as she realised what this woman's occupation must be. An occupation that would most probably be decidedly unwelcome in the City of Ladies. She recalled a line from the beginning of the book: *Only ladies who are of good reputation and worthy of praise will be admitted into this city. To those lacking in virtue, its gates will remain for ever closed.*

A jumble of disturbing images danced into Maria's mind and she was profoundly shocked to realise that what she felt was not disapproval. It was envy.

Her face flamed.

The woman looked up and saw her embarrassment. 'I'm so sorry, Signora,' she said, pushing the book back into Maria's hands.

'Why do you apologise?'

The woman hesitated. 'I'm imagining . . . by your expression . . . that . . . that you have just worked out my occupation,' she said. 'And that perhaps, having determined what it is that I do, you no longer wish me to look at your book.'

Maria felt her colour deepen still further. She put a hand up to the side of her face, the heel of her palm across her mouth. And then an idea struck her. This woman would know. Maria drew in a breath, held it for a moment. She might never have the opportunity again. She had to do it. Her need for information became so intense she felt quite breathless. She felt her mouth opening and closing, but the words seemed to have jammed somewhere at the back of her throat; it was as though they had braced themselves against eviction and were determined to stay put. There was a long silence. Maria saw the woman shift her weight uncomfortably and wince as, presumably, the twisted ankle pained her.

She felt a tear spill over and run down her cheek. The woman reached out and took her hand, but, embarrassed, Maria pulled away from her grasp. The woman said, 'Signora, what is it? What's the matter? Why are you crying? Is it something I said?'

Her voice sounded kind.

Maria began to mutter, more to herself than to her companion, 'I can't ask anyone I know – I simply can't! There's no one. But you'll tell me – I'm sure you will. You'll understand. You're . . . you're a . . .' The final word faded away and Maria stared down at her lap, winding her wedding band around and around her finger.

'Ask what?'

Maria looked up at the woman. She imagined her questions, hanging loud in the quiet air between them, and her courage drained away. She shook her head and said nothing.

The church bell tolled the hour, and the woman in the crimson dress glanced up at the clock. 'Oh,' she said. 'I really should be getting back to my children.'

Maria's heart pinched with envy. 'You have children?'

'Two. Twin girls.' The woman picked up her *chopines* and made to stand, but she stumbled on her first step, gasped, and then swore again under her breath.

Maria stood too. 'Please – let me help you home. Do you live far from here?'

The woman explained.

'That's no distance. I can go with you. Take my arm, Signora.'

The woman smiled at her.

A matter of yards from the Via Santa Lucia, in sight of the sea, the two women saw a small group of people outside a tavern. A young girl, no more than sixteen, Maria thought, dressed in an extravagant and tattered orange dress, was leaning insolently against a wall, clearly enjoying the admiration of a group of young men in varying stages of inebriation.

The woman in crimson stopped. 'Look,' she said. 'I've had an idea. Can you wait a moment?' She raised her voice and said, 'Excuse me . . .' and the group turned as one to see who had spoken. The girl, still leaning on the wall, raked her from head to foot with an appraising, disdainful sneer; Maria she ignored completely. The men's attention shifted quickly from the girl to Maria's companion – their stares were unabashed and openly lascivious. Maria's skin crawled, but her companion seemed to take no notice. 'Might you be able to find a use for these?' she said, holding up the shiny *chopines*.

The girl's pretence of superiority vanished. Like a greedy child, she gasped, and her eyes stretched with longing.

'Don't you want 'em?' she said, staring at the shoes. 'Whass wrong wiv 'em?'

'Nothing. They don't fit me any more.'

The girl stepped forward and snatched at the shoes. With her tongue protruding from the corner of her mouth, she kicked off her own wooden pattens and slipped a grubby foot into one of the chopines. Then, wobbling a little, she balanced on the impossible shoe and put on the second, smiling widely. Her admirers clapped. She made no attempt to thank her benefactor, and after a few seconds, the woman in crimson turned to Maria. 'She seems happy enough, Signora. Shall we go?'

Maria smiled and nodded, and the two women limped on, leaving the young men eagerly assuring the girl that they needed to see a very great deal more of her legs, to appreciate fully the beauty of the strange new footwear.

Sixteen

Luca della Rovere eased his arms into the sleeves of the doublet Signora Zigolo held out for him, pulled the two halves of the front together and roughly laced it closed. He flexed his shoulders, raised and lowered his arms, twisted from side to side. He smiled at the seamstress.

'It's perfect, Signora. Thank you so much. I imagine it must have been something of a challenge to mend?'

'Ooh, nothing I could not manage, Signore,' Bianca Zigolo said happily. She raised a plump forefinger in cheerful admonishment. 'And I had *not* forgotten it, Signore, though it was a pleasure to see your son when you sent him to see me the other day to remind me about it. It is to be quite an evening, from what he tells me.'

Her face radiated curiosity. Gianni could not have told her much – he knew next to nothing about the night to come himself. Luca said, 'Yes, it will be an impressive gathering, Signora. Though it doesn't happen often, when it finally organises such an occasion, the university does like to create a spectacle.' He raised his hands in mock apology and smiled as he said, 'I am afraid that as a mere lowly academic I am not thought important enough to be party to any of the details, though I believe there is to be performance of a play and a quite certainly overindulgent and disgustingly extravagant meal, which we will all no doubt thoroughly relish.'

The seamstress blew an appreciative breath out through pursed lips, shaking her head as though struggling to accept the idea of such opulence.

Luca said, 'And I shall enjoy the evening all the more for being so finely dressed, Signora. Thank you again. Now . . . how much do I owe you for your labours?'

She told him, and (privately astounded that anyone could survive on so pitiful an income) Luca paid her, inclined his head in a brief bow and left the shop with the newly mended doublet over his arm.

He walked slowly back to the house, thinking about his sons.

The continuing tension between the two boys was unsettling. In itself, it was not unexpected: Carlo and Gianni had been uneasy playmates since early childhood. Over the years there had been frequent, usually petty quarrels (most often occasioned by Carlo) and seldom had they seemed truly to enjoy each other's company. Their troubled relationship saddened Luca, more acutely since Lisabeta's death. His sweet-natured wife had always been able to reconcile the differences of her two sons – either with smiles or scoldings – and whatever their issues with each other, both boys had unreservedly adored their mother. He saw again in his mind their uncomprehending devastation on the day of her unexpected death and thought with tearing guilt of his own inability to comfort them from within the shattered shell of his own grief.

He too had adored Lisabeta.

With the loss of the woman he had so fiercely loved howling around him and deafening him, he knew now that as that first year of bereavement had trailed past, he had entirely failed to hear the plaintive pleas of his sons for his attention.

When, months later, the tumult died down and he could step outside his head again, he turned his thoughts back to his boys. But he found unexpected changes. Seven-year-old Gianni's cheerful confidence had shrivelled without his mother; nervous and mistrustful, he now watched the world through wide eyes and spoke little, and Luca found that he missed Gianni's happy chatter almost as much as he missed his wife. And there was worse: clever, vivid little Carlo seemed to have withdrawn – even in those short months – inside a hard carapace Luca could not now penetrate. Carlo hardly spoke to his father. Within his shell the boy had become devious, manipulative, cunning, and Luca found himself almost afraid of his older son, whom – to his great distress – he found he no longer entirely trusted.

He remembered thinking at the time that something like this must be the experience of sailors who come back from months – years – at sea, to find that in their absence their home life has altered beyond recognition and that they no longer know people they thought irrevocably familiar.

He walked on for some moments, tangled inside a buzzing jumble of uncomfortable thoughts.

'Oh, Luca – how lovely to see you!'

Luca started at the voice, and then smiled to see the diminutive figure of his friend, Serafina Parisetto crossing the narrow street towards him. Hardly taller than a child and impossibly narrow shouldered: it always amazed Luca that such a tiny woman could have successfully borne two children. She stopped close to him, placed a hand on his arm and smiled up into his face. He had to stop himself from crouching to bring himself down to her height.

'I have been wanting to see you for weeks, Luca – ever since you sent us that invitation. I know Piero has told you we should simply *love* to come, but I've been very anxious that you have been thinking me most *dreadfully* remiss not to have spoken to you myself.' She hesitated, and then her mouth opened and she sucked in a little gasp, as though she had just thought of something very shocking. 'He did speak to you, didn't he?'

Luca laughed. 'Yes, Serafina, I saw him some two or three weeks ago.'

Serafina puffed a breath out again. '*Santo cielo* – I thought for one frightening moment that he might not have done and then you should have thought us the rudest friends anyone could possibly have.'

'Which of course you are . . .'

Serafina caught her lip between her teeth to stop herself smiling, and smacked Luca's forearm. 'You are a *horrible* man, Luca della Rovere,' she said. 'I don't know why Piero and I ever agreed to come to this play with someone so totally unlikeable!'

Luca laughed again.

Serafina said, 'But, seeing that we are being forced to spend an evening with such a *canaglia impenitente,* perhaps you can tell me a little more about what we may expect . . .'

Her phrase 'unrepentant scoundrel' made Luca think unwillingly of Carlo. He pushed the picture of his elder son back out of sight.

'Do you have the time to come back to the house, Serafina?' he said.

'I most certainly do. Piero's mother is at home.'

'I'll tell you as we walk then.'

Despite the fierceness of the sunshine outside, the light in Luca's small *sala* was cool and dim. The shutters were, as usual, firmly closed to keep out the heat of the afternoon; they would not be opened again until the morning. Little of the bustling noise of the street below penetrated either, and the *sala* had a peaceful, composed air about it – rather as though the house were drowsing in the warmth with a shady hat over its eyes. Several large tapestries, depicting busily peopled scenes from mythological stories, covered two of the three un-windowed walls and a long, scrubbed table ran the length of the room. The day being so warm, the fireplace was empty – clean and cleared of the detritus of the previous blaze, though a faint smell of burned wood still hung in the air.

'And shall you be coming to this marvellous evening of entertainment, Gianni?' Serafina asked. She replaced her glass on the table and folded small hands in her lap.

'Possibly, Signora.' Gianni flicked his hair out of his eyes. Pushing back his chair, he crooked one foot up onto the other knee, resting one arm on his thigh, hand hanging loosely.

Luca watched as one of the cats appeared and stood in the half-open doorway for a moment. It crossed the room to the table, where it snaked around the legs of Gianni's chair and pushed its head up into his palm. Gianni fingered the creature's ears for a moment. The cat began to purr.

'And why only "possibly", *caro*?' asked Serafina.

'I have to make a trip to Bologna for my studies, and my tutor has not yet told me when I am to travel.'

'How tiresome of him. Well, I hope very much that your dates are settled soon and that we shall be able to have the pleasure of your company, Gianni,' Serafina said with a smile.

'I hope so too, Signora.' Gianni turned to Luca. 'Papa, can you excuse me – I have one or two things I need to finish before tomorrow.'

'Of course – off you go – but would you be able to walk Signora Parisetto home when she's ready?'

Gianni nodded. 'I'll be upstairs when you need me, Papa,' he said. He smiled, bowed briefly to Serafina and left the room.

As he left, the cat walked silently around the table and jumped up into Luca's lap. He scratched the back of its neck; the cat's claws stretched and curled in pleasure, needling into Luca's leg and making him wince.

'Oh, Luca, Gianni is such a lovely boy,' said Serafina. 'If Paolo and Benedetto grow up to be even a quarter as delightful as he is, I shall be entirely overjoyed.'

'They will, Serafina – they are enchanting children, as you well know.'

'Yes, well, they are only three and one, so we have many years for things to change.'

Luca laughed. 'Why do you always seem so very determined to see the absolute worst in your lovely boys—'

'The worst? Oh, heavens – if you want to know the worst – just listen to what my darling Benedetto did last night . . .'

The pair of them discussed the tribulations of parenthood with animation and amusement for a few moments until Serafina sighed and pushed back her chair. Luca stood too.

'I must go, Luca – my mother-in-law will be anxiously waiting for me to get back, I am quite sure. Patience has never been her most obvious virtue.' Serafina raised an eyebrow and Luca laughed again. Serafina said, 'Thank you for your hospitality, *caro* – I do hope the time between now and the banquet, or play, or whatever it is, passes quickly. I simply cannot *wait* to see Filippo again, and to meet his cousin. Poor thing: I cannot imagine *what* I should do if I were ever to lose Piero—' She stopped abruptly, one hand across her mouth. 'Oh, *cielo*, Luca . . . how *appallingly* tactless of me.'

Serafina threw her arms around Luca in consternation, but he kissed the top of her head, placed his hands on her shoulders and held her away from him.

'Stop it, Serafina – don't think of it for a moment. For goodness sake, it is – what? – nearly eleven years now. I am . . . quite mended now, I think.'

'Well, nevertheless, it was horrible of me to be so thoughtless. I am sorry.'

'You don't need to be. Don't think of it. Wait – I shall just call Gianni for you.'

Luca leaned against the door jamb, swinging his spectacles in one hand. He watched the two figures move away up the street: his long-limbed son and a woman whose head barely reached Gianni's shoulder. Luca could see that she was taking two steps to every one of Gianni's slow strides. Gianni carried Serafina's big basket.

He smiled at the sight, turned back into the house and closed the front door. Does one ever fully accustom oneself to the sight of one's replication in one's children? Seeing Gianni now, it was as if he saw himself at seventeen. The over-long legs, the tangled curls, the slight stoop – Luca had not forgotten wanting to hide his height at Gianni's age. Gianni's eyes were Luca's, his straight nose, his wide mouth – at times the resemblance was unnerving. The day Gianni needed spectacles, the picture would be complete.

And Carlo? Luca sighed. Carlo most closely resembled Lisabeta's Venetian father, he thought. Slight, good-looking; much fairer-complexioned than he and Gianni. Carlo did not look Neapolitan at all.

Did physical similarity or difference influence filial closeness?

For he and Gianni understood each other; liked each other. They laughed and wept at the same things, could thrash out a discussion for hours, keeping easy pace with each other – both were fascinated by the intricacies of the law and, stupidly, both even shared a marked aversion to broad beans.

But Luca had very little notion of what happened inside the

head of his older son. He had almost no conception of how Carlo earned his money, or of the identity of his friends. Shadowy individuals occasionally visited the house, but never stayed to talk, and Carlo carefully avoided the particular if he was ever asked about what he was doing. Rarely, if ever, did Carlo seem truly happy, except perhaps at odd moments (and usually at someone else's expense). He remained a worrying mystery to his father, and over the years Luca had spent many, many painful hours in fruitless arguments with himself, trying to decide whether or not he should blame this unsettling separateness of Carlo's upon his, Luca's, miserable withdrawal from his children at the time of his bereavement.

He consistently pushed from his mind his almost certain conviction that his older son was a sodomite. The terrifying threat of the agonies of the *strappado* – or the stake – should this be the case, and should Carlo ever be accused – and convicted – made Luca feel physically sick. He knew he was wilfully forcing himself to ignore the possibility of Carlo's unpalatable predilections, simply because he could not face their reality.

'Papa?'

Luca started at the sound of Carlo's voice, and felt himself reddening, as though he had been caught rifling through his son's possessions.

'Carlo.' He made himself smile.

Carlo slid onto a chair where he sat with one knee twitching. 'I wanted to tell you, Papa – I have to be away for a week or so: I will be gone from tomorrow for about ten days.'

Luca waited to see if Carlo would expand upon this sparse information, but though his son smiled at him, he offered no illuminating detail. Luca, however, wanted to know. He said, 'Where will you be going?'

'Rome.'

Luca's desire to know more about the trip seemed to swell inside his chest, and he felt his hands ball in tension as he fought not to question Carlo further. He did not wish to be seen to interfere.

But nevertheless on one matter he could not help himself. 'Carlo?'

A raised eyebrow.

Luca said slowly, 'What is it that is causing this distance between you and Gianni? Why did he hit you?'

A long pause.

Carlo finally said, irritably, 'He can't take a joke.'

A cold thread slithered through Luca's head. 'What have you done, Carlo?' he said quietly.

Carlo shrugged. 'Nothing of any consequence, Papa. Gianni simply lacks a sense of humour. He always has. I need to pack.' And with that, he crossed the room, eeled through the door and ran lightly up the stairs.

Luca's gaze rested on the empty doorway.

'If that boy were not my son,' he said to himself, feeling rather ashamed of his admission, 'I am not sure I should care to know him.'

Seventeen

The two women arrived at a house in a narrow street near the church of Santa Lucia a Mare.

'There we are, Signora,' the woman said. 'That's my house there –' She pointed.

Maria's heart began to thud. The only chance she might ever have to find answers to her increasingly unbearable questions was about to walk away from her. She was about to let it slip through her grasp.

She stopped, feeling her grip on the woman's arm tightening.

The woman turned to her. 'Signora – is there something wrong? I hope that you are not now feeling inconvenienced – our journey has perhaps taken longer than you had expected. You must be tired. I'm sure I have been horribly heavy on your arm.'

'Oh, no – it's nothing like that.'

'But there is something troubling you, isn't there?'

Maria nodded. She was breathing through her mouth now – shallow, frantic little breaths like someone in pain. She had to speak. And it had to be now. Feeling sick, she said, 'I have to know. I just have to. You're the only person I've ever met whom I could even think of asking.' She hesitated, unsure how to phrase what she wanted so badly to say. Then her words came rushing out of her like vomit. 'I'm afraid,' she said. 'Afraid that my husband may have . . .' she felt her voice fade almost to nothing '. . . unnatural appetites.'

The woman's expression hardly changed, though Maria felt sure she saw a gleam of prurient interest in the wide brown eyes. The woman said quietly, 'What makes you think that, Signora?'

Maria put her free hand over her face and spoke through her fingers. 'I can't believe it is natural . . . for him to wish to lie with me . . . so . . . so very often.'

'How often?'

'I see it in his eyes all the time. Every day.'

'How often does he ask you?'

Maria shrugged, unable to say anything, feeling tears behind her eyes, building up like swollen water pressing against a too-fragile dam. She could feel her bottom lip trembling, and bit it. It wobbled against her teeth.

The woman smiled. She took Maria's hand and squeezed it. 'I would say that all the men I have met – *all* of them, Signora – quite certainly wish to –' she paused, and then laid a gentle emphasis on the next words '– to *lie with* their wives every day, if not more frequently. They don't always get their wish, of course, but it doesn't stop them wanting it. And the less they do it, the more they think about it. I don't think that what you describe sounds unnatural at all.'

Then Maria saw her smile fade. The woman hesitated, checked to either side, as Maria had done before, and said in a lower voice, 'Signora, does your husband ever . . . ever hurt you?'

Shame flooded into Maria's face and she stared down at the ground. How could she tell this woman what it was like between Filippo and herself? How could she explain that their every attempt to do what she understood most people enjoyed was – for her – never anything more than a struggle to avoid allowing

Filippo to see how much pain she was in. She said to the hem of her dress, 'He never means to hurt me. Never. I'm sure of that.'

'But?'

Maria looked up at her companion, paused and then said, 'It always hurts.'

'Do you tell him?'

Maria shook her head.

'Has it always been like this?'

Wiping her eyes with the tips of her fingers, Maria nodded and said, 'I've read the poets' accounts of love, and I've seen artists' depictions of it. I know what people say about it, but I simply can't equate that with . . . well, with what happens.' There was a long silence. Then she said, 'Does it hurt *every* woman?' Surely now she would hear the truth. A whore would be honest about whether there was in fact a conspiracy of silence amongst women, a silence that she, Maria, knew nothing about, with everyone actually enduring the same pain she did but simply managing to conceal it with more stoicism than she could, or whether in fact the horrible truth was that she was alone.

Her companion's expression was suddenly one of pity and compassion. She shook her head. 'No, Signora. It doesn't. Some people sometimes, but not everyone always.'

Maria pulled in a long breath through her nose, and let it out again slowly.

The woman in the crimson dress said, 'Forgive me if I seem impertinent, Signora, but . . . do you care for your husband's company in other ways? At other times?'

Maria nodded. She knew she did. Despite everything. She loved him.

'I think you've been so brave – to talk to me like this. Much braver than I could have been.' The woman smiled. 'Look, I've

174

been working a long time, Signora. There have been many, many occasions when it hasn't . . . been easy. Times when it's been . . . terrible.'

Despite herself, with a tightening of the skin on her neck and arms, Maria began to imagine what those occasions might have been.

The woman continued. 'There are tricks that you learn, when things become too difficult, as in any profession, I suppose. Perhaps . . . perhaps one or two of mine might be helpful to you, Signora.'

Maria felt her colour deepening still further, but, trying to smile, she nodded. She had to know.

'Now we are here at my house – why don't you come in and have a drink with me in my *sala*. I'd like to sit down – my ankle is hurting like the very devil – but I have things to tell you. Things that might help. Would you care to do that?'

Maria drew in a breath and hesitated.

The woman saw her hesitation, paused and then said, 'I don't . . . work here. Ever. This is where I live, with my children.'

Maria felt her face burn. 'I should very much like to come in, if I may,' she said.

The woman smiled. 'Good. Then could you kindly knock for me?' she said.

Maria leaned forward, knocked and waited; the weight of the red-sleeved arm still lying heavy upon her own. Now that they had stopped walking and she no longer felt responsible for preventing her companion from falling, Maria became uncomfortably aware of the warmth of the slim body within her encircling arm: they were pressed together and the woman's peach-scented arm lay snug around her shoulders. Their two faces were on a level, and now standing still, they were almost cheek to cheek. It occurred to

Maria that this was probably as sustained a contact with another body as she had had in many years. It was not unpleasant. But, embarrassed now, Maria pulled her arm back from around the woman's waist, and stood a step to one side, nonetheless keeping a supporting hand beneath the bent elbow.

The door was opened by a plump servant, with a big slab of a face; her hair was quite hidden by a carelessly wrapped length of linen.

The woman spoke. 'Ilaria, can you take my arm? I fell in the street outside the cathedral and wrenched my ankle. The Signora here has been so kind – she's helped me all the way home. I've asked her to come in for a moment. I'm taking her up to the *sala* – perhaps you could fetch us something to drink.'

The linen-wrapped servant said nothing, but eyed Maria suspiciously as she stepped down into the street. Maria stood back. Taking the woman's wrist in one hand, and cupping the crimson elbow in the other, the woman called Ilaria began to help her limping mistress up the step and into the house, muttering irritably about the foolishness of walking barefoot in filthy streets.

Her heart now beating up in her throat and making her feel quite sick, Maria followed the woman and her servant up to a small but well-appointed *sala*, in which a bright fire was blazing. Two pretty little girls were sitting by the hearth; a square board lay in front of them, and one of them was shaking a small leather pot which sounded as though it contained dice.

They looked up as the three women came in.

'Good, Mamma's home,' one of them said to the other. Then, seeing her mother's limp, her smile vanished. She sat upright. 'Oh, Mamma! What have you done to your leg?'

The woman limped across to a chair near the fire and sat heavily. She said, 'Nothing much – I fell over and twisted my ankle.' She looked across at Maria and added, 'This kind lady helped me home.'

Maria's face flamed again as the two children turned to stare at her. She watched as they scrambled across the hearthrug to where their mother sat, and pressed up against her legs. One of them lifted the hem of her mother's dress to inspect the injured ankle. Sounding surprised, she said, 'But, Mamma! You're not wearing any shoes! Your feet are all dirty – have you been walking barefoot? You're always telling us not to. "The streets of Napoli are far too filthy to go barefoot" – that's what you always say.'

The woman leaned forwards and kissed the top of her daughter's head. 'You're quite right. But Beata, Bella, listen – I need to talk to the Signora. On our own. Could you go with Ilaria, and help her choose us something to drink? You can each have a comfit, if Ilaria will get them down for you.'

The little girls nodded and stood without a word. They left the room with the servant and Maria heard their fading footsteps on the stairs.

The crimson-clad woman smiled at her. 'Come and sit down, Signora,' she said. Maria sat. Wincing a little, as she shifted her weight, the woman began to talk. And Maria listened, rapt and open-mouthed, swallowing the advice and the instructions as though they were a life-saving physic offered by a compassionate apothecary. Which, she supposed on second thoughts, perhaps they were. And as the woman spoke, describing with ease – even humour – things that normally froze Maria into paralysis, she found that an odd sense of release was trickling down through her, unnerving and unsettling, but oddly refreshing.

Walking slowly away from the house in the Via Santa Lucia, Maria thought through every astonishing thing that she had just been told. It seemed to her that a window had been opened in the barricade behind which she had been imprisoned for so long. It was a small window, she knew, and awkwardly placed, high in the wall – not easy to reach – but fresh air from outside was already blowing through it. The heavy mass of congealed fear and guilt that had lodged for so long in her chest like a malignant growth, seemed somehow to have shifted, lightened. Like a persistent background noise that only becomes apparent to the listener upon its cessation, it was only now, as she felt the familiar burden of her anxiety lift a little, that she realised how weighted down by her worries she had been for such a very, very long time.

She pondered on how extraordinary this encounter had been. The woman she had just met had not been in any way what Maria had expected. Had she ever really stopped to think about it, she realised now that she would have presumed a whore to be brazen and vulgar, unthinking, unlettered, crude, and flamboyantly predatory. Maybe some of them were. But her new companion had been kind and considerate, hospitable, softly spoken – and clearly a loving and capable mother. Those little girls had been quite charming – well-behaved and polite.

Maria did not know what to think.

She looked back once at the facade of the woman's house, and then, determined to make the purchase that the woman had suggested, before her resolve failed her, she quickened her pace, heading towards the long row of shops in the Via Toledo, *The Book of the City of Ladies* held tightly in her hand.

Eighteen

I am standing with my back to my big mirror and I twist around to look at my reflection over my shoulder. 'What do you think?'

Modesto runs an appraising eye over my new blue dress, with its high neckline, discreet lacing and simple, unslashed sleeves. My hair is parted in the middle, and drawn back tightly into a simple knot at the nape of my neck. I have Filippo's string of pink pearls around my throat and more pearls hang from my ears. A single plain ring adorns my right hand. My face is pale. I have left it untouched: I have neither put colour onto my lips, nor pinched it into my cheeks, and on this bleached canvas my eyes are quite different from usual – bigger, sadder, more wary, it seems to me. It is as well that the dress fully covers my ankles: one of them is still heavily strapped, and continues to hurt like the very devil.

'Mmm,' he says. 'I would say . . . chaste, virtuous and entirely unlike a whore.'

'Good.'

'And . . . quite delicious, Signora.' He is trying not to laugh.

'That is *not* so good. I'm in *disguise*, Modesto – if anyone recognises me for what I am, or worse – *who* I am – Filippo will be in complete disgrace, his friend will never speak to him again and we will probably both be kicked out onto the Spaccanapoli like a couple of scoundrels.'

179

Another laugh. 'Like the couple of scoundrels you both actually are, then?'

'That's enough, *sfacciato*! Remember who pays your wages.'

Modesto shrugs. 'Well, *you* remember who procures the means to provide you with the money to pay my wages, then.'

'Not always.'

'Can you tell me the last patron you actually—'

'Oh, stop it!' I can never win these stupid arguments: Modesto can always find one more point to balance on top of the teetering pile, and it always seems to end by falling on to *me*.

Modesto says, 'Don't expect me to excite myself over an evening during which you are not planning on earning a single *scudo*. If the truth be told, I wish you weren't going. Are you intending that the Signore should pay for his entertainment, when he brings you home?'

I redden. He has guessed correctly and his scornful expression makes me feel foolish.

'I shall only say it once, Signora. Let word get out that you ever – *ever* – fuck *gratis*, and your standing in this city is in shreds. You lose your status as a courtesan and, in the eyes of potential new patrons, you become no more than a loose-moralled trollop who can be had by anyone. You know I'm right, I'm sure.'

I try to justify my decision. 'But Filippo is taking me to this banquet. It seems only reasonable to offer him some sort of recompense . . .'

'Recompense?' Modesto says, pityingly. 'Recompense? Is that how you see yourself?' He shakes his head and his eyes flick heavenwards. 'What has happened to this sense of rivalry between you and the others? Does your reputation no longer matter to you? Do you imagine that Malacoda or Emilia Rosa would offer themselves – their *expensive* selves, in charitable *recompense* –' he says the word as if it tastes bad '– to anyone who performed some slight service for them?'

I say nothing.

I feel foolish now for ever agreeing to attend this ridiculous affair with Filippo and I suddenly dislike my deceitful disguise. The unfamiliar image I see in the mirror cannot be me – it is some virtuous creature who resembles me but whose wholesome life I can scarcely imagine. Perhaps I have become that sweet-natured woman from another world – the world of the virtuous – who came to my aid when I fell the other day. Unlike her, though, with her naïve and compassionate curiosity, this unknown person in the glass is scowling at me, as though her contemplation of my harlot's existence is distasteful to her – something disgusting she would prefer to pretend does not exist.

But it does exist, and (amongst much else) I am still Filippo's whore. I have promised Filippo I shall go with him to his party and, despite Modesto's scorn, I shall not disappoint my needy patron. I wish Modesto would go away. I want a few moments to practise my disguise before it is time to leave.

'Can you leave me alone for a while?' I say, frowning critically at myself.

Modesto nods. I can see him behind me, reflected in the mirror. He says, 'You may think I lack respect, Signora, but I don't. It is just that I shouldn't want anything to damage what you –and I – have worked so hard to achieve.'

I shrug.

'Don't lie with him *gratis*. It'll be damaging in the future.' He is almost pleading. Irritatingly, I think he is probably right.

'Very well. But you tell him, Modesto. I can't. He'll be here in an hour – perhaps a little more.' It is Modesto who shrugs this time; he leaves the room.

I turn to the stranger in the glass and wonder what it can be like to be truly as wholesome as I now appear to be. 'Chaste, virtuous and entirely unlike a whore,' Modesto says. I try to imagine myself as that sweet woman from San Giacomo. What would it be like to be in her position – beholden only to the desires and wishes of one man, cherished and cared for, walking securely along a virtuous path, rather than dancing up to the very edges of the pit, as I do every day? I think it would probably be very much easier than the life I lead. But her astonishing admission of her . . . her miserable *imprisonment* within her fear of her own body astounded me. Astounded me perhaps as much as her realisation of the true extent of my licentiousness shocked her.

'Oh, perfect, Francesca. How absolutely perfect. I would never have believed you could look so . . . so . . .' Filippo struggles to find the word, then smiles and says, 'demure.' He is obviously pleased to have found the perfect description. 'That is the word. Demure.'

I cannot help smiling. This is not a word I have ever heard used about myself.

'They will all love you.'

'All? Who will be—?'

Interrupting me, Filippo begins to describe the small group of his friends, but before he has got further than explaining that his friend Luca is a widower, Modesto appears in the doorway.

'Signora, can I ask you to go downstairs a moment? Lorenzo wants your approval of tomorrow's choice of dishes.' Modesto widens his eyes at me and flicks his gaze to the door. He wants to speak to Filippo.

I limp down to the kitchen, where Lorenzo is gazing lovingly into a large copper pan, smiling to himself, and tunelessly crooning a line from one of Modesto's favourite songs. Although my kitchen is spacious, Lorenzo's enormous body seems to fill the room with its soft bulk. Despite his size, though, my cook walks lightly on small feet and his hands are delicate. Neat-fingered, they do not suit him: they appear to belong to someone else entirely, and protrude as though from thick, fleshy sleeves at the end of Lorenzo's massive arms. A savoury steam is rising from the pan; Lorenzo lifts a large wooden spoon and tastes his soup, eyes closed, a frown of ecstasy puckering the skin between his brows.

He turns to see me in the doorway and says, 'Ah, *merda*, that's good, *padrona* – would you like some?'

I smile and nod. Lorenzo scrapes the back of the refilled spoon on the lip of the pan and holds it out to me, other hand cupped below to catch any drips. Holding my skirts back and out of the way, I lean forward.

A blast of rich flavour, subtle and savoury. God, that is truly wonderful.

'Oh, Lorenzo – one of your best. You are an artist. What's in it?'

With an expression of rapt delight, Lorenzo begins to reel off the long list of ingredients. *Romagnola beef, olive oil, tiny red onions, Signora – they cannot be more than* that *big or the flavour is spoiled – melanzana, borlotti beans, parsley* – I quickly lose the thread, but Lorenzo continues his luxurious litany as though caressing me with it. It occurs to me then that he and I both, in our different ways, are equally adept at indulging the senses. It might be that I use eyes and tongue, legs, fingers, breasts and buttocks to seduce those I choose to indulge, whilst Lorenzo uses only his legions of herbs, spices and fragrant oils, but we are both true *virtuosi* and I know we take equal pride in observing the pleasing effects of our skills.

For a moment, and not for the first time, I imagine the roles reversed, and smile to myself at the picture of a startled Vasquez struggling with unexpected and suffocating mountains of soft flesh whilst I work alone down in the kitchen, singing to myself as I concoct some fragrant pot of something delectable.

I say, 'We won't be home until much later, Lorenzo. I understand there's going to be some sort of meal at this concert tonight, but will we be able to have some of the soup if we are still hungry when we arrive back here afterwards?'

'I should be grossly offended if you did not, Signora.' Lorenzo folds his arms (with difficulty) across his wide chest, and feigns hurt feelings, but he cannot sustain the pretence for long: his face soon folds into a broad smile and the swell of his cheeks reduces his eyes to knife cuts in the dough of his face.

'Listen,' I say, 'if I end up having stuffed myself like a sucking pig and can't manage another mouthful when I return, I *promise* I shall be sure to have some soup tomorrow, *caro*.'

He laughs.

Modesto's face appears in the kitchen doorway and Lorenzo's laughter dies away. They exchange their usual glances of mutual dislike. Modesto clears his throat. 'Signor di Laviano now understands the situation, Signora,' he says drily.

I kiss Lorenzo on the cheek (it feels like kissing a warm, damp mushroom) and cross to Modesto. 'Oh, *caro*, what on earth did you tell him?'

'The truth. I organise your money and your diary, and I won't let you fuck *gratis*.'

Lorenzo shakes his head, but turns back to his soup and says nothing.

'What did Filippo say?'

'Not much. He wasn't pleased, but, then nobody is forcing him to stay after the party if he doesn't wish to part with his gold, are they?'

'You are hard on him, Modesto.'

'You're too soft and someone needs to redress the balance.'

We leave the kitchen and Modesto helps me up the stairs. I turn towards my chamber and he carries on up to his own rooms. He stops on the stairs and calls back, 'The carriage will be here before long – I'll call you when it arrives.'

Filippo stretches out an arm to help me down from the little carriage. The great basilica casts a deep violet shadow across the Piazza San Domenico Maggiore, and the sun has already dropped below the roofline. A number of people, obviously dressed for a night's entertainment, are already making their way into a long, low building to the right of the church, whose many windows glow yellow in the dusk, and I feel a shiver of anticipation at the sight. Within moments I shall be presenting my newly acquired persona to Filippo's friends: I hope I shall not let him down.

'Let me see you . . .' Filippo says; he puts a hand on each of my shoulders and crouches to bring his face on a level with my own. Without my *chopines*, I am fully a head shorter than Filippo. He strokes my hair flat, fiddles the pearl earrings until he is satisfied and then stands back to admire the effect.

'You look entirely delightful, Francesca,' he says. A hungry grin twists his mouth. 'I think I shall have to ask you to dress like this on other occasions – the thought of corrupting an innocent such as you appear to be tonight, is really most appealing . . .'

He reaches forward, but I draw back and hold my hands up in front of me. 'Stop it, Filippo! I am your *cousin*, now, remember, and you can have absolutely no interest in corrupting close members of your family in front of your friends. Do you want me to be able to convince them?'

'Of course!'

'Well, keep your hands to yourself then, and take that greedy grin off your face, or you'll give the game away in an instant.'

'Oh.' He deflates visibly. 'Was it that obvious?'

I raise an eyebrow and say nothing.

His face falls, and I laugh and peck a cousinly kiss onto his cheek. 'Well, *cugino*, are you going to take my arm and lead me in to meet your friends? Or am I going to have to limp in there unaided?'

'*Andiamo, cugina!*' he says with an extravagant bow. He holds out his forearm and I put my hand on his sleeve. Together, we make our halting way inside.

The great hall is lit by what appears to be at least a thousand candles, and the effect is exquisite. With no hangings at the windows, the candles reflect in the black glass and it seems to me as though each pane is studded with diamonds. The room is already bustling – guests in their bright evening best and servants in livery – and a dozen musicians are in place at one end of the room, tuning their instruments and assembling their music. Behind them an enormous square gilt-painted archway frames an elaborate set stage. Light shines somehow from behind the arch, making it glow, and the scene is lit from below as well, across the front of the span of the arch, by twenty or thirty candles in fretted silver covers. A tree – large as life and seemingly in full leaf – stands to one side of the stage and the floor beneath it is scattered with rocks and boulders. I gaze at the scene and wonder how it can be that it seems to stretch so much further back from the great golden arch than can feasibly be possible. As I stand and stare, the mosaic of voices and the fractured harmonies wrap around me, loud and insistent and I am quite enchanted by the entire spectacle – I allow it to wash over me; my worries about the propriety of my deception begin to fade.

But, as it turns out, my new sense of ease lasts little more than a moment.

'Luca!' Filippo calls across the room, and I wonder which of the group will answer. A man turns to see who has addressed him. He is tall and dark. As he turns, a lock of heavy hair falls across his forehead; he flicks it out of his eyes with a sideways shake of his head and my insides turn over as, for a second, I think I am looking at Gianni. This man's features and that gesture both seem familiar – but I am mistaken: he is much older than Gianni. His face splits in a broad smile when he sees Filippo, and, without taking his eyes from us, he pats his companion on the shoulder and begins to cross the hall, weaving his way through the knots of other guests.

'Filippo – you're here at last! I was beginning to wonder if you had decided not to come,' he says, grasping Filippo's hand.

And then he sees me.

'Signora,' he says, inclining his head in a little bow. He takes my hand as he straightens, lifts it to his lips and kisses my fingers.

'Luca, this is my cousin – Francesca. Signora Francesca Marrone.'

I can hardly breathe.

Around me the room freezes into silent immobility, like a gaudy tableau in a festival pageant. This man is staring at me with eyes like Gianni's and as he stares, images from that night with Gianni flicker across my mind and down through my body, though it is this man Luca's face I am seeing, not Gianni's.

'*Your shift has no laces . . .*' he says.

'*How would you . . . imagine . . . taking it off, then?*'

'*Perhaps you would do that for me – I should not want to presume . . .*'

I see Luca's mouth – Gianni's mouth – and feel again that warm pressure of lips on my scar. The tender compassion I was shown for the first time that night looks out at me again from within Luca's steady gaze.

A sensation of helplessness I have never known before pushes its way through me, dissolving me, threatening to overwhelm me: for no reason that I can understand, I want this man. This stranger. I want him more than I think I have ever wanted anything – I don't understand what is happening to me.

I see desire in his eyes and unwillingly think of Vasquez.

The Spaniard's desire for me has never been more than a selfish, animal wish for hedonistic gratification. His dribbling greed has entertained me, though. Reinforced my sense of my own powers. Look at me! Look at what I can do! Look at the sorceress, able to bewitch at will. See the temptress, playing her catch with such consummate skill, enjoying the game as both bait and fisherman.

But now I am neither. This man Luca's gaze has disarmed me entirely. Left me helpless. And I don't think I am alone. In his eyes I see desire, yes, but also a vulnerable bewilderment – even fear. Perhaps a similar tumult is whirling through his mind.

'Where are we sitting, then, Luca?'

Filippo's voice. Unaware that anything untoward might be happening right under his nose, he shatters the glittering web of silence that encloses the two of us, with his cheerful question, and the noise and colour of the party surge back into life. 'Are Piero and Serafina here yet?'

Luca turns his head towards Filippo at least a second before he can pull his gaze from my face.

'What? Sorry, Filippo . . . what did you say?'

'Piero and Serafina – are they here yet?'

'Er . . . oh, yes. They arrived some moments ago. Come – let's go and find them. They will be so pleased to see you. Signora?' He turns back to me and it is only then that I realise that he is still holding my fingers. He glances down at our hands, seemingly as surprised as I am that they are still clasped together, and lets go.

I begin to walk and Luca frowns in consternation to see my limp. He bends towards me and speaks quietly.

'Please, take my arm, Signora. What have you done to your foot?'

I can feel the muscles in his arm tense as I lean my weight upon him. I look up at him and say, 'Nothing, Signore. Carelessness and uneven cobbles. I tripped the other day and wrenched my ankle. No more.'

My heartbeat is so frantic in my throat that my voice sounds distorted.

'I will get you a chair as soon as we find the Parisettos.' He lays his other hand on my fingers, where they are gripping his forearm.

Our progress across the great hall is halting and slow, but we soon draw near to a small group of people: a tiny woman and a stocky, older man turn from their conversation and smile as we approach.

Filippo is beaming. 'Serafina! Piero! How lovely to see you – Piero, do you know, I do not think I have seen you since you challenged me to a game of *palla maglia* last summer, and I broke your father's best mallet by attempting to use it as a crutch and then tripping over one of the hoops . . .'

Piero throws his head back and laughs. 'I remember it well, Filippo – and Papa has certainly neither forgotten nor forgiven!'

The tiny woman then reaches out and takes Filippo's hand. She says to her husband, 'Yes, well, your father excels at grudge-bearing, Piero, does he not?' She turns back to Filippo. 'Don't even think about it for a moment, Filippo, *caro*, I do not think Piero's papa has ever forgiven *me* for bringing such an abysmally small dowry to our marriage, and *that* was six years ago!'

Filippo stretches out an arm towards me and says, 'Serafina – Piero . . . this is my cousin: Signora Marrone. Francesca. Francesca – Signor and Signora Parisetto.'

Piero bows briefly, and Serafina smiles. 'I am so glad you were able to join us, Signora. I was very disappointed not to be seeing Maria, but meeting a new member of Filippo's family is a great privilege. Oh – Luca? Where are you going?'

He has left my side and is striding away from our party, but at Serafina's words he turns back over his shoulder and says, 'To fetch the Signora a chair. She is injured.'

Serafina draws in a soft breath and lays a hand on my sleeve. 'Oh, *cielo* – what have you done?'

'The Signore exaggerates. I twisted my ankle a few days ago. Nothing at all interesting I am afraid.'

'But however boring an injury may be, it can still be quite unaccountably painful.' Serafina smiles at me sweetly and takes my hand in hers. The second time in a week – the second time in ten years – that an honest woman has sympathised with me and spoken to me with unthinking kindness, as though I were . . . a virtuous citizen like herself. I feel included, comforted. A warm sense of camaraderie drapes itself around my shoulders like a friendly arm, and the smile I offer back from behind Signora Marrone's mask is unexpectedly genuine.

I think of the sidelong glances of the penitents at San Giacomo every week; of the sneering determination of passers-by to ignore my plight when I fell in the piazza. I am being offered a glimpse through a half-open door of a world I have never even imagined – a world of kind, affectionate friendship and loving solicitude.

Suddenly, the familiar landscape of my daily life seems loveless and tawdry by contrast.

Luca returns, gilt-painted chair in hand, and he and Serafina settle me into it. She crouches down next to me, though in fact she is so small she hardly needs to, and Luca stands just behind me.

'The boys not with you, Luca?' says Filippo, some way above my head.

Luca is resting a hand on the back of my chair and I can just feel his fingers behind my shoulder. His voice is warm and slow. 'No. They are both away, as it happens, on very different missions – one academic and one purely commercial, I am afraid. Though the exact details of the latter venture escape me. Irritatingly, Carlo is never forthcoming about his business.'

'He quite definitely doesn't seem to want to follow you into the law, then, Luca?'

I can hear a smile as Luca says, 'No – apparently not. One fledgling advocate will have to be enough for now . . . Oh, they are coming over here. I think the play might be about to start.' He helps me to my feet. 'We are lucky, Signora, they have put out seats for us tonight. Last time, we were on our feet the whole evening.'

'Marvellous!' says Filippo. '*Orlando* is about to become "*furioso*"! Do you know the story, Piero? I cannot say I am particularly familiar with the works of Ariosto.' They begin to talk together as liveried servants bustle from group to group, telling us to move to our seats. Luca smiles at me and holds out an arm which I take with my heart beating fast. I stand and we walk together. Filippo walks ahead of us, deep in conversation with Piero Parisetto. Serafina has come up upon my other side; she holds my elbow, though being so very much smaller than I am, she in fact offers little support.

Everyone takes their seats. I have Luca upon my left and

Serafina on my right, and a large gentleman with white hair fluffed out like spun sugar sits directly in front of me, effectively blocking my view of much of the stage.

Filippo leans across Serafina and pats my knee. 'Enjoying yourself, *cugina?*' he asks with a grin. I manage a smile, but do not trust myself to speak. For a few moments, the enormous room hums with an almost palpable collective anticipation and then silence descends.

The musicians begin to play.

A woman – who I suppose must be being played by a boy – walks out onto the stage and begins to speak. The words are musical and beautiful, but I do not listen to what is being said, for my thoughts are tumbling over themselves in scrambling confusion.

My hands lie in my lap apparently calmly, though the dark patches in the middle of my nails give away the fact that I am gripping the fingers of one hand with those of the other – my desire to reach across and slip them into Luca's palm is so intense that I have to clench my teeth to stop myself doing it. I dare not look sideways at him in case he catches my eye and I betray my confusion, but I cannot prevent myself from leaning just a little towards him as though to see past the sugar-haired man in front of me. If Luca but knew it, despite my earlier enthusiasm, I now could not be less interested in the performance.

I am quite lost in a foreign country. I stand at a crossroads, unable to communicate; in an instant entirely ignorant of language, customs, expectations. Never before – never – have I been in close proximity to a man I have wanted – as I find I want this man – and not known what to do, what to say. I am a whore, for pity's sake! I have been a successful whore for more than ten years – I know all too well how to play the men I want. I work them like a virtuoso instrumentalist. And I rarely fail. In fact the game has become quite predictable – I have never doubted my skills.

But now . . .

I cannot even contemplate ensnaring Luca with my usual tricks.

This man would never lie with a harlot – I am quite sure of it. His compassionate wholesomeness is as obvious – and as charming – as was Gianni's a few weeks ago. God! Luca would no more pay to enter a courtesan's chamber than he would spit at a priest at the altar. Oh, I am certain he knows about love – I saw it in his eyes when he looked at me just now – but I know too, as clearly as if he had written it to me in a letter, that he would never, never *pay* to enjoy what is not his by legitimate right.

He has no idea what sort of woman I really am.

I imagine the horrified incomprehension in his eyes if he were to discover my true identity and I have to bite my lip to hold in a cry of what feels close to despair.

Nineteen

Luca glanced sideways at Signora Marrone and saw, with a catch in his chest, that her lower lip was caught between her teeth. Tiny lights glittered along the line of her lashes. He reached across and laid a hand on her sleeve, then bent towards her so that he could whisper close to her ear without disturbing his neighbours. 'Is your ankle hurting you, Signora?'

She turned her head and looked at him. Her lip slid out from under her teeth and with a rush of unexpected longing, Luca found that he very much wanted to kiss her. He was shocked at the unprecedented intensity of his feelings. This chaste-looking, vulnerable woman, newly emerged from mourning, would be appalled if she were even to suspect what he was thinking. The light from the stage caught the pearls that hung from the Signora's ears; Luca held his breath as she shook her head a fraction in answer to his question. 'You seem troubled,' he whispered again.

She shook her head once more. 'It's nothing,' she mouthed. They held each other's gaze for a second and then she looked at her fingers which were twisted together in her lap. Luca gripped her arm briefly and withdrew his hand.

He turned his attention once more to the stage. Dressed in a flaming red doublet, spangled and glittering, the unwittingly enchanted Rinaldo was addressing the audience, declaring his undying love for the beautiful Angelica, apparently unaware that the object of his desire was hiding up in the branches of the tree above him, listening with obvious disgust to his proclamations of affection.

Luca's mind raced; he was not listening to a word.

It was years since he had felt anything more than a passing interest in a woman. In all the time since Lisabeta's death he had never even contemplated remarriage – had never met anyone who had stirred him – beyond occasional disinterested, vaguely lustful, musings. He had over the years seen faces he thought beautiful, bodies that intrigued him, met women whose wit – or lack of it – had diverted and entertained him. But none had truly touched him and he had long ago resigned himself to a life without the love of a woman.

What had Filippo told him? The Signora was now out of mourning . . . she had two children; she lived with her daughters and a couple of servants in the Via Santa Lucia. He knew little more than these few bare facts. He had no idea what sort of man her late husband had been, or in what circumstances he had left his widow. She was well-dressed and elegant, though there was a certain fragility about her that belied the serenity. Bereavement had been hard for her – he could see that.

She was so very beautiful. He found it quite charming to see such an unusually attractive woman make no attempt at all to use her physical attributes to her advantage; the Signora seemed, by contrast, to be deliberately ignoring the potential impact of her looks. Perhaps she genuinely did not realise how lovely she was. She seemed vulnerable, lonely, in need of someone to take care of her, and the longer Luca sat so close to her, the more intensely did the notion strike him that he should very much like it to be he – Luca – that took upon himself this delightful task.

He began to chew his thumbnail to stop himself reaching across and taking the Signora's hand in his.

Up on the stage, Angelica, abandoned by the incompetent Rinaldo, backed away from the rapacious King of Circassia, to find herself pressed up against the trunk of the tree. Her eyes were wide with fear for she quickly understood his intentions.

'Well! What a very strange play!' said Serafina, as they all took their seats at one of several long dining tables. 'Signora – please be honest, now – did you have the slightest notion of what was happening?'

Luca saw Francesca start at being addressed. She smiled at Serafina. 'If I am forced to be truthful . . . I'm afraid I did find it a little difficult to follow the progress of the plot . . .'

Serafina beamed. 'There, Piero, it was not just me being completely stupid!' she said, as her husband came up behind her and sidled his way between two tables, down towards his seat.

'I'm sorry, but it was perfectly obvious what was happening, Fina . . .'

'Be careful, Piero – now, too vehement a protestation will insult our new companion,' Serafina said. 'She has just agreed with me that it was all but impossible to understand. What about you, Luca?'

'I'll admit I was not always entirely focussed upon the action on the stage,' Luca said, looking at Francesca. She caught his eye and he thought he saw in her gaze a comprehension of the reason for his distraction. A slow ribbon of heat slid down through his guts and he smiled at her. She compressed her lips in a brief smile and then she looked down at her hands. Luca was charmed by her diffidence.

'Francesca, you are very quiet this evening,' said Filippo, as he sat down upon Francesca's left side. 'Are you enjoying the occasion?'

'Of course, *cugino*, I am really very grateful to you for inviting me.'

'And I am quite delighted you were able to come – as I am sure everyone else is too!' Filippo said. 'Now, I don't know about all of you, but *I* am extremely hungry. As we all seem to be voicing honest thoughts about the play we have just watched, to add my opinion to the general pile, I confess that I thought the piece rather lengthy. My stomach has been quietly complaining about its lack of contents for some time.'

'Quietly, Lippo?' Francesca said, glancing at him.

Luca laughed.

Filippo spluttered with mock indignation. 'You are always quite unaccountably rude, *cugina*! Always! See what appalling tribulations I have to endure from my ill-mannered family, Luca?'

'Perhaps it is not rudeness at all, Filippo, but rather . . . accurate observation.' He raised an eyebrow.

Everyone laughed at that. The servants reappeared to place dishes of buttered asparagus before them and all along the tables, knives and forks were picked up.

'This should quieten the protestations of your innards, Filippo,' said Piero.

'I think the less said about my innards now, the better,' Filippo said, laying down his cutlery again and picking up a dripping stem. He tipped his head back and lowered the asparagus, bud first, into his mouth. A glisten of melted butter gleamed on his lip and he let out a groan of ecstasy.

Luca smiled at him and then turned to Francesca. She speared a stem with a narrow, two pronged fork, cut off a bite-sized piece with her knife and put it into her mouth.

'Good?' asked Luca.

Francesca swallowed and nodded. 'Very good,' she said, touching the corner of her mouth with the tip of one finger.

'Tell me a little about yourself, Signora,' Luca said. 'Describe for me a typical day in your household. I always enjoy discovering something of the way of life of a new acquaintance.' He saw her pause, loaded fork halfway to her mouth. For a moment she seemed wary – even frightened – but then she smiled and said, 'I fear I might disappoint you. Daily life with two children can be frustratingly uneventful.'

'Oh, Signora, I cannot agree more!' cried Serafina, leaning in from the opposite side of the table. She reached across and laid her hand upon Francesca's. 'Paolo and Benedetto – who are three and one – seem *never* to sleep except when I most wish them to stay awake, and have an apparently unending fount of energy for making mess, noise and confusion wherever they go.'

'My girls are somewhat older,' said Francesca, 'and perhaps a little more decorous. But they have other equally effective methods of disruption. They have recently begun to ask questions – questions about absolutely everything – I often have to find satisfactory answers to at least a hundred questions from each girl each day. "*Why are tomatoes red, Mamma?*" "*Why does the moon move across the window each night?*" "*Where is it going and why has it gone in the morning?*" "*Why don't women grow beards?*" "*Why do I dream, Mamma?*"'

Serafina laughed and said, 'I will look forward to it, Signora – but I fear I had better start keeping a collection of suitable answers, tucked away in a box under the bed, ready for when the onslaught begins. Either that or simply redirect both boys towards Piero each time they need a piece of information.'

Luca said, 'I remember those years very well, though it was

some time ago – both my boys are grown now and rarely ask my opinion upon anything at all. They are both entirely certain that they know considerably more than I do. And, most irritatingly, they are often right.'

Francesca smiled, and Luca, his eyes on her mouth, fought down a renewed fierce longing to kiss her.

The meal continued. The university had been lavish in the preparation of its annual banquet. The asparagus gave way to sardines, dressed with sweetened orange slices; great dishes of pike and crayfish; bowls of fresh egg pasta, stuffed with a variety of fillings; plates piled high with pyramids of sparkling sugared fruits.

While Filippo and Piero Parisetto both ate heartily, Francesca hardly touched her food. Serafina seemed not to notice her companion's lack of appetite, but Luca watched Francesca covertly, feeling a moment's anxiety that her unenthusiastic response to her meal might signal ill health of some sort. Then, remembering the wrenched ankle, he comforted himself that Francesca's painful foot might be the cause.

He sat back in his chair for a moment as Serafina leaned across the table again and spoke to Francesca. 'Now listen, Francesca, before we all disappear at the end of the evening, I want to arrange for you to come to our house very soon. Piero has just had the *belvedere* repaired and we can sit up there and watch the boats. The back of our house overlooks the harbour. You must bring your children, too. I know Paolo and Benedetto are so much younger than your girls, but perhaps they will still entertain each other whilst we talk, nonetheless.'

'Beata and Isabella love babies,' Francesca said.

Luca struggled to keep his face impassive as a vivid picture he could not prevent flashed across his mind – of a drowsy Francesca lying amid rumpled blankets, sleepily cradling a baby. His baby.

'Good. That is settled. Would you be able to come on Saturday afternoon?' Serafina asked. Francesca smiled and accepted the invitation with obvious pleasure.

As the final plates were cleared away and chairs were pushed back from tables, Filippo laid his hand upon Francesca's.

'Francesca, *cugina*,' he said, 'we must go. I have to work in the morning, and I must see you home.'

Luca smothered a stab of envy at the thought of his friend's easy familiarity with this woman who had so entirely and unexpectedly filled his mind this evening. He helped Francesca to her feet and, with a raised hand, summoned a servant to fetch her coat. Serafina kissed Francesca's cheek and gripped her hand as she bade her farewell.

'Signora,' Luca said, as Filippo took Francesca's arm. 'It has been such a pleasure to meet you. I feel sure we will see each other again soon.'

'I should like that very much,' Francesca said. Luca heard a slight tremble in her voice. She opened her mouth as though to speak again, but closed it without saying a word. Luca smiled and Filippo began to steer his limping cousin across the room towards the tall double-doors, cupping her elbow in the palm of his hand.

Luca ran his fingers through his hair as he watched them go.

Twenty

'You were superb!' Filippo cries as we leave the building, and stand in the darkened street. 'Quite superb – even *I* believed you to be the virtuous widow! You are a wonder, Francesca. Indeed, you played your part with *far* more skill than any of those idiots up on that stage!'

I do not know what to say. My mind is in pieces. I want to go home.

'Come on then – *cugina* – let's get back quickly. I want to get all these modest and entirely inappropriate garments off you as quickly as possible so that I can ... well ... so that I can thank you properly.' He chuckles. 'I shall find us a carriage.'

I freeze. Oh, dear God. I can't do it.

'Filippo ... I—'

'What, *cara*, what is it?'

'Please, I really do not think I can do any more tonight. I ... I ...' I am struggling to avoid blurting out the fact that even the thought of fucking with Filippo tonight is now so abhorrent to me that I think I might weep.

'Francesca?'

'My foot is horribly painful, and I really am very tired. Please, Filippo, I just need to sleep.'

'You sound like Maria,' he says and his voice is suddenly cold.

'Don't be like that, Lippo. Please, I really just don't feel well.' I am struggling to contain my distress, but despite my best efforts, my voice cracks and the tears I cannot prevent begin to spill over.

Filippo is shocked. In a more sympathetic voice he says, 'Oh, Francesca, I'm sorry. Oh, dear, you are looking pale. This isn't like you, I do hope it isn't anything you've eaten. What a dreadful shame after this lovely evening. I'll call for a carriage and take you back to the Via San Tommaso.'

'No, Filippo, please don't come in. I can put myself to bed. I just want to sleep. Thank you. And thank you for this evening – thank you very much for taking me.'

'Well . . . if you're certain . . .' He looks doubtful. 'I am not sure that I should leave you alone . . .'

'I'm not alone. Modesto is here, and Lorenzo will arrive in the morning.' *Oh, God, Filippo, please just go!* 'I shall be well looked after, if I need anything.'

At last he leaves and I close the door behind him. I push the bolts home and lean up against the wood, my forehead and both palms pressed hard onto the cool oak. After a moment, I slide down the door until I am sitting on the floor in a wide puddle of crumpled blue damask; I put my face into my hands and begin to weep.

Once I start to cry I cannot stop.

A door opens upstairs. I continue to sob into my sodden palms.

'Dear God, Signora! What's happened to you?' Modesto crouches at my side and takes my wrists. He tries to pull my hands from my face, but I press them in harder, and the next sob sounds more like a howl.

'Who's done this to you? Has somebody hurt you? Was it di Laviano? If that bloody man has laid even a finger on you, I'll kill him.'

He puts heavy arms around me and pulls me in close to him. With eyes still screwed shut, I grip fistfuls of Modesto's shirt and press myself against the warm, damp, sweat-smelling linen. I cry until I am exhausted. My chest heaves as I gulp ragged breaths. I feel Modesto's fingers smoothing my hair away from my face and as my sobs begin to fade, I look up at him.

'What the hell has happened? Why are you crying like this? You never cry. I've never seen you like this. What's gone wrong?'

I tell him.

In halting gasps I explain what has happened.

He says nothing until I have finished, but watches me steadily with troubled eyes.

'. . . and I know I can't do it any more, Modesto. I can't let any of them even touch me again. Oh, God – I want this man so much.' I bend forwards until my head is between my bent knees, clutch handfuls of my hair and pull until my scalp hurts. My voice comes now as a sort of muffled scream, smothered in my skirts. 'Oh, God, even supposing that he has any feelings for me at all, what will he do when he finds out that this apparently decorous widow he seems pleased to have met is nothing better than a filthy whore? What am I going to do? Oh, Modesto . . . tell me what to do.' I press my fingers over my mouth.

A cold draught slides like a blade under the lower edge of my front door.

Modesto watches me for a full minute without speaking, and I gulp down several more shuddering breaths as I wait for him to say something.

'What does he think of you, this man?'

'I don't know.' My voice sounds muffled, coming out from behind my hands. 'I think I saw a regard for me, in his eyes – well a regard for the woman he thinks I am – and he was most attentive

203

to me all evening, but . . . oh, dear . . . I'm so confused now, I begin to doubt my own mind.'

Modesto tucks another lock of hair behind my ear, saying, 'Just sleep on it, Signora. See how you feel in the morning, when you're not so tired. Nobody's visiting tomorrow, so you can rest properly. See what you think about this man then. Before you make any big decisions.'

Oh, God – he thinks this is just a whim – that it'll pass. I have to make him understand. 'Modesto, I'm serious,' I say, and my voice cracks. 'What's just happened is like nothing I've ever known before. It sounds completely ridiculous, but right now, I feel as if I might die without Luca.'

After a pause, Modesto says, 'Well, could you not just take him on as a patron, might that not be a possibility? You could have him as often as you like, then – well, as often as he could afford, I suppose.'

'No! Never!' This comes out as something close to a shriek. 'I couldn't!'

Modesto holds his hands up, leaning back from me, clearly surprised by the vehemence of my response. I stare at him, my eyes stinging, my face puffy and hot, and a long silence stretches out between us. The tailends of my last few sobs catch in my throat. Then Modesto says slowly, 'I suppose if you are serious, you could sell the house.'

'What?'

'Sell it. Sell this house, sell the furniture, paintings – sell all of it. Well – perhaps keep the jewels for the future. You never know, do you? Put the money away safely with everything else you have saved so far, and stop whoring. Become the virtuous widow you've just pretended to be.'

I stare at him.

'Well,' he says, raising an eyebrow at me. 'If you say you cannot contemplate continuing to fuck for a living – if you really mean it – then there's no reason to keep this place, is there? That's all you do here, is it not?'

I nod.

'Let's be practical, Signora. You maintain this house and its contents solely to provide you with an opulent establishment in which to sell – to carefully chosen gentlemen – privileged access to your extraordinary body.'

I wince.

'Don't be coy. It doesn't suit you. It is how you've lived for years and, as I see it, you are seriously considering destroying everything you have worked for, simply because you think you have lost your heart to a man you know would never set foot inside a den of iniquity such as this one. You cannot have him as a whore – because you know, instinctively, that he would never lie with a whore – so you need to find some other way of capturing him.'

The tears begin again. 'You make it sound sordid and horrible, Modesto.'

'I don't mean to. I just want to make you face reality. Make sure you are quite certain about what you want to do, before you do it. Because if you sell the house, give it all up, there'll be no coming back.' He pauses. 'If you stop everything and sell up, and then discover he doesn't want you after all, I cannot imagine you will be able to find your way back to where you are now – even if you wanted to start again. Word gets about in this business, as you well know. Your patrons won't return once they've left. And you might not want to hear this, but you're not young enough, any more, to start again from the bottom, somewhere else. And I doubt you'd want to return to the streets.'

There is a long pause.

'I know I have to stop, Modesto.'

He stares at me, his expression unreadable. I have to try to make him understand, though I'm not sure I understand it myself. Hesitating, feeling my breath catch in my throat, I look down at my fingers and manage to say, 'I think it all started the evening I met Gianni.'

Something shifts in Modesto's expression but he says nothing.

'He . . . made me start to see things differently. He was so tender and diffident, and . . . well . . . then something happened . . . he did something that made me wish that . . .' I try to explain, but tears are thickening my voice, and I don't think Modesto can properly hear what I am saying. I clear my throat, and wipe my nose on the back of my hand. 'It's all seemed so pointless since then. Everything. As if it's just a stupid game. And there's something else – I didn't tell you. The other day, when I hurt my foot – this woman helped me up from where I'd fallen, and she walked back to Santa Lucia with me, holding me up. Oh, Modesto, she had worked out that I'm a whore, and it shocked her, but she still helped me.'

Modesto remains silent.

'Then tonight,' I say, more quietly than ever. 'When I saw him – Luca – it was like an earthquake. Something shifted. Something enormous. I don't know why . . . but the world just feels different. I can't go on like I have done.'

Modesto's gaze is steady and searching. He seems to be thinking hard for a moment, and then he says quietly, 'Very well. We'll sell the house, then.' He lays a hand on my cheek and wipes some of the wetness away with his thumb.

'What if Luca discovers the truth?'

'That is a risk you will have to take. You might change your ways, but you cannot make your past completely disappear.'

A horrible thought lances through my head. 'Oh, God!'

'What?'

'Filippo, and Michele and Vasquez, and – what am I to say to them?'

Modesto pauses, frowning. 'Let me think about that one. Feign illness for a couple of weeks. Give yourself some time. Go back to Santa Lucia, and be "unwell" for a week or two. Don't leave the house more than you have to. In the meantime, I'll try to find a lawyer who can help us value this place and shift it for us.'

'I don't know what I would do without you . . .' I say, clutching Modesto's hand.

His face is suddenly stiff and expressionless.

'What is it?'

'You say you cannot do without me. Without this house, though, maybe you won't need me any longer . . .'

'Oh, Modesto.' I throw my arms around his neck. 'I can't imagine managing without you. You'll have to come and work for me at Santa Lucia.'

'You already have two servants there.'

I sit back. 'Well, I shall dismiss them, then. I don't like either of them very much anyway. Ilaria is always grumpy and irritable and Sebastiano drinks too much.'

Modesto snorts softly.

'I want both you and Lorenzo.'

A raised eyebrow.

'You don't have to talk to him. Often.'

An irritable sigh. 'I suppose that fat old lump of cold dripping can cook – I'll give him that.'

'He is a genius.'

'As I say, he can cook.'

A thought strikes me. I say slowly, 'But what about you? Shall you be happy still to work for me under new conditions – as manservant to a sober widow – knowing me as you do?'

I speak seriously, and Modesto continues to look steadily at me but then his mouth suddenly twitches and he begins to laugh. His laughter shakes his heavy shoulders. Despite my tearing anxiety, his mirth infects me and within moments the two of us are helplessly convulsed. He puts his arms around me and we sit on the floor in my hallway and laugh until we ache. I say, through gasping breaths, 'Why are we laughing? What's funny?'

He sighs deeply and says, 'Oh, just the thought of me becoming the decorous servant of a virtuous, well-behaved widow, and trying to forget about all the time I've spent over these last years rubbing soothing oils into the smacked and smarting arse of that same "widow".' He smiles at me. 'Trying to forget how often I've gazed in speechless admiration at your beautiful breasts as you have acted the strumpet with such consummate skill and how many times I've stood there watching you parading yourself stark naked before your panting admirers like bloody Aphrodite herself. *Cazzo!* It won't be easy to give up such intimacy, Signora. Perhaps not so easy for you, either, though you might not think so just at this moment.'

I am shocked at this sudden outpouring. 'Oh, Modesto. If . . . if you would rather not . . .' I hesitate.

'No,' he says, suddenly serious. 'I would *not* rather not. I suppose I will simply have to accustom myself to . . . to sobriety. And distance. And so will you. Don't imagine for a moment that many women of good families would allow the sort of intimacy between mistress and servant that you have positively encouraged, Signora. Much will have to change, if your new identity is to be credible for an instant.'

'I know. I do understand. None of this is going to be easy. But

I have to do it, Modesto. I know I have to stop whoring. I know it sounds mad, but I can't face rutting for money ever again. Because of him – this man. Luca. I just know it. If it happens that he doesn't want me, or won't have me, or can't have me, then I'll just have to find another way to survive – but I won't fuck for a fee again. Not ever. Please, *caro* – just find me a lawyer. I'll tell Sebastiano and Ilaria tomorrow.

Relief makes me feel quite weak.

When Lorenzo arrives for work the next morning, Modesto, on my instructions, brings him upstairs to my chamber, where I am sitting curled in my favourite chair, dressed in my wrap. My eyes are puffed and gritty, and my mouth feels like a dried-out sponge after so much weeping. I am sure I must look quite dreadful. I have not dared confront my reflection, but Lorenzo's startled intake of breath when he sees me confirms my suspicions.

He frowns and says, '*Padrona*, are you unwell?' His voice is kind.

I smile and hope I sound reassuring. 'No, not at all – just rather tired.'

'Why have you asked me up here? Is there something wrong with the food? Have I displeased you in some way?' he asks, his chins wobbling like a poorly set milk pudding. Tiny beads of sweat gleam along the line of his brow and across his upper lip. My attempts at reassurance were obviously not a success. 'Oh, no, Lorenzo!' I say. 'Nothing like that at all. It is simply that—' I stop. I am not sure how to explain the situation to him.

Modesto steps forward from where he is standing in the doorway. 'The Signora has decided to sell this house.'

Lorenzo's mouth falls open. 'Why?' he asks.

It all sounds so extreme, now that the wild panicked desperation of the previous night has calmed. But I am still certain. I unfold my legs and put my feet down on the floor. 'I am going . . . to give up the work I do here,' I say, my voice as firm as I can make it.

'Give it up?'

I nod.

'But, *padrona*, I don't understand . . . Just last night, you were . . . What has happened? Why?'

'Lorenzo, forgive me if I don't unravel all the details of the situation for you just now. I will soon, I promise.' I take a deep breath, which still trembles in my throat in an echo of last night's sobs. 'But . . . something very significant happened to me yesterday – something rather complicated and uncertain and potentially far-reaching – and it seems to me that the only thing I can do to respond to this . . . this event . . . is to change the way I live, completely.'

A ridge of damp flesh pushes up between Lorenzo's brows as he frowns. Then he says, 'What I am going to say may seem to you to be taking an unwarranted liberty. Perhaps it is not for a servant to say such a thing, and in another household perhaps I should not dare suggest it. We have often spoken frankly to each other, though, Signora. I beg your forgiveness if I am mistaken, but I am imagining that . . . could it be that you met someone last night who does not know you are . . . are a . . . does not know what you do for a living?'

I stare at him.

'And might it be that . . . you would prefer that this person never found out?'

Modesto says, with a flicker of admiration in his voice, 'You perspicacious old bastard . . .'

Lorenzo raises an eyebrow and for the first time ever, Modesto looks at my cook with an expression on his face other than dislike.

I avoid a direct response. 'Lorenzo, *caro*, would you . . . would you consider continuing to cook for me at my other house? I am not sure I could bear to lose you. But . . .' I hesitate, needing to know, but not wishing to give offence. 'Shall you be truly able to keep my secrets?'

He shakes his head, and at first I think he is refusing my request. But then he says, 'I will continue to cook for you. And I will keep your secrets, of course I will, *padrona*, but . . .' He pauses. 'There are so very many people in this city who know who you are, and what you do. How can you swear them all to silence?'

Something of last night's panic begins to scuffle again in my head, but Modesto says quickly, in his honey-calm voice, 'Listen: so far as I can see, today's tidbit of exciting gossip is nothing more than tomorrow's nugget of abandoned irrelevance. Napoli will not think of it for long. We take these changes one day at a time.'

His words ought to soothe my anxiety, but my mind teems suddenly with images of Luca. A crowd of his friends surround him, congratulating him on his good fortune in finding such a lovely new wife (my insides writhe at even the thought of such a future) and – here I see Serafina and Piero – they all tell him how fitting it is that two such deserving people have found each other after their respective bereavements. What a fortunate evening that was at San Domenico, they say; how lucky it was that you met. You both deserve happiness, after all your grief. Luca's two sons – who, in my ignorance, I imagine resemble their father – appear delighted at Luca's joy. Everyone is eating, drinking – there is noise and music and laughter. I see myself and the twins, welcomed into the family; but behind my smiles they all have no idea that I am almost choking on my guilt at such ill-deserved approbation.

And then the image shifts and I see disgust on a hundred faces – those that I know, those that I can only imagine – as they discover the true identity of Luca's new spouse, this new mother to his two lovely sons. *Luca has been lying with a whore*, they say to each other in hushed voices, their features distorted with incredulous revulsion. *How could he not have guessed? Surely it shows? Did he not realise when . . . when they . . . you know?* They widen their eyes and imply the improprieties they imagine, with eyebrows lifted into their hair. They shun poor Luca as quickly as they turn their backs upon me. His friends stare at him with a jumble of pity and embarrassment splashed across their faces. They no longer have any idea what to say to him.

Yet another image takes its place. I see Luca look at me. He does not smile. He opens his mouth to speak and I dread hearing what he will say, but before he can say a word, Modesto's voice cuts into my reverie.

'I'll take you back to Santa Lucia, Signora. Get yourself dressed, and we can go straight away.'

He and Lorenzo leave my chamber, and I pick up the dress that I wore last night. The dark blue, modestly cut disguise. The only garment Luca has seen me wear. He will think I dress in such clothes every day. I put it down and open a painted wooden chest. Squatting on my heels, I breathe in the scent of cedarwood and finger the extravagant silks and velvets it contains, the fur-trimmed coats and the glittering, beaded bodices, including the red and gold bodice that reveals so much of my breasts – the one I wore to seduce Vasquez. What would Luca think of me if he saw me dressed in my usual finery?

Shall I mind abandoning such gorgeous garments? Will it be possible to be content to be . . . *unremarkable* for the rest of my life?

I drop the things back into the chest and cross the room to the long mirror: one of my first presents as a courtesan – from the Conte di Vecchio. In its elaborate gilt frame, it reaches almost to the ceiling of my chamber; the huge sheet of flawless Venetian glass reflects the whole room. As I allow myself to think about the catalogue of acts of licentiousness that have been witnessed by this huge and sumptuous *specchio*, I undo my wrap and let it fall to the floor.

I stare at what I see.

My face is still uneven and swollen from last night's tears and my hair is tangled into a fuzzy cloud. My gaze moves downwards. What is it about this body that has entranced so many men? Why do they tell me it is so beautiful? So 'extraordinary'? To me – trapped inside it – it is simply the vehicle in which I go through my life. Like everybody else's body, at times it aches or pains me, it frustrates me when illness weakens it, I marvel at its patient ability to withstand all the demanding tasks I ask it to perform so regularly. Is its inexplicable attraction simply how it appears, or is it rather what I have been prepared to do with it, for them? Why should it be different to that of any other woman? Looking at myself dispassionately, I see narrow shoulders, visible *clavicola* bones, full breasts with brown nipples. My belly is still surprisingly flat and smooth, despite the twins' former residence beneath its skin. My hipbones jut, and below and between them lies the dark arrowhead of soft hair, that has pointed the way to euphoric gratification for so many, for so long.

So many.

I want now to scrub them all away. Scour out my body from the inside, to rid it of what it has contained. If there was some draught I could drink – something I could take to flush out every trace of every man who has ever paid to enter it – I would give every *scudo* I have earned across the years to obtain it. To rid myself of what has so suddenly become entirely abhorrent to me. The vague dissatisfaction Gianni's tender compassion began in me has, in the few hours since last night, become a vivid, screaming disgust – with myself, with my patrons, with my life. I realise as I stand before my mirror that from this moment, whether or not Luca will ever care for me at all, I cannot continue the life I have been leading.

This shocking, frightening, unprecedented sense of revulsion swells in my chest and I begin to feel physically sick. I think I might scream. A hot pressure builds behind my eyes until, letting out a sort of wordless yowl, I swing round and grab a big glass pot from the table near the bed and hurl it across the room. It hits the far wall and shatters into a thousand glittering shards. The noise of the glass hangs in the air accusingly and I step back and stare at what I have done, with my hands over my mouth.

I know now what it is that I want. I must at last properly admit to myself what was shut away in that locked box: what was released when it was cracked open by Gianni's tenderness. An awareness of it flashed into my mind the night it happened, but until now I have not dared allow myself to think too carefully on it.

I want to be loved.

I want to wake in the mornings, wrapped in the arms of a man who will be content to hold me, warm and lazy beneath passion-crumpled blankets; who will kiss my hair and watch me as I go back to sleep. Someone who will eat with me, drink with me, cry and laugh and love with me, someone who will treat my girls with kindness – a man who will not simply gaze at me, wet-lipped with lascivious admiration as he pushes his way between my thighs and demands his money's worth.

I want that man to be Luca.

But there is something else. Something that I have never known and never expected. I want Luca to know that I will love him, too. He needs to be loved. I saw in his eyes in that first moment at San Domenico a sort of stoic vulnerability, a loneliness, that has made me want to pull him into my arms and comfort him. I want us to be lovers, yes – oh God, yes – but perhaps even more than that, I want us to be friends.

If I chose to, I am quite sure I could seduce Luca, as Modesto suggested last night. I could with ease break down his barriers of gentility and virtue and persuade him to lie with me and learn to revel in the heady delights of harlotry. But to do that I would have to change him. And once changed, he would no longer love me. He would become like all the others. He would see me as they do. Oh, God, I know he may *never* love me! I may be pathetically deluding myself, and entirely mistaken in imagining Luca has any sort of regard for me. But surely it would be better to know that he had never loved me, than to discover that he had indeed once done so, but that his feelings for me had been destroyed by disgust at my pleasure-seeking attempts to corrupt him. He will love me on his own terms or not at all, I know that.

The door pushes open, and Modesto peers around. I see the whites of his eyes glint in the glass, as he stands in the gloom by the chamber door, but I do not turn around. I continue to stare at my naked self in my mirror.

'What happened? Did something break?'

I shrug.

I watch Modesto's reflection eyeing the mess of broken glass on the floor.

'I'll find a broom,' he says softly.

I don't move.

'Are you . . . quite certain that you still want to do this, Signora. None of them knows anything. You don't have to go on with this. Everything could just continue as it always has – Signor di Cicciano's due tomorrow. The Spaniard is expecting you on Saturday and—'

'No!' His words make me nauseous again. I drop my arms to my sides and curl my hands into fists.

'You are quite sure . . .'

I nod again. Behind my reflection, at the back of the room, Modesto's gaze rests on my buttocks. Looking up and catching my eye, he swallows and says softly, 'The new Signore is a very lucky man. He'd be a fool not to want you. I'll be back in a moment with a broom.' There is a pause and then he says, 'Be careful not to tread on the glass,' as he pads noiselessly out of the room.

A tear trickles across the bridge of my nose as I bend to pick up my wrap. I clutch the silk in both hands as though I mean to tear the thing into two pieces, and then press it hard against my cheek.

Twenty-one

'What do you mean she's not here?'

'The Signora is unwell, Signor di Cicciano. I'm very sorry to disappoint you, I know you were expecting to see her this evening, but I am afraid she is . . . indisposed.' Modesto's voice was calm. He stood in the doorway, one arm across the width of the frame, hand resting on the jamb.

'What's wrong with her, then?'

'I believe she ate something that disagreed with her.'

'How long is she expecting to be "indisposed"?' Michele di Cicciano's voice sounded scornful and unsympathetic.

'She has a high fever. I doubt she will be fit to leave her house before the best part of two weeks has elapsed, Signore.'

'Two weeks?' The Signore's eyes flashed and his mouth tightened to a thin line across his face. 'Send word when she is well again,' he said abruptly. Turning on his heel, he strode away up the street.

Modesto raised his eyebrows and shook his head as he watched the visitor round the corner and disappear. 'She's well rid of you, if nothing else,' he said. 'Arrogant, self-opinionated, conceited bastard.' He spat onto the dust of the street, pulled the front door closed and went back into the *sala* where, sitting down on one of several folding chairs, he pulled a quill from an iron ink pot.

Several sheets of paper lay in a loose pile in front of him; he straightened the pile and frowned down at what he had written, the end of the quill against his bottom lip. Having perused his scratchy lines of writing for some moments and added a word here and there, Modesto then put the quill back into the pot, picked up the papers and pushed his chair back from the table. As he stood, though, the door to the *sala* pushed wide and Lorenzo's doughy face peered in.

'Are you hungry?' the chef asked.

'Are you offering some form of remedy for that, if I am?'

'There is a large quantity of pork, which the *padrona* has not even touched, and which ought to be eaten by the end of today; there's the remainder of that soup, and a couple of loaves of bread which will be fit for nothing by tomorrow morning.' Lorenzo was strangely deflated; his skin seemed to hang more loosely around his great moon face. Modesto felt a stab of sympathy for a man he had never liked and said, 'I'll come down to the kitchen in a moment. I just want to make sure I have finished this room.'

'When does the *padrona* need the inventory finished?'

'She hasn't said, but I want it done by tomorrow morning – I have a lawyer meeting me here at midday and I want to have everything clear in my own mind before he arrives.'

Lorenzo nodded and left the room.

The cook's footsteps receded; Modesto crossed the room to the window. 'There's no point in even thinking about it,' he said aloud after a few moments. 'It's what she wants.' He tried unsuccessfully to suppress the thought that was swelling up into his head like a black thundercloud, and attempted to rationalise the situation. He had (at times literally) witnessed her bedding countless customers. For years he had watched her – seducing the reluctant, enthralling the enthusiastic and exhausting the unprepared – and though it had often been difficult for him, he had always been comforted by the fact that though she *liked* some of her patrons well enough, she had *loved* not a single one of them. It had always been a job to her. Nothing more. None of them had ever touched her heart. That boy had come close, he admitted to himself – she had been quite distracted for days after his visit. But until now it always had been the two of them: him and her, the eunuch and the harlot, ranked together *contra mundum*.

He realised now how precious that solidarity had been to him.

Modesto was acutely aware that living in the opulent shadow of so much exuberant and immoral sexual activity had somehow mitigated the miserable absence of it in his own personal experience. The voice of an angel, they had all said he had had as a child. And angels don't need to fuck, do they? They have better things to do, generally. He had always been revolted by his perception of his own 'otherness' and, though he understood that many *castrati* did in fact manage some form of physical union, he had never had the courage even to try to find out if it were a possibility for him. He was too frightened of the humiliation of failure. Especially with her. After his singing career had faded, Francesca's offer of this position had, he knew, rescued him from a life as the butt of predictable jokes about his lack of sexual potency: his intimacy with a creature of the Signora's beauty and standing had drawn grudging admiration and envy from many that he met, despite their understandable horror at the thought of his affliction.

But now this was all about to be taken from him and he would – if the Signora's hopes were fulfilled – be reduced to the status of a formal manservant, kept at arm's length, spoken to with politeness and warmth; still well-liked, perhaps loved, but no longer taken into intimate confidences. Pictures raced through his mind: Francesca climbing into his bed and holding him whilst he wept; the two of them sitting side by side on the staircase, leaning against each other and laughing aloud at some piece of pointless nonsense that had caught both of their imaginations; himself, standing in her chamber watching her unabashed nakedness, shaking his head in wonder at the perfection of the exquisite body.

He might never be allowed to see it again.

If the future were to unfold as she wished, these were all things she would share only with the new Signore, and her bond with this man would be of an entirely different order from anything either she or Modesto had yet experienced. Something inside Modesto's chest swelled painfully as he contemplated the future, and he was ashamed to admit to himself that he felt certain that he would find it difficult to like the new Signore, whatever sort of man he turned out to be.

'Yes, Signore, I understand. As soon as possible.' The lawyer leaned back in his chair and frowned down at Modesto's inventory.

'Do you know of any potential buyer?' Modesto asked.

'It is not really within the remit of what I do, Signore – I am not a broker. But, as it happens – in the course of a case I am handling at present, I did the other day happen to hear of a gentleman who might indeed be interested, and I will certainly be happy to inform him—'

Modesto interrupted. 'We need to move fast, Signore. My mistress would like to sell the place as quickly as possible.' He could see curiosity fighting propriety across the man's face but he did not offer any enlightening information. A few seconds passed, then the lawyer said, 'Might your mistress be interested in letting the house? There are always far more people in Napoli willing to take on a place for a short time; finding someone to buy the house outright may well prove much more difficult, if my gentleman turns out not to be interested.'

'I would have to ask her, Signore. She is, I know, wanting to sell it.'

'It's a fairly reliable source of income, you might tell her – letting, I mean.'

Modesto nodded.

'It's a lovely house. Well-maintained . . . and the decorations are . . . well, they are almost *opulent*, aren't they?'

Modesto raised an eyebrow and watched the lawyer gazing around the large, low-ceilinged *sala*. He seemed impressed. In other times, perhaps, this well-heeled gentleman might have been a potential new patron.

Out on the roof garden at the Via Santa Lucia, the setting sun was turning the white-painted walls of the house a rich ochre, and the bustle of the city was just beginning to die down. On the low table several candles were burning. Moths fluttered into and out of the pools of light; one of them caught the tip of a wing in a flame and instantly fizzled into powdery nothingness.

Modesto watched his mistress run the heel of her hand over her forehead. Her eyes were shadowed from lack of sleep and she was chewing at the corner of her lip.

'I don't know, *caro*. I did really want to sell the place outright – I want it out of my life. I don't want to have to think about it. About all the things that have happened there.'

'I know you don't. But it's a source of income, if—'

'Don't say it!'

Modesto reached for her hand. Gripping her fingers, he said, 'I *will* say it, because it has to be said. Listen to me – letting that house will give you a source of income, something you and those little girls can rely on, if all this comes to nothing.'

'Please don't say it.'

'Do you want to see them on the streets?'

He held her gaze for several seconds. She looked appalled.

Modesto said, 'You have to be practical. You've set every-thing in motion now. You've written to Vasquez – I delivered the letter not an hour since; I've said I'll tell Signor di Cicciano myself, which in his case I think will be more effective than a letter, and you can inform Signor di Laviano in due course, because obviously you can't write to him at his house, but I think with him, it'll come better directly from you than from me. So, now that—'

'But—'

'No – it's simple, Signora. You listen. You're risking every-thing – everything! – on what's actually nothing more than a possibility. You're about to pull your own house down around your ears – I just think you have to put as many practical props in place as you can before you pull out the last of the cornerstones, don't you?'

A flurry of footsteps on the stairs startled them both.

'Mamma! Look! Look what we've got!'

'Ilaria gave them to us!'

Modesto watched the two little girls run from the stairs, across the roof garden to where Francesca sat, both waving what looked like a little bouquet of white feathers, each bunch tightly tied to the end of a small cane.

'Ilaria said they're for dusting!'

'Can we do dusting up here?'

Modesto saw his mistress smile, though her eyes gleamed with a sudden flash of tears.

'No,' she said. 'Not up here – but why don't you dust the bed-chambers instead?'

Both girls murmured their approval of this suggestion, and wheeled round as one, heading back towards the stairs.

'You could dust me before you go, if you like, just to practise,' Modesto said with a grin, and the girls squealed with delight and stopped in their tracks. Giggling, and holding their little clumps of feathers up in front of them, they flicked them over Modesto's upturned face, neck and shoulders, down his doublet front, along the length of his thighs and over his knees, whilst he maintained an expression of statuesque ecstasy.

They completed their task. Modesto shook his head, and, jutting his lower jaw, blew upwards over his nose. 'Oh, my goodness, that's better,' he said, as the girls stood back, breathless with laughter. 'I haven't been that clean for a long time. Thank you! What marvellous dusters you both are. I'll look forward to seeing the bedchambers in a few minutes! Go on, get on with it! I'll be in to check how well you've done, before you can say "feathers"!'

Giggling again, they both ran off.

'You are so sweet with them,' Francesca said, running one finger along under her lashes.

'They are sweet children.' Modesto leaned forwards and pointed a forefinger at her. 'And if you want them to continue to have nothing more frightening to do in bedchambers than *dusting* for the next few years, then you had better bloody well listen to advice and agree to let that house of yours.'

There was a long pause.

Francesca put her face in her hands for a moment, then looked up. 'Very well. Just arrange it, will you? And . . . thank you, *caro*.'

'Huh . . .' Modesto said gruffly. 'I'm off, now. And you can spend a bit of time practising being a proper Neapolitan housewife. Your servants need telling a thing or two – that Ilaria is a lazy trollop. You'll be well rid of her.'

Twenty-two

Miguel Vasquez dropped his quill back into its pot with some force. Ink spattered in tiny droplets across his doublet sleeve and over the corner of the table. He blotted, reread and then folded the sheet on which he had been writing, then pushed his chair back from the table, and crossed to the window.

'Every month the same,' he muttered, in Spanish. 'Every month. Why do they never, *ever* pay up in time? The bastards. Do they imagine I have endless funds? I will run out of money eventually and it will end in mutiny – they're fools if they think otherwise. Unless—' He stopped, frowning as a thought struck him. 'Unless it is no accident that it always seems to be me to whom they turn. Perhaps this is their idea of a suitable retribution for . . .' Vasquez paused '. . . for . . . for Milan. The bastards.'

He strode over to a carved cupboard in the far corner of the room. Unlocking it, he took from a lower shelf a heavy box made of iron-banded oak. This too was locked. It needed both hands and a fair amount of strength to carry it across to the table, where he put it down with a bang. Pushing a hand down into his breeches pocket, he pulled out another key and unlocked the box. Inside, beneath a large number of leather pouches fastened by drawstrings, the box was filled with gold coins.

From the top of a pile of papers, Vasquez picked up a sheet, on which was a list of names. His soldiers. None of whom would receive a single *scudo* from the Crown this month. Yet again. Possibly the tenth month in a row. All of the men would be looking to him to save them from starvation. Lucky for them and for the Crown that he had the funds available, he thought angrily. Running a finger down the list, he assessed numbers. Rapidly calculating what he could afford to give each man, he snatched the quill back out of the pot and spent a few moments scribbling figures down on a scrap of paper.

Then, striding across the room to the door and leaning out, he shouted, 'Juan! *Donde estàs?*' Pausing, he added, a little louder, '*Ven aquì!*'

After no more than seconds, his servant appeared. '*Maestre?*'

Vasquez motioned to him to come with him to the table, then pulled out a second chair. As Juan sat down, he held out several sealed letters. 'These arrived a few moments ago, Señor,' he said.

Vasquez snatched them from him, and put them to one side unopened. 'I have to pay the men again myself this month,' he said, glaring down at a letter bearing a large be-ribboned seal. 'Yet again, it seems that no official funds are forthcoming. I've worked out roughly how much I can give them – can you help me count it all out? As you did before?'

'*Si*, Señor.' Juan nodded. He reached across to the open strongbox and took out the leather pouches. Laying them down neatly, in rows, he picked up the first and held it ready. Vasquez took a clinking handful of coins from the box and started counting them out into the other palm. Each time he reached the requisite amount he handed it to Juan, who slid it into the bag, drew the strings tight and laid it to one side, while Vasquez scratched out the name on his list. Vasquez counted again, Juan bagged the coins, Vasquez scratched out the name. And again. And again.

At last, Vasquez put his quill back into its pot and puffed out a breath. He ran a hand around his beard. '*Gracias*, Juan. Let's hope the bastards cough up in time for next month's salaries, eh?'

'Let's hope so, *Maestre*.'

'I shall be inspecting troops after this is all delivered tomorrow, so I will be away from the apartment for the day, and might possibly stay overnight in the garrison building. But I will definitely be back on Saturday in time for the evening meal – can you make sure that is catered for?'

'Yes, *Maestre*.'

'I'll be entertaining Señora Felizzi – please inform the kitchens and arrange for the other servants to keep away, as usual.'

'Yes, *Maestre*.'

Juan took his leave, and, after locking and replacing the strong-box in the carved cupboard, Vasquez wandered back through into the room with the golden *lettiera*. Sitting down on the edge of the mattress, he pulled off his boots, swung his legs up onto the bed and lay down. Hands behind his head, he closed his eyes and, hoping to put his money worries aside for a time, he pictured his courtesan. It was a pleasing image. He saw her clad in the red-and-gold dress she had worn on that first visit – the delicious one which exposed so much of her breasts – and then in his mind he undressed her. Slowly. Smiling complacently to himself, with one hand tucked inside his codpiece, he worked his way through her garments, one by one, taking his time in imagining the unfastening and removal of each piece.

And then he allowed his now quite fevered imagination free rein.

Several minutes later, now very much looking forward to his assignation that Saturday, Vasquez straightened his breeches and stood up, aware that, if he were to be fully ready to go out to the troops on the morrow, he ought to go through the correspondence Juan had handed him earlier.

'Come on, man,' he muttered, seating himself back at the polished table in the adjoining room. 'It won't take long.'

The first two letters were important, but dull. Vasquez searched for answers amongst his papers, then scribbled responses, folded and sealed them and put the letters to one side ready for later dispatch.

Then he cracked open the seal on the third missive.

He read it. Then, brows puckered in surprised disbelief, he read it again.

Miguel – I must beg your forgiveness. We have barely had time enough to establish a proper liaison, I know, and I would assure you that those times that I have been fortunate enough to spend in your esteemed company have been entertaining and pleasurable. But the circumstances of my life are ever complicated. I neither wish to explain myself in detail, nor feel at liberty to do so, but please understand, Miguel, that I am ceasing to work as a courtesan. That part of my life is over, and I am, I hope, setting out on a very different course to that upon which I had presumed until even a few days ago. You and I will not lie together again. Please be assured of my high estimation of both your character and your – how shall I best express it – 'abilities'.

The letter was signed and sealed. Vasquez had no doubts that it was indeed from Francesca. Feeling angrily foolish now, after his indulgent few moments just now in the other room, he stared for several moments at the words his erstwhile courtesan had penned, then screwing the sheet into a tight ball, he threw it across the room. It bounced off a window ledge and fell to the floor behind a chair. A *'very different course'*? What did she mean? What had happened? Why had she changed her mind? He sucked in a shocked breath and his hands balled into fists as a thin blade of cold panic caught him in the throat – might she be with child? Was that what she meant by his *'abilities'* – the ease with which he could manage to father bastard offspring? Getting to his feet, he crossed the room in a couple of strides. He pulled open the door and, taking the stairs three at a time, left the house, slamming the front door behind him as he ran out into the Via dei Tribunali.

Twenty-three

A thin stripe of light moved across Luca's face as the early morning sun passed a gap in the shutters. He opened his eyes, then screwed them shut again and rolled to face away from the window. Pressing his face into his pillow for a moment, he frowned as he tried to retain a dream that had been interrupted by the sunshine, but despite his efforts, it seeped away from him like water through cupped palms and within seconds he could recall none of it.

He sat up.

The dream quite gone, he began to think of the evening before. Flowers. He would buy her flowers. It suddenly seemed urgent. The thought of Francesca's beauty and her air of vulnerability tore at his heart and he felt – with a sensation akin to panic rising in his chest – that he had to make some move towards her as soon as possible. To claim her for himself, in case anyone else had designs upon her, now she had emerged from the sequestrations of mourning. He suppressed the thought which now pushed its way into his mind: that this notion was unpleasantly like that of a farmer putting his mark upon a beast he had chosen at the market.

He could not believe his reactions. Here he was, a grown man – a widower with two adult sons – and he had thought until last night that he was past passion. He had had his share of it during his ten-year marriage, and had been resigned to a life without it since Lisabeta's death. But last night's encounter had smashed through his calm composure like a battering ram through castle ramparts and he felt at once defenceless and exposed.

He pushed back blankets and bed-hangings and climbed out of bed. Padding over to the window, he opened the casement, unfastened the shutters and pushed them wide. Bright, white light filled the room like a shout and Luca screwed his eyes against it. He scooped a couple of handfuls of water from a large pewter jug and rinsed his face, pushing wet hands through his hair. Droplets splashed cold on his bare shoulders and spattered across the wooden floorboards, glittering as they fell in the light from the window. He dried himself with yesterday's shirt, dressed hurriedly and, still fastening the laces of his doublet as he went, made his way to the kitchen, where Luigi was grumpily finishing his breakfast.

'Signore,' Luigi said, without looking up.

Luca heard his manservant's mournful tone and closed his eyes for a second. Since Luigi's illness – could it be as much as a year ago? – the old man had been increasingly taciturn and incommunicative, frequently withdrawing into impenetrable silences for hours at a time. Luigi's presence frequently cast a dark pall of pessimism over the household and Luca often wished he had the resolve to dismiss him. On several occasions he had actually opened his mouth to issue the dismissal, and then an image of a miserable, ragged Luigi, unemployable and reduced to begging and foraging for scraps in the backstreets of Napoli, had pushed its way into his mind, and Luca had simply closed his mouth again and swallowed his irritation without comment. He was aware that he and Gianni often performed tasks which should by rights have been done by Luigi, but short of sentencing his father's old servant to live out his remaining years in undoubted penury, he could think of no other way of running his household, for on his academic salary he could certainly not afford a second employee.

'Luigi,' Luca said, sitting down next to him at the table, 'I need to buy some flowers. Where do you think I should go?'

Luigi frowned and considered. 'This time of year you'll be lucky to find any,' he said after a moment.

'But surely there must be *somewhere* in the entirety of this city where I can buy something as simple as an armful of flowers?'

'Doubt it.'

Luca suppressed a brief desire to thump his manservant and said as calmly as he could manage, 'What else do you suggest I might buy someone, as an impromptu gift?'

Luigi considered again and said, 'Fruit.'

It was Luca's turn to frown. 'Where?'

'Market, Signore. They had figs there yesterday, and little sweet melons. Market in the Piazza Girolamini.'

Luca's irritation with Luigi vanished. He clapped a hand on the old man's shoulder and said happily, 'Perfect, Luigi, what a good idea. I'll go as soon as I've eaten.'

The soft raffia basket bulged. Luca put his face to the contents and sniffed. Half a dozen tiny, sweet-smelling, orange-fleshed melons, a pomegranate and a handful of velvety apricots would make a pleasing present, he thought to himself with a smile as he walked briskly across town towards Santa Lucia.

He found the Signora's house, and knocked on the front door, his heart beating in his throat. The door was opened by a short, plump woman, reddish-skinned, her hair loosely wrapped in a linen cloth.

'Signore?'

'I hope I have the right house, Signora,' Luca said politely. 'I am hoping to see to Signora Marrone.'

He expected a smile, but the woman with the linen head-covering took a step back, frowned up at him, clearly suspicious. Luca started to wonder if he was mistaken in the address. The woman opened her mouth to speak, but before she could utter a word, a movement behind her caught Luca's eye and he looked past the woman into the depths of the house. Francesca, coming up out of the shadows at the far end of the room, saw Luca in the doorway and started visibly. She looked confused for a moment, then limped forward and said, 'Thank you, Ilaria, I will talk to the Signore.'

The linen-wrapped woman shrugged and stepped away from the door. Francesca smiled at Luca, her face flushed. She was tired, he thought with concern: there were deep shadows below her eyes that had certainly not been there last night.

'Signore,' she said, smiling. 'How lovely to see you again.'

'I . . .' Luca faltered. All his carefully prepared greetings left him. He had no idea what to say, felt suddenly as tongue-tied as an inexperienced boy. 'I wondered . . .' he tried again, but as he spoke, two identical, beautiful little girls appeared, each clutching a small white feather duster; they stood one on either side of Francesca, gripping her skirts with small fingers and looking up at him. 'I . . . I brought you some fruit,' Luca managed to say at last. He held up the basket.

Francesca's blush deepened. 'Thank you, Signore,' she said. Luca's desire to kiss her returned, with ferocity.

He held out the basket and she peered into it.

'Oh, girls – a pomegranate! Your favourite.' Both children leaned forward to see, then turned their faces up to their mother's in mute entreaty. She turned to Luca. 'May they?'

'The fruit is yours, Signora,' he said. He inclined his head and smiled.

'Go on then, you two, take it. You can share it between you,' The two girls eyed each other, then one of them put down her duster, reached into the bag and brought out a shiny, pink-tinged globe like a blushing skull; the fingers of both her hands stretched carefully to hold the treasure without dropping it. 'Take it out to the back step – and don't leave bits of peel everywhere!' Francesca said.

Both children ran off.

Luca stood on the step. He still did not know what to say. Then he saw Francesca shift her weight awkwardly and his insides jumped. 'Oh, Signora – your ankle! Is it still as painful as last night?'

'Er, no. Thank you. I think it's a little better today,' she said.

'I won't keep you,' Luca said. 'Perhaps we can arrange to see—'

'But . . . why don't you come in for a moment now?' Francesca stood back to let him in to the house. He hesitated, then crossed the threshold.

They climbed the stairs to the *sala*. It was modestly, but elegantly furnished, and was well-lit by three large windows which opened onto the street. There were several hanging tapestries and a large carved fireplace took up much of the furthest wall. Several folding wooden chairs stood to one side of the *sala*, one of them piled untidily with childishly worked embroidery, and in the middle of the room was a large square table, covered with an elaborately worked cruciform carpet, which hung neatly down to the floor on all four sides. A big white maiolica bowl stood empty in the middle of the table and Luca watched as Francesca carefully took the melons and the apricots from the basket and placed them one by one into the bowl.

'They're gorgeous against the white. What lovely colours. I haven't had melon in weeks. Thank you so much, Signore,' she said. She picked one up and held it cupped in her hands up to her nose, hunching her shoulders around the scent. 'Oh, that smells so good. Please, do sit down.'

Luca crossed to the folding chairs and seated himself in the nearest.

'I . . . I trust you slept well, after your late night, last night.' he said.

Francesca reddened again. She said, not meeting his eye, 'Well enough, thank you, Signore.'

Luca was not sure what to say. He looked at the shadows under her eyes and found that he did not believe her; he wondered what it could have been that had so disturbed Francesca's night.

There was a short pause.

'What beautiful girls,' Luca said then. 'They are so similar!'

Francesca smiled fondly and said, 'I can tell them apart, of course, but I don't think many others can – I have to admit that they quite shamelessly use their likeness to their own advantage fairly frequently.'

Luca laughed. 'And so would I in their position.' He paused, then added, 'They are very much like their mother.' As the words left his mouth, though, he heard his voice from a moment before, praising the girls' beauty, and he hoped Francesca did not think he was being inappropriately forward.

They were interrupted then by voices from below, and the sound of the front door being closed. Heavy footsteps climbed the stairs and then someone knocked on the door to the *sala*.

Francesca said, 'Yes?'

The door pushed open. A stocky man of about Luca's own age, with dark hair and large, slightly protuberant black eyes, leaned into the room, one hand on the handle, the other on the jamb.

'Oh, Signora, I'm sorry – I didn't realise you had company.' A strong Roman accent. The black eyes rested on Luca for a moment, then turned back at Francesca.

'Don't worry, *caro* – is there a problem?'

Luca's heart jumped at the affectionate title she gave the new arrival.

The man shrugged. 'No, not at all. I'll come back later.' He disappeared, closing the door behind him.

'I'm sorry,' Francesca said to Luca.

Her colour rose again. Her lips were slightly parted and as Luca watched, the tip of her tongue appeared briefly, leaving a gleam of wetness behind it. He looked up at her eyes, but she in her turn had let her gaze fall to his mouth. And then their eyes met. Seconds passed and a taut-wire tension stretched out between them. Neither of them spoke and Luca's guts writhed as he fought his growing need to kiss her. Francesca caught her lower lip between her teeth as she had done in the hall at San Domenico and Luca looked back at her mouth.

It was too much.

He began to stand, determining to tell her how he felt, when the door to the *sala* burst open again and the two little girls ran in. Luca quickly sat back down. The girls had purple-stained fingers and faces, and both were smiling widely as they approached their mother.

'We've eaten our pomegranate,' one of them said.

'Already?' Francesca said, smiling.

Both girls nodded. 'It was lovely.' They spoke in unison. Even their voices seemed identical to Luca.

'Good. I'm glad you enjoyed it,' Francesca said. She sounded husky. 'Have you collected up all the bits of peel?' More vigorous nods. 'You can thank the Signore for bringing you such a special present.'

Both children turned at once to Luca and bobbed hasty curtsies. He smiled at them.

'But just look at the pair of you!' Francesca said then. 'Go and ask Ilaria to help you wash your faces and hands,' She reached forward with both arms and ran a thumb down each girl's cheek. The two children eyed each other's blotched mouths and dirty hands, giggled, then turned and left the room.

Luca stood up. His chair scraped loudly on the floorboards. The moment to declare his feelings seemed to have been snatched from him, and he felt suddenly awkward. 'I should go, perhaps,' he said.

'Oh. Do you have to?'

He thought he saw a flash of entreaty in her eyes and was instantly rocked by a vivid image of himself, all caution abandoned, taking her into his arms. He sucked in a breath and closed his eyes for a second, then swallowed. What if he were wrong? What if his desire for her was clouding his judgement? Perhaps, if he made any such move towards her she would – rather than respond as he had just imagined – be appalled at his temerity and demand instead that he leave her house. He cleared his throat.

'I think I ought to go – I have a number of pressing errands to run today.' Luca heard these lies as though listening to someone quite separate from himself. And then he surprised himself by saying, without having planned the invitation at all, 'But perhaps you would care to come and dine at my house one evening soon?' With a moment's unease, he thought of Luigi's increasing inability to cook anything remotely edible. He would probably have to prepare the meal himself.

'Oh. I should like that very much,' Francesca said. She sounded genuinely pleased.

Luca's face felt suddenly warm. 'Would tomorrow be a day you could manage?' he said. 'I shall be teaching this afternoon but—'

'Teaching?'

'Yes – I teach law, at the university. Did Filippo not tell you?'

Francesca shook her head. 'He told me almost nothing.'

'Probably far too excited about the evening's entertainment.'

Francesca reddened again.

'Anyway,' Luca said, 'perhaps if tomorrow were possible for you. My sons will be there . . .' He tailed off.

Francesca frowned for a moment, then smiled and nodded. 'I have promised to visit Signora Parisetto earlier in the day, if you remember, but I shall be home long before the evening. Thank you – I should very much like to come and eat with you and your boys,' she said.

'Good. Come at about the hour of the Angelus, then. Will you need to bring the little girls with you?'

'Oh, no – it would be far too late for them and they will probably be tired after playing with Signora Parisetto's children. They can stay here with Ilaria.'

'As I say, my boys will both be back from their various activities by Saturday and they'll eat with us. They'll be so pleased to meet you.'

He explained his address to her, and described the simplest way of finding it.

'I will look forward to it very much.' Francesca smiled at him again.

She showed him to the front door and they bade each other farewell.

Just as he turned to step down into the street, Luca saw the stocky man with the black eyes walk up into the hallway from somewhere at the back of the house. Francesca flicked a glance back at the man, nodded, and then turned back to smile and wave to Luca as he left.

Luca's head buzzed with a confusion of conflicting thoughts as he walked slowly home.

Twenty-four

The Parisetto's house is small and new and, as I was told at San Domenico, it is only a short distance from the sea. Its pale stone front gleams in the sunshine as the twins and I stand on the step, and the bright, salt-smelling air around us is full of the vulgar laughter of gulls and the slap of water against stone.

'Can I knock?' Bella asks.

'Go on then.'

She reaches up and bangs the wood with her knuckles, looking back at me for reassurance as the noise she has made sounds out into the quiet. Straight away, a flurry of activity sounds inside. Feet hurry towards us. A crash is followed by a wailing sob, and a fumbled scrabble at the fastening on the front door. Then the door opens, and Serafina Parisetto, rather pink in the face, smiles at the three of us, a howling baby astride her hip. He is little more than a year old, but even so, being so small, she has to lean away from his weight to balance. The older boy stands behind her, clutching her skirts and peering around at us, wide-eyed.

Away towards the back of the house, visible through a vista of two or three doorways, several other women and an immensely tall, roughly dressed young man – are busily occupied, taking no notice of our arrival. The clatter of their activities and the hum of their conversations punctuates the exchanges between me and

Serafina. The tall boy, a large flat tray tucked under one arm, edges past us without a word and leaves the house. Beata and Bella's heads swivel to watch him as he goes, clearly impressed by his height.

'Oh, Francesca, how lovely to see you. I'm so sorry –' Serafina gazes affectionately at the screaming infant '– poor Benedetto fell over on the way to the door.' She kisses the top of the baby's damp head. 'Please, come in. Oh, you must be . . .' She pauses, smiling at the girls.

I say, laying a hand on each head as I speak, 'Beata and Isabella.'

Serafina says to them over the howls. 'I expect you must get very cross with people telling you how alike you are.'

They both look up at her and nod seriously.

Serafina stands back and we step into the house.

'Come upstairs,' she says. 'Piero's mother, and her –' she rolls her eyes '–her *retinue* will be in and out of the *sala* and the kitchen, so perhaps we can sit out on the belvedere and hope that we won't be too badly disturbed.' We follow her and the little boys upstairs. We go in to the *sala*, which is large and brightly lit by the sun. Half a dozen elderly ladies are busy with embroidery frames and – by the sound of it – with a great deal of gossip. They look up at us, mouths a little open, needles held up in bony fingers, pausing in their chatter as we pass through. Serafina speaks to them briefly, and their heads bob a brief acknowledgment of the presence of newcomers to the house, but otherwise they make no attempt at conversation. I wonder briefly at the reaction to my presence that would ensue were they to guess my real identity. At this thought, a nasty twinge of guilt stabs at me accusingly – Serafina's friendship is open and welcoming and yet I am deceiving her. She would be appalled at the truth.

I glance around the room as we pass through. It's very pretty, it looks out over the light-flecked harbour, and its walls – and indeed the old women – are all dappled with beautiful, shifting water patterns. An open door in the furthest wall leads out onto the *belvedere*; Serafina shepherds us all across and out onto this sun-filled balcony and pulls the door closed behind her.

The *belvedere* is beautiful: wide and long, roofed over but airy – and fragrant with orange blossom from trees which are fairly bursting from several large terracotta pots. Three or four carved animals lie on the floor. Seeing them, the baby on Serafina's hip curls backwards away from his mother, bending precariously, stiff arms stretched in entreaty, though he says nothing. Serafina sets him down on the floor and he staggers across to them, rolling from foot to foot like an aged seaman. He plumps down onto his bottom, gathers a wooden horse into his arms and begins to suck its muzzle, the last of his sobs still shaking his fat little shoulders.

Smiling, I glance at the twins. They are staring at the baby, fascinated.

'I'm so glad you were all able to come,' Serafina says. 'Girls, I have some games you might like to play.' She steps back into the *sala*, and comes back a moment later with a wooden box, inside which proves to be a velvet bag, closed with a drawstring. 'Do you know how to play *Zara?*'

Both girls shake their heads.

Serafina lays on the floor a square chequered board like a chess board. 'Open the bag and tip the pieces out,' she says, and Bella obeys. A scattering of wooden stars, circles and squares of all colours plinks down onto the tiles. Benedetto, the baby, immediately puts down his horse and crawls over to see what he is missing; he reaches out with splayed, shrimp-like fingers, grabs a star and puts it straight into his mouth.

'Spit out,' Serafina says firmly, and Benedetto opens his mouth, letting the star drop back down onto the floor. The older child sits near the twins. He scoops up a handful of the coloured pieces, one eye on his little brother, whose face immediately crumples as he sees this; he sucks in a long breath ready for a new sob.

'Girls,' I say quickly. 'Why don't you lay the pieces out in patterns? The little boys might like that.'

Beata and Bella start ordering the shapes along the edges of the tiles. Noticing these two new small strangers properly for the first time, the boys' attention is caught and they watch the twins with rapt fascination, their heads swivelling from one to the other, obviously startled by their intriguing similarity. Serafina comes to sit down in the chair next to mine.

'They are so pretty, your two girls,' she says.

I smile. 'And your two are quite charming.'

Serafina raises a sceptical eyebrow and does not reply. I laugh.

'Now, quickly – while we have a moment's peace – would you care for something to drink and eat? Piero brought up a couple of bottles of wine from the cellar this morning for us, and I made some bread earlier on. We need to eat that while it's warm, as any bread I make seems to be quite inedible within a matter of hours!'

She busies herself as she speaks, pouring out two glasses of a tawny-coloured wine and passing one of them across to me. The bread proves to be light, salty and quite delicious.

'Oh, goodness, that's better,' Serafina says, taking a mouthful from her glass, tipping her head back and closing her eyes. A brief moment of sweet-scented respite from the endless chaos of her boys. A second or two later she opens her eyes again and smiles at me. 'Now,' she says, reaching across and laying a small hand on my arm. 'Now that you're here: I have something to confess.' She lowers her voice and glances across to the closed door to the *sala*.

'I have to admit that I spent quite a bit of last night wondering about what your secret can possibly be.'

My heart jolts up into my throat. With difficulty, I swallow the piece of bread I am chewing, which suddenly seems to have doubled in size and dried to the consistency of old carpet.

'Secret?' How can she know?

Serafina raises her eyebrows at me and nods; there is a gleam in her eye and she suddenly reminds me of Bianca, about to reveal some tasty titbit of gossip. It is not a reassuring image.

'Yes. Your secret. I've had a lot of time to think about it – you see, my little Benedetto was perfectly horrible last night – weren't you, *carissimo*?' She smiles fondly at her smaller son. 'And of course I ended up spending simply *hour*s trying to settle him to sleep, and, while I was sat there beside his crib, I found myself thinking about you.'

Her smile is frank and open, and her eyes are dancing – but my pulse-beat is now painfully fast.

'Because,' Serafina adds, in a lowered voice – little more than a whisper, 'I think you had quite an effect on my lovely friend, Luca, the other night.'

It is as though boiling water is rising up inside my face. My eyes begin smarting. 'L . . . Luca?' I say.

'Luca,' she agrees, smiling more broadly. 'Bless him, he seemed to be having terrible trouble dragging his eyes from your face all evening. Do you know, I don't think he took in a single word of that play or thought for more than a second about his food! Do you normally have that effect on people?'

Oh, dear. What do I say to that?

'Erm,' I stammer, feeling horribly sick. 'Erm . . . I really don't know . . .'

But even as I speak, Serafina's eyes widen and her smile fades.

She puts her fingers up over her mouth. 'Oh, *cielo*!' she says. 'Oh, dear, I must be the most tactless person in the whole of Italy! In all the excitement, I quite forgot – oh, *Dio*! How simply dreadful of me! You must think me *so* unkind.'

I am now completely bemused. 'What do you mean?' I say.

'To ask you something like that . . . when you are so recently out of mourning. How *could* I? What must you think of me?'

Mourning? Oh, dear God – I had almost forgotten my 'widowhood' myself – thank *God* she reminded me! I say, 'Please, don't trouble yourself. It's—'

She interrupts me. 'It's unforgivable, that's what it is. Oh, if Piero knew what I'd just said. I said something just as stupid to Luca a few days ago, too – I am *so* thoughtless.'

All four children, hearing the distress in her voice, stop what they are doing and look across at her.

'Please,' I say again. 'Stop it – don't think of it. I should be flattered, rather than insulted, after all, by what you've just asked me, shouldn't I?'

Serafina gives me a rather wan smile. 'You're really not offended?'

'No. Not at all. Honestly.'

The children return to their activities with the wooden *Zara* pieces.

Serafina says, 'Thank goodness. Because I *did* think it remarkable. Luca is such a lovely man. S*uch* a good friend, and I do worry about him – he has been on his own for so very long, and then last night he seemed quite different to how he has been, and I couldn't help noticing, and I was so pleased, Francesca! *So* pleased. I thought to myself – Oh, this is just what Luca needs, and . . .'

She tails off, clearly embarrassed at her outpouring. I feel fairly certain that she is longing to ask me if I have any reciprocating feelings for Luca – perhaps to validate her desire to broker a suitable match for her friend – but she says nothing; instead she reaches for her glass.

Wanting to reassure her, but afraid of giving away too much, I say carefully (and untruthfully), 'I cannot say that I noticed what you've described, the other night.' I pause, and then add, 'But . . . if . . . if Luca were indeed to be interested in me, I . . . I think it would be fair to say . . . that I don't think I should be too displeased. He . . .' I hesitate. Feeling somehow that I am allowing out something very tender and naked and vulnerable, I say, 'He's invited me to his house for supper this evening. To meet his sons.'

Serafina draws in a delighted breath and reaches for my hand again. 'Oh, Francesca – I am *so* pleased. Oh, that is wonderful! You are *so* perfect for each other.'

Perfect?

A wholesome widower and a deceitful whore?

Twenty-five

Smoke was starting to wisp out around the carved larchwood jut of the fireplace hood. Luca looked across at Luigi and drew in a long breath. The old man's forehead was deeply furrowed as he bent over a copper pot that was hanging above glowing embers. Luca saw that the hand holding the long iron spoon was shaking, and little splashes of gravy were falling and staining the brick floor.

Luca closed his eyes for a moment, opened them again and said, 'Luigi, you must be tired. Why don't you rest now? I am quite happy to finish off the meal. You've worked so hard over the preparation – it's just a matter of waiting an hour or so now . . . I'm really very grateful for all your help.'

For a moment, Luigi appeared not to have heard, but then he turned and gave one curt nod. 'If you are happy, then, Signore, I will go. I am a little tired, you are quite right.' He frowned at the long spoon in his hand as though not quite sure why he was holding it, then put it back into the pot. Nodding at Luca once again, he shuffled across the kitchen in ill-fitting shoes and, fumbling for the handle, left by the side door. Luca turned his face up to the ceiling and pushed the heels of his hands into his eyes, his fingers in his hair. 'Oh God!' he groaned. 'Heaven knows what this hideous potful will taste like – she will probably never speak to me again!' He picked up the spoon, raised it to his mouth and, blew gently across the steaming contents. Tasted it. Pushed his bottom lip out in surprise and relaxed a little. He added salt, however, and pushed a large, rather twiggy bunch of rosemary down into the bubbling sauce; he then put a lid on the pot.

Luca spent the next few moments moving between kitchen and *sala*, laying the table for his meal with Francesca. He opened the *credenza* and took out one of three white linen cloths, which he flapped out and smoothed over the table. On this he placed a basket of cut bread and a big, white, tin-glazed fruit bowl. This was filled with peaches, grapes, apricots and a handful of cherries – a couple of which Luca now picked out and ate, spitting the stones into his palm and then throwing them into the fireplace. He laid two places: knife, small two-pronged fork, and glass for each person. Then three candles in brass holders in a line along the centre of the table. Standing back, he examined the effect, leaned back in towards the table and straightened a fork.

Two places.

No sign of either of the boys. Luca hoped Francesca would not think poorly of him for not letting her know in advance that they would be dining alone.

It was cool enough this evening for a fire. Luca ran down to the back door and collected an awkward armful of logs; after carrying them back up to the *sala*, he busied himself for a moment laying and lighting a fire. The evening being still and quite windless, it took time and the careful application of the bellows to get it to catch, and there was a soft haze of smoke hanging up near the ceiling by the time Luca was able to leave the fireplace and return to his bubbling pot of *peposo*.

Luca tasted his stew again. He sliced and laid out a plateful of tomatoes. He shredded and dressed a salad. Cursing quietly when he caught the end of his finger with the knife, he sliced the ends of a dozen stems of asparagus and laid them out ready to be placed in hot water at the last moment. He poured himself a glass of red wine, sat down at the kitchen table and sucked in a long mouthful. His heartbeat was quick in his throat as the Angelus struck outside.

Some moments later, he heard a soft knock at his front door.

She was accompanied by her manservant. As he opened the door, Luca saw her turn to her companion and smile, saying, 'Thank you so much for walking me, *caro*.'

'Do you want me to come back and fetch you?' the man said in his heavy Roman accent. Luca coughed and interrupted before she could answer. 'Thank you, Signore – please don't trouble yourself. I will be delighted to walk the Signora home.'

The dark eyes rested on his face for a moment, with an expression he could not read, and then Francesca said, 'There you are, I told you he would.' She smiled at her companion, who nodded, turned, and began to walk back up the street.

Luca watched him until he turned the corner and was lost from view, then he took Francesca's hand and kissed her fingers. 'How lovely to see you,' he said over her knuckles.

She smiled and said, 'I've been so looking forward to tonight.'

Luca stood back to let her in. 'Come upstairs,' he said. He took her coat from her and laid it over a chair, then held her hand and moved to the staircase. 'The fire is lit, the room is warm, and the food is almost ready. I'll find you a chair, and then I must check that our stew isn't burning.'

'Have you cooked it yourself?'

Luca smiled. 'My cook is getting rather elderly,' he said, a little conspiratorially, 'and his . . . grasp of seasonings is becoming . . . somewhat *unsubtle*, shall we say. I've suggested he might like to go to bed and leave me to finish the preparations.'

Francesca laughed. 'I am very impressed that you feel able to tackle such an undertaking, Signore.'

'I'd save your admiration until after you've tasted it.'

They went together into the *sala*. 'Oh, what a lovely room!' Francesca said. 'Such beautiful tapestries. Where did you find them?'

Luca paused before saying, 'My late wife made them.'

'Oh.' Francesca hesitated. 'How grateful you must be to have them.'

For a second, Lisabeta's presence – and her absence – hung in the air between them, unwelcome to Luca for the first time since her death. He silently apologised to his memory of his wife and changed the subject. 'You are walking more freely – is your ankle mended?'

'Oh, yes, almost completely. Thank you.'

He held Francesca's gaze, and found himself suddenly aware of how difficult swallowing had become. She smiled at him, and for a moment Luca was unable to speak and found that he had to think quite carefully about the mechanics of breathing.

She was wearing the same blue dress he had seen her wear at San Domenico. Perhaps it was the only one she had for special occasions – again, he reminded himself, he had no notion of the circumstances in which her late husband had left her. It was certainly a pretty dress – but it struck him now that a woman this beautiful should not be wearing something so . . . so understated. She should wear silks and silver, he thought, fabrics that glittered, and—

'The table's only been set for two. Where are your boys?' Francesca's voice broke into his musings. 'Are they not coming? I was looking forward to meeting them.'

Luca started. He said, 'I'm so sorry – I should probably have sent word . . . there has been no sign of them so far. I've rather given up on them for this evening. I do hope you don't mind that it will just be the two of us. You may think it improper . . . I'm so sorry . . .'

Francesca smiled. 'Not at all.'

Luca breathed in, and the smells from the kitchen reminded him of his duties as cook. He said, 'I should really check the food. Can you excuse me for a moment?'

'Of course – I shall be very happy taking stock of all the lovely things you have in your beautiful *sala*.'

Luca smiled at her, and hurried to the kitchen. He put splayed hands on the kitchen table and leant his weight on his arms. Closing his eyes for a moment, he breathed slowly through his nose.

'You are behaving like a bloody child!' he muttered to himself. 'She'll think you're a complete idiot.'

He placed the asparagus into a small pot of boiling water, then tasted the *peposo* again, added a pinch more salt and threw in a handful of chopped parsley. He ladled it carefully into a large maiolica pot, onto which he placed a lid. Steam rose pleasingly through a small hole in the lid. Luca put the pot onto a wooden tray, along with the plate of sliced tomatoes, the salad and another plate. Draining the now-cooked asparagus, he placed this onto the empty plate.

He backed out of the kitchen with the tray in his hands and crossed into the *sala*. Putting the tray down on the top of the *credenza*, he saw that Francesca was standing by the fireplace. The shadows on her face were slate blue against the warm peach of her flame-lit skin and her eyes were enormous. An orange dot glowed in the centre of each of the pearls hanging from her ears. An insistent hunger for her quite smothered Luca's appetite for his meal, but he smiled at her nevertheless and said, 'I think the food is as ready as I can manage. Would you care to come and eat?'

'I should love to. I put a couple of logs on the fire, I hope you don't mind.'

'Very sensible. Come – sit down.'

He pulled a chair out for her and then ladled some of the *peposo* onto her plate.

'It smells wonderful.'

Luca sat down with his own plateful, reached across and passed Francesca the basket of bread.

'Mmm. What's in this?' she said, tasting the stew. 'It's lovely.'

'Nothing exciting – beef, pepper, garlic, possibly too much red wine, and a great deal of rosemary.'

'Exciting or not, it's delicious.'

Luca watched her take her next mouthful, saw the tip of her tongue picking up a stray drop of gravy from her lip, thought to himself how very, very much he would like to leave the table right now, pick Francesca up in his arms, carry her out of the *sala* and up to his bed.

'Tell me about the university, Luca,' she said, wiping the corner of her mouth with the tip of her little finger and then sucking it, a torn piece of bread in her other hand.

Luca pulled his gaze from her mouth and said, 'I'm not sure where to start.'

'Well, tell me about your teaching.'

'Oh, dear, there really isn't much to tell. I have weekly meetings with various groups of usually disenchanted young men, who have vague hopes of becoming advocates. I describe to them the nit-picking details of aspects of the law that have not yet occurred to them; they more or less retain what I tell them, and then they regurgitate it at a later date to prove their academic prowess.'

Francesca laughed. 'I am sure you do yourself a disservice. It must be such a horribly difficult subject to teach . . .'

'Not at all. Things are only difficult if they are unfamiliar.'

'I suppose so.' She paused, frowning and then shook her head. 'But . . . no. I'm not sure I agree with that. Surely some things are, by their very nature, just more difficult to understand than others.'

Luca considered. 'I'd say that familiarity unravels most tangles – but I suppose I'll accept that it might in fact take longer to become familiar with some subjects than others.'

'I don't think it's as easy as that. There are many things in life that I can't imagine I could *ever* learn to do, however familiar I was forced to become with them.'

She ate another mouthful, her gaze still on his.

Luca puffed a soft laugh in his nose. 'I doubt that that's true.'

Francesca smiled at him and his insides turned over again. Struggling to keep this from showing on his face he said, 'How are your little girls?'

The smile widened. 'Oh, let's see . . . they are charming, entertaining, exhausting, constantly hungry and seemingly endlessly energetic.' She counted the girls' attributes off on her fingers.

Luca raised an eyebrow. 'That's not quite what I meant,' he said, 'but I suppose what you say is unsurprising – how old did you say they are?'

There was a momentary pause as Francesca swallowed another mouthful of wine. 'Nearly nine,' she said.

'As you say, an age of endless curiosity and boundless energy – I remember it well with my own two.'

'How old are your boys now?'

'Twenty, and almost eighteen.'

'Very grown-up. Do tell me about them – is there anything I should know before I meet them?'

'Well . . .' Luca began.

Francesca lifted her glass and drank the last mouthful it contained.

Seeing this, Luca paused and said, 'Would you like a little more?'

Francesca nodded, smiling her assent. Luca reached across the table for the bottle, but in doing so, caught the edge of the bread basket with the underside of his sleeve. Snagging on the fabric, the basket flipped up to the vertical and a dozen pieces of bread cascaded across the table, past Francesca's plate and onto the floor. Francesca gave a little gasp.

Silently cursing himself for his clumsiness, Luca jumped to his feet and hurried around the table; Francesca slid off her chair and knelt, her blue skirts crumpling around her legs as she began to collect up the scattered morsels.

'Here – let me do it!' Luca said, crouching down beside her. He looked sideways at Francesca; his eyes were on her face as he reached for the bread, and his fingers touched not the crust he expected but the back of Francesca's hand.

They both froze.

She turned towards him, twisting her hand up inside his own until they were pressed palm to palm. Holding Luca's gaze, she ran her fingertips down the length of his hand and traced a circle, moving across his palm until he felt his thumb being softly wrapped inside her fist. She squeezed and pulled his thumb gently upwards and Luca held his breath. He leaned towards her, his eyes on her mouth.

Then Francesca tilted her face up.

And Luca kissed her.

She laid her hand on his cheek and, while Luca kissed her mouth with a slow and careful deliberation, he felt her fingers stroking in and around the folds of his ear. He moved his lips down onto her neck, and Francesca's head tipped back; she rested her forearms on his shoulders and Luca slid one hand up into her hair at the nape of her neck and put the other around her waist, pulling her in towards him. He lipped the soft skin beneath her chin and breathed in the warm scent of her hair.

A movement by the door startled him.

His mouth still on Francesca's throat, Luca looked past her, across the room.

Gianni stood in the doorway, eyes wide with shock.

The two of them stared at each other for several long seconds, then Gianni turned without a word and shut the door behind him.

'Damn!' Luca said softly.

Francesca opened her eyes. 'What is it?' she said.

'My son. I didn't hear him come in. He was watching us. I don't know how long he had been there.' He ran a hand over Francesca's hair, and kissed her mouth again. 'I should go and talk to him.'

Francesca stared up at him. 'Do you want me to go home?' she said.

'Dear God no!' Luca said, cupping both hands around her face. 'If the truth be told, I don't *ever* want you to go home – but you must certainly not go now!' He pulled her in towards him and wrapped his arms around her. 'It was a shock for him, I suppose. I haven't so much as looked at a woman since his mother died, let alone kissed one, but he's not a child any more . . . he will just have to accustom himself to changes.'

'I'm sorry if—' Francesca began, but Luca interrupted her.

He held her upper arms. 'Sorry? Sorry for what? Listen – I have been wanting to kiss you since I first set eyes on you at San Domenico. I have been trailing around my house like a lovesick schoolboy for days, wanting you so much that I've been good for nothing. Don't apologise, Francesca! I'm the one who should be apologising.'

'You? Why?'

'For rushing you – I'm sorry – you might not—'

'You haven't rushed me.' She hesitated. 'You . . . you are not the only one who has been good for nothing for days.'

There was a long pause.

Then Luca said, 'Can you bear to stay here for a moment whilst I go and find Gianni. I need him to come and meet you properly.'

Francesca started at his words. Luca kissed her again.

'Don't worry – he'll love you, *cara*. It was just the shock.'

Francesca did not seem reassured. She said nothing.

'I won't be a moment.' Luca hesitated. He badly wanted to keep kissing Francesca, but saw in his mind Gianni's shocked stare and knew he should go to his son. 'Please – don't worry. He will understand. I just need to speak to him.'

Francesca nodded.

Gianni was folding a doublet. A large, painted chest stood propped open under the window, and his coat and saddlebags lay across the end of the bed; the contents of the bags were strewn untidily across the covers. Gianni's face was pale, his eyes huge and black in the fitful light from a single candle.

'Gianni—' Luca began.

Gianni ignored him. Turning away from his father, he placed the doublet into the chest, then reached across the bed, picked up a crumpled linen shirt and began to fold that.

'Signora Marrone is my friend Filippo's cousin. We met at that play at San Domenico.'

Gianni turned back and stared at him. The shirt hung from his hands. He said nothing, but Luca felt the anger and accusation as clearly as though his son had hit him. A picture of Carlo's bleeding nose flickered across his mind.

'She is waiting in the *sala*, Gian. I should like you to meet her.'

'Signor di Laviano's cousin?' Gianni said. His voice shook.

'Yes. She was widowed a while back. Has two daughters.'

'Oh, has she? And just what else do you know about her?' Gianni dropped the shirt and glared at his father, and Luca felt a sudden wave of irritation at his son's aggressive tone.

'What else do you *want* me to know? What is this? What the hell is the matter with you, Gianni? Why are you interrogating me like this? I'm sorry you saw what you saw just now – but for God's sake, Gian, you're not a child! I've finally met someone I like very, very much. It's a long time since your mother died, and—'

'It's not that!' Gianni said scornfully.

'What is it then?'

Gianni stared around his room as though trapped in it, his arms folded tightly across his chest, shoulders hunched. Luca wondered if he were trying not to cry. It seemed a ridiculous overreaction.

Luca said, forcing himself to speak calmly, 'Gianni, I am going back downstairs to Francesca. Please come and introduce yourself as soon as you feel able. We'll be waiting for you.' Luca strode out of the room. The door banged shut behind him and he ran two-at-a-time back down the stairs to the *sala*.

Francesca was standing once again by the fireplace, staring into the flames, chewing her thumbnail. She started visibly as Luca came in.

'What did he say?' she said, sounding almost breathless.

Luca shook his head. 'He's more upset than I thought. I'm not sure why. I hope he'll come down later, but—' He broke off, reached for Francesca's hand and squeezed it. 'Please, please, *cara*, don't worry.' Her fingers felt stiff within his own, and he realised with a little jolt of shock that she was shivering. Surprised at the intensity of her anxiety, he turned her to face him, took up her other hand and held them together, clasped inside his own.

'Listen, *carissima*,' he said, 'It simply doesn't matter what Gianni thinks – he'll get used to the idea. Please, there's really no need to—'

The handle of the door to the *sala* clicked.

Francesca snatched her hands away and pulled back from him.

Gianni stood, pale and wide-eyed in the doorway. His eyes on his son's face, Luca reached again for Francesca's fingers.

'Thank you for coming down, Gianni,' he said. 'I would very much like you to meet Francesca – Signora Marrone. Signor di Laviano's cousin. Francesca, this is my son Gianni.'

Twenty-six

It was a full moon, bright as a new-minted coin. The light caught along the edges of the shrouds, turning them to spun silver, as the *Għafrid* rolled gently in the swell of the incoming tide. The youngest member of the crew, on watch up in the sharp bows of the ship, picked out a haunting tune on a home-made pipe; the sound hung above him for a moment, like a wisp of woodsmoke, and then drifted out over the water and disappeared.

Down in his cabin, Salvatore Żuba leaned back in his chair and fingered the beaded braids beneath his chin.

Carlo della Rovere was insistent. Żuba watched him run the tip of his tongue along the edge of his upper lip as he said, 'So, you would consider it then, would you?'

'As I said, *Sinjur*,' Żuba said slowly, running a thumb over the stumps of the missing fingers on the opposite hand, 'I find that it pays to keep an open mind on most things.' He paused. 'I thought I had made it quite clear to you that it's not a venture I have undertaken before – I have always presumed that *inanimate* cargo would be far less demanding to maintain – but, as I explained to you just now, this gentleman in Tunis did say several times that it would be well worth our while to consider it. If the opportunity were ever to arise. And it is, as he pointed out, much safer than the demanding of a ransom.'

'I'll bear it in mind, then, Signore,' Carlo said with a grin. 'If, as you say, the opportunity were ever to arise.'

'But – to more immediate concerns,' Żuba said. 'How much did you get for the alum?'

Carlo tipped his chair back onto two legs, and, arching his back, wriggled a hand down into a pocket in his breeches. He pulled out and held up a bag, which clinked as he dropped it onto the table in front of the privateer. Żuba loosened the strings and poured the coins out onto the table.

'Good. Well done. And the diamond?'

'Disposed of successfully – not a chance of its being traced. The money will be with me by Friday.'

'A certain transaction?'

'Absolutely.'

'You've done well.'

'I told you I was good.'

Żuba looked at him. 'Yes,' he said. 'You did. And you shall have your commission.' With one finger, he slid a number of coins across the table towards his open palm, then handed them across to Carlo. 'That's for today – there will be more when the money for the diamond is in.'

Carlo nodded, clearly pleased, and then said, 'What is the next venture to be?'

'We set sail in a few days' time, *Sinjur*. Our supplies are nearly complete, the refit of the galley is finally finished and the repairs to the mizzen mast are well under way – not much more than a couple of days' work remain, I think. Of course, now that we have such a generous Letter of Marque –' he smiled and nodded towards a small chest, in which lay his prized document '– we can set our sights on considerably higher earnings than we have done in past years. So, I have it in mind to go back to Tunis.'

'Tunis?'

'Aye. Or possibly down as far south as Chebba. I'll try to pick up the best of the wind off the coast of Syracuse, take the *Għafrid* down past the Isola di Lampedusa and hopefully – if my inform- ants are correct, which they most often are – we might very possibly be set to encounter several overladen vessels on their way back from Tripoli who might possibly be . . . *persuaded* to part with some considerable part of their excess cargo.'

'And when shall you be back in Napoli?'

'That will depend entirely upon what we discover on the way out.'

'I wish I could come with you, Signore.'

'You would always be more than welcome, *Sinjur.*'

Carlo's eyes glittered.

Twenty-seven

Oh sweet Jesus! This simply cannot be happening. Small wonder Luca's face seemed familiar at San Domenico . . . God has finally run out of patience with me. For so many years I have been so terribly afraid of dying – of going to Hell. But perhaps not quite frightened enough. It now seems I don't need to worry about death after all. I am to be punished for my wickedness *before* I die.

God must hate me so very much. He's going to take Luca away from me. I knew it would happen. He's given me just this one tantalising glimpse of . . . of what I want so very much . . . just to show me what I've been missing, and then – *oh, Dio!* – He's going to snatch it all away from me.

I think I might be sick.

'Gianni,' Luca says, 'I'm glad you've come back down. Forgive us if we finish our meal. Do you want some?'

Gianni shakes his head.

My plate is still half-full of Luca's lovely *peposo*, but I know I won't be able to eat another mouthful. Luca and I sit back in our places, whilst Gianni pulls out another of the folding wooden chairs from where it stands against the wall; he shakes it open and sits down at the far end of the table.

'Signora Marrone has been kind enough to come and keep me company for supper this evening.'

Gianni stares at me. I can feel my heartbeat shaking my whole body.

Luca has either not noticed the horrible tension shuddering between Gianni and me, or he is deliberately ignoring it. He says, 'Tell us about your trip. How was your journey?' His voice has a brightness about it, but then, when I look at the fork in his hand, I see a tremor in his fingers. Gianni doesn't answer immediately: he cannot take his eyes from mine. Will he say something? Will he give me away and ruin everything? He is holding me out over the edge of a precipice by my wrists and could let go at any moment. A long way below me lie jagged rocks.

He finally drags his gaze from my face and turns to his father. 'It was long, Papa. Very long. Piccione lost a shoe about thirty miles out of Napoli, and we had to walk for a couple of hours until we could find a farrier.'

'Were you able . . . ?'

Gianni nods. 'He's quite sound again.'

'What about Bologna?' Luca asks.

Gianni shrugs. He picks up and begins to fiddle with one of the pieces of bread that lies on the cloth, pulling the soft crumb into tiny shreds. 'I am not sure how helpful it was. Signor Trotti set me various tasks – most of which I've managed to accomplish. But I shan't really know until he has seen and commented on what I have written. Perhaps you could cast an eye over it all for me, Papa, before I give it to Trotti.'

Luca smiles, nods and says, 'Would you like a drink, Gianni?'

'Thank you, Papa.' The bottle on the table is all but empty. 'There's not much left in that one,' he says. 'I'll go down to the cellar and get another.'

'No – I'll go, Gian – take a moment to talk to Francesca whilst I run down and get another couple of bottles.'

Gianni and I stare at each other as Luca leaves the room. His footsteps ring clear on the stairs.

There is a moment's screaming silence.

My face burns with shame as I remember the warmth of this boy's mouth on my scar, the feel of my legs wrapping around his waist, the taste of his skin, the exquisite, shivering conclusion of our coupling; and then he pushes back his chair. He walks across to the window, and, leaning his head upon the glass, says coldly, with his back to me, 'How much has he paid you to be here?'

My head is icy and hollow. 'Nothing.' My voice comes out as a whisper.

He turns to me, arms folded across his chest, shoulders high. 'Nothing? Then why have you come? I didn't think you did it *gratis.*' His voice cracks.

'He doesn't know, Gianni. He doesn't know I'm a— He doesn't know about any of it. I gave it all up the day I met him. I'm not whoring any more. Oh, God, Gianni, please, *please* don't tell him!'

He frowns. 'What do you mean – you've given it all up?'

Tears are blurring my vision.

'It's because of him. Your father. I can't explain now – it's too complicated. He'll be back in a moment. Please . . .'

I hear footsteps; I quickly wipe my eyes and nose with my fingers, expecting to see Luca as the door opens. But a slight, fair-haired young man leans in through the doorway, a twisted smile lifting one corner of his mouth. I stand up.

'So, he's found himself a woman after all this time . . .' the young man says. 'If you don't mind my saying so, Signora, you don't appear to be particularly happy about it.'

There is a loud pause and then Gianni says stiffly, 'Carlo – this is Signora . . . Signora Marrone.'

The man called Carlo bows with an exaggerated flourish and Gianni turns to me. 'Signora, this is my brother.'

The man whose money paid for Gianni's defloration.

Oh, dear God – this is a nightmare!

'And the two of you have been getting to know one another. How nice,' Carlo says. Gianni reddens. Carlo sees his flush and grins. Leaning in close to Gianni's ear he says quietly, though with his eye on me – he means me to hear – 'I know you've developed a bit of a taste for it, after your encounter with that beautiful bitch of Michele's, but this one here is Papa's, Gian. Hands off, I'd suggest.' He pats Gianni's cheek softly with the flat of his hand.

Gianni swears, glares at Carlo as though he is trying not to hit him, and then, with a last swift glance at me, turns on his heel and leaves the room, slamming the door behind him.

It opens again a second later, and an anxious-looking Luca, a bottle of wine in his hand, says, 'What in God's name is the matter with Gianni now? He almost knocked me down the stairs.'

'Told you the other day, Papa, he lacks a sense of humour,' Carlo says. His mouth is still twisted in amusement. 'Excuse me – I have things I should be doing. Delighted to have met you, Signora.' He bows ostentatiously to me once more and, walking with a curiously boneless gait, leaves the room.

Luca puts both bottles down on the table. 'I'm so sorry, Francesca. Oh, *cielo* – it was probably a dreadful idea in the end, our having our meal together on the night the boys came home.' He turns towards the closed door of the *sala*. 'I have no idea what's got into Gianni.'

I stare at him, the explanation for his son's behaviour screaming inside my head.

Luca stands in front of me and strokes my hair. My longing for him is stronger than my fear, and without my deciding to do it, my arms slide around his waist. He bends and kisses my mouth once more, pulling me in towards him with one hand, pressing the other hand up between us and onto my breast. His knee pushes in between my thighs. A little noise of longing escapes me and I cling to him as though I were drowning. This might be as much of him as I will ever get – I'm going to snatch every second I can have.

But, after a moment or two, Luca takes his mouth from mine, shakes his head and says, 'No – I am going to have to take you home, Francesca. In another moment or two I'm not sure I'll be responsible for what I am doing. I don't want to do anything to compromise your reputation.'

Oh, God. My reputation? I am close to weeping.

'Come on, we'll take our time walking, shall we?' Luca says.

The night is warm, and a faint wind from the south carries a smell of salt, tarred rope and fish up from the dockside. It hasn't rained for weeks: the street is blurred with dirt. The place is almost empty – there are very few people out, though a couple of ragged little boys are sitting astride a low wall, kicking the stucco with grubby bare feet and staring unabashed at the two of us as we pass them.

Luca and I walk side by side, not touching, as close as propriety permits in the open street.

'I'm so sorry,' he says.

'Why? What for?'

'For my son. His behaviour was quite . . . Oh, Francesca, I don't know what to say! It simply never occurred to me that he would react like that – he is normally so good-natured . . . I just . . .' He tails off and I stop walking and turn to him.

'You don't have to apologise for him. He isn't you. It's you I want – not him.' My words hang glittering in the air between us as though I have shouted them at the top of my voice. My unthinking, nakedly honest words, blurting out a sentiment horribly inappropriate for the sedate widow I am supposed to be. Luca stares at me. We stand there in the street, facing each other and not speaking.

Luca does not respond to my outburst directly. He says, 'Perhaps I can see you again. On Monday?'

I cannot speak. My mouth opens, but nothing comes out of it, and I close it again.

My head feels stiff upon my neck and I wonder if I shall be able to move it. But then I manage to nod.

'What are you thinking?' Luca asks.

'That . . . that you know so little about me.' I am an empty eggshell, a stupid, fragile nothing that he could crush with ease in the palm of one hand.

He smiles and lays a hand on my cheek. 'I know as much as I need to know for now, *carissima*. I will have leisure enough in the future to discover the rest. And if it comes to that, the obverse is also true – you know next to nothing about me.'

A melting feeling of warm longing starts in my throat, catching behind my nipples on its way down through my body, when I see the deep laughter lines curving around his mouth.

Luca says, 'It is getting late, *cara*. I should get you home. I will come and find you on Monday morning.' His smile broadens. 'I'm going to take you out. If you are happy to, I should like to take you to see a seamstress friend of mine, the redoubtable Signora Zigolo, and you can choose cloth for a new dress.'

My heart jolts as though I have missed my footing on a flight of stairs. Bianca? Oh, *cielo*! I can just imagine the expression on her face when Luca and I walk into her shop together. I will have to send a note round to her straight away – and hope to God she keeps her mouth shut.

'So that boy who came here that time, is his *son*?' Modesto leans back in his chair and runs the fingers of both hands through his hair. '*Cazzo!*'

I nod. 'Oh, Modesto – it was so terrible,' I say. 'When Gianni walked in, we just looked at each other, and – Oh, *God*!' I cover my face with my hands and bend forwards until my knuckles rest on the tabletop.

'But he said nothing?'

I shake my head. 'No. I think he thought at first that Luca had paid me to be there.'

Modesto says nothing, but there is a new stiffness about his expression that has been there much of the time since I returned home from the play and first told him about Luca. My hovering suspicions about Modesto's feelings are growing stronger by the day, but I cannot think too deeply upon this right now: my heart is in too fragile a state just at present, to withstand much probing or investigation.

I ask him for paper and quill.

'Luca is taking me to Bianca's on Monday morning,' I say. 'He has no idea that I know her, and I simply have to warn her to keep her mouth shut, before she sees us together. You know what she's like.'

'Write her a note, Signora,' Modesto says, placing paper, pen and ink in front of me on the table, 'and I'll take it round tomorrow.' He turns away, but I catch his hand.

'Thank you, *caro*,' I say.

He holds my gaze, then squeezes my fingers and smiles. 'Let me know when you're ready,' he says.

I dip the quill into the ink and begin to write. I write too quickly: the nib catches on the paper and a little spatter of tiny droplets flicks across one corner of the page.

Bianca, cara — *I write in haste. Forgive my poor handwriting, but my fingers are shaking. Be prepared for the unexpected, Bianca, and if you have ever considered yourself my friend, for God's sake heed what I tell you now. You hold my future in your hands. I shall be seeing you tomorrow, but I shall not be alone . . .*

And I write as much as I dare.

Twenty-eight

Cristoforo di Benevento leaned out of the window of his apartment in the Castello Svevo and, in a voice that blasted out with ease across the already noise-filled morning, roared his disapproval. 'Hey! You! What the *hell* do you think you are doing?'

Fifty heads snapped round and looked up, searching for the source of the interruption to their activities.

Cristoforo pointed down towards an ill-dressed youth, almost out of sight behind a palisade, holding a heavy black horse by a taut length of dirty rope. The horse was pulling away from him, snorting and stamping. The boy's left hand, held out sideways, clutched a thick switch. 'Yes! You! Holding that Murgese mare! Put that fucking stick down! And stay right where you are!' Slamming shut the casement, snatching his doublet from the back of a chair, he ran from the room.

The scruffy youth hung his head and stared at the ground as Cristoforo shouted. As he yelled, Cristo took in the boy's fear, saw his shame and his ignorance, and pitied him, but there was a weal on the mare's flank, and Cristoforo had watched her shy away from the boy, eyes white-rimmed in frightened pain as the lad had hit her; the boy's actions had been unforgiveable and he had to know it.

His reprimand complete, his anger abated, Cristoforo pronounced sentence. Half rations for a week and two days under lock and key. He watched the boy led away in one direction, the mare in another, turned, and went back inside.

Heavy footfalls followed him up a flight of stone steps. He turned to see an unwashed and thick-set young soldier. '*Capitano*?'

'What?'

'Message for you, Signore.' He held out a note, folded and sealed.

'Thank you.'

Cristoforo carried on up the stairs back to his apartment, unfolding and reading the letter as he went. Cursing at what he read, he entered his room and sat back down at his table. 'Why? Why now?' he said aloud. 'Nearly two weeks it took to get here – and a good week more it will take to get back to Napoli. And I'm needed here! What are they playing at?' Wanting advice, he called his lieutenant. 'Alberto!'

'*Capitano*?' Alberto Maccari peered into the room. Middle aged, mild mannered and self-effacing, but, Cristoforo knew from experience, this was a wise soldier, ferocious in battle, with many hours combat under his belt and someone he was always happy to consult *in extremis*. Cristoforo held out the note. 'Take a look at this.'

Alberto strode across and took the note. 'Are they mad?' he said, looking up.

'Probably.'

Alberto shook his head in disbelief. 'With Soliman stockpiling on the Turkish coast – I know for a fact that a dirty great fleet of galleys has been seen in the harbour at Smyrna within the last two months – we should be consolidating, here in Bari, should we not? Not losing one of our most experienced officers for a month because of some bloody stupid logistical piece of nonsense back in Napoli.'

Cristoforo pushed fisted hands down in the pockets of his breeches and swore.

'Just get the job done quickly, *Capitano*, and return as soon as you can. You can go to Napoli, meet with Alfàn, help him come to a decision, and be back here at Svevo within four weeks. Three if you're lucky.'

Cristoforo stood up and, smiling grimly, clapped his lieutenant on the shoulder. 'You're right, as always, Alberto.'

'You have no choice, *Capitano*, in any case. This is direct from the Crown.'

'It is indeed. I'll just be as quick as I can.'

'I'll look after things while you are away.'

Cristoforo smiled his agreement, dismissed Alberto and strode off into his bedchamber to pack. He would take the opportunity to visit Francesca, he thought, as went. He could find out how her liaison with Vasquez was progressing, and make sure the little Spaniard was treating her as he should.

Twenty-nine

When Luca arrives the next morning, the sun is already high and the sky is a cloudless blue; in the bright light of the street outside, Luca's shadow lies pooled around his feet like a inky puddle. He smiles at me as I step back to let him into the house, and the sight of that smile instantly has my heart thudding up into my throat. Feeling rather sick, I search his face for any trace of accusation or anger, but see none – Gianni cannot yet have spilled out my secrets. A pulse of relief balloons inside my head – I have at least one more day with him.

He takes my hand as he comes into my front room, leans towards me and kisses my mouth. It is a brief, chaste kiss, quite unlike the barely contained insistence of last night, but his grip on my fingers is tighter than politeness dictates and I see yesterday's longing still bright in his eyes. I know that the fire which ignited within both of us then, is still burning as fiercely in Luca's belly as it is in mine.

'Come up to the *sala* for a moment, Luca,' I say, feeling the words push their way up and around the suffocating pulse-beat. 'I'm not quite ready.'

'Oh, dear . . . am I too early?' he says, as we climb to the upper floor.

I lay a hand on his arm. 'No, no – I have just been helping the girls with their lessons, and everything has taken rather longer than I thought it would. It's my fault – you're not too early at all.'

Beata and Isabella look up from their hornbooks, quills in their hands, and stare at Luca as he follows me into the *sala*.

'May I see what you've been doing?' he asks the twins politely.

Both girls nod, their faces rather solemn. Luca crosses the room, and crouches down between where they are both sitting at the table; he carefully examines first one, then the other girl's work. This morning they have been copying the alphabet in both Gothic and Latin letterings into their hornbooks.

'Well, I'm very impressed,' he says, standing again and smiling at them. 'You're both considerably more accomplished than either of my naughty boys were at the same age.'

They both peer up at him and smile, shyly.

'Hmm,' I say, looking at the three of them together with an uncomfortable knot of affection, longing, guilt and fear tightening itself in my chest. Hoping I sound less confused than I feel, I say, with as much of a smile as I can manage, 'Yes, well, practising their letters is the lesson they always seem to enjoy the most. They have something *quite* different to do whilst we are out, though, haven't you, girls? Something about which they are generally *much* less enthusiastic . . .'

Beata and Bella giggle.

I widen my eyes at them and nod towards the big basket under the window. They both put their pens back into the ink pot, then they scramble down from their chairs, grab their hornbooks and run over to the basket; each girl puts her hornbook into it, and each brings out a round, wooden tapestry frame. These are stretched across with linen and are in the process of being – I was going to say 'embroidered' with coloured wools, but in truth the word 'disfigured' would be more accurate. This is not my daughters' most

274

accomplished activity; though, being one in which any lady is supposed to be easily proficient, I'm determined that they will improve. They glance down at the frames, realise they each hold the other's work, and exchange them, pulling a face at each other as they do so. They come back to sit back down in their chairs.

'Come on, then. Let's get you started, and then Ilaria can help you with your stitching while Signor della Rovere and I go out for a short while.'

Luca sits in a chair on the opposite side of the table and watches as I thread their needles, knot their wool, and then start each girl on the next section of her masterpiece. I have to admit that I am hardly more gifted in this art than are the girls – but then, not ever having been much of a lady, I suppose, dexterity with a needle has not often been expected of me. Cobbling together a couple of little twig dolls is one thing. Careful stitchery is quite another. My fingers feel clumsy and awkward as I see Luca watching my every move, and several times I fumble the needle as I struggle to begin stitching. I think of the beautiful tapestries in Luca's upper room, worked by his late wife, and my face burns at the thought of my incompetence.

I imagine a pretty woman bent over her embroidery, her needle flickering in the light from a handful of candles as she stitches with the steady speed of the truly accomplished; Luca watches her from the other side of the fireplace, wearing an expression of fond admiration.

I feel, in the face of this image, entirely inept.

I may, until a few days ago, have been increasingly widely considered as highly skilled in my own profession – but of course I now no longer wish to admit to such dissolute expertise. I realise, with a cold drench of shame how very much my sense of my own worth has been bound up in nothing more than my awareness of men's admiration for my body. As the well-born widow that Luca presumes me to be, I know that I should have been accomplished at a variety of domestic skills for years, but, now, trying to sew under Luca's steady gaze, I feel shamefully useless, and I wonder briefly if I have ever actually been any good at *anything* other than fucking.

At Bianca's workshop this morning the shutters have been pushed back, and the sun is slicing the place in two: a thick shaft of yellow light, seething with dancing dust, lies diagonally across the room, gilding everything it touches. The long back wall is lined with deep shelves, stacked with bolts of cloth: calicos and linens, velvets, silks, lawns and damasks. Those that lie in the path of the sun now gleam bright as gems, while others lie more sombre in the shadows. The polished wooden window seat on which Bianca sits to stitch glows golden, and the almost-finished russet doublet upon which she must have been working just before we arrived, gleams in the light like hot embers.

Bianca stands behind her long, scrubbed table, one plump hand shading her eyes. She is smiling – her other hand fingers a long length of a green figured velvet, which lies piled in loose folds in front of her.

'Signore, what a pleasure to see you again so soon!' Bianca says, beaming at Luca. By the merest twitch of a half-glance which she flicks towards me, I understand that she received and read last night's note.

Luca, who is holding my hand, grips my fingers and smiles back at Bianca. 'Signora Zigolo – I'm just as pleased to see you – I have a new commission for you. Can I introduce Signora Marrone?'

Bianca bobs a nod towards me, smiling broadly.

'I'd like the Signora to choose cloth for a new dress.'

Bianca strokes the figured velvet. 'Do you have anything particular in mind . . . Signora?' she says, her eyes dancing.

I can imagine the bubbling laughter she is concealing: subterfuge like this is something I know she will be relishing. I can just imagine her thinking of the sumptuous beaded silks, and the gorgeous, gold-stamped, Genovese velvets she has turned into dresses for me in the past; the shifts she has made me in lawn so fine it is almost entirely transparent. We have sat together in this very room and delighted in planning garments to shock, dresses to thrill, underclothes to delight, and I have of course often enjoyed recounting stories of all the licentious acts I have committed, dressed in Bianca's beautiful creations.

She, as a former whore, has always found my tales diverting and amusing.

I can hear my stories and Bianca's laughter as if they float like cackling imps in the very air around me, and I can hardly believe Luca is not hearing them too. I look across at him, half-expecting to see a worried frown puckering his brows, but he is smiling at me. His smile is so trusting and happy – he makes me feel shamefully traitorous.

But, despite my doubts, I reach forward and run the green velvet through my fingers. 'This is very beautiful,' I say, truthfully. It is a rich leaf-green and feels like the softest peach skin. 'Would you be able to make me something with this – or perhaps you have others like it?'

Bianca says, 'I only received the velvet from the wharves this morning . . . er . . . Signora.'

For a heart-stopping moment, she seems on the point of addressing me as she usually does – as 'cara' – but, thank God, she manages to swallow down the potentially catastrophic familiarity.

'I'm afraid I don't have many other velvets, just at present, but . . . now, you might like this . . . I've a very pretty rose-pink damask, sent down from Florence a couple of weeks ago . . .' Bianca winds the green velvet back onto the bolt, and puts it on its shelf. She then reaches up and pulls down this damask; the heavy bolt lands with a soft thud and she shakes it out across her table, running it lovingly through her fingers. It is really exquisite: thick and soft with a muted sheen. I rub it between my finger and thumb; it is smooth and cool and whispers beneath my hand, and I know I have found what I want.

'Oh, that's gorgeous,' I say. 'It's beautiful. Luca, would you be happy if I chose this one?'

Luca takes my hand again. 'I'd be delighted with whatever you chose. But, since you ask – yes, I think that's particularly lovely.'

'Very well, the rose damask it is!' says Bianca, beaming at both Luca and me. 'Come on, Signora, into the back room now, and I'll take your measurements.' She points towards the little back room in which I have so often stood for fittings, and Luca crosses the room to sit down on Bianca's work bench.

'I'll wait for you here,' he says.

I go before Bianca into the back room. Turning round and leaning her ample weight on the door, bumping it closed with her behind, she says in a hissed whisper, her eyes positively bulging with curiosity, '*Cazzo!* Francesca, you outrageous, scheming little strumpet! How in the name of heaven did you manage this one?'

Thirty

Filippo felt winded. He sat down heavily on one of the cross-frame chairs in Francesca's front room, and stared, open-mouthed, at the black-eyed manservant. A high-pitched whine of panic began somewhere in his head: how was he going to survive this? What would he do? Without his hours here each week, he wondered if his chronic frustrations might drive him, at best, to ill-advised folly, at worst, perhaps even to madness. He rubbed his fingers backward and forwards along the arm of the chair until the wood began to feel hot.

'Can I see her?' he said.

The manservant eyed him inscrutably. 'You have to know that her mind is irrevocably made up, Signore,' he said. 'She's said she wants to talk to you, but she's told me to tell you not to expect any sort of change of heart.'

'Can I see her now?'

A nod. 'She'll be down shortly.'

Filippo felt a jolt in his chest: he had presumed he would be shown up to Francesca's chamber to talk to her. Her chamber . . . with her bed in it.

The manservant left the room and Filippo stayed in the chair. He felt quite numb. As he sat thus swaddled in unthinking insensibility, he realised that his groin was aching. He had arrived here some ten minutes before, more than ready for his eagerly antici-pated hours of wanton indulgence: the familiar need for relief had been thick in his throat and swollen in his breeches, and he had smiled cheerfully and unsuspectingly at Francesca's eunuch as he had been shown in off the street. But, instead of taking him upstairs, the eunuch had sat him down in here and . . . and . . . pole-axed him.

He was now, he realised, in physical pain.

Filippo heard voices on the stairs. She was coming down. He stood up.

The door opened.

Francesca was wearing a dress he had seen her wear once before – a tight-fitting, dark-green one; thin black lacings fas-tened the bodice across the front like a ladder, with a wide stripe of her shift showing beneath. These were new laces, he supposed miserably: she had let him cut the old, gold ones clean through, with scissors, on that previous occasion, rather than have him take the time to unfasten them properly. As though she couldn't bear to wait. Something uncomfortable shifted in his belly at this thought.

As Filippo looked at her now, though, it struck him that, although she was wearing the familiar dress and her hair was braided much as it usually was, something about her was different. He could not quite work out why.

'Filippo . . .' Francesca said. Her mouth lifted in a tight, wary smile.

He could feel again the texture of that gold lacing between the blades of the scissors. Remembered the sound of it snapping; saw again the edges of the bodice springing apart as the tension was so suddenly released. He swallowed awkwardly.

'Filippo, I'm so sorry,' Francesca said.

He wondered if he would be able to speak at all. After a moment, he managed to say, 'Why?'

'I'm not planning to tell anyone else the truth, but I know I have to tell you.'

Why did she have to? Was he somehow special to her, in a way that her other patrons were not? His heart lifted a fraction.

And then plummeted, as she said, 'Because you introduced me. He's your friend. You have to know the truth.'

Filippo frowned. What was this? Who was she talking about?

'I'm in love with Luca.'

A long pause. The words hung suspended in the air between them.

'And . . .' She hesitated. Bit her lip. Breathed in a long breath. 'And, I believe he cares for me.'

'Does he know? Know about . . .' He tailed off, jerking his head upwards in the direction of the bedchamber.

She shook her head slowly. 'He fully believes me to be your cousin.'

Filippo could feel himself sagging, like a punctured bladder. His shoulders drooped, his face felt heavy; it seemed as though his insides were all shifting downwards; they might even fall right out of him, he thought: they might soon be no more than a glistening pile of abandoned entrails, a greyish-purple heap, stinking, and buzzing with flies.

And then a horrible, sickening sense of its all being his own doing swept through him, hollowing out a cold space in his head as it went.

If.

If.

If.

If he had not invited Francesca to that play – if he had just gone alone, as he had done before, as he could so easily have done this time – Francesca would not have met Luca. If she had not met Luca, she would – at this moment – be upstairs with him, unlacing her clothes and preparing herself to entertain him.

He supposed that God must be punishing him at last for his years of selfish and self-indulgent infidelity.

Francesca now crossed the room and held both Filippo's hands in hers. Up close, he saw that her eyes were wide with entreaty and – unexpectedly – with fear. Her voice quivered as she said, 'I have to ask you, Filippo – no, not ask . . . *beg*. Please, please, *please* . . . I'm *begging* you – keep my secrets.' She paused, then said, 'It wasn't ever going to be possible to hide this from you. Oh, God! I am going to have to ask you to lie for me – for who knows how long. You're Luca's friend, Filippo – if things turn out well for Luca and me, we'll no doubt meet in times to come, you and your wife, and Luca and me. With one unguarded sentence in the wrong company, you could destroy any future Luca and I might ever have together. Any time I ever see you, Filippo, I'll be waiting and watching, trying my best to smother my fear of what I know you could do. I know that. But, I know too that you're a good man. A kind man, and—'

There were bright tears in her eyes.

And he realised what it was about her that was different. Her assuredness – her brazen, libidinous, energetic assuredness – was quite gone.

The courtesan was dead.

A vivid sense of a loss of opportunity clanged in the newly emptied space in Filippo's head and a slightly nauseous lurch of anger rose and fell in his throat. But then, much to his surprise, shoving their way past his aching groin, past his wretched, frustrated disappointment and the stabbing of his fears for the future, came striding a pair of unexpected emotions: sympathy and compassion. He put his arms around Francesca, in a way he had never done before: in tenderness. Holding her against his chest for a moment, he said softly onto the top of her head, 'What sort of man do you imagine I am, Francesca? What can you think of me? Do you really think that – out of pique, or spite, or a desire for revenge, or whatever it is – I would ever deliberately spoil your chances of real happiness?'

Francesca pulled back from him, stared up into his face for a moment and then began to cry.

Filippo was glad that Maria was asleep when he arrived home. He had stayed only a matter of another few minutes at Francesca's – it had still been light when he had left her house – but, not feeling robust enough to face his wife, he had wandered through the city and down to the sea, where he had sat on a low wall, staring out over the water until well after dark.

He intended to spend that night – as he often did – in the smallest of the three bedchambers. The bed in here was narrow and the mattress was thin. He usually pretended to curse the lack of comfort, although he knew in his heart that in fact he rather relished the aggrieved sense of martyrdom it offered him: it had always been a way of sweetening the sourness of his guilt. A sense of shame at his infidelity was something which had hung around him like a bad smell ever since he had first been introduced to Francesca, but, as he lay on the lumpy bed and thought about it now, he realised that, over the years, the increasing familiarity with the routine of his Wednesday visits had somehow given his licentious disloyalty an air of artificial respectability.

Now it was over, though, he wondered in hindsight if it had actually just been rather grubby.

Filippo had always tried to convince himself that his arrange-ments with Francesca provided the least disloyal solution to the intransigent problems of his and Maria's marriage: it might be that Francesca asked for payment for her favours, but he had never quite been able to see her as a whore. She was more like a *friend*, he had always told himself, a friend who understood his needs and his difficulties; a friend who was happy to offer him a solution to his frustrations, without hurting Maria. It was not, after all, as though they had been lovers. Francesca had never even made a pretence of loving him – he was sure of it, and glad of it. He had never loved her – not the way he knew he loved Maria. He and Francesca had never coupled other than as a commercial transac-tion and now he was grateful for that, too. He had been astounded by her beauty; frantically aroused and joyously liberated by her flamboyant lack of inhibition; he had been comforted by her con-sistent refusal to judge him. But though his body might have been all but possessed by her, he knew now that this beautiful woman had never truly reached his heart. This was, he supposed, why he had never felt that he had betrayed his wife.

Now the thought of Maria sent a knife through his guts as he sat down on the edge of the bed and removed his shoes.

He pictured her lying asleep in the next room, entirely unaware as usual of where he had been and what he had been doing. He imagined her sleeping face and wished – with a racking feeling of longing – that he could just open the door to her chamber, climb into bed with her and tell her . . . everything. He realised as he imagined the scenario, what a relief it would be to unburden him-self.

Maria, however, was not asleep and she was certainly not unaware of where Filippo had been. She was sitting up in her bed, a wrap around her shoulders, writing in her vellum-bound notebook, and the words she was writing were sending a thin, wire-like thrill of arousal down through her insides.

If you can't say it or do it, just think it and write it, the woman in the crimson dress had said that day, amongst other, more intimate, advice. *Whatever it is, and however guilty you might feel committing it to paper — just write it. Nobody need ever see it, unless you choose to show them . . . and you'll find that writing can be the most extraordinary release.*

She had bought a notebook that very day, and had determined to write as soon as she had retired to bed. Book, quill and ink at the ready, propped up against her pillows, she had wrapped a shawl around her shoulders, and, with a breath-held sense of fear, heart thudding as if she were about to excise a festering wound on her own leg, she had nipped the end of her tongue between her teeth and stared at the first blank page in her new book. The words she wanted to write had hung in her head, shouting out their robust refusal to leave her pen, and she had pressed herself back against her pillows in suffocating desperation, her loaded quill trembling in her fingers, tilting her chin high to hold back scalding tears.

She had stared at the paper, transfixed by its blankness, and the tip of the quill had hovered above it, pulsing minutely with her heartbeat. She had placed the nib on the page. One tear had spilled over, slid down her cheek and dripped onto the paper. Slowly and painfully, she had scratched a short sentence.

I think my husband is fucking another woman.

That one forbidden word had shrieked inside her head, shocking her with its bald vulgarity, and for a moment she had not been able to breathe.

And then the dam had burst. She had started to write, had

written for over an hour, staining her hands with ink, freckling with black her night shift and the bedcovers around her, cramping her fingers as she penned a minute description of the activities in which she presumed Filippo had been indulging during his hours of absence, week after week. Her long-fettered imagination had crept out through its newly opened door and, blinking in the unaccustomed light, had begun to explore the many acutely painful possibilities that it found right outside. She had resolutely begun peering into forbidden rooms full of sounds and sights that sent shards of shame, like fragments of broken glass, deep into her guts, and, much to her surprise, but just as the crimson-clad woman had predicted, the sense of release was profound.

Perhaps, she had written, as the thought had occurred to her, *shame is only powerful when it is locked away – like a frustrated guard dog, which, tethered night and day, finds that its snarling ferocity builds in intensity, simply because it has no means of release.* Maria imagined this dog, set free to run through the hills, galloping on and on until physical exhaustion finally brought it down, all aggression vanished; she pictured its heaving sides, its lolling tongue, imagined its exhilaration and its sense of freedom. *He will sleep where he falls*, she wrote, *there on the sun-baked earth, savouring the novelty of an exhaustion borne of physical release rather than that of pent-up frustration.*

'I have to let it out,' she had said, aloud. 'Everything I have locked away. I have to let it out. I have to let it race up into the hills and run itself to exhaustion.'

And so she had ranked in her mind a gallery of images – collecting them from all the forbidden rooms she had just discovered, and displaying them as though along the length of a long wall. They were images that she knew from experience would evoke the usual churning, smothering feelings of shame as soon as she saw them, but rather than avert her eyes, as she always did, she would, she had decided, make herself walk along the display; she would force herself to examine each one, until she had confronted them all.

And she would write down what she felt each time, in meticulous detail.

Fully aware of Filippo's presence in the smallest bedroom on the other side of the wall, Maria wrote and wrote until her fingers ached. Finally, rereading her last paragraph for the third time, she put down her pen and the book and stared at the bedchamber wall for several long seconds. 'Now it seems that I *can* think it and write it,' she said to herself. 'And that is a considerable achievement. But it will be of no use at all, unless I can find a way to say it and do it.'

Putting her book, pen and ink into a box, she got out of bed and put the box into the long wooden chest that stood at the end of her bed. A folded blanket lay on the end of the bed. This Maria picked up and placed in the chest on top of the box. She closed the lid of the chest, got back into bed and pulled the covers over herself.

Thirty-one

The door to the inn burst open, and a buffet of sea-smelling air pushed its way into the smoky interior. All the candles guttered; a few went out. Along with some half-dozen others, Carlo della Rovere looked around to see who had arrived.

'Cicciano!' he called across the room, raising one hand.

Michele di Cicciano strode towards where Carlo was sitting. Pushing past seated drinkers and kicking aside an empty chair that stood in his way, he slumped heavily onto a bench on the opposite side of the table, breathing loudly through his nose.

After a moment, he said, 'Get that effeminate little *bardassa* of yours to bring me a fucking *grappa*, will you?'

Carlo called over his shoulder, 'Marco?'

Over on the far side of the room, the thin boy with the greasy pigtail jerked his chin in acknowledgment.

'Two more, can you? In fact, bring us the bottle, why don't you?'

A nod.

'So,' Carlo said. 'What's the matter?'

Michele chewed the inside of his cheek and said nothing.

A pause.

'Has something happened?'

'Seems my money's not good enough for her any more.'

'Who?'

'That fucking, *fucking* Felizzi bitch.'

Frowning, Carlo said, 'Is that such a problem to you? She's only a whore. Fair enough, a bloody good one – a bloody expensive one! – but a whore none the less. Can't you just find another? Surely there must be at least one other woman in this city prepared to lie back and endure, for the amount of gold you might possibly throw at her?'

Michele hunched his shoulders and clamped his folded arms across his chest; one knee began twitching furiously. With his jaw jutting and his breath still audible in his nose, he suddenly reminded Carlo forcibly of an irascible bull. He half-imagined steam coming from Michele's nostrils, and smothered a smirk.

Michele said, his voice obviously deliberately quiet, 'I don't care to be told what to do by a fucking *doxy*!'

Marco, arriving at their table, leaned past Carlo – rubbing his arm along Carlo's shoulder as he did so – and placed a full bottle of grappa and a second glass down on the tabletop. Michele snatched up the bottle even as Marco's fingers released it, splashed a measure into his glass and swallowed it down in one mouthful. Grimacing against the strength of the spirit, he refilled the glass. Emptied it again.

Carlo and Marco both watched Michele for a moment as he refilled and emptied the glass yet again, then Marco laid a hand briefly upon Carlo's sleeve and left.

Attempting to fill the ballooning hollow of silence, Carlo said, 'She has children, Cicciano, did you know?'

No reply.

'Extraordinary things. Twins. Completely bloody identical. I'd be surprised if *she* can tell them apart, let alone anyone else.'

Another silence.

Michele glared at him and said, 'Just why the fuck do you think I'd be interested in her children?'

'No reason.'

A pause.

Carlo went on, 'I saw them the other day. With that eunuch of hers.'

Michele seemed not to be listening. Apparently talking to himself rather than to Carlo, he hissed, 'Bloody, *bloody* bitch! Sends the fucking servant down to tell me that she no longer wishes to see me. Won't even *talk* to me herself.'

'What was the reason?'

Michele's voice quivered with anger. He spoke in what was clearly an imitation of the black-eyed servant's voice and accent. 'She no longer wishes to . . . entertain . . . for a living.' A pause. In his own voice, thick with sarcasm, he then added, 'Apparently.'

'So it's not just you?'

Michele flashed him a look. 'Apparently not.'

Carlo let out a soft breath of surprise. 'She seemed enthusiastic enough the other week, according to my brother,' he said. 'I wonder what's changed her mind so suddenly.'

'The *bitch*. I could just—'

Carlo watched Michele's fingers curl and tighten. He thought of Gianni, face crumpled with anger, punching out at him with his unpractised fist, and fingered his nose, which was still tender. That had all been about the Felizzi woman too: she certainly provoked strong feelings in those people she allowed under her skirts, he thought. Or didn't allow, either, it now seemed.

He thought then, with biting irritation, of the large amount of gold he had lost to this Signora Felizzi, on the occasion of Gianni's defloration. Remembering the conversation he had had a week or so before, with Żuba the little privateer, an idea blossomed in his mind. Carlo felt a slow smile stretch the corners of his mouth, as a possible means of teaching Michele's whore a lesson she would never forget, and of recouping his losses at the same time, began to take shape.

'And what the fuck are you laughing at?' Michele snarled.

Carlo told him. His gaze flicking around the inn to ensure they could not be overheard, he outlined his idea.

Michele stared at Carlo, mouth slightly open. He looked deeply shocked for a moment, but then, his expression hardening, he nodded.

Thirty-two

Luca will be here in a matter of minutes. He told me yesterday that he wanted to take me out on the water this morning – his friend Piero Parisetto has a boat, apparently, which Luca says he sometimes borrows when he feels the need to get away from the bustle of the city. It's only small: not large enough for us to take the girls with us, he says, so they'll stay here with Ilaria today.

I hope they don't mind. Poor Ilaria has been looking thunderous all morning. I have told her and Sebastiano that they are to be dismissed and, although I have offered them both a more than generous sum of money to cushion the blow, Ilaria quite obviously feels very poorly treated. (Sebastiano has said nothing, but then I would have been astonished if he had: he rarely gives his opinion on anything.) Neither of them has actually complained openly, but there has been an unpleasant atmosphere of aggrieved resentment seeping through the house since my announcement, like some noxious marsh gas.

They are leaving on Saturday, and Modesto will be moving in to their room next week. The girls are delighted: they are very fond of Modesto.

Eyeing myself in the mirror, I fiddle a stray wisp of hair back into the complicated web of braids I cobbled together this morning, and fiddle my lower lip between my teeth to redden it. My dress is an old, plain, brown one that I haven't worn for years – it's the most suitable thing I have, I think, for an outing in a small boat. It's been difficult to decide what to wear ever since all this happened: so much of my wardrobe is of course so entirely unsuitable for the supposedly sober Signora Marrone. I have been reduced to three or four dresses, and with two of these, I have had to replace their opulent gold lacings and fastenings with much simpler and plainer ones in an attempt to make them seem a little less frivolous.

All this deceit is making me feel desperately uncomfortable. I'm lying to Luca – God! I hate doing it! Luca is so transparently honest that my duplicity seems doubly shameful, and I feel ever less worthy of his affections. But even the *thought* of confessing the truth fills me with dread: it would be catastrophic.

My heart starts to race as I imagine how the conversation might go How would I set about it? I suppose I would begin by admitting: *I have something to tell you* . . . I'm sure Luca would smile at my trite words, an affectionate air of unsuspicious curiosity on his face. Eyebrows raised, head tilted slightly to one side, he would wait to hear what I had to confess, certain that whatever I was dreading revealing could not be anything very terrible. *I don't know how to tell you this,* I would say, *but* . . . *I am not what I have told you I am.* I imagine myself hesitating, and stammering, and struggling to speak. Luca's brow would furrow at the sight of my genuine disquiet, with the first intimations of real anxiety. And then the horrible truth would all burst out, like being sick. *I am not a widow. I have never been married. My children are not – as I have implied – the legitimate orphan daughters of a respectable merchantman, but are, rather, the bastard offspring of the fifth duke of Ferrara, whose paid mistress I was for eight years, before I ran away from him and set up here in Napoli . . . as a courtesan. I have made a great deal of money.*

Neither this house and its contents, nor my other house in the Via San Tommaso were in fact left to me by my late husband, as I have led you to believe; rather, one was given to me by a grateful patron, and the other was bought, with my own earnings and you should know that every scudo *was earned . . . the hard way.*

I can just imagine the hurt in his eyes; can see him stepping back from me, physical pain and disgust distorting his sweet features. Dear God! How can I ever tell him the truth? But then, if I don't . . . how am I going to be able to live with the guilt of my deception . . . and with the constant fear of discovery? Every time I see Luca, I find myself searching his face for signs of a change of heart. I wonder each time if Gianni, or Filippo – or God knows who else – has told him the truth, and I have to admit that I am finding living like this not far from unbearable. I am balanced on the crumbling edge of this abyss, with incipient panic thumping away in my chest half a dozen times a day – and it is proving to be more arduous than I could ever have imagined.

But I can't walk away from it. It has been less than a fortnight since Filippo took me to San Domenico Maggiore, and turned my life upside down, and already, I simply cannot imagine life without Luca.

It will all quite certainly crash around me eventually. The only thing is – when? How long do I have left?

There is a knock at the front door.

My heart balloons up into my throat, and I pull in a long breath, trying to force it back down to where it should be. I can hear the girls scrambling for the stairs, bickering: they both want to be the one to open the door. Thank heaven, they seem to have taken to Luca, and spend as much time as they can when he is here trying to sit or stand as close to him as they can reach, fiddling with the material of his doublet and peeping up at him coyly from under their lashes. He is lovely with them – funny and kind, and always seemingly interested in what they have to say.

Little feet thud on the stairs again, coming up this time.

'Mamma! He's here!' Bella says, sounding breathless as she pushes open my bedchamber door.

'Tell him to come up to the *sala*,' I say. 'And then go and find Ilaria. I'll be there in a second.'

Bella runs back downstairs, and I give a last tweak to my hair, chew my lip once more, and, leaving my chamber, cross to the *sala*.

Luca's smile is wide and warm when he sees me.

I relax.

Before saying a word, he cups my face in his hands, and kisses me – slowly and with obvious longing; one hand then slides down around my back – and I find myself arching forwards and pressing up against him. Perhaps it's as well that the girls are here or I might not be able to prevent myself from pulling his doublet laces undone.

He stands back from me, drawing breath. 'Looking forward to your boat trip?' he says.

'Very much.'

'I thought we might work our way round the coast to Mergellina, if you'd like to . . .'

A smile and a nod.

'The coastline round there is lovely. I know a place where we can stop and eat our food and then . . . well, let's see what we want to do after that, shall we?'

I think I know what I might want to do.

Beata and Isabella stand on the door sill and wave an enthusiastic goodbye, as Luca and I make our way up the street. Luca is carrying a bag of food – sliced pigeon breast wrapped in waxed paper, bread, cheese, grapes, a couple of peaches and a big bottle of wine. Turning, I call back, 'I'll see you this evening. Be good!'

They continue to wave until we are right at the end of the street. Just before we round the corner, I turn back, kiss my finger tips and blow the kiss towards them. Bella jumps up, pretending to catch it, and Beata tries to snatch it from her sister. Luca laughs. Ilaria, however, standing behind them, stares mulishly at me for a moment, before shepherding both girls back inside.

Luca told me that Piero's boat was small, but when we arrive at the waterfront it seems both long and heavy to me, and I'm more than a little impressed that Luca is happy at the thought of rowing it as far as he plans to. I think Mergellina is at least three or four miles away. The boat is tied up in front of the Parisettos' house, and, much to my delight, it is painted a bright and vivid yellow. Two huge oars are stowed along its length, and two shiny, polished seats – Luca tells me they are called 'thwarts' – cross from side to side. I know nothing whatever about boats, and have absolutely no idea of the seaworthiness or otherwise of this little craft, but it appears to have been beautifully made, its yellow colour is sunny and cheerful, and – best of all – it offers me the prospect of a whole day alone with Luca away from the city, uninterrupted by anyone I know.

'Like it?' Luca says.

I nod. 'It's lovely.'

'Piero and Serafina aren't here but Piero said just to take the boat and go, whenever we wanted. So . . .' He inclines his head towards the boat, holding out a hand to help me in. I take it, and gingerly step across into the boat, which shifts alarmingly under my feet. Settling down onto one of the thwarts, I shift my bottom to free the crumpled material of my skirts and, rather awkwardly, stow the bag of food underneath my seat.

'Comfortable?' Luca says, as he steps into the boat himself. Sitting down, he pulls off his doublet and rolls his shirt sleeves up above his elbows. He folds the doublet and pushes it out of sight.

I nod again. As it happens, I'm not, but I should not dream of saying so.

With the confident ease of the much-practised oarsman, Luca unfastens the rope securing the boat to the shore, picks up one of the oars and, using the end of the blade, pushes against the jetty-edge. He takes up the other oar then, and deftly begins rowing out into open water. For a few moments the only sounds are the slap of the water against the side of the boat, and the soft 'clop' of the oars dipping and lifting.

The close-packed houses that jostle one another right down to the water's edge begin to thin out as we make our quietly purposeful way westwards. Clustered together in joyous disorder, these waterside dwellings are grubby and dilapidated but teeming with life: half a dozen bare, brown-skinned boys are jumping into the water, shouting with ebullient pleasure, pulling each other in and then slithering out up onto the decrepit old jetty, all angled arms and legs. They glitter with sun-filled water droplets as though encrusted with diamonds as they pause in their play to watch us pass, catcalling and waving at us. Several women look up from washing clothes and stare, and at least a couple of dozen men are busy preparing their boats; they take absolutely no notice of us whatsoever.

'About another mile or two westwards, and the coastline is almost deserted,' Luca says, his voice jerking a little in rhythm with the oarstrokes. 'There's a little inlet just past the main harbour of Mergellina – I'm going to take the boat up there.'

We row on, alternating between easy, companionable silences and entertaining conversations. We discuss music and art and history, we talk about poetry and politics — wonderful, fascinating, important things about which no one, not even Modesto, has ever, *ever* cared to hear my opinions.

And we talk about each other.

Well . . . no. That's not quite true. It would be more accurate to say that, in answer to *my* questions, Luca tells me much about himself, and in answer to *his*, I — well, I tell him mostly about Signora Marrone. Sparks of guilt ignite at every lie I invent, but I carefully snuff each spark out as it flares, and, as if in reparation for my deceit, I do my best to offer Luca as many truths as I can risk uttering.

'Tell me something about what you like to do,' Luca says, smiling. 'I think I asked you that day at San Domenico — but I seem to remember that you very successfully wriggled out of answering.'

He rests from his rowing for a moment, balancing the oars horizontally under his forearms; the water running from the blades glitters like tiny shards of glass as it falls back into the sea, and the boat tilts up and over a wave.

I hesitate, thinking fast. What *do* I like to do? Now I am asked, I have no idea.

After a moment, I say, 'I play the lute.' That is just about true.

Luca's smile widens, and he says, 'I love the sound of a lute. Will you play for me one day?'

'I should love to — I'm not very gifted, though.'

'You have to be more gifted than me — I don't play an instrument at all.' He hesitates, then adds, 'Having said that, when I was a boy —' another pause '— I did learn to play the *zampogna* . . .'

He reddens a little as he admits this, and, hearing in my head the dying-cat moaning of that tuneless bagpipe, I cannot help laughing. Putting my hand over my mouth, I try to smother my amusement.

'You're very rude,' Luca says, pretending to sound hurt. 'I was often told I played extremely well!'

'By whom?'

'By my mother.'

I imagine a sweet-faced, dark-haired little boy, awkwardly embracing his great, stiff octopus of an instrument; his cheeks bulge with the effort of producing a sound and he is squinting at a sheet of music, watched by rapt and smiling parents – who seem quite deaf to the horrible sound he is producing.

'Your parents must have been very proud of you,' I say, loving the image, and meaning what I say.

'No prouder than yours must be of you.'

Oh, God. The shock of this is like a douse of cold water and quite wipes the smile off my face. My father, proud of me?

I cover my discomfiture with a counterfeit cough, and hope that the colour I can now feel flaming in my cheeks will be taken by Luca as self-conscious modesty, rather than the biting shame it really is.

I have to change the subject.

'Do you like to read?' I say.

'Oh, dear. I should read much more widely than I do – but there always seems to be so much legal documentation to fight my way through, preparing work for my students.' Luca pauses a moment and then adds, 'Do you know, I'm not sure I would have said so before, but since the day of the play at San Domenico, I think I have something of a fondness for Ariosto.'

I smile at him. 'I couldn't say *what* I think of his work,' I say. 'I don't think I listened to a word of that play.'

'I'm not sure I did either, now I come to think about it.' He is looking at my mouth. 'I was concentrating on quite other things.'

'Perhaps, if we had listened more carefully,' I say, and Luca's gaze lifts back to my eyes, 'we would find that we neither of us care much for Ariosto at all.'

'Perhaps not, but I shall always be particularly grateful to him, whatever the quality of his verse.'

He leans forward, over horizontal oars, now seeking my mouth with his own. He tastes of salt and his lips are cool and wind-dry.

I sit on my uncomfortable thwart, watching Luca's hands on the oars, feeling as content as I think I have ever felt in my life. The rhythmic sounds of the oars are comforting; pleasing. Droplets of water flick from the blades as Luca rows, landing like little cold needles on the sun-warm skin of my arms and the light dazzles as it catches on the ruffled surface of the water. Luca rows on and on. I watch the muscles in his forearms shifting as he pulls at the oars. Our knees bump together on every stroke.

Mergellina, when we arrive, proves to be a tiny fishing village, nestling between a bank of imposing rocky hills and the sea. The harbour is small and neat, and is packed with little boats, both moored and sailing. There seem to be no more than a couple of streets leading away from the waterfront, and a ribbon of a road leads out of the village, obviously heading back towards Napoli.

We row on past the harbour entrance.

'There,' says Luca, holding the ends of both oars with one hand and pointing. 'Can you see over there behind that big rock?'

A pause, whilst I follow his outstretched finger, and nod.

'Just between the rock and that dark patch of headland — that's the inlet. We're almost there. Hungry?'

Oh, yes, I think, as I nod. Yes, I am. Very. But not necessarily for food.

Thirty-three

Beata and Isabella Felizzi sat on the doorstep, each girl's face wearing an identical scowl. Beata scuffed at the dust with the heel of her shoe, and watched as a pebble skittered away from her. Bella picked irritably at a scab on the back of her hand.

'I'm *glad* Ilaria is going. And Sebastiano,' Beata said. There was a short pause and then she added, 'Sebastiano smells of fish.'

'And Ilaria's always cross,' her sister agreed.

'Always.'

'I'm glad Modesto will be coming here instead of them,' Bella said. 'And Lorenzo.'

'Even if he is so fat.'

The girls, despite their ill temper, looked at each other and smothered a snorted giggle.

'I wish Desto was here already,' Bella said, her smile fading again.

Beata fiddled with the fastening of her shoe. 'Why don't we go and see him?' she said.

'When?'

'Now.'

'Ilaria won't want to go.'

Beata paused, licked her lips and then said, quietly, 'Ilaria needn't come. It can be just us.'

'Ilaria told us to stay here,' Bella said.

'She won't notice, if we don't stay too long at Desto's house. She hasn't spoken to us for ages.'

The twins stared at each other as the enormity of their disobedience mushroomed up between them. They both turned and looked over their shoulders in at the open front door. Ilaria was nowhere to be seen.

They stood up.

'We don't know if Desto will be at his house . . .' Bella said.

'If he's not, we can just come home again.'

'We must be back before Mamma gets home.'

Imagining her mother's anger, and determining to avoid provoking it, Beata nodded, and took Bella's hand; they glanced up and down the street, checked behind them once more and set off, hand-in-hand, towards the house in the Via San Tommaso.

Ilaria sat heavily down onto the taller of the two stools in the kitchen. Reaching towards the basket of cannelini beans, she grasped a handful of beanpods and dropped them into her lap. She ran a dirty thumbnail down the outer seam of the pod, pushed her thumb into the slit, levered it open down the length of the bean, and pattered the contents out into a small pewter bowl.

'A disgrace!' she muttered. 'Two good years I've given that woman and now it's dismissal without a word of warning! A disgrace, that's what I call it . . . When you *think* of what I know about her and her carryings-on. Shameless, she is. Quite shameless!'

Ilaria flung the now empty pod onto the floor at her feet.

The pile of podded beans in the small pewter bowl grew steadily larger, the heap of pods on the floor spread wider, and Ilaria continued to mutter angrily under her breath as she worked.

She paid not a moment's heed to the two children she had last seen sitting on the front door sill as she had passed through the hallway from the *sala* upstairs.

Weighing the pommel of a short-bladed, damascened sword in the palm of his hand, Carlo della Rovere, a calculated sneer of pitying incredulity on his face, said to the armourer, 'You're actually being serious? You're expecting me to pay that much – for *this*?'

The armourer shrugged; entirely unconcerned by Carlo's critical tone, he scratched the back of his neck with a short length of unworked iron. 'If you don't wish to buy it, Signore, there are plenty who do.'

'Good. I'm delighted to hear it. I'll leave it to them, then.' Carlo stared at the armourer for several seconds. The armourer, tall, bulky and solidly muscular, stared back, unabashed. Finally, Carlo handed back the sword. He turned away, and began to walk down the Via San Giacomo, sensing the armourer's gaze upon his back. Fully aware that he had lost face, he tried to swagger, attempted to present an unconcerned back view, but nonetheless ducked down the first side street he came to. He pushed his hands into his breeches pockets and strode on past covered shops and stalls, ignoring the handful of chickens and ducks that scattered out of his way with a clatter of irritable wings as he walked.

Some few seconds further on, however, he checked, as two little girls started and sidestepped at his approach. Seeing them there, he recognised them at once, and, realising that this time they were alone, he smiled. An entirely mirthless smile. The ill-thought-out plan for retribution against Signora Felizzi that he had suggested to Michele the other day – a plan which, until this moment, he knew had been little more than an intoxicating idea – seemed suddenly entirely possible. Fate appeared to be smiling upon him, for a change. The hairs on his arms rose as he remembered the details of the conversation he had had that day with Żuba.

'So, tell me, Signore,' he says to the little privateer, 'tell me about your most . . . interesting . . . voyage over the last few months.'

Żuba stares at him without speaking for a moment, twisting the little plaits beneath his up-tilted chin around his forefinger, then says, 'I prefer not to discuss past successes, Sinjur.' He smiles – a twisted smile, showing the gap in his teeth. 'We seamen are superstitious, Sinjur. The sea is a capricious mistress and we try never to do anything to annoy her; anything that might ever tempt her to exact any sort of revenge upon us. Boasting of past exploits might seem to her to be . . . presumptuous.'

'All right then,' Carlo says. 'Tell me about something you might do in the future.'

'Mmm. Well. That would be asking for trouble too, do you not think?'

Irritated now, Carlo swallows the remains of his grappa and says, 'Well, just tell me something interesting. Anything.'

A pause.

'I suppose I might be able to tell you about a discussion I had, a few months ago.'

Carlo raises an eyebrow.

Żuba leans back in his chair. He links his fingers together and stretches his arms up above his head, cracking his knuckles. He says, eyes fixed upon Carlo's face, 'Now, at the end of a mission, Sinjur, the hold of the Ghafrid is usually stacked with gold. Or silks, or spices, or other . . . ill-gotten gains. Inanimate things we've collected, which lie uncomplaining in barrels or boxes, ready to be unloaded at the end of the voyage and then passed to ricettatori, Sinjur, such as yourself.' He pecks a nod towards Carlo in acknowledgment.

Carlo frowns, unsure where Żuba is heading.

'Well, Sinjur, some six months ago, we were stranded for several days in a little port a few miles up the coast from Tunis. Pretty place. Hot, mind. And — from time to time — windless. We were there near on two weeks. Spent a fair bit of my time ashore, and one night I found myself in conversation with a most interesting gentleman who- after discovering something of my way of life — made me an interesting suggestion. How shall I put it? He suggested that, should I ever chance upon any . . . any fair-skinned young ladies who might — or then again might not — wish to travel out his way, he might be able to reimburse me and my men quite handsomely for the privilege of having transported these ladies so far from their homes.' He pauses, then adds, 'The younger the better, apparently. So the gentleman said.'

A shiver of slightly nauseous prurience runs down into Carlo's belly. 'And have you ever . . . ?' He finishes his question with a nod and a raised eyebrow.

'No, Sinjur. I have not. As I say, I always seem to have the hold full of inanimate merchandise. Rather than . . . living cargo.' Żuba licks his lips. 'But that's not to say that I wouldn't,' he adds. 'If the opportunity ever arose.'

'*Buongiorno, Signorine*' he said to the two children, bowing.

They stood still and silent, and stared at him.

'Where are you going?'

No reply.

Carlo began to think fast. 'Anywhere interesting?' he said, smiling more widely.

One of the little girls said, in a voice hardly louder than a whisper, 'Desto's house.'

Not recognising the name, Carlo fished for information, hoping that his hunch might prove accurate. 'I saw you with him the other day, didn't I?'

Two identical nods.

'Is he expecting you?'

Two identical head-shakes.

Carlo breathed a silent sigh of relief. Possibility became feasibility. A brief pause. How best to accomplish what he wished to do? 'He's not at home, just at present,' Carlo said, thinking fast. 'I happen to know where he is though – I saw him earlier on. Would you like me to take you to see him?'

The little girls said nothing, obviously suspicious.

Carlo waited. 'He said he'd love to see you, when I saw him just now. He was just talking about how much he likes your visits.'

At last, one of the girls nodded. 'But we mustn't be long,' she said. 'We have to be back before Mamma gets home.'

'Oh, don't worry, we won't be long,' Carlo said. 'Come on, we'll go and find . . . *Desto*.'

He reached out and took one of each girl's hands. The smallness of their fingers in his palms surprised him. Looking down at each child in turn, he attempted another brotherly smile; they merely stared back at him, wide-eyed and solemn.

They all began to walk together towards the end of the narrow street.

Thirty-four

Luca stows the oars along the length of the boat, and stretches, hunching his shoulders and flexing his fingers. He smiles at me. The boat shifts up and down as it rides the beach-edge wavelets.

'Well. We're here,' he says. 'Shall we find somewhere to eat?'

'This is so beautiful, Luca,' I say. 'Thank you. Thank you for bringing me all this way.'

He leans forward, one knee on either side of my legs, holds my face in his hands and kisses me. 'You don't need to thank me. Just enjoy it.'

He stands up, vaults over the side of the boat, splashing down into the shallow water, and scrunches the little craft up onto the gritty sand. Reaching out with both arms, he lifts me onto the shore. I stand back then and watch him as he tugs the boat a little higher still, trying to imagine how I would see him if I were a detached passer-by. What would I think of him: this tall, dark, untidy-haired man, shirt half-untucked and doublet discarded, his hands strong and capable as he crouches and fastens the rope to a large rock on the beach? I can only imagine that I would see him as I see him now – with a giddy grasp of wanting making my insides dance.

'That should hold for a couple of hours,' he says. 'The tide's almost on the turn.'

I reach back into the boat for the bag of food. Luca takes it from me.

'Come on,' he says, pointing. 'That's where we're going.' And, holding my hand, he starts walking with me along a narrow, rocky path, away from the little inlet. The bag bumps against his leg on each step. We climb for a while, sometimes hand in hand, sometimes one behind the other, until the path flattens out, and divides in two.

'Which way?' Luca asks.

'You've been here before – which way is better?'

'You choose.'

I am charmed by his gentility. 'That way, then,' I say, pointing.

We take the left-hand path, which, within a couple of hundred yards, leads to a secluded grassy clearing. Heavy, tussock-tufted rocks loom up behind us, casting a pool of purple shadow across half the clearing; the other half is brightly sunlit. We are screened from almost all sides by thick, scrubby bushes, beyond which the hillside we have just climbed runs steeply down to the sea.

We could be the only two people in the world.

'Perfect,' Luca says. 'You chose well.' He puts down the bag of food, and we sit next to each other on the scrubby grass. He has been rowing for over an hour – his hair is damp, his shirt is clinging to his back and arms, and now, sitting this close to him, I can actually feel the heat coming from him; he smells of sweat and sun and salt and sea.

'Happy?' he asks.

'What do you think?'

Luca rummages in the bag and brings out the waxed-paper package of pigeon breast, the bunch of grapes, the bread and the wax-covered cheese, placing them all down in the narrow space between us. Opening up the packet of meat, he dips into it, picks up a small piece and holds it out to me. I am irresistibly reminded of Vasquez, and a little worm of shame crawls into my belly at the memory. But I take the piece of pigeon from Luca directly into my mouth, holding his fingers with my own as he touches my lips. My gaze fixed on his, I reach between us for the bunch of grapes and pick one. This I hold up for him to take from me. Smiling, he lips it from my fingers. I offer him another. Murmuring his pleasure as he eats it, he tears off a piece of bread. Pulling it open, he tucks another slice of pigeon inside it, hands it to me and then repeats the process for himself.

For a moment we eat, saying nothing, each watching each other's face, each feeling the proximity of the other's body tugging like the irresistible pull of a lodestone.

Then, 'Drink?' Luca says.

'Please.'

He leans away from me, looks in the bag and says, 'Damn!'

'What?'

'No cups. How stupid – I forgot to bring any.'

'It doesn't matter. We can drink out of the bottle.'

'You don't mind?'

'Of course not.'

Luca smiles at me, his gaze flicking from my eyes to my mouth, and then, easing out the cork, he hands me the bottle. The wine is warm and strong and I drink gratefully. But then, concentrating more on watching Luca than on what I am doing, my hand slips and wine splashes down my chin and onto the front of my dress. Cursing under my breath, I sit forward, holding the bottle away from myself and wiping my face with the back of my hand.

Luca pulls a linen kerchief from the bag; he reaches out with it, and wipes the wetness from my chin. 'There you are,' he starts to say, 'no harm done.'

I look down at the stained front of my dress, feel it with my fingers, and then feel Luca's hand tilting my face back up. 'Stop it. It doesn't matter, *cara,*' he says. 'Don't think about it.'

I cannot take my gaze from his mouth.

It has to be now.

No one can see us.

No one will know.

Thirty-five

Luca saw the colour rise in Francesca's cheeks. The wine she had spilled was wet on her chin; it had splashed like a bloodstain down onto her pretty dress, and he could see her embarrassment flaring in her face. He pulled a cloth from the bag, and reached forwards to dry her face for her. She looked down at her stained bodice.

'It doesn't matter, *cara*,' he said, putting his fingers under her chin and tilting her face back up. 'Don't think about it.'

But then it suddenly did matter.

She was staring at his mouth and her lips were parted and he could see the red-wine stain rising and falling as her breathing deepened and he knew that he was not going to be able to resist. Her tongue-tip ran along the edge of her lip as she lifted her gaze to his.

He had intended to wait. To do everything properly.

But now . . .

He did not think waiting was any longer an option.

As he sat up and leaned towards her, she lay back, eyes fixed upon his. He bent over her. She reached out and began to pull on the fastenings on his shirt; Luca let out a little noise of longing and slid one knee up and over her legs. Francesca undid his shirt and took it off. He held her by the upper arms and rolled, pulling her with him, until she lay above him. Her hipbones pressed into his belly, her knees gripped on either side of his legs. With her fingers and her mouth she began to move hungrily over his skin – across his chest, his arms, round the curve of his shoulders, up the side of his face and into his hair, and he welcomed the greed of her touch, murmuring his pleasure as she worked.

She crawled back then, sliding off him, lipping and licking along the thin seam of dark hair that ran down from his navel, undoing his breeches as she went. Easing them open. Sprawled across his legs now, she twisted around and settled herself. And then he wound his fingers into her hair, closed his eyes and abandoned himself to her.

She stopped. Too soon. Much too soon. Desperate now for her to complete what she had begun, Luca propped himself on his elbows and looked down at her. She lifted her head and gazed back at him, wide-eyed and wet-mouthed.

'Come here,' Luca said. He reached down and took her hands, pulling her back up towards him, and rolling with her again until she lay on her back and he was above her. He wanted her now. He pushed one hand around and under her back, searching for the laces of her bodice; the other moved down towards the hem of her skirts. The linen puffed and crumpled around his arm as his fingers began searching upwards.

And then – with a sharp thrill of shock – he saw that she had tears in her eyes. He froze. 'Oh – *cara* – why? What is it? What's the matter?'

She made no answer, but the tears swelled and began to spill over onto her cheek. She put her hands over her face.

A hot pulse of self-recrimination stabbed through him. He had rushed her. She had not been ready. He had pushed her into a situation she was clearly now regretting – what must she think of him? The first man she had kissed since the death of her husband and he had done this to her. He had been overwhelmed by his own feelings and had thoughtlessly coerced her into compromising her reputation, and now – oh, God! – she would be quite justified in never wanting to see him again. Cursing himself, dreading seeing rejection in her face, he pulled her into his arms.

She began to sob.

Thirty-six

I only wanted to give him my very best. A courtesan's best. I just wanted him to believe himself to be the most fortunate man in Napoli: a man who, after so many lonely years, had found himself an unassuming 'widow', ripe for the picking, a woman who seemed in every way modest and respectable – but a woman who could nevertheless fuck like the king's prize whore. What more could he ask for? *But it's happened . . . you've begun believing your own lies, you silly bitch. You're tricking him. That's all. Corrupting him. Don't fool yourself. The most fortunate man in Napoli? Hardly. Possibly only the most deluded. First the son, now the father. And you think him lucky?*

I am so stupid.

I never used to cry. Until the night of the play, I think I could have counted on the fingers of one hand the number of times I have cried in the past ten years, but now I seem to find myself weeping at least two or three times every day. I'm like a hermit crab, pulled from the safety of its armour: soft and naked and vulnerable without its stolen carapace.

A life of whoring builds you a strong shell. It's never a pretty one – or a comfortable one – but it's tough. You shelter inside it or die. And now Luca has tugged me free of mine for good. I can't imagine ever being able to get back inside it.

The whole of the last ten years blatters at my head as I cling to him, and my tears are hot and slippery against the skin of his chest. A circle of leering, jeering faces surrounds me: every man who has ever paid to bed me is leaning over me and laughing at my pathetic attempts to leave my past behind me, and the tighter I curl myself up against their onslaught, the more completely do I find myself shut away from Luca.

He is muttering soft, soothing nothings as he holds me, one arm pulling me in against his chest, the other stroking my hair. He rocks a little, back and forth, as though I were a frightened child. 'Shh, shh, shh, it's all right,' he murmurs into my hair and his words hiss hot on my scalp. 'It doesn't matter. It was all too soon. It's my fault. It doesn't matter.'

Oh, dear God but it does. Oh, Luca, you have no idea how much it does matter.

My sobs finally subside into shaky, wobbling breaths, and Luca cups my face between his hands, his thumbs stroking my cheekbones. I sniff, and press my fingers up under my nose. Without a word, Luca hands me his shirt. I wipe my face on it and a ragged breath hiccups in my throat. 'I don't deserve you,' I say.

'Don't say that. How could you think such a thing?'

How? Because you deserve better than a soiled, second-hand, immoral trollop who has spent the last ten years doing little more than being fucked – by more men than she can remember. Including your son.

'You are so good, and so kind,' I say, 'and you deserve more than—'

'Stop it!' Luca says, putting his fingers over my mouth. 'I'm not good and kind. I've made you cry. I *deserve* nothing. But I *want* a great deal. I want *you*. What can you possibly have done that could make you imagine yourself undeserving?'

I stare at him, unable to speak.

Luca gazes back at me for a full minute and then says, 'Marry me.'

I hear the words, but I hear them as though I were eavesdropping on someone else's conversation. They cannot be meant for me.

'What?' I say, stupidly.

'Marry me.'

I continue staring at him.

'I've wanted to ask you to marry me since that day you first came to supper, but in the circumstances it seemed wrong to suggest it so soon. I thought then that it would perhaps be better to wait a while – to give my proposal at least a semblance of propriety. I didn't want to rush you. I seem to have spoiled that today, though, so I suppose there's no point in waiting any longer. So will you? After what I've just done – do you think you can still consider it?'

I feel numb.

How can I? How can I accept? If I marry him, I will be sentencing him to a life of shameful lies – if my past remains secret, that is – and if the truth is ever revealed, then I will be condemning him to the probability of being ostracised by everyone he holds dear – I can't do it. Oh, sweet Jesus, I can't bear it! How can this be happening? I am going to have to refuse him. I am going to have to turn away what I want more than anything I have ever wanted. Ever. It cannot be worse than this to stand on a pile of faggots, tied to a stake, with a bag of stinking gunpowder round your neck, watching someone walk towards you with a lighted torch. I open my mouth to say what I have to say, but nothing comes out of it.

Luca looks stricken as the silence stretches out. He stares at me for long seconds, and then looks down at his hands. He says to his fingers, 'Do you think you might be able to consider it, at least, and give me an answer later, when it has had time to sink in?'

I manage to nod.

'Thank you.' He pauses. After a seemingly endless silence, he says, 'Perhaps we had better go back to Napoli now. The tide will be turning soon, and it will be harder work rowing against it.'

Luca's knees keep bumping against mine. On the way out to Mergellina this sent a thrill through me each time it happened – a fizzing sense of expectation – but now it's just making me feel sick. I can't meet his eye. He is avoiding mine. I have no idea what to say to him.

He wants an answer.

But I don't know what to do.

I've never lied about who I am and what I've done, however terrible it's been. And it's been truly terrible at times . . . those first days on the streets at the age of seventeen, lifting my skirts and spreading my legs for pathetic handfuls of coins . . . being at the beck and call of the Duke of Ferrara – the paranoid and homicidal father of my twins – for the best part of eight years . . . and for the past two years I have been struggling up the ladder towards the coveted title of *'cortigiana onesta'*. That's the word – *'onesta'*. I've always been honest about who and what I am.

Until Filippo made his suggestion a few weeks ago.

Of *course* I want to marry Luca. How could I not? I love him. But the horrible truth is that the woman Luca wants to marry is Signora Marrone. Not me. He doesn't know I exist. And unless he can ever truly want to marry Francesca Felizzi – with all her faults and her murky history – then I don't believe I can accept his proposal. How can I?

He has to know the truth, that's all.

I'll tell him when we get home.

Not here – not in the boat. I want to be in my house. I'll tell him everything. Then I'll know, one way or the other. Yes – as soon as we get home, I'll tell him.

Thirty-seven

Modesto drained the last dregs of his wine and put the cup back on the table. He looked around the kitchen, stripped now of all the colourful pots, copper pans, bunches of herbs, and glittering ranks of glassware that had filled the room until a few days before. Everything but the table, two chairs and this last bottle had been wrapped in straw, packed into wooden crates, nailed down and stacked in the front room.

Leaving the kitchen and climbing the stairs, he mentally ticked off the last few remaining items on the inventory. He peered in through each door on the upper floor: the *sala* was quite empty, the small antechamber was no more than a wood-panelled box, and, the big bedchamber had been cleared of everything but the Conte di Vecchio's great mirror and the bed, both of which the Signora had said were to be left in the house. A couple of crates remained, still open, with the last of the Signora's personal belongings carefully packed in them. Not a problem, Modesto thought; the boxes were too big for him to carry downstairs by himself, but he would arrange for the boy with the cart, who had been commissioned to remove the crates to the other house, to help him tomorrow. He did not want them forgotten.

He stood for a moment, regarding himself critically in the

enormous glass. Stocky and barrel-chested, black-haired, dark-eyed; Modesto scowled at his reflected image.

'It's over,' he said aloud, pointing at himself with an accusatory forefinger. 'That chapter's over now, and there's no point regretting it.'

Deciding that he had better get himself over to Santa Lucia to ensure the Signora was ready to receive all these boxes in the morning, Modesto ran back downstairs, grabbed his coat from the back of one of the kitchen chairs, and left the house.

Some moments later, halfway down the Via Toledo it lanced through his mind that he could not remember locking the front door. He debated upon whether or not he should go back to make sure, but, thinking it through, he decided that, given the fact that he would be away a matter of an hour at most, and given, too, how few items were left in the building, there was little need to concern himself.

There was no breeze, and the streets were thick with warm, stale air. Modesto walked briskly, his doublet over one shoulder, side-stepping every now and again to avoid the scattered rubbish and excrement that always seemed to be an inevitable, fly-infested hazard on any journey through the city. Turning down an alleyway so narrow he could have touched the houses on each side had he stretched both arms out sideways, he arrived in the small piazza at the top of the Signora's street.

Her front door was open. Nobody seemed to be concerned with keys today, he thought. He walked down towards the kitchen, and saw Ilaria chopping onions with a long bladed knife. Her eyes were streaming, and her big face was blotched and puffy.

'The Signora not back yet?'

Ilaria shook her head, pressing the back of one hand to her eyes.

'Where are the little girls? Did she take them with her?'

'No. They were out on the front door sill a little while ago. Did you not see them as you came in? Naughty little things, they were playing me up all morning.' Ilaria shook her head. 'I was glad of a bit of peace when they stopped all their bickering and carryings-on.'

Modesto frowned, and walked back into the hallway. He stood with one hand on the banister rail and called upstairs, 'Beata! Bella!'

The lack of response did not immediately alarm him. They quite frequently played hiding games. He ran up the stairs and peered first into the *sala*, into the girls' room, and then into the Signora's chamber, listening each time for the expected breath-held, stifled giggles.

Nothing. He called again, sharply now, with no response.

Back downstairs, he knocked on and then opened the door to Ilaria and Sebastiano's chamber, which proved equally empty.

'Are you sure they are not with their mother?' Modesto said to Ilaria, leaning back in through the kitchen door.

'Yes, I told you – they were on the step, not more than an hour since.'

'Well – they are nowhere to be seen now.'

Ilaria put down the knife and wiped her hands on her apron. 'I'll go next door. They've probably gone in to aggravate poor Signora Bellini in the next house.'

She hurried off while Modesto went from room to room once more, banging open doors he had opened no more than a moment before, lifting covers, snatching back hangings he knew hid nothing and calling pointlessly into silence.

The hair on the back of his neck stood up when Ilaria came back into the kitchen, breathless and clumsy in her agitation: her eyes were now fearful and her hands were twisting together.

'She's not seen them. I . . . I don't know where they are, Signore,' she said, her voice high and sharp.

'How long since you last saw them?'

The dull flush that suffused Ilaria's face implied longer than the hour to which she admitted.

'Where's your husband? Might they be with him?'

She shook her head. 'He's away. He went down to Sorrento two days ago to see his mother, and—'

'You stay here,' Modesto interrupted, 'in case they come back, and I'll start searching. They can't have gone far.' Attempting to believe his own reassurance, he pushed his arms into his doublet sleeves, and ran out of the open front door.

'Trotti said he wants those outlines finished by next Tuesday,' Gianni said. 'Have you done yours yet?'

'Are you mad? I haven't even started it!' The young man spoke cheerfully, and, looking across at Gianni, he grinned. 'Trotti can whistle for it. I'll get it done as soon as I can, but . . . well . . . other . . . erm . . . other *things* seem to be taking precedence at the moment.'

Gianni laughed. 'One of those *things* being the lovely Signorina Tacciarello?'

The young man smirked. Gianni shoved at his friend's arm, pushing him off balance, and he staggered, before righting himself and reaching to push Gianni back. Gianni, however, sidestepped neatly out of reach and, both laughing now, they broke into a run. Reaching the end of the street, they vaulted over a low wall, and set off across a dilapidated, weed-infested square towards their preferred tavern, outside which several wooden benches were already peopled with a noisy assortment of drinkers. The boys sat down in the only two available seats.

'Do you want an ale, Raffa?' Gianni asked.

'Yes – but I'll get them. You paid last time. Stay here – I'll go and find Fat Massimo.'

'You'd have to be blind to miss him.'

Laughing, Raffaele handed Gianni his things – a roll of paper and a large wooden-backed book – and strode off towards the tavern door in search of the landlord. Gianni leaned back in his seat, closing his eyes and crooking one foot up onto the opposite knee. The conversations of the other drinkers drifted past him; he listened with half an ear.

'. . . *and before I had taken more than two steps outside the house, she throws a bloody pitcher full of wine into the street after me! Full! What a waste! As if any of it had been my fault!*'

'*Does she admit to having been there?*'

'*Cazzo! Are you joking me? My Caterina admit to a fault?* Il Papa *is as likely to admit to a belief in witchcraft!*'

Gianni smiled to himself and opened an eye. At least twenty men were milling around outside the tavern: most were seated on the benches, a couple of them had sprawled on the ground and one had perched a bony buttock on the edge of a table. In one group of some half dozen drinkers, the husband of the self-righteous Caterina was red-faced and gesticulating, though, despite his obvious discontent, he seemed to be rather enjoying being the centre of the group's attention.

But then a very different voice pushed through the deep-toned male hum of conversation. A softer, much higher-pitched voice. Anxious. A child. 'How long will it take to get to where Desto is? We mustn't be late for Mamma.'

'Not long – I told you.'

Gianni's head snapped round at the sound of the second voice. A shiver trickled like cold water across his scalp and down the back of his neck. Carlo. Carlo was walking quickly across the top corner of the square, hand in hand with two identical little girls. Gianni was certain he had seen these children before – but where? Why were they familiar? He stared at the trio, leaning forward on his bench seat, searching his mind for some clue as to where he had seen them.

And then a memory . . .

Two little girls are threading beads, sitting on the floor of Signora Zigolo's workshop. Their similarity is enchanting – Gianni stares openly for a second, quite entranced by the sight of the extraordinary replication of such overt prettiness.

They look up.

'Buongiorno,' he says, bowing. Both little girls smile at him – identical smiles. 'Forgive me for staring, Signorine – but I was quite taken aback by your beauty,' he says, with a creditable attempt at solemnity.

Both girls giggle behind their hands.

'Hmm!' says Signora Zigolo. 'Pretty they might well be, but make no bones about it, Signore – this is a pair of very naughty little minxes – and there is no hope for them: for they are just like their even naughtier mother!'

Gianni laughs and the little girls wriggle with pleased embarrassment, and giggle even harder. Charmed, he bows again, then straightens, thanks the Signora, and leaves the shop.

Why? What the hell were these children doing with Carlo? Whoever they might be, they were certainly nothing legitimately to do with his brother – he was quite certain of that. Getting to his feet, without realising what he was doing, and dropping his and Raffaele's books onto the ground, Gianni started walking away from the tavern, ignoring the muttered comments of the drinkers.

One of the little girls was sniffing, wiping her nose and eyes with the back of her hand. She tried to push her hair out of her eyes with the hand held by Carlo, and he jerked it irritably back towards himself. Gianni could see that Carlo's boneless, loping stride was too fast for the children, who were trotting in their attempt to keep up with him.

He heard his brother say crossly, 'It's not far now – we're going down to the water. You like the docks, don't you?'

'Is that where Desto is?'

'We'll see him when we get there – I told you.'

A pause.

'I want to go home. I don't want to see Desto any more.' There was a whining sound in the child's voice now, and when Carlo spoke again, he sounded more irritable than ever.

'Well, we *have* to go there now. He's expecting us.'

Even from the other side of the square, Gianni could see that both girls were now struggling to pull their hands from Carlo's grip, but Carlo's white knuckles implied an equal determination not to let go.

Gianni sped up, but a second later, Carlo and the children rounded a corner and were lost from sight. Gianni began to run. He reached the same corner in seconds, but they were nowhere to be seen. He listened, but could hear nothing.

Raffaele edged his way out of the tavern, a pewter mug of ale in each hand and a flat loaf of bread tucked under one arm. Looking across to where he had left Gianni, he saw only an empty space on the end of the bench, and their three books abandoned on the ground. One book was bent and scuffed, and several pages had torn free. The rolled papers had blown across to the opposite side of the square. Of Gianni, there was no sign at all. Raffaele stood staring around him, bewildered.

At the end of a dingy alley that opened out onto the dockside, a thin young man with a greasy pigtail leaned against a wall, his weight on one foot, scuffing down into the dirt with the toe of the other boot. He was scowling: a deep frown had creased between his brows, his lower jaw jutted, and, somewhat surprisingly, the gleam of a tear flashed along the lower edge of one eye. He bit his lip.

'Marco!'

The boy looked round to see one of his fellow tavern workers.

'Hey, Marco! Thought you'd gone off to . . . er –' the new arrival grinned and waggled his eyebrows '– to meet the lovely *Signor Stupendo*.' He pushed his tongue into his cheek so that it bulged out sideways for a moment. 'Where is he, then? Not turned up? Lost interest?'

'Fuck off!' Marco hunched his shoulders and turned away. A vivid picture of Carlo's sneering dismissal the day before came into his mind. '*For God's sake, Marco – what did you think? That I was in love with you or something? A cheap little* bardassa *like you? Please! Allow me a touch more sophistication!*' Remembering the pleading tone in his own voice that he had not been able to prevent, he felt a sickening lurch of shame creep up into the back of his throat like a cold slug.

He slouched off down towards the water, trying to pretend that he was not hoping to bump into Carlo. He was well aware that he was being foolish even *thinking* of attempting to see him again so soon, but he couldn't help wanting to. It was like having a full bottle of *grappa* within reach on a shelf, when you badly needed a drink, and not reaching for it. Carlo could well be here, Marco thought, trying to convince himself that he merely wanted to catch a glimpse of his friend. He wouldn't talk to him, or touch him or anything. It would just be good to know . . . whether he was on his own . . . or with someone. If Carlo *was* on his own, Marco told himself, then he would stay out of sight, go home, wait a few days, and then try to win him round again. He knew the tricks – he'd be sure to be able to manage it. It had worked before. He would have to play a different game this time, though – convince Carlo that he only wanted a bit of fun. Nothing more. All those things he had said before had been a big mistake, he knew that now.

He sat down on an upturned barrel some yards down from the tavern entrance, in sight of the curve of the dockside, and, lifting one hand, began to fiddle with his pigtail, winding it round and round his forefinger, wondering how long he would have to wait for a sight of his friend. He had resigned himself to being there for some time, so it was with a frisson of shock that he saw Carlo almost immediately, coming towards him from the far end of the dock. He held his breath.

Carlo was not alone.

Marco stood up, puzzled. Carlo was scowling, and he was hand in hand with two little girls. They were moving fast – Carlo striding, the little girls almost running. Some few yards away, their eyes met; Carlo's scowl became a not very pleasant smirk and the stride slowed to a swagger.

'Still hanging around waiting for me, Marco? After everything I said?'

Marco could feel his cheeks flaming. 'I wasn't waiting for you.' Despite his best intentions, his voice sounded petulant and he wished he had kept his mouth shut.

Carlo gave a faint, contemptuous snort.

Marco wanted very badly to turn away and ignore him, but his curiosity was too much for him. 'Who are they?' he said, nodding towards the children.

He saw Carlo cast them a strange, hard, greedy look. 'Hopefully,' he said, 'the key to a small fortune.'

'What do you mean?'

'I can't stop to talk now, I'm in a hurry,' Carlo said, 'but . . .'

His next few words raised gooseflesh on Marco's arms.

The front door of Francesca's house was unlocked.

Michele di Cicciano pushed it and stepped up into the hallway. He called and listened. No reply. The place was empty. Wandering down towards the kitchen, his footsteps echoed on the wooden floor, and, when he tried clearing his throat, the noise sounded overloud in the stillness.

Michele climbed the stairs. The *sala* had been stripped out, he saw: the tapestries had gone, the furniture and ornaments were no longer there. The windows were bare.

She had moved out.

The bedchamber door was ajar. Pushing it open, Michele's gaze took in the bare-mattressed bed, and the great floor-to-ceiling looking-glass in its ornate gilt frame. He stared at his reflection for a moment or two before turning to the bed. Up near its head were two big boxes, packed with straw and a number of Francesca's belongings.

'Ah. So you've not quite left the place yet,' Michele muttered, pushing aside the straw at the top of one of the crates. On top of a number of other objects lay a painted wooden box. This Michele picked up. He turned the small protruding key, and opened the lid.

'Well, well, well – you deceitful little bitch! So this is where you hid it!' he said softly, picking out a slim, needle-pointed knife and testing the edge of the blade carefully against his thumb.

Reaching back into the box, he found three vellum-bound note-books. He thunked the blade of the dagger into the wood of the bed head, and then picked up the uppermost book.

'*Book of Encounters* . . . Hmm. That sounds as if it might make for a bit of entertaining reading.' Michele grinned and sat down on the bed; he hutched himself up to lean back against the wall, and, flipping the laces undone, he opened the book. He licked his lips, rubbed his groin absentmindedly, and began to read.

Modesto stood at one entrance to the Piazza Mercato, and stared about him, his heart beating frantically in his ears and up in his throat, his breath catching in his throat. He felt sick. The city had never seemed so big, so crowded or so labyrinthine. A clock struck three. The Signora would be home at any time. He had to go back to the house. He could not leave it to Ilaria to break the news.

Thirty-eight

'Oh, God . . .' I whisper. My face is numb and my mouth no longer seems able to form words. I manage to mumble, 'How long ago?'

Modesto swallows awkwardly. His gaze is fixed upon mine. His breathing sounds heavier than usual, as though he has been running. 'I got here about an hour ago,' he says, 'and . . . and Ilaria told me that she hadn't seen them for at least another hour before that—'

A white-hot anger slices down through my belly at the thought of Ilaria's unforgivable negligence. I remember the mulish expression on her face as Luca and I left for Mergellina . . . and the kisses my children blew towards me as we left. My hands are trembling as I look across at her, but she is staring resolutely at the ground, her face a dull, purplish red, her fingers twisting together. 'Has anyone been up to San Tommaso to see if they're there?' I say, in a voice that does not sound like my own.

Modesto says, 'I went straight away – they weren't there, so I came back here.'

'But they might have got there after you left.' *Please let that be what has happened.*

Luca takes my hand. I look up at him. What happened in Mergellina seems a thousand miles away. He squeezes my fingers, and says, 'San Tommaso? Do you mean the Via San Tommaso d'Aquino?'

I nod. Luca clearly wants to know more, but I don't know what to tell him. Hesitating, I glance across at Modesto, who says straight away, 'She means my house, Signore. The little girls like coming to visit.'

Luca nods. 'But is there anywhere else they might be – any favourite places? They're most likely to be somewhere familiar.'

'The waterfront. They like the boats,' I say, trying to force back images of sodden little bodies floating face-down in dark water between berthed ships.

'We need to cover as much of the city as we can, as quickly as possible. Someone should stay here, in case they come home. I'll run down to the docks,' Luca says.

I nod. Luca's voice sounds as though it is coming from the other side of a shut door. I say, in the same unfamiliar, flat whisper I managed just now, 'I'll go up to San Tommaso.'

'Are you happy to go there on your own?' Luca says. 'Would you rather I—'

'No.' I interrupt him. 'You go to the docks. You said – as much of the city as quickly as possible.'

I don't want him anywhere near that house.

'I'll go there now, then I'll run home,' he says. 'If Gianni and Carlo are there, they can help search.'

'Is there any point in telling the *sbirri*?' I say, knowing the answer already.

Modesto runs his hand through hair already standing up on end. 'That bunch of useless degenerates? No, they're worse than nothing – bloody vandals. We'll have to manage ourselves. I'll go up to Girolamini – to the market. They like it there. I've been twice already, but it's so busy at the moment, I could easily have missed them.' He turns to Luca. 'Signore—'

I hear him begin to explain where on the waterfront we like to take the twins. I see Luca nod, feel him put his arms briefly around me as Modesto stops talking. My head feels as though it has been wrapped in gauze: I can neither see nor hear the people around me clearly. Everything is moving too slowly and sounds no longer seem to be coming from expected directions.

Luca leaves with Modesto; I hear their footsteps running together, up the street towards the docks and the market. I turn to Ilaria before I go myself, jabbing towards her with my finger, and hear my own voice saying, 'Don't you leave this house, Ilaria – do you hear me? You have to be here – in case they come back.'

She starts to say something in reply, but I have already left and do not listen. I begin to run, skirts clutched in both fists, feeling my chest swelling against the tight lacing of my bodice. The streets are busy, and people react indignantly as I push past them.

'Cazzo*! Mind where you're bloody going, woman—*'

'*What's the hurry,* mignotta*?*'

Checking frantically to right and left as I run – what if they are there, and I miss them? – I run through familiar streets as though I am a complete stranger in the city. I call and call. The girls' names crack in my throat. The words thud out in painful pieces around my running footsteps. People turn round and stare, but nobody offers to help. I can't remember how to blink. My eyes are stinging.

The front door of the house in the Via San Tommaso is open.

'Beata! Bella! Are you here?' A second's desperate hope. 'If you are in this house, you two, you come down here now, do you hear me?'

Silence.

My chest is heaving from the running, my throat is raw and my rasping breath is loud in my ears. But that's all I can hear. They're not here.

And then a door clicks open upstairs.

'Girls?' It comes out as a shriek. I run up the steps, two at a time, skirts bunched in my arms, to see the door to my bedchamber slowly opening.

It is not the twins.

Michele. He leans lazily against the edge of the doorframe. 'Good. I hoped I'd see you,' he says. 'I've been here some time – reading your diaries. Very entertaining.'

I don't understand. How . . . ? Why is he here? 'Have you seen my children?'

'Why? Should I have?'

'They're missing – I have to find them.'

'Well, they're not here.' Michele's voice sounds scornful. Then he says, raising an eyebrow, one side of his mouth lifting in a smile, 'Maybe Carlo has them – he said he might be able to—'

I interrupt him. 'Carlo? Who's Carlo?'

'A friend. I don't think you know him – but I believe you've met his little brother. Gianni, I think his name is.'

Gianni? Then, yes, I have met Carlo. *'This one here is Papa's, Gian. Hands off, I'd suggest.'*

'I don't understand,' I say. 'Why . . . why would this Carlo have my children?'

The expression on Michele's face is frighteningly calm. He pushes out his lips in a *moue* of consideration. 'Well. Let's see now. You've upset quite a few people recently, *cara* – me included. This friend – Carlo . . . well, he lost quite a lot of money because of you, the other week – I think he's hoping to find a way of making it back.'

'What . . . what do you mean?' I am struggling to breathe.

'Ooh, well now . . . very pretty little creatures, Carlo told me your girls are. And he said that a mutual friend of ours – a rather

334

successful little privateer – told him the other day that little girls such as—'

'No!' I grab Michele's doublet sleeves and shake him. 'Where is he? Where has he taken them? You get them back!'

He flaps his elbows out sideways, knocking my hands away. Snatching at my wrists, he pulls my arms up in front of me. His twisted smile now quite gone, he holds me in close to his chest and says, 'I've really no idea where they are – if he has them, that is. But perhaps . . . a little later on . . . I might be able to help you search.'

He dips his head forward, seeking a kiss.

'You bastard! Oh God, you bastard!' I turn my face away from him and try to wrench my arms out of his grip, but he is too strong for me. 'Let go of me! Michele, let go! I have to go – I have to find my children—'

'No. Not yet.' He speaks through closed teeth.

'*Vaffanculo!*' I try kicking him, but my skirts are too thick and too heavy, and when Michele starts walking backwards, back into my bedchamber, he pulls me with him with ease. Modesto's voice sounds somewhere in the back of my mind – *You've always just been too bloody proud to ask for help when you need it, he'll go too far one day* – but Michele has reached my bed and swung me around to lie across it; he holds me down with one knee and Modesto's voice vanishes. I push hard at the heavy knee, and say, trying to sound irritated rather than frightened, 'Get off, Michele, stop it! Let me go! I told you I've stopped working. I'm not doing this any more.'

Michele holds my chin tightly between finger and thumb, and tips my head backwards. Bending down to put his face close to mine, he says, 'No, *cara*, that's not quite true. *You* didn't tell me that, actually. Your eunuch did. *You* did not have the courtesy to tell me anything, if you remember.'

It is hard to speak with my head pushed backwards like this, but I manage to spit out, 'Fuck off! I have to find the girls.'

'Not till I get what I want, *troia*. And this time, I'm having it *gratis*.'

'Get *off*!' I shove as hard as I can at his leg, and it slips off me, but, before I can sit up, he reaches out and grabs at something that is sticking out of the bed head.

I freeze.

My head is a hollow sphere.

In his fist is the knife I took from him the other week. The silver one with the little round 'ears'. The one I've been keeping in my box. Modesto said he would dispose of it for me – but I stopped him. Michele touches up under my chin with the very tip of the blade. It stings. The scar on my back twinges in sympathy.

'You'll not tell me what I can and cannot afford, this time, *cara*,' he says.

Air from the open casement blows cold on my legs. Then, as he tugs awkwardly at his breeches, one-handed, his right arm jerks and the blade snicks in a bit further. A little noise of panic smothers itself somewhere inside my head. I cannot take my gaze from Michele's. I cannot speak. I swallow, and feel the lump in my throat move the knifepoint sideways. He is too strong for me – and I can do nothing to stop him. The needle-point of the blade catches under my chin; where the point is digging in, it no longer stings – it is just achingly sore.

Detach my thoughts.

I have to block him out. Block Michele out. I can't rid him from my body but I can force him out of my head. I've done it before. Think. Think of what? Luca. Think of Luca. Luca rowing. Luca's hands on the oars and the sun on the water. Luca's hands on my face. He says he wants to marry me. He has no idea who I am but he wants to marry me anyway. Marry me. Marry me, marry me. The rhythm of Michele's assault becomes quicker, more insistent, and then, unthinking, his hand slips and a hot flash runs up from my throat, past my ear and up into my hair. I hear a sharp cry, which I think might have come from me. I press a hand to the side of my face. Michele seems not to notice. His eyes are unfocused and his mouth has twisted, almost as though he is in pain. But at last he pulls away from me, standing quickly, a strangely triumphant look of distaste distorting his face, as though he has just successfully accomplished a task he found entirely disgusting throughout.

'I'm going now,' he says. 'Now I think about it, I don't think I have time to start searching for any children now, but if I see my friend Carlo, I'll tell him you want him.'

He strides to the door of the chamber. I have turned my head away from him, but I hear him pause in the doorway, and he adds, 'By the way – as I was saying just now – I had a chance to read some choice extracts from your . . .' he pauses, and then says with a sneer '. . . *Book of Encounters* while I was waiting for you this evening. You really are a grubby little bitch, aren't you?'

I hear him spit onto the floor, then he leaves the room. His feet are loud on the stairs, and then the heavy latch on the front door clatters; there is a blurt of sound from the street outside, and then the door bangs shut again.

A silence.

I have to find the girls.

God knows how long I have been here. I can't stay. Now he's gone, I have to find them. It's getting dark. A grubby bitch, he said. A bitch. Is that why they've taken my children?

I try to stand, but my knees are shaking and, as I slide off the edge of the bed, they crumple under my weight, and I am sitting on the floor. The side of my face hurts. I reach for the place with the tips of my fingers: it is warmly wet, and my own touch makes me feel sick.

'Get up . . .' I say aloud.

But I don't seem to be able to get up.

There is a soft noise in my ears, a quiet hissing, like running water.

I lean against the side of the bed and close my eyes.

I suddenly feel very tired.

Thirty-nine

Gianni stopped and looked about him. The alley he was in was narrow and cramped – it was strewn with rubbish, and smelled of salt and dirt and stale fish. An old woman peered out at him from a shutterless window – an lightless opening like a crack in a rock; she glared suspiciously at him for a second, her knobbed fingers gripping the broken sill, and then she drew her head back inside, muttering to herself.

'Where the bloody hell are you, Carlo, you bastard?' Gianni muttered aloud, looking around him. 'Where have you gone?' Ducking down into a gap between two buildings on his left, he headed towards the docks.

Sunlight was dancing in sparkling fragments on the wavelets out in the bay; but between the berthed ships, the water moved more sluggishly – it was a slow-swelling, brackish brown, and as it shifted and lifted, sodden flotsam pushed up almost silently against the bellies of the ships and moved away again. A greasy-looking rat walked gingerly along a taut rope down towards a bollard. Eyeing Gianni for a second, it jumped down onto the cobbles and skittered away beneath a pile of broken boxes.

The dockside was quiet, almost empty, apart from a couple of nut-brown sailors, an elderly man in a filthy, salt-encrusted doublet, and a scrawny, pigtailed boy about his own age; the boy was sitting on an upturned barrel, wiping his eyes and nose on his sleeve.

Gianni ran up to the sailors.

'I'm sorry,' he said, breathlessly, 'but have you seen a man – a young man about that tall?' He held up a horizontal hand. 'He has light-brown hair, he's wearing a doeskin doublet and he's with two little girls?'

One of the sailors shook his head, raised his hands apologetically and said something incomprehensible in a language Gianni had never heard before. Gianni forced a smile of thanks, then strode across to where the old man in the dirty doublet was splicing the end of a fraying rope without looking at it.

He repeated his question. 'He's with two little girls. Have you seen them?'

The old man gazed up at Gianni with milky eyes and shook his head, frowning doubtfully. 'I'm sorry, lad. He might have been here, but I've not been noticing.'

Gianni nodded, feeling sick, and ran down towards the boy on the barrel.

'Might have done,' the boy said in answer to Gianni's question, swallowing what sounded like the tailend of a sob.

Gianni's heart thudded. 'Please – which way did they go?'

The boy wiped his nose again and stared down at his smeared hand. 'Why do you want to know?' he said, looking back up at Gianni. His gaze raked Gianni from head to foot. 'Interested in him, are you?'

Gianni frowned. 'What? What do you mean? He's my brother.'

The boy's expression changed. 'Your brother?' he said, now sounding surprised.

'Yes – does it matter? I just want to know where he is.'

'He told me he was going to the tavern round the corner,' the boy said, jerking his head in the direction of the entrance to another filthy little alley. 'But from what he said, I don't think he was planning on staying long.'

'Thank you,' Gianni said over his shoulder as he began to run again. 'I'll try there now. Thank you very much.'

Gianni grabbed the old tavern-keeper by the upper arms and shook him. 'But don't you understand? It's urgent!' he said. 'He's my brother, and . . . and he's . . . he's in danger. I have to catch up with him and warn him.'

The lie seemed plausible enough.

'Someone told me he had come in here,' Gianni said, still gripping the tavern-keeper's arms. 'He was with . . . our two nieces. Have you seen them? They don't seem to be here. Could they have gone upstairs? Please – I have to find them! Do you know where they might have gone?'

The old man stood still, saying nothing but staring pointedly at Gianni's hands on his sleeves – first the right, then the left. Gianni let go, stood back a step and held his hands up, palms forward, as though in apology. The tavern-keeper shrugged, and jerked with his chin towards the far end of the room.

'They went down there,' he said.

Gianni pushed his way through the busy tavern and saw, almost hidden behind a table, a steeply descending set of ladder-like steps. He scrambled down, and opened the tiny door that stood at the bottom. The narrow corridor that led away from the door was long enough to disappear out of sight, and was entirely lightless.

'Oh, God!' he said with a lurch of his stomach. 'He's taken them into the *sottosuolo.*' His father's voice, sharp with anxiety, rang in his ears from years before as he stared now into the blackness. *'Don't you ever let me catch you going in there, do you hear, Gianni?*

341

People get lost in the sottosuolo. *Lost for good. People go exploring and never find their way out again. And some people actually live down there – wicked people running from justice.*' People like Carlo, Gianni thought. Swallowing down a smothering feeling of panic, he hurried back up to the cramped back room of the tavern and squeezed his way through the crowded tables to where the old man was now standing with a pewter jug in his hand.

'Please,' Gianni said, trying to keep his voice calm. 'Please – do you have any sort of lantern I could take?'

The old man put the jug on a nearby table, lifted down a thick torch from a wall-bracket, its end wrapped in flaming, pitch-soaked sacking, and handed it to Gianni. His face was quite expressionless as he said, 'Mind you don't let it go out. I doubt you'd find your way back in the dark.'

Gianni nodded, and, holding the torch above the heads of the many drinkers, pushed his way back to the steps.

The corridor into which he stepped now, had long ago been hacked out of the tufa stone on which the whole of the city was built; it was narrow – hardly wider than Gianni's shoulders – and he had only inches of headroom. The torchlight sent black, flickering shadows dancing across the walls. Gianni held his breath, straining his ears as he walked. He could hear nothing but his own hissing pulse-beat.

Creeping forward, moving sideways, holding the torch out behind him, he picked his way carefully as the ground began to slope more steeply downwards. The stone was damp and slippery, and a sharp smell of mould hung in the air. The tunnel meandered down another few hundred yards, then bent sharply to the right, where a short flight of steps, carved as precisely as if they had been in a cathedral, dropped the level of the tunnel another dozen feet or more.

At the bottom of these steps, Gianni stopped. In front of him, a square of denser black a few feet ahead indicated that some bigger space lay before him. Holding the torch up high, he saw a vast cavern. Its walls soared up twenty, thirty feet, and the floor stretched away from him into blackness; the cave could have held a crowd of a thousand, with room to spare, Gianni thought, panic beginning to lump uncomfortably in his throat.

He pulled a linen kerchief from a pocket in his breeches and, crouching, tucked one corner under a stone. Having thus marked his way out, he walked into the emptiness, looking around him, searching for Carlo. His own shadow lay out to his right, long and black, rippling over the uneven floor as the torchlight bobbed and swagged.

The cavern was empty.

Carlo and the two little girls were nowhere to be seen and the cave was silent, but, as Gianni stared around, now holding the torch above his head, he saw the mouths of another three tunnels, leading out of the cavern at the far end.

Which one had Carlo taken?

And where did it lead?

He walked across the cavern, glancing down over and over again at his feet, treading carefully over the rubble and rocks that made up the floor. All he could hear were his own tentative footsteps and the skittering clatter of small lumps of rock, dislodged as he walked.

And then a long, wailing moan sliced out into the air around him.

Gianni froze.

Every street Modesto saw teemed with children, and every child he saw was one of the twins; his heart jumped in his chest at each sighting, then plummeted with sickening disappointment. Every person he asked gave the same shrug, the same frowning, apologetic headshake. *'No, Signore, I'm so sorry – I've seen nothing.' 'What do they look like, again, Signore?' 'I hope you find them, Signore.'*

He began to walk back towards the house in Santa Lucia.

Ilaria was sitting on a stool by the ashes of the untended kitchen fire when he arrived. Her swollen face and tear-blurred eyes gave him the answer to his unspoken question.

He said, 'The Signora not back? Nor Signor della Rovere?'

'No one.' Her voice was thick and distorted.

'I'll go back up to San Tommaso.' Keeping still was unbearable. 'See if she's still there.' He could not stay and wait. Banging back out through the front door, Modesto began to run.

It took him no more than a few thudding moments to reach the other house. The front door was unlocked.

Wheezing a little, he pushed it open. Stepped up into the entrance hall.

Silence.

'Signora?'

Nothing.

'Are you still here?'

Nothing.

He turned to leave.

The faintest sound from upstairs. The softest murmur and a shifting of something along the floor. Hardly more than the rustle of fabric. Modesto ran up the stairs two at a time. The door to the Signora's former bedchamber was wide open. Holding the door handle, he leaned in – and froze.

She was crumpled on the floor at the side of her bed, her head leaning up against the mattress, and, around where her face was pressed against the brocade covering, a dark stain had soaked out like a poorly executed map. A thin trickle of darkening red ran down her neck and the top edges of her shift and bodice were discoloured. Her eyes were closed.

'*Porca Madonna!*' he said under his breath. Then, running to her and crouching beside her, pulling her up into his arms, he said, 'Signora? Francesca! Francesca – open your eyes! Oh, Christ! Look at me!'

Her head hung back over his arm.

Under her chin was an untidy, ragged-edged wound about the size of his thumbnail; a long cut sliced upwards from this, running in front of her ear and up into her hair, which was stiff with dried blood.

'Oh, God – please, no!' Modesto muttered. 'Francesca!'

He touched near the edge of the cut with a tentative fingertip. Her skin was warm. Looking down at the red-stained dress, he saw, with a vertiginous swoop of relief in his belly, that her chest was rising and falling. He shook her gently.

'Come on, *cara*, open your eyes!'

Her mouth opened a little. A soft, wordless noise sounded somewhere in her nose. Her eyes opened. And closed.

Modesto pushed one arm further around behind Francesca's shoulders, and tucked the other in underneath her knees. Pulling in a breath and holding it, he lifted her, staggering a step backwards as he shifted her weight up into his arms. He put her down gently onto her bed.

'What's happened to you? Who did this?' he muttered, unsure what to do first. 'Water,' he said then. 'I need water. That cut needs cleaning.'

He ran back down the stairs and into the kitchen. Everything crated and packed in straw. Nothing useful, though – no water, no cloth. Nothing.

'*Merda*!'

For a moment, he stood irresolute, then ran back upstairs.

'*Cara*, can you hear me?' he said, softly, crouching down once again at the side of the bed.

Francesca made another soft noise in her nose, and then he saw her run her tongue along her lower lip, which was split and swollen. She opened her eyes.

'Have you found them?' she said in an almost soundless whisper.

'Who did this?' Modesto said, deliberately ignoring the question.

'Have you found them?'

He did not know what to say. 'We . . . we're still searching. I've not seen Signor della Rovere – he might have them.'

She turned her head away from him.

'Who did this to you? What happened?'

There was a long pause. Then she said, so quietly that he had to lean close to her face to hear her, 'Michele.'

'Oh, no . . . no . . . no. The bloody bastard!'

'Please,' she said then, reaching for his hand.

'What? What is it, *cara*?'

'Get Luca. I want Luca. Michele said Carlo's taken them.'

'I don't know where he is . . . Signora.' He paused. 'Who's Carlo?'

She ignored his question. 'Please, find Luca for me.'

'I don't want to leave you on your own . . .'

'Just find him.'

She curled on her side and closed her eyes again. With another nauseous lurch, Modesto looked at the gaping cut around the edge of her face and at her ashen colouring. He took off his doublet and laid it over her shoulders. 'I'll find him, Signora – I'll be quick.'

He ran down the stairs and left the house, taking care this time to lock the front door.

The voice that cried out into the silence of the cave was high pitched – clearly that of a child. Swearing softly to himself, Gianni began to run, stumbling and tripping on the uneven ground, but the noise stopped before he reached the far side. Facing the three tunnel mouths, he stood, irresolute, looking from one entrance to another.

'Oh, God – which one?' he said aloud, his voice sounding flat and deadened in the vastness of the cavern. Holding his breath as he tried to decide, he heard a cough, coming from the central tunnel. He started to run, but the flames from his torch streamed out backwards and he slowed, holding the light out as far to the side as he could to keep it from catching his hair. The tunnel was narrow and dank, and the knuckles on his outstretched hand caught against projecting lumps of rock as he walked.

Some hundred yards further on, the tunnel suddenly widened. As Gianni slowed his pace and lowered the torch, there was another cough, and a voice called out. 'Who's there!'

Gianni stopped.

Carlo's voice said, 'I can see your light. Is that you, Cicciano?'

Gianni held his breath. He heard footsteps, and then Carlo's face appeared, underlit by a small, flickering lantern. Seeing Gianni, he gasped and swore.

Holding his torch high again, Gianni said, 'What the hell are you doing down here, Carlo, and where are those children? What have you done with them?'

'None of your business.'

'I mean it, Carlo. Where are they? Come to that – *who* are they?'

Carlo looked mulish. 'Like I said – it's none of your fucking business.'

Gianni's right hand balled into a fist and he moved in towards his brother. 'You tell me. Who are they?'

'You really want to know who they are?' Eyeing Gianni's fist, Carlo sounded suddenly defensive. 'They belong to that over-priced bitch of Michele's.'

'I don't— *What?*' A wild jumble of images of Francesca flashed into Gianni's mind. *His fingers on her breasts. The taste of honey. The puckered skin of the little scar on her back.* And then the picture that had been haunting him for days: *his father on his knees on the floor of the* sala, *with his hands in Francesca's hair and his mouth on her throat.*

Gianni shook his head. 'I don't understand. Why? Why have you brought them down here?' he said.

'Fuck off, Gian! It's nothing to do with you!'

Dropping the torch, which rolled away across the rock floor, its flame licking out horizontally across the stone, Gianni grabbed Carlo by the neck of his shirt. '*Why?*' he asked again, both fists pressed up under Carlo's chin. Carlo's voice was distorted by the pressure of Gianni's hands, but Gianni heard his scowling mutter, 'Justified retribution.'

Gianni pulled the neck of his brother's shirt upwards, dragging him up onto his toes, and Carlo dropped his little lantern. It landed on the rock floor with a clatter and the flame went out. Gianni pushed Carlo back against the tunnel wall, shoving his brother hard up against the wet tufa. 'What do you mean? Where are they? You foul, despicable, disgusting little *shit!*' He banged Carlo's head back against the wall on the last word. 'I'm ashamed to think you're my *brother*.' Another bang. 'Where *are* they?' Bang.

'Fuck off!' Carlo shoved at Gianni's chest, trying ineffectually to push him away. 'Fuck off and leave me alone!'

'Tell me!' Gianni shouted, with another, harder bang. 'What have you *done* with them?'

Carlo kicked out at Gianni, aiming for his groin but catching him on one thigh. Momentarily unbalanced, Gianni let go. As he righted himself, Carlo scrambled away but, grunting with the effort, Gianni threw himself at his brother. He caught him around the waist and together they fell to the ground, where, in scuffling confusion, they rolled across the uneven rock. Taller and stronger than his brother, it took little more than seconds for Gianni to pin Carlo down. With one knee on his brother's chest, he clutched the neck of Carlo's shirt in both fists. 'Where are those girls, Carlo?' he said through his teeth.

There was a pause, and then Carlo muttered, 'They're in the next tunnel. She cost me all that money, didn't she? Their bitch of a mother. And Cicciano's friend Żuba said he could . . . could . . . get a . . . good price for—'

Gianni felt a nauseous leap in his guts. He scrambled to his feet, backing away from Carlo as though he had been burned, and then stood staring down at where Carlo lay sprawled on the rock. 'Where are they? What have you done? Am I too late?'

Carlo didn't move. Gianni kicked him. 'Where *are* they?'

Carlo grunted. Scrambled onto all fours. Stood up slowly.

Gianni's fists were up; he flexed his fingers, re-fisted them. 'Go on – where are they?' he said, picking up the still flaming torch and held it high. Carlo reached for his extinguished lantern and then began to walk back down the tunnel towards the cavern. Gianni followed.

They re-entered the cavern. Carlo crossed to the next tunnel entrance. He nodded towards it. 'They're down there.'

'Go on then – show me.' Putting his free hand in the small of his brother's back, Gianni pushed Carlo, who stumbled over a loose rock and fell onto hands and knees. 'Get up!' Gianni said. Carlo pushed himself back up onto his feet. This new tunnel was narrower than the first, and the low roof was a smooth arch. Bending slightly, to avoid hitting his head, Gianni followed Carlo and together they walked along the tunnel as it curved around and down.

A second later, the keening whimper broke out again. It echoed through the tunnel, a sound of terrified despair, raising the hairs on Gianni's neck and arms. 'Oh, God. You bloody bastard, Carlo,' he muttered.

They rounded a final corner, and the tunnel came to a dead end. Gianni pushed past Carlo, held the torch up and saw the little girls, sitting pressed together on the rock floor. Their eyes were wide and black in the torchlight and they had their arms around each other. One of them was crying. Seeing Carlo, though, the weeping stopped; they both scrambled to their feet, and shrank as far back as the tunnel would allow, uttering incoherent little sounds of terror.

'You wait back there!' Gianni hissed at his brother, and Carlo stepped backwards into the shadows and slid down the wall to squat on his heels. Gianni laid the torch down, crossed to the children and crouched in front of them. He held out a hand towards them, but they cowered away from him and their whimpering grew louder.

'I promise I won't hurt you,' Gianni said softly. 'Do you remember me? I met you at Signora Zigolo's that day. You were playing with beads. I know your mamma – I know where she lives. I'll take you back to her. You're quite safe now.'

The girls stopped crying, but did not move.

'Has Carlo hurt you?' Gianni asked. 'That man. Has he done anything to hurt you?'

Neither child replied or moved. They just stared at him, huge-eyed and silent. Gianni said, 'Listen: I'd like to take you back to your mamma now,' he said. 'Will you come with me?'

Two brief nods.

'And *you*.' Gianni turned back to Carlo. 'I don't even know what to *think* about you, let alone know what to do. God alone knows what Papa will say . . .'

Carlo said nothing.

Gianni said, 'I'm taking these children home now, and we're taking the torch with us. Come with us, or stay here and make your own way as best you can – to be honest, just now –' Gianni felt his voice quiver in his throat '– I don't give a two-*scudi* shit what you do.'

He stood, staring at Carlo for several long seconds. Carlo stared back, swallowing awkwardly, grimacing as though it hurt to do so. Then, gaze still fixed upon Gianni's face, he got slowly to his feet. Gianni saw the two little girls cower as Carlo stood up.

'Don't worry,' he said. 'He can't do anything to you now. You're quite safe.' He took one child by the hand, and she in turn grabbed for her sister. They followed Gianni past Carlo, flattening themselves against the opposite wall of the tunnel as they passed him.

'Wait a moment,' Gianni said. 'I'm going to light his lantern for him. Though he doesn't bloody deserve it.' Picking up the still-burning torch, Gianni crouched down and tried to relight Carlo's lantern. Twice it simply sputtered and went out, but on the third attempt, he succeeded, and he placed it down on the floor of the tunnel. It threw a feeble, dirty-yellow light across a few feet of rock.

Gianni looked from the lantern to where Carlo still stood slumped against the wall. One of his eyes was puffed and bruised; his lip was split, and he was holding his head awkwardly over to one side, shoulder hunched. His brother's usual swaggering insolence had quite gone, Gianni realised; Carlo was small and broken, sagging against the tufa like a bag of damp grain. A faint sensation of sympathy rose in Gianni's throat, but the little flutter of compassion was quickly drowned as a wave of sickening anger broke over it.

He opened his mouth to say something to Carlo, but then closed it again.

Glancing back to make sure that the lantern he had left was still alight, Gianni held the torch high and then reached out with his free hand towards one of the two children. She took it, and in turn grabbed hold of her sister. Together the three of them made their way back to the tunnel mouth, where Gianni's linen kerchief was still tucked under its lump of rock. He picked it up, pushed it back into his pocket, and, one behind the other, he and the children walked back up towards the door to the tavern.

Gianni did not allow himself to turn around to see if Carlo was following.

His mind was racing.

Almost unable to believe what he had just discovered, he felt physically sick at the thought of what might lie ahead. He had no idea what to do. Should he report his brother to the authorities? Was he morally obliged to do so? Carlo had abducted Francesca's children . . . had intended to hand them over to be *sold* into . . . into . . . God knows what fate. He would have to be punished, Gianni thought, but might such a crime be serious enough to merit burning? Might he hang? Could he, Gianni, really do it? Really hand his brother over to the thuggish and unreliable *sbirri*? Or –

another thought struck him – would it be the Spanish who would mete out whatever form of justice Carlo's actions deserved? Where would Carlo go now? What would he do? Gianni pictured Carlo, alone with the feeble lantern in the *sottosuolo*, and his head teemed with painful images.

'Are we nearly there yet?'

The little voice from behind him was tremulous and tired; Gianni sensed the child's exhaustion and found a smile for her. 'Yes. Nearly back at the tavern, and then we'll go up into the city.' He squeezed her fingers. 'We'll find your mamma, shall we?'

'Do you know where her house is?'

'I think I do, but I've only been there once. If we can't find it, though, we'll go to my house and Papa will help us. He knows where your mamma lives. I think you know my papa – his name's Luca. He's – he's a friend of your mamma's.'

They both nodded.

Ahead was the narrow door to the tavern. Gianni let go of the child; transferred his torch from one hand to the other; opened the door. Light from the tavern flooded into the corridor; a hum of unthinking conversation hung thickly in the smoke-filled air above them.

Some way down the Via Toledo, Modesto stopped running. Leaning against a wall, one hand fisted against his doublet front, he felt his breath rasp in his throat. Damn his bloody chest! He had run too far today. Losing his singing career had been one thing – but possibly losing the Signora because he could no longer run for more than a few yards without wheezing like a pair of bellows was quite another. He closed his eyes and drew in several long, uneven breaths.

'Modesto!'

Modesto's eyes snapped open and he stood up away from the wall. The Signore was running up from the direction of the waterfront. Alone.

'Have you found them?' the Signore called as he ran.

Still wheezing, Modesto shook his head. 'No. But you have to come. Come with me – now.'

The Signore frowned. 'Why? What's happened?'

'No time to explain. Just come now.'

Forty

Luca dropped to his knees at the side of Francesca's bed. With fingers that shook, he pushed her hair back from her face, picking from the gash on her cheek a few stiffened wisps that had become caught in it and soaked. Her eyes were closed. 'Oh, *cara* . . .' he said, in little more than a whisper. 'How did this happen? Who could have done this?'

Francesca made no reply.

Modesto appeared in the doorway with a pottery jug in his hand. 'Water, Signore,' he said, putting the jug down on the floor near the bed. 'From the house next door.' He pulled a length of linen from his breeches pocket. 'And a cloth.'

'Thank you,' Luca said. He dipped the cloth into the water and squeezed it out. Wrapping it around his fingers, he gently dabbed at the dried blood that was already crusting at the edges of the long cut. At his touch, Francesca sucked in a breath and opened her eyes. She reached up and took the hand in which he held the wet linen. 'Luca,' she said, softly. 'Thank God . . . you're here. Are they with you?'

Luca glanced at Modesto and swallowed. 'No, *cara*,' he said. 'We . . . no – no they're not.'

Francesca sat up, eyes wide. Luca held her hands and said, 'But I know we'll find them. Let me wash this for you.'

Pushing him away, Francesca let out a wordless, wire-thin wail that stabbed like a blade into Luca's chest. He saw her run her fingers into her hair, but she cried out as she touched the cut on her face, and held her hands up beside her head. Moving her fingers in jerky agitation, she said, 'No! We can't stay here – we have to find them! We have to go, now, keep looking! They could be anywhere!'

'I'll go, Signora,' Modesto said. 'I'll go now. The Signore should stay here with you: you're not fit to—'

'No! Modesto, no! I have to go too ! Help me up – I can't just sit here like this!'

Luca began to remonstrate, but a loud banging on the door interrupted him. Modesto left the room.

Voices in the hallway. Two male voices. And then, from the stairs, a shriek, 'Mamma!'

Scrambling footsteps.

Luca stood up. Francesca was off the bed and across the room in a second, but, unsteady on her feet, she stumbled and grabbed for the edge of the door to hold herself up.

'Mamma! Mamma!'

As Luca took a step towards Francesca, the twins ran in and threw themselves at her. She sank to her knees; the girls sank with her, and in a moment, they had wrapped themselves around each other. Tears stung behind Luca's eyes as he watched Francesca gather her children into her arms. None of them spoke, or cried, or moved for more than a minute. Then one of the children turned her head, reached upwards, and unwittingly caught the cut on her mother's cheek. Francesca gasped, winced and pulled back, and the child let go of her. 'Oh, Mamma – your face!' she said, her voice high-pitched with distress. The second child scrabbled around. Seeing the cut, which had started to bleed again, both children began to cry.

Luca crouched down next to them. They jumped, and stared around at him, whimpering and clinging again to Francesca's skirts. 'It's all right,' he said. 'Mamma has hurt her face, but she'll be fine. Shall we help her back up, and let her lie down on her bed? And then . . . then perhaps you can tell us where you've been.'

Both girls nodded. They stood back, fingers over their mouths as Luca gathered Francesca up into his arms and put her back onto her bed. She lay back against the pillow, and closed her eyes.

'Would you like to come and sit by her?'

They scrambled onto the bed and sat curled up, one on either side of their mother. Eyes still shut, she put an arm around each and pulled them in close.

'Mind her face,' Luca said, sitting on a chair near the bed. One of the girls lifted a hand, and touched her mother's cheek near the cut, with the tip of her forefinger. Francesca smiled and stroked the child's hair.

Luca wanted to hold her. He ached to wrap his arms around her and comfort her. But now, he told himself, was not the moment. She would marry him – he was sure of it. He had seen it in her eyes just now. There would be time enough ahead for him to hold her – for now, she needed her children and far more importantly, they needed her. He contented himself with reaching out and squeezing her fingers. At his touch, Francesca moved her hand away from Beata's shoulder and gripped his fingers in return, turning her head and smiling at him with a melting tenderness. Then she released his hand, and pulled her daughter in close once more, closing her eyes again.

The two male voices were still rumbling downstairs. With a stab of shock, Luca realised that he had no idea how the children had come to be here. Francesca had said this was her servant's house. Who was that downstairs? Whoever it was must have brought the girls – but where the hell had they been? He stood up, determining to discover who the visitor was, and why they were all here, but before he could take more than a step towards the door, he heard someone running heavily upstairs, and the door to the chamber banged open.

Looking flushed and dishevelled, Gianni strode into the room. He stopped dead, staring at Francesca and the twins. '*Porca Madonna*!' he said, sounding hoarse with shock.

'Gianni—' Luca began.

'What the hell has happened?' Gianni said, staring at the blood on the bed and then up at Francesca's cut face. 'Dear God – who did that?' He turned to where Modesto had appeared in the doorway. 'Who was it, Signore? Was it one of her—' He stopped abruptly, and what looked like guilt flooded his face.

A cold stab of anxiety caught in Luca's throat. 'Gianni?' he said again.

Gianni swallowed awkwardly. 'Papa.'

'Why on earth are you here?'

Gianni did not answer.

'What did you mean – "*one of her*"? Her what? One of Francesca's what?'

Gianni shook his head. He muttered, 'Nothing, Papa,' and looked back at Francesca. She was sitting upright now, wide awake, staring at Gianni. She mouthed the word '*please*' at him, and shook her head, almost imperceptibly. Luca looked from his son to Francesca and back. 'Gianni,' he said, 'what did you mean? Francesca, *cara*, do you know what he's talking about?'

Francesca gazed up at him, saying nothing.

Modesto crossed the room. Leaning in towards the bed, he spoke softly to the children. 'Beata, Bella, could you come with me for a moment?' he said. 'I want you to do something for me. For

Mamma. It won't take long.' He smiled and raised his eyebrows, his expression promising a treat, and the children nodded, slid out from under Francesca's arms, and crossed the room to where he stood. He took one small hand in each of his. They walked with him towards the door.

Just before he reached it, however, he stopped. Luca saw him bend down behind the bed and pick something up from the floor. He tucked whatever it was into a bag, which he swung over his shoulder. Taking the girls by the hands again, he left the room and closed the door behind him.

Forty-one

The silence was close and congealed: it filled the room, seeping thickly into Luca's ears and mouth, and when he spoke at last, it felt as though he were forcibly pushing the words out into the air around his head. 'What's happening here?' he said.

Gianni and Francesca both immediately looked away from him. Francesca dropped her gaze to her hands, and Gianni stared at the floor; his colour deepened. Francesca was paler than ever, and the gash on her cheek stood out black against her pallor. A sharp jab of fearful anger caught painfully in Luca's throat. '*Santo cielo!*' he said, his gaze flicking from one to the other, 'What the hell is going on? What are you two hiding from me?'

Francesca put her hands over her face.

'Gianni?'

Gianni shook his head.

Feeling now as though he were facing an adversary in court, Luca heard himself say, deliberately calmly, but feeling his voice tremble as he spoke, 'Francesca, do you know who hurt you this evening? Was it someone you know?'

Putting her hands back down into her lap, she nodded.

'And . . . do you know *why* this person might have done this to you?'

Another nod.

Gianni's gaze was still fixed upon the floorboards.

Struggling to keep his voice steady, Luca said, 'Do you think you might be able to tell me anything about it? Gianni seems to have some idea already . . . but . . .'

With a sickening twist in his belly, he stopped speaking, it having suddenly occurred to him that it could have been Carlo who had hurt Francesca, but, in a voice barely more than a whisper, he heard her say, 'It was a man called Michele di Cicciano.'

Gianni gasped.

Luca frowned. 'Cicciano? But . . . but I know that name. Cicciano's a friend of Carlo's. How do you? I . . . I had no idea that *you* knew him.' Oh, *Dio* – she had another lover. Dreading what she might say, he said, 'Has there been something between you and this man? Did you – *do* you – love him?'

He steeled himself, ready to see guilty confusion on her face at his question, but to his relief, a naked, transparent dislike was all too obvious in the shudder that shook her and in the twist of her mouth as she said, 'No. I don't love him. And I never have. Never.'

'Then how—'

She interrupted him. Held up both hands. Drew in a long breath. And, in a voice that shook, she told him how.

It took several minutes.

He could not take his eyes from her face as she told him what he realised immediately was the truth: as she shattered into razor-edged fragments the exquisite, blown-glass bubble of the past few weeks. Her voice was low and – almost – steady, but she trembled visibly as she spoke, and Luca felt – for the second time in his life – a liquefying sense of disbelief that tore through him and left him light-headed and terrified. He stood unmoving, as he had done ten years before at the foot of his wife's bed, gazing down at Lisabeta's newly lifeless body – and he knew again the suffocating enormity of a truth too big to comprehend. 'Then,' he said, trying to order his thoughts, 'how was it that you came to be at the play at San Domenico that day?'

'It was just a stupid idea of Filippo's, something that he suggested when his wife didn't want to come with him.'

'Filippo? Then . . . ?' Luca could not finish his sentence.

Her eyes brimming with tears, Francesca nodded.

The smothering silence draped itself over the three of them again. Eventually, Luca looked away from Francesca to where Gianni still stood, hunch-shouldered and stiff in the doorway, and, as he caught his son's eye, Gianni reddened still further and bit his lip.

The liquefaction in Luca's belly turned in an instant to ice.

He stared at his son and then at Francesca. 'Oh, God, no. Please, Francesca, tell me I'm mistaken . . .'

Nobody spoke.

Luca felt sick. 'When?' he said. 'When, Gianni?'

After another long, screaming silence, Gianni said to the floorboards, 'A few weeks ago.'

Fighting to keep his voice steady, Luca said, 'Just once?' He faltered. 'Or was this a regular occurrence?'

An almost inaudible mutter. 'Just once.'

Luca saw that Francesca's face was now slick with tears.

'I gave it all up the day I met you,' she said, her voice distorted with the effort of controlling her weeping. Her lower lip was visibly quivering. Despite everything, seeing that quiver sent a hot little thread of wanting down through his belly.

She said, 'I gave it all up *because* I had met you. I sold this house – my house, not Modesto's – sold all my things, knew I would never have any more to do with any of it.'

Luca stared at her. His mind was quite numb. He had no idea

what to think. He listened to what she said, but hardly heard her. He continued to stare at her but hardly saw her. A courtesan. She was a *courtesan*. Had been. Was. Which was it? Did it matter? She had lied to him. Not a widow. A courtesan. A *whore*. He thought back a few hours, remembered how the two of them had spent that morning – could it possibly be only that morning? – lying together on the springing grass in the little clearing at Mergellina. A judder of irrepressible longing physically shook him as he remembered Francesca's fingers and mouth moving over his body, awakening his senses in a way he had never known before. He had been astonished at her inventive dexterity, entranced by the touch of her lips and her tongue and her fingers on his skin, marvelling at the thought that fate had introduced him to such a creature and that such a creature actually seemed to care for him.

And then she had wept and, at the sight of her tears, he had cursed himself for causing them, for compromising her reputation so thoughtlessly. Luca felt another wash of nauseous anger sweep through him. Her reputation! 'Reputation' was hardly the word – 'notoriety' might be more apposite. She was a professional. An amoral professional. Had she done these same extraordinary things . . . to Gianni . . . a few weeks ago? Here? In this room? And to Filippo – how many times had she entertained *him* in that way? And Carlo's friend Cicciano, who had been so angry at the withdrawal of his pleasures that tonight he had exacted this painful revenge? What had been *his* preferred choice of activity? And – Luca could hardly bear to even think it – how much had all these men *paid* her? They and how many others?

A horrible, distorted image of Francesca pushed its way into his mind. She was facing away from him, naked but for a glittering, beaded wrap that hung loosely, low on her back; jewels glittered at her throat and wrists, and her hair was down. She turned to look at him over her shoulder and he saw that the sweet smile he had come to love so much in these last few weeks had gone – in its place was a twisted mask of lascivious invitation.

A sense of betrayal and anger, of confusion and incredulity swelled and billowed in Luca's head. He raised his hands, balled them into fists and held his breath, as the sensation expanded within him.

'No! Papa, please!'

At the sound of Gianni's voice, at the sight of his son stepping forward protectively from the doorway, the glittering courtesan he had conjured vanished, and he saw instead an exhausted, frightened, ash-pale woman, flinching and pulling back from him to sit huddled against her pillow, her face soaked and swollen with tears. Her mouth had opened and she was staring at his fisted hands, holding her breath, quite obviously in expectation of being struck.

For a moment he stood irresolute, his insides crawling, then he uncurled his fingers and put his hands over his face. He pressed in hard against his skull. For long seconds he stood unmoving, in the hot palm-darkness, feeling the rise and fall of his ribcage against his elbows, then he lowered his hands.

'Were you . . . were you ever going to tell me?' he said.

She nodded. 'I wanted to. From the first moment. I've hated lying – but I didn't know how – I didn't know what to say. I didn't know how to do it.'

A long pause.

'No. I can see that.'

'After everything that happened this afternoon, after . . . what you asked me' she said, ' I had decided to tell you as soon as we arrived back at the house. Whatever the outcome, I was going to tell you the whole truth. I wanted you to know everything.

Whatever it meant. And then we arrived back, and . . .' She tailed off.

Luca looked across at Gianni. Through the numbness that seemed to be paralysing him, he felt a sudden flare of naked jealousy: for a second Gianni was not his son, but simply another man – a rival – and a fierce and painful desire to knock him down filled Luca to the point that he struggled to breathe. But then a tear swelled, broke and ran down Gianni's cheek into the soft fluff of hardly visible downy beard that ran around the edge of the boy's jaw, and Luca's anger left him.

He was empty. Dry and hard and empty like a shrivelled gourd skin. If he moved now, he thought, his insides would rattle inside him like a handful of desiccated seeds. 'I'll take you home,' he said to Francesca. 'You need time to rest and heal. You can't stay here, in this empty house – you or the children.'

The children . . .

He stopped and turned to Gianni, and said for a second time that evening, dreading further unbearable revelations, 'Why are you here, Gian? How is it that you came here to this house, with those children?'

Gianni's mouth opened, but no words came out. He closed it again.

Luca's heart beat faster. 'Why, Gian?' he said again. 'Where were you? Where have you been? Why were they with you?'

Gianni swallowed uncomfortably. He flicked a glance at Francesca. 'Papa, Carlo had them.'

'Carlo?' Luca said, frowning quizzically. 'Carlo? Then . . . where is he now?'

'I don't know. I left him – down in the *sottosuolo*.'

'The *sottosuolo*? But – I don't understand. Why? Why did Carlo have Francesca's children?'

Gianni swallowed again, and shifted his weight from one foot to the other. He breathed in slowly. Luca's pulse raced. What in heaven's name was Gianni struggling to admit? Francesca, he saw, was now staring from him to Gianni and back. 'Why, Gianni?' he said again. 'If you know, please tell me. Why did Carlo have the twins?'

Still no answer.

With a creak, the door to the bedchamber opened a little wider. Luca, Gianni and Francesca all turned to see who was there.

Modesto stood foursquare in the doorway. The little girls were pressed against him, one on each side, each with a wilting handful of flowers in her hand. Speaking clearly, in a voice that quivered with suppressed dislike, Modesto said, 'Forgive me for interrupting, Signore, but, as I've just discovered, it appears that your elder son was planning on handing these two over to a privateer friend of Signor di Cicciano's.'

Luca could think of no reply.

'Luca,' Francesca said into the silence, her voice quivering with tears.

Luca turned to her.

'Michele told me. He said he thought Carlo might have them. He just sneered at me. He said they would be taken away. Over the sea. And . . . sold.'

Luca looked at the little girls. They were huge-eyed and silent, clinging to Modesto. Francesca was tear-soaked and trembling. And Gianni – across Gianni's face Luca could see the same confused mixture of horror and guilt that he was feeling himself. That Cicciano could have spoken so heartlessly of such a proposition was terrible enough, but to think of his son – his own son – actually carrying it out . . . Luca thought he might be sick.

Hardly aware of what he was saying, he looked from Modesto

and the children to Francesca and said quietly. 'I was going to take you back to Santa Lucia, but I think now you had better come with me back to my house. You'll all be safe there.'

He saw Modesto nod his approval of this suggestion.

'But . . . *he* . . . *he* won't be there, will he?' Francesca said.

Seeing her fear, Luca's insides twisted painfully. 'No,' he said. 'I'll make sure Carlo doesn't come anywhere near you.'

Forty-two

It soon became clear to Maria that Filippo was unhappy. Since the previous Wednesday, when her husband had crept into the house, well past midnight, trying to avoid waking her – as he had so often done on Wednesday nights – he had been uncharacteristically taciturn and lethargic. He had not been in to work, he had risen late in the mornings and retired early each evening – always to the smallest bedchamber. He had barely spoken to her, had avoided catching her eye whenever he could, and so had consequently spent much of his time in the house over the previous few days staring either at the floor or out of the window.

'What on earth is the matter with Filippo?' Emilia said to Maria after a few days of this miserable lassitude, as the two women stood together in the kitchen, preparing vegetables for a soup.

Maria heard the lack of compassion in her sister's question and swallowed down a bite of irritation. 'I don't know. Perhaps he is sickening for something,' she said. Or perhaps, she thought to herself, he is sickening *because* of something. Or someone. She cut down hard through a chunk of carrot, gripping the handle of the knife so tightly that her knuckles stood out white.

'You may be right,' Emilia said. The problem was clearly not troubling her excessively, for she added in a voice of supreme indifference, 'If that's the case, then a nice bowl of soup might cheer him up.'

If he is here to eat it, Maria thought. Its being a Wednesday.

But, much to Maria's surprise, Filippo stayed at home that evening, and it was quickly apparent that the bowl of soup he had been offered had done little, if anything, to raise his spirits. He pushed his spoon about in the bowl a great deal more than he lifted it to his lips, and he shredded far more of his bread than he ate. Maria watched him; she said nothing, but felt, as she watched, a strange tension in her limbs and a tightness within her chest as though she were physically restraining her own body from reacting to her husband's obvious misery. Though why don't I react, she thought, as her left leg began to twitch. Why do I not just ask him what's troubling him? Hold his hand?

She thought through some of the things she had written in her vellum-bound book. She had read and reread her own sentences so many times she knew many of them by heart: unfettered outpourings of bitter self-criticism, tentative explorations of her own opinions, and of course the long passages of vivid – if clumsy and probably ignorantly inaccurate – descriptions of what she had imagined her husband had been doing during his regular Wednesday evening absences. Looking at him now, as she had done countless times, she pictured Filippo, doing those things she had described; imagined his hands; imagined – with a shard of ice in her throat – the expression on his face as he did them. Imagined the unknown woman. Having no idea who the woman might be, but finding that she needed to put a face to the invisible threat, Maria had, over the weeks, begun to picture her husband's anonymous lover as the beautiful whore in the crimson dress, who had fallen that day outside the church of San Giacomo. The woman who had told her to write. Her leg twitched a little faster and her heartbeat quickened.

It was the first Wednesday in well over a year, Maria thought, that Filippo had remained at home. There had to be a connection between that alteration to his routine, and this palpable misery. Had the woman – whoever she was – told him that she no longer wished to see him? Another thought struck her: had she perhaps *died*? Maria felt slightly sick. Was Filippo *grieving* for whoever it was? This thought hurt in her chest, like a painful breath dragged in after too much running.

'I'm very tired, Maria. I think I'll go up to bed,' Filippo said then.

Maria looked at him. He held her gaze.

'You didn't eat your soup,' Emilia said from the other side of the table.

Filippo shook his head and, though he answered his sister-in-law politely, he still looked at Maria. 'No. I'm sorry – I don't seem to have much of an appetite just at the moment. Nothing to do with the soup – it . . . it was a very good soup.'

Maria breathed in slowly.

The woman in crimson had told her that day that writing down her thoughts – even her most shameful, forbidden thoughts – might help her to unlock the barricades behind which she had hidden herself for so long. And for weeks now, she had done what the woman had said – she had written, page after page, in her vellum-bound book. Much of it, whenever she read it back, embarrassed her very much and made her insides creep, as though she had a fever, but she knew that somehow the woman had been right. Committing to paper what had been festering inside her for so long, had changed her. She might still be sequestered behind her barricades, but, even if they were still locked, Maria thought that she might now have fashioned herself a key. She just had to summon the courage to use it.

She said, her eyes still fixed upon Filippo's, 'I had thought I might go for a bit of a walk before I go to bed, Filippo. To get some air. Would you like to come with me? It might help you sleep.'

Filippo didn't answer, and Maria wondered if he had heard her. She wondered too if he could 'hear' anything of what she was not saying, and, fully expecting a refusal, she sighed, feeling her shoulders droop.

But Filippo said, 'Yes. I think a little air might do me good.'

'What?'

'Thank you. I'd like a walk.'

Maria's pulse raced. 'Good,' she said. 'I'll fetch my coat.'

Above them the sky was the greyish blue of the heart of a candle flame, but nearer the roofscape of the city, the blue had softened and blurred into a deep, pinkish red. The sun had already sunk out of sight. Within minutes, Filippo thought, it would be quite dark. They walked without speaking for some moments along the Via Santa Chiara, Maria's skirts rustling rhythmically with her steps. Filippo found himself soothed by the sound.

After a time he looked sideways at her, just in time to see her risk a glance at him.

She flicked her gaze back to the street in front of her feet, with a little jerk of her head, but then looked back up at him and said, 'I'm sorry you are not feeling well at the moment.'

'I'm not unwell.'

'But you are not happy.'

'No.' Filippo gave Maria a tight smile. 'No, I'm not very happy at the moment. I'm sorry.'

There was a short pause, and then Maria said, 'Is it anything I have done?'

Filippo answered with an emphatic negative straight away, but realised, in the brief hiatus of silence that followed his reply, that he supposed the entire situation was in fact – at least partly – his wife's fault. Then, feeling that thus apportioning complete blame would be horribly unfair on Maria, he allowed that his own appetites were probably to some degree equally as responsible for his current unhappiness as was Maria's lack of them. These thoughts, though, made him feel confused and awkward, so he kept his eyes on his shoes as they continued walking. At every step a deep horizontal crease appeared across each shoe, the leather creaked quietly and a little corner like a dog's ear pushed in and out as each foot rose and fell.

He knew Maria was curious. Tension was emanating from her like heat: she was, he thought, almost crackling with it. And, much to Filippo's surprise, he found this tension fleetingly arousing. He looked across at her again and saw, with a jolt of his insides, that she had tears in her eyes.

'What on earth is the matter?' he said.

Maria ran the tip of her finger under her lashes: first one eye and then the other. 'I hate to think of you being unhappy,' she said.

Filippo stopped and turned towards her. In a flash of confused emotion, he saw not Maria, but Francesca as she had been the other day, crying and begging him to keep her secrets from Luca. He saw himself, putting his arms around his courtesan and comforting her even as he acknowledged his own yawning fear of a future without her ministrations. He felt again Francesca's warm body trembling within his embrace.

And then he saw Maria.

His wife.

His face burned as he remembered how long it had been since he had last held Maria in tenderness, as he had held Francesca that final time. Every touch he and Maria had shared – for years – had been tainted with tension, taut with anxiety, weighted down with the threat of yet another possible failure. He had been quite hollow with loneliness for a week, wrapped up in his own misery, but now it struck Filippo that he had not given a thought – in nearly two years – to her possible feelings of isolation. A cold drench of shame washed over him.

'Please,' he said. 'Don't cry.'

And he reached out towards her.

She stared at him for a moment, then stepped forwards. Filippo folded his arms around her and held her in close to his body. She was small and angular, and the points of her shoulder blades jutted against his forearm.

Forty-three

Luca has not been up to this room, or indeed spoken a word to me since we arrived here nearly an hour ago. He was silent all the way back from San Tommaso. He carried me all the way here – and it must be at least half a mile – but he didn't speak to me.

Gianni and Modesto carried the girls, who were, not surprisingly, exhausted and confused and tearful. Before we left, Gianni told me where he had found them. I can hardly believe it. If Gianni hadn't been there . . . My poor darling little girls – left alone in the dark like that, while Luca and I were . . . no, no I can't bear to think about it. And it's all my fault – oh, God, it's all my fault! I might have dressed like a duchess and feasted like a princess and been fêted like a queen for years, but it's all just a pile of shit. Behind all the tawdry trappings, I have to face the fact . . . that I'm nothing but a whore. I earn my *scudi* on my back. Strip me of my finery and I am no different from any street *puttana*. And my poor Beata and Bella are no more than two little whore's bastards, innocent hangers-on, who have today been lucky to escape paying the price for the depravity of their mother's life.

I don't deserve to be a mother.

I look at where they are sleeping, lying curled together on a mattress beneath a couple of woollen blankets: their eyes are tight shut, mouths slightly open. Beata's thumb has fallen from where she has been sucking it, and a glistening line of spittle has slid down her chin. Their sweet faces are, thank God, untroubled, innocent, ultimately undamaged. They're safe. No thanks to me. I've lived for years in a vicious world amongst vicious people fuelled with vicious intentions, and my children have truly been fortunate to survive in it unscathed for so long.

They deserve a better mother.

And Luca deserves a better wife. I knew in my heart it would never happen. He's disgusted by me now and I cannot blame him. How could I? I would be disgusted by me, if I were him.

I walk back and forth across this little bedchamber in which I have been left to rest. My legs and belly are still aching, but I can't sit still. Think, Francesca. Try to think. Try to think about something else, or you'll run mad. About what? The room. Look at the room. I'm not sure, but I think this room – a small one on the second floor, up under the eaves – might belong to Gianni. It's a pretty place, although it's only sparsely furnished; the walls are painted a warm crimson. There is only a narrow bed, a huge carved chest and a table, on which stands a delicate casket, made of some sort of gilded wood. It's beautiful – I wonder if it perhaps belonged to Gianni's mother.

Luca's wife.

No – not that. Don't think about that.

There are hangings at the window – faded and obviously quite old, but they must once have been lovely.

Oh, stop it! This is just *stupid*! Why do I *care*? Why am I even noticing the furnishings in this room, when I feel as though the very walls have already fallen in upon me and are slowly smothering me? I am trapped beneath the rubble of the shattered future Luca and I might have had together, unable to move, unable to breathe, not knowing whether or not Luca will ever even *want* to stretch out a hand to try to pull me free, let alone be *able* to do it.

Though . . . if everything were indeed totally hopeless . . . would Luca have brought us here? If he truly despises me now, would he not have just left me with Modesto in the Via San Tommaso? This morning, he wanted to marry me.

Oh, God, I don't know – I simply don't know what to think.

I sit down on the edge of the bed, fold my arms up and over my head and put my head between my knees, trying to stifle down the scream I can feel building up in my chest.

A knock at the door. My heart jolts. I sit up.

'Signora?' Modesto leans into the room, one hand on the door jamb. He is holding a candle in the other. His eyes are quite black in the candlelight. He smiles. 'I'm leaving in a moment. I just wondered how you were, Signora.'

I shrug.

'The twins still asleep?'

I nod. 'Thank you,' I say. 'Thank you for helping with them. Helping to find them.'

Modesto nods in acknowledgement of this. Then adds, 'Do you want anything before I go?'

I want to scream at him. Yes! Of course I do! I want Luca. I want him to be here in this room, with his arms around me, telling me that he doesn't care about any of this – assuring me that this appalling revelation of my lurid history is of no importance to him. I want him still to want to marry me. I want my face not to be hurting so very much, and my legs and belly not to ache. I want not to have to think about what Michele did. I want the whole of the past few hours not to have happened. But . . . but I suppose I'll settle for a glass of wine.

Modesto smiles when I ask him. He is absent a few moments,

then returns with a pewter cup and an uncorked bottle of red wine. He pours out a generous measure and hands me the cup.

'There you are, Signora. Look, I have to go. I'll come and see you in the morning.'

We stand without speaking for a moment, and then Modesto sighs and shakes his head; he drops something that he is carrying, crosses the room and hugs me. He holds me very tightly in his big arms, smelling reassuringly familiar – of warm leather, linen and sweat – and, as he holds me, a hollow place opens up inside my chest: a chill empty sphere of homesickness. I cling to him. With a soft splatter, most of the contents of my cup, still in my hand, spills onto the floorboards.

Pulling back from Modesto, I stare down at what I have done. He drags a large linen kerchief from his breeches pocket and crouches down to mop up the dark puddle.

'You were never a very tidy drinker,' he says, with a wry grin. He refills the cup and hands it back to me. I suddenly wish with all my heart that he could stay here with me tonight. Curl up in my bed with me and hold me until I fall asleep. But before I can even finish the thought, he has reached out, squeezed my hand, and left the room.

The front door bangs a moment later.

I sit down on the edge of the bed with the cup held in both hands, staring down into the dark-red liquid.

I can hear voices from the floor below: a deep rumble that I imagine must be Luca and Gianni.

Opening the door to the bedchamber a little wider, I stand just outside the room, straining to hear what is being said downstairs. Gianni's words are hard to distinguish, but Luca's deeper voice carries easily. My heart starts thudding up in my throat.

'. . . actually *admitted* that was what he was planning to do?' Luca says.

Gianni's reply is inaudible.

'But, how did you know where he was?'

An indistinguishable murmur.

'. . . left him down there?'

More from Gianni that I cannot hear.

'I have to go and see if I can find him. You stay here with Francesca and the children.'

The door bursts open and Luca strides out, shrugging his arms down into his doublet sleeves as he goes. He glances up – and sees me standing there. For a brief moment he stops and stares. His mouth opens a little. Even from here I can see that he is holding his breath. I feel as though I have been turned to stone. I cannot move at all. I can't even blink. Neither, it seems, can Luca. We stare at each other for endless seconds, and then Luca drags his gaze away from my face as though it hurts to do so, rubbing at one eye with the heel of his hand. He shakes his head and winces, and then runs downstairs and leaves the house through the front door, banging it shut behind him.

I stare down at where Luca was just standing. My longing for him feels like a fist in my chest: tight, hard, punched through from the outside, but, somewhat to my surprise, after all my recent tears, I find that I no longer seem to be able to cry.

Gianni glances upwards and sees me. Dear God, he looks like his father.

'Come down here, if you'd like to,' he says stiffly.

I do not reply but, after glancing back into the bedchamber to see that the girls are still sleeping, I walk down the short flight of stairs, towards where Gianni is standing. He goes back into the *sala* and, when I enter the room, he is standing with his back towards the fireplace, though there is nothing in it at present but ash.

There is a long pause. I can think of nothing to say to him and, as he too remains silent, I can only imagine that he is experiencing a similar problem. I pull in a long breath like a wobbly sigh, and then let it out again.

Gianni has the corner of his thumbnail in his mouth. He bites at it for a moment or two and then finally he speaks around his thumb. He says, 'I'm sorry.'

'What do you mean?'

He takes his hand away from his face. 'I'm sorry for what I said. I gave away your secrets. You asked me not to.'

'It's not your fault,' I say. 'You didn't mean to.'

He shrugs. 'But – I'm sorry, anyway.'

I swallow and say, 'Thank you,' almost inaudibly. And then, dreading the answer, I say, 'Has he said anything?'

Gianni raises an eyebrow and when he speaks, his voice sounds hard. 'Did you really expect him to? He's just found out that the first woman he's taken an interest in since my mother died is not the sweet little thing he had presumed her to be, but has in fact been fucking everything that moves, for years. Including his younger son. He's also just discovered for certain, after suspecting it for a long, long time, that his elder son is an amoral little shit. What do you think he's going to say? Especially to me.'

Tears sting. I have no idea how to answer.

'Why did you have to interfere in his life?' Gianni says. 'Wasn't it enough for you, what you had before? You seemed happy enough, the day that I . . .' He tails off, reddening, and drops his gaze to his boots. He starts chewing his thumbnail again. 'I'm sorry,' he mutters around his thumb a few seconds later. 'I'm sorry – I shouldn't have said all that.'

'Don't apologise. I deserve everything you've said. It's all true.' I sit down on one of the folding chairs, and run my fingers along the grain of the wood of the table. A cat appears from the shadows. He pushes up against my skirts, purring, and stretches his head towards my hand, clearly yearning to be stroked. Reaching down, I scratch between his ears with the tips of my fingers; his tail lifts and sways sinuously, and the purring intensifies.

'No,' Gianni says. 'I *am* sorry.'

'Look, I wasn't expecting to feel the way I do about your father, Gianni. It was as much of a surprise to me as to anyone.'

Gianni says nothing. He looks very young.

I say, 'I agree that I must have seemed happy enough, the day that you came to see me; I think that perhaps I was, in a way. But then you made me see things differently—'

He sucks in a shocked breath. 'So it's all *my* fault?'

'No! No – that's not what I meant!'

'Then what?'

I hesitate, and then say, 'The life of a courtesan is one of glitter and glamour and exhilarating excitement – but that's like a . . . like a sparkling crust over a swamp. Under the crust it's different. It's dark and dirty and dangerous. It's like an endless rush towards the inevitable wreck of your life, in a runaway cart, unable to stop however clearly you see the dangers around you.'

Gianni watches me, silently.

'You slowed the cart for a moment, Gianni, that day you came to me in the Via San Tommaso. Slowed it enough to make me start thinking about what I really wanted. And then I met your father, and he tipped it over entirely. Just before it reached the cliff edge.'

There is a long pause, and then Gianni says, 'I suppose it would be hard to get back into it again after that.'

I nod.

The two of us sit in silence for a while now, and then Gianni clears his throat. 'I'm sorry for what Cicciano did to you.'

He has hunched his shoulders again, and his arms are folded

tight across his chest. The quick-flicked glance he now makes down towards my breasts, and the uncomfortable way he swallows, makes it clear to me that Gianni has guessed just what revenge Michele chose to take upon his traitorous whore. Gianni looks at me as he did that night when he discovered my scar – with a sort of anguished compassion, as though he is ashamed of the brutality I have experienced at the hands of others of his sex; as though he feels somehow responsible and wishes he could find a way to atone for it.

I wonder if his father will ever be able to see it as he does.

Forty-four

A pallid puddle of light from the lantern lay across a few feet of the tufa rock, bobbing softly in a faint draught. Carlo sat on the ground for some moments after Gianni and the children had left the tunnel, staring at the light, feeling along his split lip with the tip of his tongue. It was swollen and salty. He touched it gingerly with a finger and winced.

He had to get out. Whatever he had said just now, Gianni might even at this moment be alerting the *sbirri*, and, should that be the case, Carlo was in little doubt that his life would be in danger. If they picked him up . . . if he was tried and found guilty . . . he knew that there was a fair chance he would hang. Or burn. He shivered. He had to leave Napoli. Even if Gianni said nothing, it would probably only be a matter of time. It was going to leak out, some-how – he had told that whining little Marco what he was planning to do, when Marco had seen him with the brats near the waterfront, for one thing. A knot of fear tightened, high in his chest.

It took him some moments to get to his feet: the strength of Gianni's fists had been a clear indication of his brother's opinions. Carlo wished now that he had never taken the children. It had been a stupid idea. Pointless. Ill thought out. It had seemed safer than the more obvious demanding of a ransom, like Żuba had said.

He swallowed. The air in the tunnel was thick and stagnant; he needed to get out. Walking to the tunnel entrance, he lifted the lantern to head height, and looked out into the cavern. To his left was the central tunnel that led down to Posilippo – he could go back down there now, as he had been planning to do before, with the children in tow, and signal to the *Għafrid*, which was still anchored offshore. Żuba would certainly take him on board and ferry him to some safe port. But, he reasoned with himself, what if he could not be seen from on board? He did not want to be found on the hillside in broad daylight. Like a sitting target. He would probably do better to get back up into the city. Easier to lose himself there, and escape undetected overland.

Picking his way over the rubble-strewn floor, holding the lantern up high, Carlo started across towards the tunnel entrance on the far side of the cavern.

'Come on, come on,' he muttered to himself as he walked. 'Get a move on.' His gaze fixed upon the tunnel entrance, he increased his speed.

And tripped.

Sprawling full length upon the rocky floor with a grunt, he dropped the lantern, which rolled away from him and went out.

The darkness was absolute.

Carlo swore. His pulse raced, thudding in his ears and making him feel sick. He could see nothing at all. Nothing. He lifted his hand; held it a few inches before his face; waved it back and forth. Nothing. Frantically trying to remember in which direction the tunnel entrance had been, he got to his feet and began to shuffle slowly, with his arms stretched out in front of him, towards where he prayed his way out of the cavern would be. Once in the tunnel, he knew it was a straightforward – if lengthy – route back to the tavern.

He stumbled again and fell onto his knees. Swore again.

The floor of the cave was rough and littered with tufa rubble. Crawling now, Carlo inched a painful way across rough rock projections and sharp-edged pebbles, catching knees, shins and palms at every step. Panic was bubbling up in his throat, and he found himself speaking aloud into the blackness: a chattering monologue of muttered attempts at self-encouragement.

It ought to be no more than twenty yards to the tunnel entrance. Terrified that, in his disorientation, he might have set off in the wrong direction, Carlo fumbled with searching fingers across the ground beneath him, his eyes stretched pointlessly wide in the utter darkness.

Endless minutes passed.

The cave, it seemed, was far bigger than he had presumed.

Then he reached a wall.

He groped upwards and stood, pressing his body up against the rock, breathing heavily, leaning his face against the cold, mould-smelling stone. It was not the tunnel entrance but it was better – immeasurably better – than the awful nothingness of the open cavern. Taking a few creeping steps towards where he prayed the tunnel would be, he tripped yet again, scraping the side of his face and grazing his knuckles as he fell. He crouched back onto all fours, feeling along the ground where the wall met the floor.

Dust. Grit. Large blocks of tufa. Smaller, angular chips.

And then something quite different.

He fingered it curiously.

A conical pile of stones, like a little cairn.

For a moment Carlo sat on his heels and wondered, then he remembered Michele, crouching down at the tunnel mouth, grinning at him and piling pebbles. Remembered his own irritable question:

'What in hell's name are you doing, Cicciano?'

'*I want to be quite certain,*' his friend had said, '*of finding my way out . . .*'

Carlo bent down and, cupping both hands around the cairn, he kissed the topmost stone. Several of the pebbles dislodged and clattered down onto the floor. A short sob caught in his throat as he straightened, stood again and reached out with waving arms. One hand caught the wall where it folded around into the tunnel entrance. Cursing, and tucking the banged wrist under the other armpit for a moment, he then pressed his hands against the two sides of the entranceway and waited for his painfully leaping heartbeat to settle enough to start the long walk back up to the surface.

Forty-five

Luca banged the front door shut behind him and stood on the step for a second, eyes closed, struggling to steady his breathing. Looking up at Francesca just now, he knew he had been perilously close to crying. It seemed, almost literally, unbearable. There she was, in his house, standing at the top of his stairway, exquisitely, astonishingly, unbelievably beautiful: so vulnerable . . . and so entirely unlike how he had always presumed a whore would look.

A whore.

She was a whore.

It was ripping him in two. Even after so short a time, the idea of life without her was appalling – her hesitancy at his proposal this afternoon had sent panic coursing through him – but, just at this moment, he had absolutely no notion of how he was ever going to reconcile himself to this discovery of Francesca's past life. He pictured her as she had been in Mergellina: her hair falling around her face, her beautiful mouth lipping down his belly. Holding his breath, he felt again her tongue on his skin.

He walked fast, away from the house, down towards the tavern by the docks.

She must have honed her skills over years, he thought bitterly as he walked. Had been paid to do so. Handsomely. She had, after all, earned enough – on her back – to own two houses and employ a handful of servants; enough to dress herself in silks and gemstones, enough to furnish her houses in a style that would not disgrace a nobleman. On her back. Fucking like a common trollop. The thought made him feel sick and, with a sudden swoop of furious, vertiginous lust, he kicked out at a small and rather shabby handcart that had been abandoned at the side of the street. The heel of his boot crashed into the painted side of the cart; it swung round away from the blow and tipped over with a clatter, sending a wooden bucket and half a dozen onions rolling across the cobbles. Horizontal now, the upper wheel rotated pathetically, creaking its protestations, but Luca paid it no heed and strode on, hands balled tight.

His rage was thick and acrid and hung about him like a fog.

And then he thought of Francesca's discovery of the disappearance of the children, her panic, her desperation to find them and then her touchingly dignified ecstasy at their safe return. She was a devoted mother. The wrenching anger in his chest changed and despair at the prospect of losing her lanced through him. His fists uncurled and he pushed the fingers of one hand up into his hair. He knew – quite clearly – that he loved her, but this knowledge was now unbearable. He had no idea how to love a whore.

She had had a terrible time today. He knew that. He thought through everything that had happened after their return from Mergellina. It had seemed to all of them, for hours, as though the children might be dead. Or worse. And then that bastard Cicciano . . . Even as he began to think about this, an idea pushed itself into the forefront of his mind. He had been sickened with shock on discovering what Cicciano had done, but now he found himself wondering whether that particular ordeal was perhaps less terrible for a whore than it would be for a virtuous woman. Francesca had said that she didn't care for Cicciano – and Luca believed her. But for years, so he understood, she had endured Cicciano's regular attentions – for a fee. Perhaps had even encouraged them. She had grown rich, had she not, bedding (amongst who knew how many others) a man she said she didn't even like, so, could what had happened tonight be *so* much worse an experience than those regular encounters?

But then Luca pictured Francesca as he had seen her not more than a few hours before, crumpled and bleeding on the bare-mattressed bed in the house in the Via San Tommaso d'Aquino, and immediately felt light-headed with shame. In that first shocked second he had thought her dead: how arrogant could a man be, to describe so dreadful an ordeal – even to himself in private – as in any way insignificant?

Both hands now laced in his hair, he gripped his skull, as though trying to prevent his chaotic thoughts from physically bursting out through the bone. He heard a long, guttural groan, and only seconds later realised that it had come from his own mouth.

Reaching the top of a dingy alleyway, he paused, breathing as heavily as though he had been running. At the far end of the street, there was a gap between the tight-packed buildings, and through it Luca could see a narrow strip of sea; points of light from the last of the sun were dancing on the very tops of the waves. Luca saw several people, apparently somewhat the worse for drink, leaving what he knew to be the tavern most often frequented by Carlo – the place where Gianni had said Carlo had entered the *sottosuolo*. The place where Carlo might be now.

Carlo.

He could hardly make himself think about what his elder son had done. On top of every other thing he had discovered today, this was the final drop of water and the jug was now fully overflowing. Pouring out and soaking everything around it. For a long moment, Luca stood staring at the tavern, feeling drained and despairing.

Then, sucking a long breath into a chest that felt as though it were heavily strapped, he walked towards where light and noise was spilling from the open tavern door, out onto the cobbled street.

It was only when Modesto had all but reached the Via Santa Lucia and a sharper breeze blew in from the sea, raising gooseflesh on his arms, that it occurred to him that he was no longer wearing his doublet. He thought back over where he might have left it and realised that the last time he had been conscious of its presence was when he had taken it off and draped it over Francesca, back in the house in the Via San Tommaso, some hours earlier.

'Damn!' he muttered, looking back up the street and trying to decide whether or not he could be bothered to retrieve the doublet. The rest of his clothes, including another two coats, were now at Santa Lucia – but the missing doublet was his most comfortable, and he knew he would almost certainly want it the next day. Huffing out an irritable sigh, he turned on his heel and set off at right angles, down a steeply sloping, brick-stepped street, taking the shortest route back towards San Tommaso.

The events of the day played themselves out in his mind as he walked; he experienced again faint echoes of the fear he had felt as he had run through the streets searching for the twins; his gut-churning shock at the discovery of Francesca's injuries; his rage at Cicciano's depravity. And then he contemplated once more the emerging prospect that Francesca's hopes of a future with the Signore now seemed set fair to crumble. Disturbed by uncomfortably conflicting emotions, he began muttering aloud. 'You are a truly unpleasant and selfish individual.' He paused, bit his lip and shook his head. 'She loves him. Yes, you poor, sad, bollockless

excuse for a man – *she loves him*. Face the fact! You really want him
to abandon her? When she so obviously adores him? You want
him to throw her back onto the stinking dungheap she's so nearly
escaped from?'

His voice must have increased in volume as he spoke. Passing
an open front door, he heard a snort of laughter. A grubby boy of
about twelve was sitting on the door sill, fiddling in the dust with
his fingers; he smirked and said, 'Who's your invisible friend then,
Pazzo?'

Modesto ignored him. Doing no more than casting the boy a
fleeting glance, he continued, in a hissing whisper, 'If you care
about her at all, you bastard, you'll want what *she* wants. Not what
you want. And what she wants is *him*. The Signore. Him – and an
end to how it's been for so long. No more patrons. No more
having to fuck for a big fat fee, night after night.' The volume
began to rise again. 'No more having to placate spoilt, arrogant
little noblemen with more money than cock in their oversized,
overstuffed codpieces.'

He elbowed past two richly dressed, elderly men, who turned
scandalised faces to stare after him as he strode on. Ignoring them
too, he carried on his furious monologue, now gesticulating with
both hands as he spoke. 'And *him*! Gutless intellectual. First hint
of trouble and he's backed right off. Oh, yes – might have guessed!
What's his problem? Scared of the pox? Frightened of scandal?
She's better off without him – he can't care two pins for her – not
like—'

The obvious end of the sentence, he left unsaid.

Modesto strode on, hardly noticing where he was, until he was
brought up short by a heavily laden cart, travelling fast down the
street, which crossed the end of the lane in which he was walking.
The carter, oblivious to everything around him, was urging his

horse to ever greater speed; the cart clattered past Modesto, missing him by little more than a foot. His hair was lifted by the wind of its passing. A cabbage bounced over the tailgate onto the ground, rolling past where Modesto stood and banging into the wall behind him with a deadened thwack. Staring up the street after the cart, Modesto saw it veer abruptly round to the right some moments later and it lurched off up towards the Piazza Francese. Turning back, he caught sight of a tall figure standing outside a tavern some yards down the road, looking in at the open door, seemingly unwilling to enter.

'So. Left her at home and come out to drown your sorrows, have you?' Modesto muttered. 'Not quite got the nerve to go in?' He snorted out a derisive laugh, and decided that he might just wander down to the tavern and – hopefully unobserved – watch a little more closely just what the Signore was intending to do. He saw the Signore square his shoulders and enter the tavern, and he walked a little faster.

The fireplace was belching out smoke, and a greasy haze hung over the crowded tables. Luca stood in the doorway and stared into the room, searching through the fog for his son. His eyes stung as he gazed around the room, unsure which would be worse: for Carlo to be here, or for him not to be.

But there was no sign of him anywhere.

A boy of about Gianni's age – skinny, unkempt, with his hair scraped back into a dirty pigtail – raked him up and down with a dismissive glance and turned away, a filthy cloth hung over one shoulder.

Luca edged further into the room, wondering if there might be any other, smaller space not visible from the entrance where Carlo might be concealed. He sidled between two tables, frowning through the smoke, but saw nothing but a narrow staircase descending out of sight in one corner of the room. He checked, remembering Gianni's description of his fight with Carlo in the darkness of the *sottosuolo*. This, he thought, must be the entrance-way the boys had used. What if Carlo was still down there, confused and frightened and unable to find his way back? Smothering a stabbing thought that if that was the case, then his amoral son deserved his fate, Luca determined to find a light and start searching.

He turned towards the torches burning in brackets on the walls; he had just taken a step towards the nearest, when a bright flash caught his eye and he spun round, peering through the smoke haze to see what had distracted him.

A long-legged, broken-nosed young man with close-cropped curls was leaning back in his chair, one booted foot up on the edge of the table. Luca realised who it was almost immediately. An empty glass stood in front of the man, next to a three-quarters-empty bottle of *grappa*, and he was holding up a small, silver-handled knife; the blade gleamed steel blue in the torchlight. He was testing its needle tip on the ball of his thumb; then as Luca watched, he ran the knife from point to hilt between his fingers, lazily flipping it over and over, repeating the action almost lovingly – as though he were caressing the blade. He was smiling.

Luca's pulse was loud in his ears.

He pushed his way through the crowded room until he stood within feet of the man with the knife.

'You fucking bastard . . .' he said, softly. He saw a moment's blankness in a gaze blurred by drink, then Michele gripped the dagger by its handle and scraped his chair back across the flags. Luca eyed the blade.

'You have a problem, Signore?' Michele said.

The buzz of conversation in the tavern died to silence. Several people stood, pushed back their chairs and backed away, leaving an empty space like a little arena around Michele and Luca.

'No,' Luca said, 'I don't have a problem. You do.'

Michele laughed.

Modesto pushed his way around the edge of the tavern room, his gaze fixed upon the two men who were now standing facing each other, some feet apart. Cicciano held his knife loosely in one hand, and the Signore had both fists clenched. Cicciano took a step backwards and bumped into his chair. Without taking his eyes from the Signore's face, he kicked out behind him and sent the chair sprawling.

An expectant buzz ran through the watching drinkers.

The Signore said softly, 'I'll see you put away, Cicciano.'

Cicciano smirked. 'Yes? What for?'

'You know.'

Cicciano paused, ran his tongue over his lower lip, then caught it between his teeth. He said, 'The treacherous little whore owed me: I collected my debt – no more than that. It's still allowable within the law to recoup your losses, I believe.' He smirked again, then started theatrically. 'But, oh, dear,' he said, eyes widening in obviously artificial surprise. 'Maybe this is news to you. Carlo's told me all about your liaison with *La Bella Felizzi*, but perhaps –' he dropped his voice to a forced whisper '– you're not yet aware of her profession? Your son knows, Signore. Knows *intimately*, as I understand it. Your younger son, that is. Carlo, of course, has . . . very different tastes.' He flicked his eyebrows up and down.

Modesto saw the Signore redden. Saw his right hand brush against the back of a chair, and then grip its top bar, white-knuckled. Modesto edged in closer, worming his way through the

393

bright-eyed crowd, who were, he saw, eagerly awaiting some sort of action. He pushed in next to a squat, broad-shouldered man in a leather apron.

'Are there any depths to which you will not stoop?' Modesto heard the Signore say to Cicciano, his face twisted with dislike.

Cicciano grinned. 'Well, now you mention it, I think I might have plumbed them tonight – fucking that traitorous little strumpet. I'd advise you to steer clear of her yourself, Signore, you might—'

But his words were cut short. Modesto saw the Signore swing the chair he was holding upwards, scything it into Cicciano's wrist.

The knife flew out of Michele's hand, and Luca dropped the chair back down onto the tavern-room floor. He heard the knife clatter across the table and onto the floor; heard the sharp intake of breath from the crowd; heard Michele's gasped oath as he launched himself forwards. Grabbing Michele's doublet front with both fists, he fell with him to the floor, the watching drinkers scattering out of their way. Michele was winded, and, in the second it took him to blink and begin to push himself upright again, Luca snatched at Michele's shirt collar, banged him back down onto the ground, and then hit him as hard as he could on the jaw.

Michele grunted.

The crowd gasped appreciatively.

Hot blood pounded in Luca's face.

Forty-six

The fire has been lit in this bedchamber. Luca's old manservant came up with me just now from the *sala*, and lit it. He seemed to find the task very difficult: he took a great deal of time and effort over it and I was astonished that the twins didn't wake, given the amount of noise he made, but, thank goodness, they're still asleep. I suppose the shock of what happened to them today has worn them out. I can feel my heart swelling inside my chest, as I think about how things might have turned out: it's as though I was under sentence of death until an hour or so ago, and their return is my reprieve.

Though if Luca rejects me, it will still be a life sentence.

The crimson walls are shivering now in the leaping firelight, and on the big painted chest the pretty little casket glitters, as though it might hold unexpected treasures. On the floor near the end of the bed is a bag that I'm sure wasn't there earlier. Made of old, scuffed leather. It's not mine, but it's familiar – I think it's Modesto's. Why has he left it here? He must have dropped it before he went earlier.

I pick it up and look inside.

Books. Vellum-bound, tied notebooks.

My heart skips a beat. I look into the uppermost. *Book of Encounters*.

Oh, *Dio* – why? Why in heaven's name has he brought these here? What was he thinking of? These books are full of the sort of lewd accounts of my past life that would damn me irrevocably in anybody's eyes. *An Intimate Portrait of a Filthy Bitch* would be a better title for them. So Michele would say, anyway. Luca simply *cannot* ever see them – it would be disastrous! When he left the house an hour or so ago and looked up at me from the stairs, it seemed that the very *sight* of me was physically painful for him. If he were to see this, I think it would be the end. The books have to go. I can't just throw them away, though – God knows where they might turn up, and what mischief they might cause. They'll have to burn.

Luigi has left a basket of logs, and there's a pair of bellows propped up by the edge of the grate. I'll need to build the flames up – I simply cannot risk anything being left legible. The thought of Luca's seeing even one page of any of these books makes me feel utterly sick. My explanations of Filippo's complicated predilections and . . . oh, *merda*! . . . my account of Gianni's visit, which is in here somewhere. No, no, no, this can't happen. Why the hell did Modesto bring the books here? I could kill him!

I kneel in front of the fire and poke the nose of the bellows into the wood at the base of the flames. They seem startled at the intrusion, and jump up a little higher. I put on more wood, work the bellows again. The flames continue to leap. I repeat the process two or three times. It's hot now – hot enough to make my eyes water. I sit back on my heels and watch for a moment. Chewing the skin on my thumb, I stare into what has become a miniature inferno: hellish little caverns and tunnels, which shift and rearrange themselves even as I watch. I half expect to see a bunch of tiny demons poking their faces out from behind white-hot lumps of wood, beckoning to me to come and join them. Perhaps it's where I belong, after all.

I pick up one of the books, determining to thrust it into the flames, but realise with a jolt that now the moment is here, I don't want to lose them. Why, though? Why am I thinking this? I *hate* them: they represent everything that stands so implacably between me and Luca. They are the embodiment of the life I now loathe. The life I wish I could eradicate from my past. But it's strange – now that I am on the point of destroying them, I feel as though I am holding in my hands some living thing: a creature that must be sacrificed to placate the wrath of the gods. Here, after all, held fast between these smooth, skin-smelling vellum covers, is *my life* – two and a half years of it – laid bare, stripped naked, staked out for scandal-hungry vultures to peck at. I don't remember which accounts of which encounters are in which book, and find myself tugged by an almost irresistible urge just to sit back down on the floor and immerse myself once again in my own pages, to remind myself – just one last time – of the person I was, before it is all consigned to oblivion.

But I know I have to get rid of them. And I must do it now.

A pair of tongs lies at the side of the fireplace. I pick these up and, two-handed, take hold of the first – the oldest – book. Screwing my face up against the heat, I reach forward and put it down onto the flames. A branch shifts and settles under its weight: I hold the tongs out, ready to catch the book if it falls, but it stays balanced where it is. Within seconds, though, the cover begins to distort: it twists and writhes as though it feels the pain of its burning. If it could give voice, I think it would scream. The creamy vellum begins to blacken, and tendrils of thick, grey, acrid-smelling smoke, like ringlets of unwashed hair, creep out around the edges of the cover. The vellum starts to shrink into a glistening black lump, pulling away from the paper beneath. My own words stare up at me from the newly revealed page,

And into the hidden crevices of how many men's lives will I have to poke my fingers before I learn enough to justify the title of 'corti-giana onesta'? Will it ever happen? How different shall I be then from the grubby little strumpet I am today? Can . . .

Checking over my shoulder, I snatch up the poker and push the book further down into the fire. With a muffled crackle, the wood crumbles and flames flare around their sacrificial victim. The page blackens, glows red around the edges and then catches. My words disappear into flame. The page beneath follows suit, and then the fire takes the book and cradles it tenderly, wrapping it around and consuming it.

I let out the breath I only now realise I have been holding in.

The heat stings against the cut on my cheek as I reach out with the tongs towards the second book. I touch the cut with the tip of my finger: the edges feel dry and slightly stiff already, and at my touch, they flash with a thin, white-cold pain. I ignore this, and grip the second book with the tongs. I place it carefully on top of the burning corpse of its brother. It groans and heaves and arches its spine: the cover shrinks, the pages buckle and scorch; then flames lick along the ash-frilled edges and slick out across the flat of the paper.

Two gone.

One left.

I reach out for the last and newest volume – one I began writing in not more than a couple of months ago. I know which one it is by the long dark blemish in the vellum on the front cover.

The book is scarred, as well as the writer.

I pick it up, but my fingers are slippery with soot from the tongs and it slides from my grasp and falls, splayed out and spine-up, onto the floorboards. I snatch for it, turn it upwards and examine the now-crumpled page on which it has landed.

Surely I will never need this carefully hoarded store of ammunition again? What possible use could it ever be? I imagine its most likely purpose now would be to cripple any fragile bond of trust that might possibly grow back between Luca and me. I ought to fear it: of course it should follow the others onto the pyre. But – a new thought trickles cold across my scalp – maybe I've just made the wrong decision. Perhaps I shouldn't have burned any of it. Then maybe I could have blackmailed the lot of them: Michele, Filippo, Vasquez, da Argenta, Salerno – all of them. One by one. Saved myself from penury that way. My heart gives another painful jolt. A few shrivelled and glistening lumps are all that remain of the first two books. No point in thinking about them – nothing will bring them back, but, though I don't understand it, I think I am going to listen to this little voice.

But here in Luca's house, to be in possession of a thing like this is like standing amongst fizzing fireworks holding a gunpowder keg. Where should I put it until I can take it back to Santa Lucia? I look around the room and see the twins. I'll wrap it in something and then tuck it in with their clothes. Luca is bound to leave their belongings to me to pack up – if he sees the book, I hope he will presume it to be something of theirs.

But where has Luca gone? Will he ever come back? To this house? To me? He left looking so anguished, so distressed. I start to picture him: drowning his misery in ale at a tavern; wandering the lightless docks and contemplating oblivion in the black water between the great hulks of berthed ships; staring after some dis-ease-ridden, dead-eyed little *puttana* and thinking of me at my worst.

I want him back. Oh, God, I want him back – so much I feel close to retching at the thought of having to live without him.

Forty-seven

The circle of watching drinkers had become a single being, Modesto thought: a many-headed hydra, gasping and exclaiming with one voice. All twenty or so heads followed the movements of the combatants in uncanny unison, shifting forward together in greedy expectation as the two men got slowly to their feet for the fourth time. To see a pair of such well-dressed and obviously well-bred gentlemen brawling across a tavern floor like any one of them, was truly an entertaining sight for the end of a Saturday evening.

Many of the table candles had gone out, and the room was in semi-darkness, lit now only by a couple of torches in brackets on the walls.

Modesto looked from Signor della Rovere to Cicciano. Both had discarded their doublets, and Cicciano's shirt was torn. Rovere had a split and swollen lip, and a cut above one eyebrow: Cicciano's nose was bleeding, one tooth was chipped and a bruise was lifting puffily under his left eye. Both were breathing heavily. Much to Modesto's surprise, they appeared to be well matched: as the fight had begun, he had presumed that Rovere – the 'gutless intellectual' – would have neither the skill nor the inclination to fight a man like Cicciano, but he had to admit that he was impressed by the way in which the Signore certainly seemed to be holding his own, even if this might in part be due to the significant amount of *grappa* the younger man had already consumed before the altercation began. And, Modesto thought bitterly, due to the energy Cicciano had already expended on . . . other activities.

Despite himself, Modesto began to feel a grudging liking for Signor della Rovere. This fight was about Francesca, after all, he thought, and he found that he was more than happy to applaud any man who would willingly take a battering like this on behalf of his mistress.

Cicciano's gaze flicked over the floor around his feet. A brief second's stillness drew Modesto's attention and he saw, at almost the same moment as did Cicciano, the steel and silver knife, lying underneath the table, its little round 'ears' glinting in the shifting light. Modesto held his breath, then edged himself to the front of the crowd.

Cicciano stepped backwards, his gaze fixed upon Rovere's face, then, with a movement far swifter than Modesto had expected, he ducked down, grabbed the knife and stood once more.

The hydra sucked a shocked breath in through its many mouths as torchlight flashed bright along the blade and the fight took on quite another dimension.

Modesto automatically put his hand to his waist, intending to pull from the inside lining of his doublet the little leather-sheathed knife he had always kept close in case of troublesome patrons. He swore under his breath as his hand met only the linen of his shirt. No doublet.

'Let's put an end to this tedious little *fracasso*, shall we?' Cicciano said softly. 'I need to get going, and you have become decidedly boring.'

The Signore did not reply, but stood, chest still heaving, gaze fixed on the knife. He flicked his head sideways, to shift a fallen lock of hair.

Cicciano took a step away from Rovere, towards the watching crowd. With a murmur, they parted, shuffling back quickly, all eyes on the blade. 'You seem to be tiring,' Cicciano said. 'It'll be easier all round if I just leave.'

'I don't think so,' the Signore said.

Cicciano laughed, and his gaze moved from the knife in his fist to the older man and back. He raised an eyebrow, ran his tongue over his lips and edged forwards. The hydra retreated. Rovere circled around to block Cicciano's route to the tavern door. His hands had curled into loose fists at chest height, ready for a further assault and Modesto could see that, despite the fatigue obvious in his face, he was still clearly possessed of a sort of weary determination. When he spoke, however, although his gaze remained fixed upon Cicciano's face, it was not to Cicciano that he addressed himself, but to the wide-eyed faces in the crowd, and his voice was calm and clear and carrying. 'Perhaps someone here would be good enough to run for the *sbirri*,' he said. 'This man is guilty of a vicious, unprovoked attack on a defenceless and—'

'Unprovoked? Defenceless? The bloody woman's a fucking whore!'

'And you consider that sufficient justification for—'

Michele laughed. 'Ha! So you don't deny she's a whore? You did know!'

Even in the semi-darkness, Modesto could see Rovere's colour rise. He watched him push one hand up into his hair, heard him swear softly under his breath. Then came a moment of stillness. Both Cicciano and Rovere stood unmoving. The silence in the tavern was complete.

Modesto held his breath.

For a second there was between the two men a bunched, quivering, elastic tension such as will spring up between two hackle-risen dogs, and, feeling the bulging swell of it himself, Modesto's pulse quickened. The wall of watching drinkers seemed to tremble.

Then Cicciano lunged towards where Rovere was standing, the knife in his upturned fist. Modesto pushed forwards, elbowing his way free of the crowd, and, with an audible grunt, he threw himself at Cicciano. He, Cicciano and Rovere all fell to the floor, scattering chairs and two tables. A sharp pain ran up Modesto's leg as one knee cracked against the floor; he was aware of a tangle of shirtsleeved arms, grunted oaths from Cicciano, and the hot, sweat-smelling bulk of both the other bodies, indeterminate in the sprawling scrimmage. Somewhere within the tangle was the knife. His hand closed on an arm – he did not know whose – and he felt it twist and wrench itself out of his grip.

Flat on his back on the tavern floor, Luca saw Michele jerk his wrist from Modesto's fingers. The blade in Michele's fist flashed for a second as he angled his arm up behind him.

Luca stared at the knife.

The scene hung frozen for a second.

And then Michele struck.

Luca squirmed sideways – but he could not move freely. Modesto's weight was heavy across his legs as he twisted himself around; Luca felt his shoulder scrape across the stone flags of the tavern floor and then something hard hit him in the ribs, winding him.

For a moment, all was confusion and chaos. His head was filled with the shouts and cries of the crowd, the grunts of the two men tangled with him on the floor of the tavern, and the wild thudding of his own heartbeat.

Somebody screamed.

The sound tore through the tavern like a ripping sheet, and the writhing confusion that was himself, Michele and Modesto was suddenly still and heavy. Luca's arm was pressed in between his body and the floor; someone's crushing weight was across his hips and he was aware, in the pulsing seconds that followed the scream, of a warm stickiness creeping in between his fingers.

A thick clot of nauseous panic lumped in his throat.

Forty-eight

Serafina Parisetto realised her mouth was open. She closed it. Her eyes wide with shock, she stared at Gianni, who said, 'And then about an hour ago, Papa said he was going to try to find Carlo; he just ran out of the house and I haven't seen him since. I daren't go and look for him – I don't want to leave her and those children on their own for long, with only Luigi, he's so useless. Please come, Signora – she hasn't asked for help, but she's horribly pale and I'm frightened to touch the cut on her face in case I make it worse.'

Serafina tried to speak. Each of several attempts failed. Then, sounding hoarse, she managed to whisper, 'A . . . a *courtesan*?'

She felt a twinge of shame in her belly, even saying the word.

Gianni nodded.

'Does Filippo know?' A pause. 'I mean . . . his *cousin*.'

Serafina saw Gianni flush and her face flamed. She said, 'Oh, no. She's not his cousin, is she?'

Gianni shook his head.

Serafina felt sick. 'Oh, *cielo* – poor Maria. And poor Luca.' Another, longer pause. She remembered the morning she had spent with – as she had thought then – her new friend, out on the *belvedere*. She had liked her so much. Pressing steepled fingers against the sides of her nose, she muttered, 'Oh, dear, I . . . I don't know what to think . . .' She felt as though she were standing in fog on the edge of an unexpected cliff.

Gianni twitched his weight from one leg to another. 'Can you come now? I don't know how long Papa's going to be, and—'

'Of course, *caro*. Of course . . .' Serafina reached out and laid a hand on Gianni's sleeve.

Leaving him standing in the hallway, she ran up the stairs to where Piero sat by the fire in the *sala*. He frowned curiously as she came in, but Serafina held both hands up in front of her as he opened his mouth to speak. 'No – Piero, please – don't ask. It's too complicated, and I have to go. Now. It's just – do you remember Francesca?' She hesitated and then managed to say, 'Filippo's cousin? From the play?'

Piero nodded.

'Gianni's at the door – he says she's . . . she's been hurt. He wants me to come and see her.'

Piero stood up. 'Hurt? What's happened? Where's Luca?'

'I don't know. I'll tell you more when I get back, *caro*. Please – I just want to get going. You'll have to stay here with the boys.'

Piero nodded again. 'But it's late,' he said. 'Gianni must walk you there and back – all the way, Fina. I don't want you out on your own this late.'

Serafina nodded over her shoulder as she hurried out to the kitchen. Rummaging through several drawers, she put a handful of small squares of linen, a couple of bunches of thyme and some sprigs of lavender into a basket, then picked up a corked bottle of lavender water and a small jar of honey, putting them on top of the herbs and the cloths. She laid another square of linen flat on the table; opening a stoneware jar, she scooped three spoonfuls of salt onto the linen, where it lay in a neat cone shape. She lifted the corners of the linen square and tied them tightly across the diagonal, first one way, then the other, making a secure bag for the salt. This she put into the basket with the other items. Then, pulling a brown, sleeveless, fur-trimmed coat from a hook on the back of the door, she swung it around her shoulders.

'She's up on the second floor,' Gianni said. 'In my room. Just opposite the top of the staircase.'

Serafina drew in a long breath, and climbed the stairs with her heart thumping. The openings to a dozen different versions of a possible conversation jostled and tumbled untidily in her mind; each she discarded in turn as rude, ignorant, embarrassing.

She knocked tentatively on the closed door.

A pause. Footsteps. The door latch lifted.

In the few moments it had taken Serafina to walk from her house to this one, she had built up in her mind a picture of the woman she now knew to be . . . a courtesan. In her mind Francesca's new expression was salacious and knowing, she was dressed in provocative and revealing clothing; she was to Serafina now entirely alien. Even frightening. But, as the real Francesca opened the door to Gianni's bedchamber, and Serafina saw her pallor, her fatigue, her tangled hair and the ugly gash running up the side of her face, all her anxieties and embarrassment vanished. She dropped her basket onto the floor, put her arms around her friend and held her. She stood still and unspeaking, aware that the woman in her embrace had begun to shake with slow, silent sobs.

'Oh, *cara*, don't cry,' Serafina murmured. 'Please, please don't cry.'

Francesca did not reply, but a sound seemed to force itself out of her – a long, low, animal groan, that instantly reminded Serafina of the cries she herself had made in childbirth: a wordless, guttural expression of exhausted desperation. Serafina tightened her hold. She stroked Francesca's back in little soothing circles, aware as she did so of her own smallness; used to the size of her two tiny boys, who were the people whose tears she most regularly dried, it suddenly seemed incongruous to be thus mothering a woman at least a head taller than she was herself.

'Gianni's told me everything,' she murmured. 'All about it. He came to find me just now, because he was so worried about you.'

'Is Luca with you?' she heard Francesca say.

'No.' Serafina stood back from her, reaching for and holding both Francesca's hands inside her own. 'No. I . . . I don't know where he is.'

Francesca looked at her without speaking for several seconds, then she said, 'You must despise me.'

Serafina stared at her. 'I think I meant to,' she said. She was surprised at her own honesty. 'I think I meant to, as I walked over here, but now it has come to it, I find that I don't.'

'I hated deceiving you. I wished I could tell you the truth.'

Serafina imagined herself with such a secret: knew how impossible it would have been to have divulged it. 'It doesn't matter,' she said. 'Don't think of it. Let me see that cut.'

She motioned to Francesca to sit back down on the edge of the bed, and then, holding a candle up close to Francesca's face, she peered at the wound left by Michele's knife and said, 'Oh, *cara*, that must be so very sore – can you let me put some salts on it? There's a chance it will turn poisonous if we just leave it.'

Francesca said nothing, but sat still and quiet, watching whilst her companion busied herself taking her herbs, honey and salt out of her little basket. Serafina laid them carefully on the chest at the end of the bed, then crossed to the door, opened it, and called down the stairs, 'Gianni!'

There were footsteps, and Gianni's face, oddly isolated in a pool of wobbling candlelight, appeared in the hallway.

'Could you boil me some water, *caro*, and bring up a cup and a spoon, too?'

Gianni nodded and disappeared.

When she turned back into the room, Serafina saw that Francesca was crouched down next to her children; stroking one girl's forehead, she was crooning a softly whispered song, murmuring them back to sleep.

Gianni appeared a few moments later, with a pewter bowl in one hand, and a small stemless cup in the other. This he put down on the chest, next to Serafina's herbs and salts. He hesitated a moment, then pecked a quick nod to Francesca and left the room again.

Serafina dipped the cup into the hot water, then stripping off some of the lavender and thyme leaves, she pushed them down into the water to steep. Into the rest of the hot water, she tipped the salt, and stirred it around with the spoon.

'We'll leave that to cool for a moment,' she said. 'I'll wash the cut with it. The salt will help to clean it – it might sting a little, though. And then I'll dress it with honey.'

Francesca shrugged, but said nothing. She sat silently whilst Serafina cleaned her torn face with one of the linen squares, soaked in the hot salt water. Other than stifled winces, she neither moved nor spoke.

Forty-nine

'Quick!'

Luca felt a hand close around his wrist.

'We have to get out of here – now!' Modesto jerked at Luca's arm. 'Come on, Signore – you have to move. The fucking *sbirri* will be here any moment.'

Luca's fingers were red and sticky. Retching, he wiped them on his breeches: they left a dark, untidy smear across the top of his leg. He looked up at the manservant. 'Cicciano . . . is he?'

'I don't know – but we have to get out of here fast.'

'I can't! For God's sake . . . he's been hurt! We have to—'

'No, we bloody don't. We get ourselves away from here as quick as we can, believe me.'

Modesto's face was smeared with blood, and the protuberant eyes were wide and anxious; when he spoke again, his voice was shaking. 'You think the *sbirri* will listen to a word you say, Signore? They're a load of bloody thugs – you know how it is! They're as like to torture the *victim* of a crime as the perpetrator to get what they want – we wouldn't stand a chance. They see a body here, and they'll—'

Luca froze.

'Come *on*!' Modesto's voice sounded almost frantic.

Luca was pulled to his feet, and together he and Modesto

pushed into the throng of people now staring down at where Cicciano lay sprawled on the floor of the tavern. Much to Luca's surprise, nobody tried to stop them: the crowd parted silently, moving back as though the two of them were diseased, the various faces all wearing the same round-eyed look of shock. Luca gave one last glance towards the figure on the floor, then he turned and ran with Modesto out of the tavern, out into the dark street and back towards his house in the Piazza Monteoliveto, running at full tilt until his breath dragged and the sharp stab of a stitch dug into his side. The front door opened as Modesto thudded up against it; both men stumbled into the hallway, then Luca closed the door and leaned against it, breathing heavily through an open mouth.

Gianni appeared at the top of the stairs, silhouetted in the doorway to the candlelit *sala*. He stared down at the new arrivals for a second, then, taking the stairs two at a time, ran heavy footed down into the hallway, his face puckered with anxiety.

'Papa?' he said. 'What? What's happened? Is Carlo with you?'

Luca shook his head, still struggling to calm his breathing, quite unable to speak.

'What's happened to you? There's blood all over your shirt . . . Your face . . . Have you been *fighting*?' Gianni sounded incredulous.

'Cicciano,' Luca said, indistinctly.

'You found him?'

A nod.

'Oh, God. Is he . . . ? Have you . . . ?'

'I . . . I don't know.'

'Papa, what are you going to do?'

'I don't know.' Luca tipped his head back, closed his eyes, and drew in several long, shuddering breaths.

'Come upstairs, Papa,' Gianni said. 'Both of you. You can't just stand here.'

Luca followed his son and Francesca's servant up the stairs. The fire in the *sala* was almost out, though several candles were still burning in brackets on the walls. The hangings had been drawn shut and, Luca thought, as Modesto and Gianni pulled out chairs and sat down, his usually tranquil room seemed in a moment to have taken on the secretive and threatening atmosphere of a bandit's lair. Not feeling able to sit down, he walked across to stand by the fireplace, his heart still racing. His thoughts were tumultuous, chaotic, fragmented, unstoppable: he felt light-headed. What was he going to do? It seemed that Cicciano might well be dead, possibly at his – Luca's – own hand. Luca felt breathless. He might have . . . might have . . . killed someone. Killed someone. The words echoed soundlessly in his head.

'Papa . . .' Gianni began.

Luca saw the compassionate candour in his son's eyes and the ground began to fall away under his feet. He leaned his head against the mantelshelf and closed his eyes. He heard a chair scrape on the wooden floor; heard footsteps crossing the room, and then felt a hand on his arm. Gianni stood at his shoulder. Luca turned towards him, and pulled him in close to his body. He said, 'I'm sorry.'

'What for, Papa?'

He pulled back from Gianni. 'For Christ's sake!' Luca heard his voice rise in volume, but felt unable to control it. 'A man is dead! My God, Gianni. Dead because of me! I could have walked away from that tavern, and he would still be alive, and—'

'No,' Modesto's voice cut across him. 'No, you listen to me.'

*

413

'Oh, God. Luca's back. That's his voice.' Francesca twitched her head away from Serafina's hand and stood up, listening. 'And that's Modesto. I . . . I have to go down there. I have to talk to Luca. I can't just stay up here.'

'Do you want me to come with you?'

Francesca turned to Serafina. Serafina saw the cut on her face – clean now and dressed neatly – but still standing out stark against the paleness of her skin; she was struck by the determination in Francesca's gaze and could not help but admire her courage.

'Yes, please,' Francesca said, and Serafina was touched by her dignity. 'Thank you. I should like that.'

'Here.' Serafina held out a hand. As Francesca took it, Serafina squeezed her fingers, suppressing a moment's curiosity as she found herself picturing all the other unmentionable things that Francesca might have done with this same hand. Would she ever be able to be in Francesca's company again without such thoughts?

And, more to the point, she supposed, would Luca?

Together, the two women crossed the room and went down the stairs towards the *sala*. Voices within the room were raised now. Francesca stopped outside the closed door. She bent forward to listen, but almost immediately gasped, pulled back and put her fingers over her mouth.

'Oh, Serafina!' she whispered. 'Oh, God! He says he's killed Michele!'

Serafina frowned, uncomprehending, a nauseous swirl of shock trickling down through her insides.

Modesto looked steadily at Luca.

'So, don't you start imagining things that might not have happened. Look. We don't actually even know if the bastard's dead, but if he is, then *I* killed him. Me. Not you.' Modesto stood up, an

414

emphatic forefinger jabbing the air. 'He had that knife. I . . . I don't know just how it happened, but I got his wrist, and then, then . . .' He paused, and then burst out, 'I couldn't just stand there and let him kill you – and he would have done, Signore, he'd have finished you, for certain. I didn't mean him to die – dear God! Despite what he's done, I hope he's still alive. I just wanted to stop him, before . . .' He hesitated. 'If he'd killed you . . . it'd just have broken her heart.'

Luca looked at him without expression.

Modesto drew in a breath and said, 'She loves you, Signore.'

Luca's gaze was steady, but he said nothing.

Modesto said, 'I know what you must think about what you've found out. But you're wrong if . . . if you think that what's she's done in the past dictates what she *is* now, in the present.' He ran the heel of his hand across his forehead. 'Signore, I've known her for more than three years, and I understand her better than anyone else does. She and I have been through a great deal together – we've shared laughter and tears, rage, terror. Make no mistake, things have been bad in the past before – very bad. I've seen her frightened and angry and unhappy – but I've never seen her like this. Never.' He jabbed the accusatory forefinger up towards the floor above. 'She's sitting up there now, broken into pieces, unable to bear the thought of losing you.'

He saw Luca wince.

'Don't let her go, Signore.' He paused. 'You'll not meet many women like her in your life.'

Luca put his head in his hands.

Modesto began to pace, his gaze fixed upon Luca. 'I know what you've been thinking,' he said, feeling a hot mixture of jealousy, loyalty, and resentment bubbling up behind his voice. He pointed back at Luca, accusingly. 'You've decided she's scum. Oh, you thought her beautiful and charming and sensitive and loveable when you met her. Just the woman for you, you thought, and almost straightaway you considered marriage, didn't you? And all the delights of a life ahead in the company of an exquisite creature like her. What luck, you thought, to have found someone so lovely, when you had resigned yourself to the life of a widower. But then it all changed, didn't it? You discovered that she's not quite what you thought she was.' He paused. 'You found out that she's been fucking for money since the age of seventeen –' he saw the boy start, and Rovere shook his head, his face still hidden behind his fingers '– and then the bubble burst and now you have no idea what to say to her. You don't even know how to *look* at her any more.'

Luca's hands were pressed together, the tips of his fingers below his nose. As though he were praying.

'But whatever she's done, the truth is that she *is* all those things, Signore. She *is* beautiful and charming and sensitive and loveable. And she's clever, too. You're a lucky man; she loves you. She'd do anything for you. You'd be a fool to lose her.'

A bottle of red wine stood on the table amidst the remains of the meal Gianni had been eating. Modesto reached across, picked it up, poured some into an empty glass, and drank it down. An ember shifted in the fireplace with a soft crumbling scuffle, and a puff of hot air hissed quietly down into the ashes.

The grudging respect for the Signore that had flickered into being as he had watched the brawl in the tavern had, in the past few moments, solidified and confirmed itself in Modesto's mind. He knew – with reasonable certainty – what he – Modesto – had done back there. He knew what he would have to do now, and he knew, too, that he would have to be quite sure that Francesca would be cared for and truly loved in his absence. He swilled the last of his wine around in the bottom of the glass for a moment, staring down into it, as it washed pinkly around the bowl, and then said, 'You *might* think that whores are scum, Signore. Well. Some of them are – I've met a fair number. But *she's* not. After all, all she's ever done is attempt to give people pleasure – however hard it is to square that with your own personal notions of morality.' He paused, waiting for a few long seconds, before he loosed his final shot. 'I suppose it's not really for me to say, but it just seems to me that you might want to think for a moment or two about your elder son before you condemn the Signora too harshly.'

Fifty

As Carlo reached the top of the *sottosuolo* steps, there was far more noise in the tavern than he would have expected: the normal thrum of conversation was sharper, louder, more jagged and confused than usual. He stared about him, warily. A large number of people were on their feet, several tables had been pushed aside, and a couple of chairs lay tipped over on the floor. Even as he registered all this, Carlo heard running feet, and the sound of the door to the tavern being opened and then slammed shut.

He paused. The climb back up to the surface from the hell of that lightless cavern had been long and tiring; he had had to sit in the blackness and rest several times, feeling giddy and with his head aching, and – though he would never have admitted it – he had been very frightened to be so entirely wrapped in that smothering darkness for so long. He felt sick with relief at his arrival back in the smoky, smelly familiarity of his favourite tavern; he needed a drink to steady his nerves and he wanted time – time to decide what best he should do. But, to his irritation, there seemed to be some sort of drama going on in the middle of the room: a drama that appeared to be absorbing everyone's full attention, something which might very well mean that his chances of being served promptly would be considerably reduced.

Determining to find the tavern-keeper and demand the *grappa* he craved, he wormed his way between the jostling bodies and peered through to see what it was that was so fascinating everyone, but, on actually seeing the cause of the disturbance, he stopped short. A body lay sprawled on the flagged floor and, as he stared down at it, several thoughts struck Carlo almost simultaneously. The first was that there was something indefinably and irrevocably broken about the silent figure in front of him; it lay quite still, crumpled and bent in a manner no living person could have sustained for more than a second or two. The second thought was that it was, quite clearly, Cicciano. The third was that Marco was standing on the far side of where Cicciano lay, his arms folded tightly, his usual dirty cloth draped over his shoulder. Marco was staring at Carlo, a ragged wince of undisguised dislike twisting his face into a grimace. Carlo stared back for a second or two, and then, unthinking, he pushed through to crouch down beside where Cicciano lay motionless.

He put his hand to Cicciano's neck and felt for a pulse. The skin was still warm, but he could determine no movement of any sort, and there was a heavy solidity to the flesh beneath the skin that proclaimed no life. The linen of Cicciano's shirt was stained red below his armpit, and, seeing this, a sick wash of dizziness swept over Carlo and he put a hand down to the floor to steady himself. The wooden boards on which he leaned were wet and sticky; snatching his hand back up again, he wiped his fingers on his shirt.

Then the door to the tavern banged open again, and four heavyset men shoved their way into the room, scattering any drinkers in their path. Dressed in scruffy, ill-assorted black doublets and breeches, and each brandishing a broad-bladed knife, they had a thuggish air about them, and Carlo – recognising them immediately for what they were – scrambled to his feet and backed away from Cicciano's body. The forcible maintenance of the law in

Napoli might have been the nominal function of the *sbirri*, but Carlo knew as well as every other man in the room that he would most likely be treated by them with an unthinking, heavy-handed lack of justice.

'Everybody stay where you are!' one of them shouted.

At least a dozen people ignored the command completely, and in a noisy scramble of poorly fitting shoes and panicked gasping, they barged past the newcomers and ran for the door of the tavern. One of the *sbirri* followed them, and, although failing to stop any of the escapees, he turned and stood square in the doorway. Holding his knife point upwards, he leaned his other hand against the door jamb and glared around him at the occupants of the tavern, jaw jutting mulishly. Nobody spoke. Nervous looks were shared; throats were cleared; feet shuffled and clothing rustled.

Another of the new arrivals – a bear of a man with an unruly black beard and unwashed, over-long hair – took the position just vacated by Carlo, down beside the body on the floor. Holding Cicciano's chin between thumb and fingers, the *sbirro* flipped the head over to face in the other direction and back, staring down at the blank features with a frown of compassionless curiosity.

'What happened here?' he said, glaring up at the crowd. 'Who did it?'

The silence in the room became absolute. Nobody moved.

'Well?' the *sbirro* said again, a bite of aggression in his voice. 'Someone must have seen something. This man's been knifed, and not more than a few moments ago, I'd say – some bastard in this room must have seen who did it!'

Suddenly aware, with a cold thrill of fear that slid from the back of his throat down into his belly, that his freshly split lip, grazed cheek, blackened eye and bloodstained hand might well appear suspicious, Carlo began to edge slowly backwards, aiming to slide through the crowd towards the steps to the *sottosuolo*. He would, he thought, go back down into the tunnel and wait, a few yards in, in the darkness, until the *sbirri* had left.

He caught Marco's eye again.

There passed between the two young men a wave of almost palpable antagonism. Carlo heard again in his head the conversation that had followed their final coupling; remembered Marco's whining entreaty as he had sulkily refastened his breeches, wiping his eyes and nose with the back of his hand. *'But from everything you said – right from the start – I was sure that you felt more for me than just—'* Irritated, Carlo had held up both hands and interrupted what had surely been set to become an embarrassingly trite outpouring. *'For God's sake, Marco,'* he had said, *'what did you think? That I was in love with you or something? Proficient in a number of . . . useful methods of entertainment you may well be, but, well, Marco, I do have standards.'*

And then . . . then he had been foolish enough to boast of his plans a few hours ago, down at the dockside.

Marco stared at him across Cicciano's body for several seconds, then, turning away, he took a step towards the nearest *sbirro* and said, in a clear and carrying voice, pointing back towards Carlo, 'That man over there. The one with the black eye and the thick lip. The one with blood on his hands. You might ask him about it.'

Fifty-one

Modesto sounds angry. I stand, quite unable to move outside Luca's *sala* door, looking at Serafina and listening to my manservant's tirade. Of Luca, I can hear nothing at all. Serafina's mouth has opened and she is fiddling unthinkingly with her lower lip.

'You *might* think that whores are scum, Signore,' Modesto is saying. 'Well. Some of them are – I've met a fair number of them. But *she*'s not.'

Scum. Flotsam. Fragments of stinking rubbish lying on the surface of stagnant water. Is this what I've been all this time? Is this what Luca thinks I am?

'You might want to think for a moment or two about your elder son before you condemn the Signora too harshly.'

Oh my God.

How has he dared to say such a thing? I wait for the explosion – for Luca to shout at him and order his immediate departure, but there is only a horribly empty pause. Serafina reaches for my hand.

And then at last I hear Luca's voice. He says, 'I do love her.'

I don't seem to be able to move.

Modesto says, his voice emphatic, 'Then tell her so, Signore. Please. Before you lose her. She needs you. She really needs you. Now. Because, after what has happened this evening, I am . . .' He hesitates. 'I am going to be leaving Napoli, straight away, before they catch up with me, and—'

I do not hear the end of his sentence. I don't care whether or not they all realise that I have been blatantly eavesdropping. I crash open the door to the *sala* with my heart thumping in my ears, and my voice comes out as something near a shriek as I say, 'Leave? Why? When? Modesto, you can't!'

All three turn and stare at me.

Luca has a cut above his eyebrow and his lip is split and bleeding. Modesto's face is smeared with blood, his shirt is torn and bloodstained. Neither man is wearing a doublet. Gianni, his gaze flicking from one to the other, seems entirely bewildered.

'Leaving Napoli?' I say.

Modesto pushes his hand through his hair and nods.

'But why?' My voice cracks.

'Did you hear what I said just now?' Modesto asks – not crossly, but because he wants to know.

I nod.

He says, 'Well. I'm pretty certain I did kill that bastard. If I stay, and they find out that I'm responsible for his death, then there's little doubt that I'll hang. Or burn. So I need to get out of Napoli – probably tonight.'

I look from Modesto to Luca and back.

I'm not sure I can remember how to breathe.

Modesto is looking at Luca. 'Just talk to her, Signore,' he says quietly, then adds, to me, 'I'll be downstairs. I promise I'll not go anywhere without telling you.' He lowers his voice still more and says, 'Did I leave that leather bag in your room? With your books in it?'

I nod.

He puffs out relief. 'Thank God for that. I wasn't sure what I'd

423

done with them. Keep them safe. They are your bloody insurance, Signora, and don't you forget it.' He doesn't give me time to tell him that I've burned most of the books, but, turning away, he nods at Gianni and Serafina and jerks his head towards the door, inviting the two of them to follow him out. All three leave the room, leaving Luca and me together.

Several heavy seconds pass. I can feel my pulse in the cut on my face. I have no idea what to say, and I can see Luca is struggling too. Then we both speak at once, each almost instantly stumbling into a clumsy apology for interrupting the other. Another silence, and then Luca says, 'I'm so sorry.'

'What for?'

His gaze moves from me to the floor, to the ceiling, to the fireplace and then back to my face again. For a second he reminds me forcibly of Gianni that first night, staring around my bedchamber in an agony of embarrassment and a clotted sob rises thickly in my throat.

Luca says, 'I'm sorry for what Carlo did. For what *I*'ve done. For being small-minded and narrow and not understanding what—'

I interrupt him. 'There's a lot not to understand.'

He smiles then – a tight, uncomfortable smile that doesn't reach his eyes. 'Your servant says I should be careful not to lose you.'

'Do you agree with him?'

He does not answer directly. He says, 'Can you forgive me?'

'*Me* forgive *you*?' His question surprises me. 'For what?'

'For having failed as a father. For having raised a son who could have done something so . . . so abhorrent. To your children.'

I hesitate, then ask the question to which I'm not sure I want a reply. 'Is what he did more abhorrent then, than my being a whore?'

Luca pulls in a trembling breath, and his words slide out through the sigh of its release. 'Before today, I'm not sure how I would have answered that question. But now . . .'

I see he has tears in his eyes.

'Now,' he says, 'the answer is easy . . . but I can hardly bear to give it.'

'You are not your son, Luca.'

'But I raised him!' Luca's face is anguished.

'Aren't we all of us comprised of much more than just our raising?'

Luca says nothing.

'I was raised well. By a mother who loved me,' I say. 'She truly loved me and she did her best for me, but she was a fragile thing – she had neither the strength nor the courage to defend me from my father; his drunkenness ruled both our lives for years. It killed her in the end, after which I was the sole target for the beatings and the ranting insults and . . .' I stop. Feeling sick, I manage to admit it. 'It was only by chance that he managed to avoid siring upon me his own grandchild.'

Luca's jaw drops.

'I ran away from him when I was seventeen. I went to Ferrara and . . . after nearly a week of miserable starvation and fearful sleepless nights curled in doorways, I was presented with a way of making enough money to live on. Not an easy way, not a pleasant way, and certainly not the way I would have chosen, had I been offered an alternative, but I didn't feel that I had a choice. It was at least something I seemed to be able to do, and something I could sustain.' I pause and then add, 'I just wanted to survive.'

Luca is staring at me, his eyes now huge and glittering.

I say, 'My mother raised me with tenderness. She wanted to see

425

me safely married – to someone who would treat me with more care than she had ever known. She taught me to read and write, and to pray, and to deal with those around me with compassion and tolerance. But *circumstances* prevented the seeds of those lessons from bearing much fruit – ale-stinking, iron-fisted circumstances that ploughed in between me and my mother's wishes, like a runaway bull.' My voice cracks then, as I say, 'If you're drowning, Luca, you grab at whatever floating branch comes near you, however filthy and diseased and cracked it might be – you just don't have time to wait for the nicely polished, carefully cleaned one to come bobbing past.'

I put my face in my hands.

Luca crosses to where I am standing and puts his arms around me. His body is hot and damp; his shirt smells of woodsmoke and blood and the acrid tang of fear-tainted sweat. My arms slide around him and, grabbing fistfuls of linen, I cling to him, pressing myself against him. One of his hands cups the back of my head and he holds it in close to his shoulder; I can hardly breathe, my face is buried in Luca's shirt, the heat of his fingers is in my hair and his arm lies heavy around my back. And then I pull back and our eyes meet, and, for the first time, we look at each other in total truth.

There is nothing left to hide.

He bends his head, seeking my mouth with his. I tilt my head back and he kisses me; speaking and kissing at the same time, he murmurs into my mouth incoherent, salt-wet declarations of love. His poor split lip tastes of blood and must be painful, but still he kisses me. One of his hands holds the unhurt side of my face, the other he pushes up into my hair. We kiss and kiss: two parched desert travellers newly come to an oasis. I silently bless Modesto for insisting that I should never lie with my patrons *gratis*. Thanks to him, I've never bedded a man without money changing hands. Ever. Luca will be my first. I am a virgin again.

Luca takes his mouth from mine, slowly, slowly, drawing away from me, as though the normal division of time into seconds has lost pace and each is taking five times as long as usual to run its course. Holding me by the shoulders for a moment he looks into my face, then hugs me close again. He is lover, brother, father, friend; he is everything I have longed for him to be from that first moment at San Domenico – and he is all those things despite my terrible truths. My tears slide between my face and Luca's shirt, hot, wet and salt-slick.

'Don't cry,' he says into my hair. 'Please, *cara*, don't cry.'

I turn up my face towards his and smile. He returns it – wincing as his lip cracks open again. Bunching up a handful of his shirt, he wipes along below my eyes, first one side, then the other.

'Enough tears now, I think,' he says, stroking my hair. 'For ourselves, at any rate.' He pauses; his smile fades and his face darkens as he adds, 'We have Carlo to cry about now.'

Fifty-two

It is just after dawn: the light sliding in through a crack in the shutters is a flat, shadowless grey, and as yet, the streets outside are still silent. The insistent activity of every Neapolitan day is still some hours from beginning, but somewhere out there, striding away towards the edge of the city, wearing an old doublet of Luca's and with no more than a handful of Luca's money, and a knot of ribbon from the sleeve of my dress in his pocket, is Modesto. A fugitive from justice. Or rather from injustice: there's no justice in this. None whatsoever. For any of us.

My stalwart, faithful, funny, tragic, dearly loved servant has gone.

I can only presume that God must truly wish to make me pay for the wickedness of my past. Perhaps my sins have been greater than even I had thought. I had foolishly imagined myself forgiven when Luca kissed me yesterday evening: God, I thought, had decided that I had suffered enough to make sufficient reparation for my years of decadence. But no. It seems I have more to endure. What has been given with one hand has been snatched away with the other.

I can hardly bear to imagine how Modesto is feeling. What he said a few moments ago shocked me. I've had my suspicions, I suppose, but I've just pushed them well out of sight: hidden them in some dark inhospitable corner of my mind where I've known I would not have to encounter them unexpectedly whilst I've been busy dealing with other supposedly more pressing problems.

'But Modesto – why? Why do you have to go like this? There's nothing to prove that you . . . that you . . . killed Michele . . .' Killed Michele? I can't quite believe what I am saying. 'And anyway, even if you did, it happened because you were trying to save Luca's life, didn't it? Surely no one can blame you for that?'

Modesto's face creases with a mixture of incredulity, pity and irritation. 'Oh, Signora, those bastards simply aren't interested in mitigating circumstances – they just want justice.' He checks, and then says, 'Well, no, I suppose it would be more accurate to say that they want someone to hang. And enough people saw that fight—'

'Then they'll have seen that you didn't start it,' I say.

Luca adds, 'Apart from which, it might just as easily have been me. We were all in that melee together – there's no proof it was you that—'

Modesto interrupts him. 'There's rather more to it than whichever one of us killed Signor di Cicciano. It may have been me, it may not. It may have been you. He may have done it himself. To be honest, I don't really care.'

He seems to be struggling to say something that is causing him some distress.

'Modesto, what is it?' I ask.

'I . . . I . . .' He turns his face up to the ceiling, sucks in a long breath and juts out his jaw as though trying to summon up the courage to speak, then he turns to me and says, very softly, 'Look, Signora, I can't stay here with you – whichever one of us killed Cicciano. It would just be too hard for me to be here with you now.'

'But . . .' I say, stupidly, not understanding what he means. 'Why? Is it something I've done? What?'

He doesn't answer immediately, but his gaze moves from me to Luca, and then back to me again. He says, 'Do you remember a conversation we had some time ago, when I told you that I would have to "accustom myself to sobriety" or whatever it was I said, if your relationship with the Signore were to develop?' He inclines his head briefly towards Luca, then says to me, 'And I told you, didn't I, that . . . you and I . . . would have to be prepared to put a stop to how things have been in the past . . . because it's . . . well, let's just say it's not been the usual sort of relationship between mistress and servant, has it?'

I remember the conversation, and nod.

'Well,' Modesto says, quietly, examining his fingernails before raising his gaze back up to my face, 'After thinking carefully about it, I don't think I'd be able to cope with your new circumstances, after all. I don't think it would be as easy as I had at first thought.'

'But . . . I don't understand. Why?'

'Oh, don't be obtuse, Signora!' Modesto says with something of his old irritability. 'Can't you work it out?'

I can do no more than stare at him.

Luca understands, thank God. I'm so grateful that he hasn't tried to comfort me, or to tell me 'it will all be for the best'; he hasn't attempted to kiss me or hold me since Modesto went, but I can see in his eyes a tender, compassionate comprehension of the extent of my loss.

He was standing behind me on the door sill just now, as I clung to Modesto. I felt Luca's warm bulk at my shoulder, as my manservant and I embraced and I heard Modesto mutter next to my ear, 'Didn't I tell you you would be greater than all of them?'

I pulled back from him. 'What? What are you talking about?'

'Emilia Rosa, Malacoda and the others. I told you you'd outstrip the lot of them.'

'But . . .'

'Do you not think they would change places with you, Signora, given the choice?' He smiled. 'Just think about it.'

I wrapped my arms as tightly around him as I could manage, and he said, his voice muffled in my hair.

'Don't you bloody dare cry, Signora. Just don't do it. Bloody whores . . . overemotional . . . sentimental . . . you're all the bloody same.'

I gripped more tightly round his back.

His words buzzed against the side of my head as he murmured, 'He loves you. You do know that, don't you? You know I wouldn't leave here unless I was sure of it.' He let go of me, stood back a step and held me by the shoulders. Looking over at Luca, he grinned, then turning back to me, said, 'Show him what a lucky bastard he is, Signora.'

Luca said, 'Don't worry – he knows. He knows exactly how lucky a bastard he is.'

I couldn't speak, but managed a watery laugh.

Then Modesto said, 'I'll be back. I promise. To visit.'

'When?'

'I don't know. When everything dies down, I suppose.' He paused, then added, 'Hug those little girls for me. Tell them . . . tell them I've gone exploring, and that when I get back, I'll bring them each a very special present. Tell them I'll try to bring them in time for their birthday – but it might be a little longer.'

I nodded, wondering what sort of understatement that might turn out to be, in the end.

And then he gave me one more fierce, brief hug, turned on his heel, and began to stride away up the street. He did not look back, but raised a hand in farewell just once, before he turned the corner and was lost from sight. I'm glad Luca was standing behind me, with his hands on my shoulders, or I might have run after him and begged him to stay.

Something is bothering Gianni. In the hours since Modesto's departure, he has been restless and fidgety: he has paced from room to room, and more than once, the twins have asked me what the matter is with the nice man who brought them back from the cave.

They cried, of course, when I gave them Modesto's message and delivered his promised hug, but, as I am sure he intended, within a very short time, they had begun discussing with each other where their friend might be going to explore, and – even more exciting – what sort of presents he might be bringing them when he returns.

The girls and I have been keeping ourselves busy, on this early morning, sweeping and dusting the downstairs rooms in Luca's house – I can only imagine that Luca's old servant is losing his eyesight, as it seems that half the dirt of the street outside has found its way unchallenged into the darker corners of the house. Though cleaning and tidying is not my usual wont, I feel so entirely disconnected from reality just now, that the tedious domesticity of this task seems to be providing a sort of comforting crutch; the girls, on the other hand, each seem to be genuinely enjoying wielding their oversized brooms and pretending to be 'wives'. Outwardly, they seem very much as they always are, and only an uncharacteristic desire on their part to cling to my skirts and not to let me out of their sight, gives any indication that they have so recently suffered such a fearful experience.

For the fourth time in not many more minutes, Gianni puts his head round the door, says nothing and goes out again.

Then, a little while later, Luca comes in. '*Cara* – can we talk for a moment?'

My heart turns over. Has he changed his mind?

He looks at the twins.

I say, 'Bella, Beata . . . can you go upstairs? The little room where we are sleeping . . . all the blankets are in such a muddle. Could you go up and try to fold them for me?'

They glance at each other, anxious at the thought of leaving my side, but I promise them that both Luca and I will be up to see how well they have done in just a few moments. Looking somewhat reassured, they hurry towards the stairs.

I look at Luca. 'What is it?' I ask.

'Gianni.'

'I thought he seemed rather agitated just now – what's wrong?'

Luca hesitates. His colour has deepened slightly and he seems decidedly ill at ease. 'He has just been talking to me. It's . . . well, since Modesto told you why he wanted to leave . . .' There is a pause. 'Gianni is . . . I think he has something of the same problem as your manservant.'

I frown at him, thinking of castration and not understanding.

'He's explained it to me, but I think he'd like to talk to you about it himself.'

'Luca, what is this?'

'He's in the *sala* – go and find him, will you?'

He takes my hand and we leave the room and climb the first flight of stairs together. At the door to the *sala*, Luca bends and kisses my mouth. 'He'll explain,' he says, winding a strand of my hair around one finger.

Gianni is standing over by the window, staring down into the street below. He turns round as I enter the room, looking every bit as awkward and embarrassed as he did that first day I met him in the house in San Tommaso.

Neither he nor I say anything for several seconds. The silence is robust and elastic and I am unsure how to break it, so I just watch Gianni and wait for him to speak.

In the end, he says, looking from me to his interlocked fingers and back, 'I've been talking to Papa.'

He does not continue; I cannot think of anything to say in reply, so again, I say nothing.

After a few seconds, Gianni says, 'I've tried to explain to him . . . why . . . why I want to break from my studies for a year or so, and to leave Napoli.'

'Leave?' I say, and my voice sounds too highly pitched.

'When . . . when your servant explained why he needed to get away, it made me think,' Gianni says. 'Made me realise.'

'Realise what?'

'That I'm not sure I can do it either.'

'Do what?'

'Be here – with you and Papa.'

'Oh, Gianni . . .'

Gianni shakes his head. He opens his mouth and tries to speak, but no words seem to come to him and he puffs out a little sigh of exasperation at his inarticulacy. Trying again, he manages to say, 'After . . . after everything we did together, you and me, on that first evening . . . at your house . . . I think I am going to find it difficult . . . to be able . . .' He pauses, and swallows, awkwardly. 'I think it might be hard for me to have to watch you and Papa together.'

'But, Gianni, this is your home! I don't want to be responsible for chasing you out of it.'

He manages a rather wan smile. 'You won't be chasing me out

of it. I'm choosing to go. And I'll come back – it's just –' He bites his lip, choosing the next words carefully. 'You and Papa need some time alone, to begin with, I think. To find out all those things about each other that people need to find out, before they can settle down and just be together.'

I am touched – as I have been before – by Gianni's compassionate wisdom.

He continues, 'I can see in your face, and in Papa's too, that each time you set eyes on each other, it's like a shock that shoots right through you: your insides turn over and it's as if you are struggling to breathe for a second.'

I stare at him, unable to speak.

'It was like that for me – that day I saw you and Papa, on the floor in the *sala*. It hurt like a knife cut inside my chest.' He presses a fist against his doublet front, his gaze quite steady – almost fierce. 'From everything I've heard, though, I don't think that feeling lasts forever. From what I remember of Mamma, I don't think it can have been like that every day between her and Papa, although they loved each other very much. I suppose after years together they were just *used* to each other and so they didn't *surprise* each other all the time, any more.' He pauses. 'When you and Papa aren't surprising each other any more, and can just be together calmly, then I think I could come back.'

I can feel sharp tears behind my eyes yet again.

There is a soft knock on the door of the *sala*. Luca comes in. It is as Gianni says: at the sight of him, a now-familiar needle-thrill of shock shoots down through me and my heart turns over. Gianni smiles. 'I'm right, aren't I?' he says, raising an eyebrow.

I smile back, and in that instant Gianni and I become friends. 'Yes,' I say, with a little laugh. 'Yes, damn it, you are.'

'Right about what?' Luca asks.

435

'Surprises,' Gianni says.

He is just about to expand on this when we are all startled by a frantic knocking at the front door. Luca races downstairs, Gianni and I following. My heart is thudding wildly all over again – something about the urgency of that sound presages yet more unpleasant shocks.

Luca fumbles with the latch, then pulls open the door. There on the door sill, breathless, dishevelled and frightened, and wearing the same green doublet in which I first saw him, stands the young man with the over-long hair who arranged my meeting with Gianni, that day on the low wall outside the Castel Nuovo.

'Nicco,' Luca says. 'What on earth?'

'They've arrested Carlo,' the man called Nicco says, leaning forward, his hands gripping his knees, his breath ragged in his throat. 'Oh God, Signore – they're saying he's killed Cicciano in a brawl.'

Fifty-three

Cristoforo di Benevento dismounted, pulled his saddlebags off the mare's broad rump and handed the reins over to a horseboy. He dropped the bags at his feet, and, stretching and rolling stiff shoulders, looked around him, breathing in the comfortable smells of horse and straw, and then wrinkling his nose at the more acrid reek rising from a nearby pile of droppings. The garrison stables was almost deserted this afternoon, he thought; as the boy led his mare away – her head hanging wearily, her coat gleaming with sweat – only one other stableman was visible, leaning against the flank of a huge gelding and bending to brush dry mud from the creature's legs. This scene was quite different from the clattering bustle of departure three weeks earlier, when some forty-five fully armed men and horses had clanked and stamped their way out onto the main road heading for the east coast and the garrison town of Bari. 'She'll be thirsty,' Cristoforo called as the boy rounded a corner with the mare. 'Make sure she has a drink, will you? And hay.'

The boy made no reply, but turning, nodded in acknowledgment, patting the mare's neck affectionately as he went off out of sight.

Saddlebags now over one shoulder, Cristoforo began to walk away from the garrison block, wondering where he would go first.

The sky was the clear blue of a thrush's egg, though a few ragged wisps of cloud hung like pale smoke overhead. The city was still drowsing after the heat of the midday and most of the streets were almost empty. But behind closed doors as he walked along the Via Forno Vecchio, Cristoforo could hear disembodied voices – men in vehement argument; the petulant squeal of a scolded child; a woman's lilting song. Seductive cooking smells hung in the air, seeping from a window in a house on the corner of the street. A group of skinny boys, barefoot, tangle-haired and wearing little more than tattered breeches, bounced and jostled each other out of a side alley, shoving and hooting and pushing as they ran, their laughter skidding across several octaves from shrill treble to a grating bass.

There was something engaging in their camaraderie, Cristoforo thought, and the prospect of the empty silence of his apartment seemed suddenly unappealing. He had not expected to be back in the city, away from his men, until well into the early months of the new year; his rooms would have an unwelcoming chill about them, he was sure, despite the warmth of the afternoon. It was more than just the empty rooms, though – thinking about it, Cristoforo realised that he wanted food, wine . . . and a woman.

He would go to Francesca's first. She might, of course, be otherwise engaged, but, already aware that what had been no more than a passing fancy a second ago was quickly becoming a necessity, he was willing to risk the possibility of rejection. And she might even let him stay. He turned right and strode quickly towards Francesca's house in the Via San Tommaso d'Aquino.

Reaching the house, he was surprised to see that the front door was ajar; pushing it open, he stepped inside into a thick and airless silence. He felt unnerved straight away – the hairs on his neck stood up. Something was not right. It was too quiet. Cristoforo peered into the kitchen, which was all but empty, then he took the stairs two at a time.

Francesca's chamber door was wide open. The manservant's chair was outside the door as it had always been, but, as Cristoforo entered the room, he saw at a glance that all Francesca's opulent furniture and decorations had been stripped out and, apart from the bed, the room was bare.

The bed.

A frisson of shock caught in his throat, and he swore softly under his breath. A bloodstain – as wide across as the span of both his spread hands – stood out dark against the brocade of the mattress. Reaching out, he touched it with the tips of his fingers. Right in the centre, it was still damp.

Cristoforo stood still for several seconds, rubbing his now red-stained fingers against the ball of his thumb, then he turned on his heel, ran down the stairs and out into the street. Saddlebags clutched in one fist, he began to run, heavy footed, heading south through narrow streets, ducking the washing strung on lines between the houses and edging between carts and laden barrows, apologising to people he jostled, racing down towards where he knew Francesca's other house was situated. He had been there once before – had once walked her home. Could he find it again? He had to know what had happened to her.

Several moments later, his chest now labouring, he stood in front of the church of Santa Lucia and tried to remember where to go. Something about the crooked wall of the house on the corner was familiar, he realised gratefully, so he headed up into the Via Santa Lucia. Several houses further on, he recognised it: Francesca's house, he remembered now that he saw it, had curving, wrought-iron grilles across the bottom half of the ground floor windows, and three steps up to the front door – the top one with a large chunk missing from its leading edge. He was sure this was right.

He banged on the door with his fist. Waited. Banged again, harder.

After several minutes, he heard footsteps. There was a sound of a bolt being drawn back, and then the latch rattled and the door opened. A woman glared out at him, her expression blurred and baleful. She was heavy featured, ruddy faced, her hair loosely wrapped in linen.

'I'm looking for Signora Felizzi,' Cristoforo said.

'She's not here.'

'Is this the right house?'

The woman frowned at him. 'It's her house, yes. But she's not in it. Who wants to know?'

Cristoforo could see – and smell – that the woman was drunk. 'A friend,' he said, trying to keep his voice calm. 'Do you know where she is?'

The woman said, 'It's because the children disappeared, isn't it?' Her voice rose in pitch and volume as she expanded upon her many reasons for complaint. 'I know they all think it's *my* fault, because I should have been watching them, but I was only doing what she pays me to do – it's not as if I was slacking. I'd been preparing her food, like I always do. When I *think* about her and everything I know about her carryings-on. Shameless, she is. Shameless. And those children! They're no better. They'd been playing me up all day, little brats. Driven me mad. No wonder I didn't complain when everything went quiet.'

'The children have disappeared?'

But the woman shrugged and pushed out her lips in a dismissive moue. 'Oh, they've found them, all right. But none of *them* thought fit to come and tell me about it – only sent some grubby little *moccioso* they'd picked off the street to deliver the news, didn't they? They've found the children, he said, but someone's finally taken a knife to *her*. Been asking for it for years, she has, if you want my opinion.'

'A knife? Dear God! Where are they? Where is the Signora?'

'Can't remember.' She stood for a moment, eyes closed, leaning against the door jamb.

'Please, Signora – please try.'

The eyes remained closed for several long seconds. The creases of the woman's frown deepened, as though she was searching her memory for the elusive information. Then she opened her eyes and said. 'Piazza Monteoliveto. That's what she said before. Monteoliveto.'

Thank God, he thought. He knew the place. 'Do you know which house?'

She shook her head.

'Can you tell me *anything* that might help me to find it?'

The woman closed her eyes again, suppressing a belch, and sagged against the side of the door jamb. 'It's only a little piazza she said.' A pause. 'Won't take you long to look. The church. She said something about "opposite the church".'

'Thank you, Signora,' Cristoforo said, swallowing down his irritation. He shouldered his saddlebags and began once again to run. Heading north, he ran on and on, up the long, straight Via Toledo, eventually turning eastwards and winding his way through several streets, taking several wrong turns and doubling back on himself, until at last he reached the place the woman had named. The flat grey facade of the church loomed darkly at one end. Cristoforo stood before it, and regarded the houses

441

opposite. He crossed the piazza, and lifted a hand to knock at the door.

No. No one here by the name of Felizzi. Sorry.

He tried the house next door. No reply.

Now with his hopes of finding Francesca fading, Cristoforo raised his hand to knock at the door of the third house down from the end of the piazza.

Fifty-four

Luca felt sick. He stared at Niccolò, then, hissing, 'Quick, Nicco, come in!' he grabbed the young man by the wrist and pulled him into the hallway, pushing the door shut behind him.

Glancing sideways, Luca saw Francesca and Gianni, standing side by side in the shadow of the staircase. Niccolò, though, appeared not to have noticed they were there; he was fighting to regain his breath, desperate to impart his news. After a moment, he managed to say, 'There was a fight, apparently, Signore, a few hours ago, in that tavern in the Vicolo Cieco, and – oh, God – Michele's dead: Michele di Cicciano. Apparently there were at least two dozen people in there – though nobody's prepared to say how it started, of course – but when the *sbirri* arrived, Carlo was standing in the middle of the room, they said. He had a newly split lip and a dirty great black eye, and there was blood on his shirt and his hands, and they've taken him in. He's refusing to say how he came to be there, or how he got his injuries, so of course they're presuming the worst. What do we do? He's with the fucking Spanish – what the hell can we do, Signore?' His voice cracked as he added, 'If they decide he's guilty, you know they'll burn him.'

Luca had read somewhere about the 'weight' of guilt, and now, in an instant, he understood entirely what that expression really meant. It was as though his chest had been filled with clay.

'He didn't do it, Nicco,' he said.

'Oh, dear – I hope not, Signore!'

'No. You don't understand. I *know* he didn't do it. *I* did.'

Niccolò froze, mouth open, staring at Luca.

Luca said, 'At least – I might have done. I was part of that fight, along with someone else – someone who's left Napoli now – and somehow in all the confusion, Cicciano was hurt with his own knife. I don't know exactly how. But I have to go and tell them. Now. I have to explain what really happened.'

'But, Papa—' Gianni sounded horrified.

'Gianni, be quiet! It's the only thing to do. He's my son, as much as you are – whatever he's done – and I simply can't allow this to happen.'

'Whatever he's done? What do you—' Niccolò began, but Gianni interrupted him

'Papa, please! Think about this. There has to be some other way.'

'But what else can I do other than go to the authorities, tell the truth and plead for clemency? I have no influence, have I? I've got nothing.'

Francesca stepped forward, and a shaft of light from one of the windows caught the side of her face. Luca heard Niccolò gasp.

She said, 'I think there's a possibility – if you'll let me try it.'

'What do you mean?' Luca said.

'I hardly dare tell you,' she said. 'But something Modesto said yesterday made me think of it. He said it was my insurance.'

'What? Insurance? I don't understand.' Luca's head was hollow with trepidation.

'If you don't want me to do this, I won't – but it might save Carlo.'

'What are you talking about?'

'I . . . er . . . oh, Luca – I don't really know how to say this.' She dropped her voice. Moving closer to him, she said, 'I *know* one of the Spanish. An army captain. Perhaps rather more . . . *intimately* than he might care to have made public. I have no idea if he's directly involved in all this, but whether he is or not, perhaps I might be able to . . . to *use* that knowledge. Play on this intimacy. Use it as a lever. Will you let me try?'

Luca said nothing. Francesca took his hand. He gripped her fingers, images of her 'intimacy' with this unknown Spaniard now battling in his mind with others – of Carlo in some godforsaken cell, awaiting an unspeakable death.

'But why would you want to do such a thing?' he said. 'Carlo has behaved unforgivably towards you and your children. Why would you even consider helping him when he tried to . . . tried to take your babies away from you? And it's not safe – would you not risk—'

She cut across his words. 'Risk doesn't matter. Because, whatever he's done, Luca, he's your son.'

Luca swallowed uncomfortably.

Francesca said, 'I can't bear the thought of your unhappiness if Carlo were to be convicted. And anyway – risk? What am I supposed to be worried about risking? My reputation?' She gave a soft little laugh. 'I don't really have one of those, do I?'

Luca stared at her, then wrapped his arms around her. 'I don't deserve you,' he said into her hair.

Nobody moved. Then, breaking away from Francesca, Luca saw that both Gianni and Niccolò were staring at the two of them – Gianni anxiously and Niccolò with an expression on his face as though he had just been slapped.

'Papa,' Gianni said. 'Listen – you can't let her do this. Francesca, you can't. It *is* a risk. What if they decide to arrest you too? For . . . for . . .' He tailed off, but Luca understood. He turned to Francesca. 'He's right, *cara*.'

'But, Luca, it might be the only we have chance to—'

'No. You mustn't do it.'

Gianni said, 'Money. What about money? Could we offer them money, do you think?'

'A *bribe*?' Francesca's expression was incredulous.

Gianni shrugged.

'Are you serious? We'd probably end up in a cell ourselves, accused of some sort of moral corruption. Isn't it obvious? My suggestion's far safer, and far more likely to succeed.'

Luca shook his head. 'No it's not. If a bribe might get us arrested for moral corruption, then you simply *cannot* turn up there and suggest what to all intents and purposes is *blackmail*. And if it were to become known how you know this man—'

He broke off, as a loud knocking shook the nearby front door, startling them. All four heads turned as one. More urgent thumps followed.

Gianni unlatched the door and opened it.

Francesca gasped.

The sunlight filtering through the closed shutters in Luca's *sala* made the figures in the tapestries appear to tremble as though they were holding their breath, listening to the conversation that was unrolling before them. They looked as though they were struggling to believe their ears. Luca looked across at the newcomer: stocky and muscular, crop-haired, with bright intelligent eyes and a twist to his mouth that suggested a dry sense of humour. In any other circumstances, this would probably have been someone Luca would instinctively have liked.

His gaze moved from this 'Signor di Benevento' to Gianni and as he did so, a singular thought struck him. There were three men in this room, and two of them had already coupled with Francesca. And one of those two was his son. They had both fucked her and he had not. For a moment Luca held his breath; he turned to look at Francesca and then closed his eyes; his cock shifted and lifted as his thoughts began to tumble wildly. She had held both of them in her arms: she had touched them, fondled them, gripped them, stroked them; she had sucked and licked and gasped and moaned and ultimately, no doubt – if he could judge by the brief glimpse of her skills he had been allowed in Mergellina – brought them both to unforgettable, quivering ecstasy. Those few moments came back to him now – after all, they were all he had had of her so far – her lips and her tongue and her fingers rousing him to a pitch of desire to which he had never before come anywhere near.

He looked back at her now. She was speaking fervently to the newcomer, splay-fingered hands held up in front of her in emphasis as though she clasped an invisible globe, her expression concerned and serious. He saw her nod to him, and then she gestured towards the floor above; saw Benevento considering what she said, and then obviously agreeing with her. Luca stared at her. His gaze dropped to the neckline of her dress. These two – Benevento and Gianni – had both seen her breasts. He, Luca, had not yet had that privilege. They had touched her breasts, held them, played with them, tasted them, enjoyed them. Luca felt them under his fingers now, imagined the look of them, the weight of them, imagined them moving under his touch, felt their softness and the silkiness of the skin. He shifted in his seat, drew in a breath and licked his lips, which suddenly felt rather dry.

*

'And you'll come with us, won't you, Luca?'

He was startled at the sound of Francesca's voice, and the vivid image of her breasts he had conjured vanished. Shifting position in his chair again, his face hot, he hoped that his unexpected but now uncomfortably pressing arousal was not immediately obvious to anyone else in the room.

He did not reply straight away, and after a second or two, Francesca spoke again. 'Please. Will you come? With Cristo and me – to see Vasquez. Now.'

Luca had no idea who or what she was talking about. Unwilling to admit to the reason for his inattention, he said, 'Of course. When do you want to leave?'

'Straight away. I'll just go and get the book.'

Francesca left the room. Luca heard her footfall on the stairs, the sound of a door latch clattering overhead, a pause, and then further footsteps. What book was this? What had they planned? She came back into the *sala* carrying a bag, accompanied by the two little girls. 'Luca,' she said. 'They can't come with us. Can they stay here?'

'Of course,' he said. 'Gianni, you can look after them, can't you? Don't leave them alone for a minute while we are out. Not for a second.'

Gianni smiled at the twins and nodded to his father. 'Don't worry,' he said. 'I shan't let them out of my sight.' The little girls crossed the room and sat down on the edge of the window recess near to Gianni's chair.

Luca stood back as Francesca and Benevento left the *sala* then, smiling briefly at Gianni and the girls, he followed the others down the stairs and out of the house.

448

Fifty-five

The darkness was thick and clotted. The only window in the cell was high in the wall and even at midday it admitted little light – now, as the afternoon lengthened, it was no more than a slightly fainter, grey, cross-barred slit in the black. On the floor, the scattered straw was damp and smelled of piss. There was no bed, no table, no chair. Carlo pushed himself as far into a corner as he could. He pressed back against the walls, feeling the stone chill through the linen of his shirt. Staring unseeing into the darkness, he rubbed at the floor with his fingertips, back and forth, back and forth, unthinking, until the skin was scraped raw; to his surprise, he found himself soothed by the burning in his fingers. It detracted from the terror in his mind.

The other occupant of the cell coughed.

With a smothered whimper, Carlo hunched back still further into his corner, drawing his knees up tight against his chest, his insides churning, afraid of a resumption of the man's insistent attentions. But since his companion's return to the cell that evening, after several hours' absence, the man had been too weak to do more than curl around his cough and retch into the straw. Carlo stared at him, his belly heaving with a churning mix of revulsion, fear, and a screaming relief that it was not he who had been dragged out of the cell that morning.

Carlo had heard whispers of what awaited him if he were to be found guilty.

In this place, rumour travelled fast from cell door to cell door – if anyone overheard a gobbet of news, however trivial, it took little more than minutes for it to slither unstoppably through the building like a bead of quicksilver. Carlo discovered yesterday that Marco had been there – to accuse him of sodomy. He knew, too, that Marco had given the Spanish all the details of the failed abduction of which he, Carlo, had boasted so foolishly to the little *bardassa*.

And he knew that they thought he had killed Cicciano.

Cicciano had been dead when he, Carlo, had arrived in the inn from the *sottosuolo*, Carlo knew that, but he was well aware that the authorities were quite certain it had been he who had wielded the knife. They would burn him for it. The thought pulsed cold in his head. After all the things Carlo admitted to himself he had done, the horrible irony was that now they were planning to burn him for the one thing he hadn't done.

He wondered if Marco would be watching. When they burnt him. A wash of nausea shook him, and he retched pointlessly into the straw between his bent knees. He had witnessed a burning once, years ago. He could see in his mind the head-high pile of wood and straw, still hear the howling jeers of the crowd and the screams of the prisoner as the flames built in ferocity – and then the terrible, shattering bang as the mercy-bag of gunpowder that had been slung around the man's neck exploded.

Droplets of cold sweat sprang out on Carlo's forehead.

Fifty-six

Luca looks pale. Poor thing – it must be so hard for him to see me like this, in Cristo's company, aware as he is of Cristo's and my history together. He seemed almost distracted back in his *sala* just now. When I reach out and take his hand, he smiles at me, but it is a brief, bleak smile. My poor Luca – if he is experiencing anything of the horror I felt while the girls were missing, I am surprised he can manage a smile at all. He squeezes my fingers, lifts my hand to his mouth and kisses my knuckles.

We are on our way to try to save the life of a man I detest. I think I loathe him as much as I love his father. God, I utterly *despise* Carlo for what he did to my girls – even *thinking* about what he planned to do with them makes me feel sick – but I love Luca. And – incomprehensible though it is to me – Luca loves Carlo. Perhaps it's that he still loves the little boy that Carlo once was. If Carlo burns, then it will haunt Luca for the rest of his life. And I couldn't bear that.

We walk on, saying little, our footsteps quickly falling into rhythm with each other. Cristo is marching, like the soldier he is, and he sets the pace. Luca, with his long legs, has no trouble keeping up, but at times, I am almost running. I suppose, of course, that I made the trip to Vasquez's apartments before by carriage, but this journey seems to be taking far longer than I thought it would. We weave our way down street after street, dodging people, animals, low-lying lines of strung washing; stepping over rivulets of filthy water and stinking piles of ordure.

There are times when Napoli feels very big and very dirty.

I glance across at Cristo. Catching my eye, he smiles and nods, but says nothing, keeping up the brisk pace he has set. 'Thank you for coming with us,' I say a little breathlessly.

'I wouldn't miss this little adventure, Francesca.' His smile twists.

'But – you're taking a risk, and—'

'Stop it!' he says. His marching steps jolt his words as he speaks. 'Listen, *cara*, I might work with the Spanish, but I'm an Italian. My loyalties are with my own. And I care about you, *cara* – we're friends, are we not?'

Friends. A strange way of describing our relationship – but it's true. Cristo has been a good friend to me.

He says, 'You need help. Help I can give. If you're on your own with him, Vasquez might play tricks with you, but he won't dare try anything with me in the room. If he's able to help you, I think he will if I'm there with you.'

Luca reaches out and takes my hand, looking across at Cristo and saying, 'I'm truly grateful, Signore.'

Cristo smiles and we all march on.

By the time we arrive, I am out of breath.

We are met at the door – not by my friend Juan, but by a servant I have never seen before: a wheezy-voiced elderly Spaniard, whose face appears to have been roughly formed from a handful of crumpled parchment. 'You wish see *Maestre* Vasquez?' he mumbles in very poor Italian.

'Yes. It's most urgent, please tell him.'

'I go ask if he see you.' The old man turns slowly and creaks away out of sight, leaving Cristo and me standing just inside the front door. Luca has elected to remain outside. He has said almost nothing since we left the house, but he held me close outside Vasquez's building, and kissed me just now with a kind of desperation. Oh, dear God – we simply have to succeed.

Vasquez is not in the great golden room with the colossal carved bed. Instead, we are shown by the parchment-faced old man into another, smaller, adjoining room, which until today I have only glimpsed through a doorway. The little Spaniard is sitting behind a long and highly polished table, which is stacked neatly with piles of papers and books, but he stands as we come into the room, and walks around the table towards me, licking his lips like a hungry dog, his eyes flicking from my mouth to my breasts with ill-disguised longing.

I am so grateful that Cristo is with me.

'I was not expecting to see you again,' he says. 'After the letter you sent me, I had presumed our liaison to be at an end. And for you to be here in such company –' he glances at Cristoforo '– I confess to a little confusion. What do you want? Have you come here to . . . to request a resumption of our relationship?'

Cristo says quickly, 'You misunderstand. We seek a favour from you, *Maestre*.'

Vasquez's gaze moves to Cristo. 'Explain.'

'A young man was arrested yesterday—'

Vasquez interrupts. 'Many young men were arrested yesterday. Napoli is rife with criminal activity. You Italians frequently seem to have a particularly frail grasp on the notion of law and order.'

Cristo inclines his head in acknowledgment of this unflattering opinion. When he speaks again, though, his voice is calm and reassuringly steady. 'This young man, however, has been detained for a crime that he quite certainly did not commit. A murder.'

'You say he's innocent? How do you know?'

I say, 'We are quite certain of his innocence because I know who *did* do it.'

Vasquez turns to me and frowns, considering. 'Who?'

'A good man. A man who didn't mean to kill anyone. He was trying to save someone else's life, but it went wrong. The fight was started by the man who died.'

'But who is he – the killer? Good man or not, he must be found.'

Thanking God for Modesto's prompt decision to escape retribution, I say, 'You won't find him. He's left Napoli – he ran from the city last night.' With a pang, I add, 'He's long gone. And he won't be back.'

'Why do you tell me all this? Why me? What has it to do with me.'

I draw in a long breath. Stepping towards him, I take his hand. 'Miguel, please, I want you to help us. I want you to plead this boy's case. I don't know who else to ask. Please do what you can to make the authorities see sense. This boy didn't do it – and if he's found guilty . . .'

He pulls his hand back out of my grasp, his expression cold. He has not forgiven me for rejecting him. 'Such things are not in my jurisdiction,' he says. 'I am a soldier, not a lawyer. As *Maestre de Campo*, I—'

I interrupt him. 'I know you're not a lawyer. But, Miguel, you *know* many of those in authority – your *money* could be influential if nothing else. You could talk to them, at least. Try to persuade them towards leniency?'

'Why should I? Are you suggesting I try to *bribe* the authorities into flouting the law? Why is this boy important to you? Is this another discarded patron? Why have you come here?'

I hesitate. I have no idea what explanation will best serve my case. After a moment's thought, I decide on the truth. I'm not sure I can face any more lies. 'I want to protect his father,' I say. 'His father is a good man. A loving and virtuous man. I know it will break his heart if his son is convicted of a crime he has not committed; if he has to watch his child punished for something he hasn't done.'

'What is the boy's name?' Vasquez says in the end.

I pull in a long breath. 'Carlo della Rovere.'

He frowns. 'Rovere?'

I nod.

'But . . . but I know of this boy. Rovere stands accused not just of murder . . . but of sodomy and abduction. I was talking to someone about him less than an hour since.'

'Believe me, I know just what he has been accused of.'

'Then why could you possibly wish me to plead for him? The boy is depraved!'

I say nothing.

Vasquez shakes his head. 'I'm sorry. I can do nothing for you. I cannot be seen to be standing in support of someone accused of such crimes. Someone in my position must be seen to be above reproach.' He pauses. Once again, his gaze travels down to my breasts, and I see in his face his growing resentment at my decision to abandon him.

Cristoforo moves in closer to where I am standing. He widens his eyes at me, and nods his head towards the bag I have in my hands. In the bag is my diary. My insurance.

'Above reproach?' I say.

'Of course.'

'Can I read you something, Miguel?'

He frowns curiously. I pull the vellum-bound book out of the bag, and hand the bag to Cristo.

'What is this?'

'You'll know when I start reading.'

I cross to a chair, seat myself in it, and, looking up once at Vasquez to make sure he is listening carefully, I open the book, flick through several pages until I find the place I have marked with a thin strip of leather, and begin to read.

When I look up again, Vasquez is staring at me. He has gone pale. His lips have parted and his eyes are wide. '*Madre de Dios*,' he mutters. 'Why did you write these things? And when? I told you about . . . about what happened in Milan *in confidence*.'

'And so far, I haven't broken that confidence. You know that my life as a courtesan has finished, Miguel. But all the time I was working, I always thought it prudent to keep a careful account of everything I did with my patrons. I was told on a number of occasions, by people with experience in such things, that a woman never knows when it might come in useful to be prepared.'

'Why do you read it to me now?'

I hesitate. 'Oh,' I say as airily as I can manage, 'just to help you to see that *no one* can be held to be above reproach.'

'Can I see the book?'

'No,' Cristo says firmly, stepping forward to stand between me and Vasquez, his hand on the hilt of his sword. 'That book stays in the Signora's possession at all times. There is another volume,' he adds (untruthfully, but with great conviction), 'with further, equally frank accounts of your liaison with the Signora depicted in it. That book has been hidden in the city, *Maestre*, lodged with people who will quite certainly take it to the authorities should anything happen to this one, or to either of us.'

Vasquez says nothing. After a long moment's silence, he crosses the room and stands looking out of the long window, out into the street below. 'What do you intend to do with these accounts?'

'Nothing,' I say. I pause, my gaze fixed upon his back. 'Nothing at all. I'll burn the books, in fact. Happily. And you can stand with me and watch them burn. If, that is, you help me now by pleading this boy's case for me. If not . . .' I pause again '. . . then I shall pass it to the authorities. I'm sure they will find it most entertaining.'

Vasquez turns back into the room and stares at me.

Several long seconds snail past. Then he says, 'This young man may not have committed this murder, but apparently there is a witness . . . a boy, whose evidence will prove the other two charges. Beyond doubt. And in any case, if Rovere's father is so virtuous, how is it that he has allowed his son to stray so far?'

Cielo, this man's hypocrisy is sick making! Trying not to reveal my contempt as I think of the vast sums of money Vasquez must have spent on wanton self-gratification since he was first introduced to me, and seeing again in my mind the poor ruined girl in the convent in Milan, I say, 'Surely God only expects each man to be responsible for his own actions. Not for those of any other.'

Vasquez colours. 'And why,' he says, 'do you care so much about this man's broken heart? Whoever he is.'

He's jealous! I say, avoiding the issue, 'What will happen to Carlo if he is convicted?'

He swallows. 'For sodomy, no doubt the *strappado*,' he says. 'For the abduction and the murder, who knows – I imagine the stake. As a public deterrent, perhaps the one will be followed by the other.'

The *strappado* and the stake. A hollow chillness opens up behind my face. Oh, sweet Jesus, what if we fail? I saw a boy endure the *strappado* once, many years ago. I was sixteen. He was hardly older than me: he was thin and dirty and had wet himself with terror. Along with most of the town, I saw half a dozen men tie the poor creature's hands together behind his back, and then push him ahead of them up stone steps to the ramparts of the city wall. They fixed the end of the rope to an iron ring. And then they threw him off. As he reached the end of the rope, some three feet from the ground, his arms jerked up behind him, dislocated, and then broke. I'll never forget the noise they made. He didn't die – but I wished for him that he had.

Feeling sick, I say to Vasquez, 'And what about you? What will happen to you, if I make public what I know? How will your superiors react to the spiciness of my revelations?'

He takes a step closer to me. Cristo stands squarely between us, arms held out sideways. 'You bitch!' Vasquez hisses over Cristo's shoulder. 'You know what was in that letter, don't you? You read it that day. I thought you had.'

He rants at me in Spanish for a moment and I am bewildered. What letter? What is he talking about? Then I remember Vasquez, bursting into the golden room and shouting at his men; screwing up the piece of paper he had been flapping in their faces, and stuffing it into his breeches pocket. I remember it falling out of his pocket at my feet whilst I was dressing and he was at his close-stool. Hoping that my ignorance of its actual contents does not show in my face, I say, 'And what if I did read it? What if I know?'

'Then . . .' Vasquez's voice seems on the point of cracking. 'Then you will know what will happen to me if any further evidence of . . . of what they term "moral degeneracy" . . . reaches the ears of the authorities.'

I almost laugh. So that's what it was all about! A final warning. They've drawn a line and he's crossed it too often. This explains the empty apartments, and his refusal to have any servants in view. He's just a wealthy, hedonistic, self-indulgent little *stronzo*, who's now had his knuckles rapped too many times. Wondering if God might finally have finished being angry with me, and might possibly now be on my side, I try to look cold and determined, despite the fact that my heart is beating so violently it's making me feel ill. 'You have nothing to worry about from me – if you help me,' I say. 'If you help Carlo, the books will be burned. I promise you.' Another thought occurs to me, and I add an outright lie. 'And I shall say nothing to anyone about the fact that I have not bled this month.'

Vasquez looks as though he has just been hit in the face. He looks almost grey. A heavy silence stretches out, draping itself over the three of us like a wet sheet. And then Vasquez speaks, and I can hear an edge of fear in his voice. 'I will help you. I promise. But I am not sure what I can do. My hands are tied,' he says. 'I am not sufficiently influential, being only an army officer – I don't have the power to effect a complete acquittal. That power lies only with Don Pedro Alfàn. It may be that this Rovere is not guilty of murder – I have only your word on that – but our witness will swear to the other charges, so I can do little about them.'

'Little? What *could* you do?'

He pauses. 'I think I could plead for banishment. I could go to Don Pedro and cite the virtue of the boy's father and plead for banishment. Would that be enough to persuade you to . . . destroy this evidence you have against me?'

Banishment? How would Luca feel if Carlo were to be exiled – sent away from Napoli? Perhaps, though, it could be the answer to everything – I am not sure I could ever stand comfortably in the same room as the man who stole my children, however much Luca loves him. A few seconds pass as I allow myself to picture Luca's reactions – firstly to his son's exile and then to the unthinkable alternative. And then I say, 'Yes. It would be enough.'

Vasquez puffs out a soft sigh of evident relief.

Cristo says, 'You say you'll plead on our behalf. But you might fail, *Maestre*. If you do, how will we know you tried? We won't be there to hear what you say. What proof will we have that you've kept your side of this bargain?'

Vasquez looks blank. He says nothing. Then an idea strikes me. Filippo. 'Take Signor di Laviano in with you when you plead, Miguel,' I say. 'I know him. I would trust him to tell me what you say.'

'Di Laviano?' Bewilderment, confusion, realization and another twitch of jealousy cross Vasquez's face as visibly as the shadow of a cloud racing over a field. He mutters, 'Have he . . . and you . . . ?'

I shrug. 'From time to time.'

He stares at me for several seconds, then nods curtly. 'Very well. I will arrange to see Don Pedro this afternoon, and, as you request, I will take di Laviano into the room with me when I go. I will do what I can. I promise you.'

'And I promise you that I will show this book to no one else while I wait to hear the outcome of your efforts.'

I don't think there is any more to be said or done.

Another awkward silence descends. I take the bag from Cristo and put the book back into it. Vasquez crosses to the door and Cristo and I follow him. We walk together back towards the front entrance of the building, saying nothing, striding fast, our footsteps ringing out in marching-time with each other. As we reach the top of a broad flight of stairs, I see the parchment-faced old man again; but this time he is accompanied by an anxious-looking boy – skinny, unwashed, his hair scraped back into a ratty pigtail.

Fifty-seven

The wind had picked up and the sky was now a hard, cloud-laden silver. The Neapolitan coastline had dwindled to no more than a thin smudge along a small section of the horizon, appearing and disappearing between swells and, even as Carlo della Rovere watched from the sterncastle of the *sciabecco*, gripping the rail with white-knuckled fingers, it vanished altogether. He could see nothing but sea.

Behind him, the great rust-coloured sails bellied out, creaking with the weight of the wind and the ship listed as the *Għafrid* heeled around to starboard. Dragging his gaze from the horizon back to the ship, and clutching at a rope to steady himself, Carlo turned and began to pick his way somewhat gingerly towards the few steps that led down onto the main deck. Several of the dozens of crewmen paused momentarily in their activities to stare at him; stumbling over the projecting wheel of a cannon, Carlo groped for the door to the companionway. He could see contempt in the men's expressions, and felt acutely conscious of the softness of his physical inadequacy, faced with these sinewy, wind-browned men with their gleaming skin and carved-mahogany muscles. He closed the door to the companionway behind him, and stood for a moment leaning against it with his eyes shut, his stomach swooping as the ship dropped away beneath his feet.

A dozen steps descended into the depths of the ship: down these Carlo went hesitantly, his insides heaving. The deck above lowered over him — a heavy, close-sparred ceiling running the length of the ship, strung with hooks and ropes, buckets, marlin-spikes and the sagging cylinders of tight-rolled hammocks, all indistinct in the almost darkness. The smells of tarred hemp and salt caught in his nostrils as he turned to a small door behind him, and knocked.

'It's open.'

Carlo turned the handle and went in. Salvatore Żuba was standing behind his table, leaning on his arms, his face underlit with stuttering lanternlight; he was studying a large chart. He looked up as Carlo came in, raised and drained a small glass, and nodded. 'Now that the wind's stronger, we'll be in Tunis before too long,' he said. 'You can disembark there, *Sinjur*, if you wish to — there's a fine living to be made in a place like Tunis, for a man like yourself, if you've a mind.'

Carlo said nothing.

'Or,' Żuba went on, 'if you would prefer, you can stay with us on the *Għafrid*, *Sinjur*, and try your hand at becoming a seaman.'

Carlo did not like the smile Żuba gave him.

He thought back to the previous day.

After nearly a week of waiting, three men had slammed opened the door to his cell. They had blocked the doorway, silhouetted against torchlight from the corridor beyond. Carlo's limbs liquefied at the sight of them and his empty stomach began churning again.

'Get up!'

He could not do it.

One of the men strode into the cell, kicking through the filthy straw. He grabbed Carlo's upper arm and dragged him upright. Carlo's legs would not hold him and the man ended up supporting him under both arms. 'Come on,' he had said. 'We have to go.'

Carlo could not walk, so they dragged him between them, slipping and stumbling, along corridors and up staircases until they reached a doorway to the outside world. He kept his eyes tightly closed, his head turned as much to one side as he could, whimpering and cringing at the thought of the mountain of wood and the howling crowd that were surely awaiting him.

But there was nothing but silence in the street and when he finally opened his eyes, no pyre could be seen. The place was deserted. Then one of the men pushed a musty woollen coat into his hands, saying, 'Go on, *vaffanculo*! You're an undeserving little bastard but, for God knows what reason, they've commuted it. Alfàn says you can go. You have two hours to get out of Napoli. Don't linger – you can be sure they'll be after you if you are here a minute beyond nightfall.'

Carlo had just stood there, staring at them, unable to move.

'Go on! Get out! Fuck off out of here, you little shit! You're someone else's problem now.'

And, retching and crying, Carlo had broken into a stumbling run.

'It won't be long until you are used to the *Għafrid*'s way of going, *Sinjur*,' Żuba said, and, looking up with a start, Carlo realised that his nausea must have been visible.

'Many of my crew are sick for several days each voyage.'

Carlo tried to smile.

'Not being much of a seaman yet, though, I thought you might appreciate your privacy,' Żuba continued. 'So I have emptied a little corner for you, *Sinjur*, up at the bow end of the ship, and I've had a hammock strung for your use. It's as private a space as you will find on a ship such as this . . . we live snug on board, as a rule.'

Carlo nodded his thanks.

'But I will warn you, *Sinjur*,' Żuba said, 'that the men know why you are aboard. They know your history. And your preferences.' He paused and licked his lips. Fingering the stringy plaits beneath his chin, he said, 'You might be the object of . . . how shall I say . . . some curiosity amongst some of the crew. I overheard Ballucci muttering about you just now. I don't think they are out to cause mischief, but I would just say . . . that it might be wise to watch your back. That's all.'

As Carlo stared at the little Maltese privateer, the ship rode up and over a big sea; he felt his insides swirl unpleasantly and, before he could stop himself, he vomited over the floor of Żuba's cabin.

Towards evening, Gianni pulled on his doublet and took another long, considering look around the room. Some fifteen feet square, its walls were a faded dove grey; the paint was bubbling and flaking away from one corner near the ceiling. An elderly and sun-bleached tapestry covered most of the north-facing wall, depicting the confused culmination of a successful hunt. On one side of the room, a low bed was piled with blankets and pillows, while opposite it were a small table, two chairs and a crumbling credenza, its surfaces liberally peppered with woodworm holes. A threadbare carpet lay rucked over the wooden floorboards. The whole place was old and shabby, there were no hangings at the windows, and a chill air of disuse hung around him, but Gianni's face split in a wide smile as he surveyed his new home. He had, entirely unaided, found somewhere to stay. In Roma.

Closing and locking his door, Gianni ran down the two flights of stairs to the street below – a narrow lane which led directly onto the long Piazza Navona. Though the sun had already sunk below the roofscape, the market stalls in the piazza were still busy, lit now by tall, flaming torches, and the place was thronging with people.

Pushing a hand into a pocket in his breeches, he clinked the coins he found there. He needed food and ale, and had a mind to try to buy a few things to brighten up his new nest – candles, perhaps a small lantern if he could find one, and maybe something to read. He would be starting his search for work in the morning, but until then, he had no commitments and he relished the unfamiliar sense of freedom. He wandered down the alleyways between stalls, conversing cheerfully with the stallholders and trying to look knowledgeable as he weighed items of food in one hand, shaking his head as if disapproving of the cost or the quality and haggling the prices down as though he had done such things all his life.

After an hour, he had successfully bought several slices of lamb, a small loaf, a portion of cheese, six apricots and a large bottle of ale. He had also found half a dozen candles, a new tinderbox and a small, pierced-lead lantern. Somewhat laden down with his purchases, he determined to return to his room in order to set up his supper and, to this end, turned back towards the far end of the piazza, walking now behind the backs of the outlying stalls.

He was nearing the turning to his street, when something caught his eye. Some way away, two men, deep in earnest conversation, were walking towards the Pasquino at the south-west end of the piazza. One of the men was elderly, slightly stooped, with thick greying hair and a beaky nose, whilst the other . . . Gianni stopped and stared. The other man was stocky, slightly barrel-chested, with protuberant black eyes. He was gesticulating energetically as they walked and whatever he was saying was clearly delighting his companion: the elderly man stopped dead and laughed aloud, shaking his head and bringing his hands together in fleeting applause. The stocky man grinned, then they both continued walking and talking. Gianni changed course, determining to catch them up, aiming to meet them before they left the great square. He tried to cut across the market place, holding his purchases up above his head. Worming his way through the melee of market-goers, he tried to keep the two men in sight, but there were too many people and he was too slow and, even as he reached the far side of the piazza, he knew he had lost them. Puffing out his disappointment, he backtracked through the market and returned to his room.

He hadn't looked as though he was passing through, Gianni thought. He hadn't had the air of a traveller; he had seemed relaxed and at home. No baggage. No hat. Doublet unlaced. Perhaps, Gianni thought, if he were to look again later – or tomorrow – he might see him again. He hoped so – he had liked Modesto very much. Smiling at the prospect, he laid two slices of the lamb on a plate, tore off a corner of his loaf and placed it and two of the apricots next to the meat. Seating himself at his table, he began to eat.

Fifty-eight

'Luca's getting married again?'

'Apparently so,' Filippo said.

Maria smiled. 'Oh, I'm so pleased,' she said. 'How lovely. He's such a dear man – I've often hoped he would meet someone. What is she like? What's her name? Have you met her?'

A small, cold hand reached deep into Filippo's guts and gave a sharp tug. 'Only briefly,' he said. 'She's very beautiful – other than that, I've really no idea.'

'How did they meet?'

Now, this was dangerous territory. Filippo toyed briefly with the idea of admitting to the 'cousinship' connection, aware that Maria might well discover it for herself at a later date, but then decided he did not have the courage to risk such a strategy. He would, he thought, give Maria no more than minimal information; everything that might be potentially catastrophic, he would withhold. Dipping into his bucket of perilous facts, he picked out what he considered might be the least hazardous. 'She came to that play I went to, a couple of months ago, at San Domenico,' he said.

Maria frowned and said, 'Oh, did she? Oh, what a shame – perhaps I should have made more of an effort and tried to go to the play, then I would have met her.'

But she wouldn't have been there, if you'd gone, Filippo

thought. And I should still have been . . . busy . . . with her . . . on Wednesday evenings.

An uncomfortable thought.

He turned his head, looked sideways at his wife and the thought retreated. Of course, had Maria come to that play at San Domenico that day, then yes, Francesca would still probably have been working, and he might well still have been one of her regular patrons, but equally, he and Maria would, quite certainly, not have been sitting like this now, in their conjugal bed together, warm and rumpled and just a little tired, and that would have been a great loss to them both.

Maria was sitting up against her pillows, her hair a mass of dark tendrils, her cheeks flushed. She was very pretty. Filippo thought back over the previous hour or so. He had to admit that Maria had none of Francesca's wild and wanton abandon – she never had, and he was fairly sure that she never would – and something within him ached at his loss of that experience of shameless liberation. But, looking at Maria now, he realised that there was something entirely – albeit quite differently – intoxicating about lying with a woman you knew for certain loved you very dearly. The tenderness in Maria's touch just now, hesitant and self-conscious though it still might be, Filippo had found really very comforting and pleasing.

He reached across to her and tucked a lock of her hair behind her ear with one finger.

Maria closed her eyes and smiled again.

That moment in the street, the other day, when he had held her in his arms – for the first time in he could not remember how long – and he had felt the shamefully unfamiliar bony, boyish slimness of her, it had seemed to him in that moment that something indefinable about her had changed. He did not understand why this was, or what the change was, exactly, but whatever it was had made him feel oddly hopeful. Aware of a shifting sensation in his breeches, he had stood back from her, and said without thinking, 'May I come to your chamber tonight, Maria?'

Only when the question had blurted out and was hanging in the air between them like an ink blot did Filippo begin to doubt his moment of hope, and wondered why he had spoken. How stupid! This would only be yet one more moment of thumping disappointment – one more of many, stretching away along an empty road into a barren future, unrelieved now by Francesca's ministrations. He had been angry with himself for asking; wished he hadn't done it. Allowing himself to be ruled by his cock yet again, he had spoiled this unexpectedly tender moment of intimacy that, until his idiotic request, he realised he had been enjoying. Holding his breath, teeth clenched, he had waited for Maria's usual stiff, awkward excuses, hoping he would be able to disguise his reactions when she refused him, as she so surely would. Having thus stirred up his own expectations, he would now, he supposed, have to relieve his frustrations alone, on the thin and lumpy mattress in the smallest bedchamber, as he had done so many times in the years before he had met Francesca.

But Maria had smiled, shyly, and said, 'If you would like to.'

He had stared at her, mouth open.

She had hesitated for a moment, and then said something else, that had astonished him even more than her acceptance of his suggestion: she had blushed, run her tongue over her lip, and said, very softly, her eyes fixed firmly on the ground between them, 'I'll try to entertain you a little better than perhaps I have done for a long time.'

Entertain?

He felt quite winded with shock.

He had hardly dared hope that Maria's unexpected announcement might presage a genuine and lasting change in her willingness to accommodate his needs . . . but as they walked back to the house together that evening, she had nonetheless allowed him to take her hand in his. She had even squeezed his fingers. And on arrival back at their house, they had proceeded straight up to the bedchamber, creeping on tiptoe and whispering like naughty children.

And once upstairs, Maria had indeed been very much more 'entertaining' than he had ever known her to be. She had closed the shutters and blown out all the candles in the chamber, her gaze fixed upon his; then, in the velvety darkness of their room, having carefully (and all but blindly) removed his wife's clothing, he had *felt*, rather than *seen*, a new determination in her, both to please, and to be pleased by him.

It had been a revelation.

He could hardly bear the thought that this new, albeit still fragile and precarious, intimacy between the two of them might so soon be shattered by revelations about his past liaisons with Luca's newly betrothed. He felt his pulse beating in his throat as he heard Maria say, 'Perhaps we can arrange for Luca and – what did you say her name was?'

'I didn't say. I believe her name is Francesca. Francesca Marrone.'

'Francesca – I do like that name. I used to have a great-aunt Francesca. She died years ago – you never met her. But perhaps we can arrange for them both to come to our house to eat with us, sometime soon, don't you agree? I should love to meet her.'

Filippo did not trust himself to speak.

Fifty-nine

The two identical profiles are facing each other on the pillow, eyes closed, peacefully unaware of the world. Beata is sucking her thumb. I stand and watch my daughters sleeping for a moment or two, and then I feel a hand on each upper arm.

Luca is smiling when I turn to look at him. He runs a thumb softly beside the line of almost-mended scarring around the side of my face. It hardly hurts now and, in candlelight at least, it scarcely shows. In fact, if I dress my hair carefully, I can hide it. The messy little wound under my chin has taken longer to heal, and is still painful, but fortunately that one is almost out of sight.

'Come to bed,' Luca says, taking my hand.

We go together to the floor below.

Luca's bedchamber – I still have trouble thinking of it as 'ours' – is lit by a single candle. The windows are shuttered. The bed is hung with green curtains that seem to be moving gently in the bobbing flame, and the candlelight is dappling the polished floorboards with gleaming blotches. In the grate, the fire has died to embers, around which the last few lazy flames are licking almost noiselessly.

This is only the second day that I have stood in front of Luca as his wife.

It was a hasty marriage, perhaps, taking far less time than is usual in Napoli. We had to dispense with much of the ceremony, though formal intentions were declared and witnessed by Niccolò as notary, presents were given (to the girls, who were delighted, of course), and a feast, cooked with love by Lorenzo, was enjoyed by all. I had no one to decide upon my dowry for me, so I made my own arrangements. It was a easy decision: I shall simply bring to this marriage everything I own. Luca has agreed that this seems eminently reasonable.

But if the earlier parts of the proceedings were somewhat rushed, we had a truly lovely Ring Day.

The evening before, I had knelt before little Father Ippolito on the other side of the partition in the dingy and sour-smelling confessional box at San Giacomo degli Spagnoli, and finally shed the weight of all the years of guilt, pouring out to him every last fear and regret, and admitting for the first time to the true extent of my terror of damnation. I'm afraid I wept as I told him that it was all over – for ever; tears of relief and shame; of fatigue and an exhilarating release from dread.

He paused for a long, long moment before offering me my absolution.

On the day itself, Niccolò came again to the house in the Via Santa Lucia. He helped Luca to put the ring on the fourth finger of my right hand, just as he should, and Luca sweetly gave rings to Beata and Bella, too. They are far too big for them – Luca bought them for when they are grown up – so both girls are now wearing their treasures on ribbons around their necks.

I had a present too. Luca gave me his grandmother's bridal belt. You don't see them very often, any more. It is truly beautiful – dark-blue velvet, decorated with dozens of delicate silver medallions — and I felt entirely honoured as he wound it three times around my waist, and kissed me as he fastened it.

We walked together, with the girls, up to San Giacomo for the blessing. I was pleased that it was Father Ippolito who gave it — after everything, it seemed fitting. He appeared a little bemused, perhaps, but despite the bashful glances he kept casting in my direction, he managed to utter the prayers we needed, and Luca and I and the girls all walked back to Luca's house as the thickening light of evening sent purple shadows crawling into every corner of every street along the way. Luca and I took our time, and the girls danced merrily along ahead of us.

Luca stands now at the foot of his bed and holds my hands in his. Pulling his arms out sideways and backwards, he brings me in towards him and kisses my mouth. For a moment we are connected only by the kiss, our arms outstretched, but, when Luca releases my fingers, we hold each other close. Then, taking his mouth from mine, he says, 'Turn around.'

I turn and face away from him.

Kissing the nape of my neck, he loosens the lacing of my dress. To use Gianni's term, he *surprises* me all over again, and that surprise shivers down through my throat and pushes deep into my belly. He pulls the lacings from their eyelets and, after a moment's work, eases my dress from me in one; it falls to the floor around my feet, leaving me in my shift. Pressing up against my back, Luca reaches around me and, holding me in to his body with his hands on my breasts, he begins to kiss me again, just below my right ear.

'Can I confess something?' he asks quietly with his mouth still against my neck. 'Something rather shameful.'

I nod, my skin prickling.

473

He lips the lobe of my ear. 'I am the most terrible hypocrite,' he says, and I *feel* the word whispering against my skin as much as hear it. I arch my back so that my breasts push out against his fingers; he draws me back in towards him.

'Hypocrite? Why on earth . . . do you say that?' I ask, struggling to concentrate on what he is saying.

'Because . . .' he says, pausing every now and then to plant another kiss on my neck, 'because, after all those uncaring things I said . . . after all that terrible, self-righteous disapproval . . .' One hand has now pulled up my shift and is sliding up towards my buttocks. I cannot suppress a little gasp. 'After all that . . .' he says. 'I have to admit to finding it . . . quite unaccountably arousing . . . to be undressing a whore.'

I turn around and look up into his face.

He pauses. 'It's been the same each time. Does that make you angry? I think it probably should.'

I pull my shift off over my head and, naked, press up against the scratchy wool of his doublet front. I shake my head. 'No, Luca, it doesn't. Not angry at all.' I take from him his doublet and shirt. Almost certain what his answer will be, I ask him, 'In all those years you were on your own, Luca, did you ever . . . ?'

He shakes his head as he takes off the rest of his clothes and climbs with me through the green hangings.

'Did you ever think about it?'

He raises an eyebrow. 'Often,' he says, with a wry smile.

I run my fingers over his body, stroking every part of him except the one place I know he will most want me to touch. The omission is deliberate. It will be worth the wait. 'When you thought about it, all those times,' I say, 'what did you most want a whore to do?'

After a moment's hesitation, Luca tells me, simply and

474

honestly. I am moved by the intimacy and charmed by the revelation. Kneeling up, I say, 'Well . . . would you like to do that now, then? Now that you have a whore of your own in your bed?'

Luca stares at me and then smiles. His eyes dance and he nods.

I open my eyes and then shut them again quickly: a thin blade of bright light, cutting through a narrow gap in the shutters, is lying across my face. I turn away from the window and reach out for Luca.

He's asleep, but at my touch, he smiles at me. 'I want you always to be here,' he says. 'Always be here with me. I don't ever want to wake alone in this bed again.'

'I don't intend ever again to sleep anywhere but where you are.'

Luca draws me in close. I curl up against him, my head on his shoulder, my legs bent up and draped over his knees. We lie like that for several long, drowsy moments. And then Luca says, 'Can I ask you something?'

Entirely unsuspecting, I reply, 'Of course. Anything.'

He pauses. 'How did you come by that scar on your back?'

I hold my breath. For a moment I am rocked by an image of Gianni's worried frown, as he asked almost the same question all those weeks ago, and remember my giddy inability even to contemplate the memory. But here, now, in Luca's arms, something extraordinary happens. I close my eyes and bring to mind what took place that day, and, although the pictures come promptly and are still vivid, it seems to me now as if that memory concerns someone else: it happened, yes, but not to me, and I find that I am recalling it dispassionately. I feel, strangely, a wash of detached compassion for the victim of that night's catastrophe, as though she were not me, but a friend – someone I knew well, I think, someone I liked, but in the end, someone who has moved on, out of my life. 'It was a long time ago,' I say. 'In another existence. A man I hardly knew. A man with rage in his heart and drink in his belly and a knife in his hand.'

Luca stares at me. Then, holding my shoulders, just as Gianni did that time, he turns me to lie on my front, and draws the covers away from me. I feel his fingers tracing along the line of puckered flesh for a few seconds, and then he too, like his son, bends and kisses my scar – once, twice, three times. His mouth is warm and dry and tender, and it seems to me now that these kisses complete in me the cataclysmic changes that his son's kiss began.

I turn back towards him.

'I love you, Luca,' I say.

He smiles. We look into each other's eyes, saying nothing, just drinking each other in. Then, 'Good,' Luca says. 'I'm so very glad you do. Because that's just as it should be.' He holds my face and kisses my mouth.

'Can I ask *you* something now,' I say.

'What, *cara*?'

'Does having the girls here make things difficult for you?'

He pulls back from me and props himself up on one elbow. 'Difficult? Why on earth do you say that? They're delightful – I love having them here! What do you mean, "difficult"?'

I hesitate. 'Because of Gianni and Carlo. Because they're your boys, and they were here and now they're not, but my children are. In their place.'

Luca takes my hand. 'Oh, *cara*, no. Don't think it for a second. Gianni is a young man, not a boy any more. I'd been thinking for some time that he was about ready to go off and explore the world. He'll be back – I am quite sure of it. And as for Carlo . . .' His face darkens a little. 'I think I lost Carlo a long time ago.'

I squeeze his fingers. He grips my hand more tightly and says, 'Don't ever underestimate my gratitude to you for what you did for Carlo. You, of all people. He didn't deserve it. You saved him from the sort of death no human being should ever even have to contemplate, despite what he had done to those girls of yours, and I'll never forget it.'

Neither of us speaks for several minutes. We lie next to each other, hands clasped, each lost in our own thoughts. Then Luca grabs me, rolls over with me until he is on his back and I am lying on top of him, and says, 'But now, there must be no more looking back. Understood?'

I nod.

'We must look forward. And the first thing we'll find when we do, is the visit of the Lavianos to this house this afternoon. Which, I have to admit, might not perhaps be the easiest of occasions.'

Sixty

The sun is already low, and the fire in the *sala* looks cheerful and welcoming. There is a knock at the door. Beata and Bella scrabble out of the room and down the stairs, bickering about who will open the door to the visitors. I lean out of the room to watch as they scuffle with each other on the threshold, but then Luca appears; he gently scoops them out of the way, and opens the door.

He is facing away from me, but I can hear the smile in his voice. 'Filippo, Maria – I'm so glad you could come. Come on in! Come upstairs.'

I watch the familiar bulky, silver-haired man being ushered into the house. His wife follows him, but, as she turns around and smiles at Luca, my mouth drops open. *Cazzo!* It's her! That sweet-natured creature who picked me off the cobbles outside San Giacomo and opened her heart to me so touchingly that day . . . *that* was Filippo's *wife*. Oh, dear God – what on earth am I going to say to her? And what will she say to me? Oh heavens, this is a nightmare! I wish I could speak to Luca before we all confront each other, but it's too late – they are on their way up the stairs.

Luca is shepherding them both up from the hallway and the twins are hopping from foot to foot on the steps below the visitors. I slip back into the *sala*, and cross to the fireplace, swallowing down a sickening feeling of dread.

'*Cara*, here are Filippo and Maria,' Luca says, as they all come into the room. He shows them in, and then runs back downstairs for wine and glasses.

'You are both very welcome,' I say a little hoarsely, a stiff smile fixed onto my face as though pinned there.

Filippo is smiling broadly and blustering a reply, but, just as mine did a moment ago, Maria's mouth has opened in shock. She stares at me, her eyes wide and her face pale, clearly dumb-struck.

'Francesca!' Filippo says, his voice sounding unnaturally hearty. 'You're looking well.'

'As are you, Filippo.'

He colours, but smiles. Reaching out a hand to Maria, he pulls her in close to him and puts a heavy arm around her shoulders. 'Francesca, this is my wife, Maria. Maria, this is Francesca. The new Signora della Rovere.'

Maria and I each manage a limp little smile.

I say, 'Come and sit down here, by the fire. It feels decidedly chilly to me.'

We all move across to where several chairs have been placed near the fireplace. Filippo helps Maria to sit, then seats himself next to her, taking her hand as he does so; my smile fades again as an awkward silence seems to fill the room. Even the twins sense it – they have curled up next to each other in one of the window recesses, and are now looking from me to the two visitors and back, cheek to cheek, wide-eyed and curious.

Luca appears then, with a large bottle of red wine and a basket of bread. He flicks a glance towards Filippo and Maria, then to me, and I can see a flash of understanding in his eyes – though he knows less than he thinks. Putting the bread and wine down on the table, he sits down in the chair next to mine, draws in a long breath and says, 'Filippo, Maria – you must be wondering about the happenings of the past few weeks.'

Filippo starts blustering, trying to absolve himself of being thought intrusive. But Luca holds up a hand, and Filippo stutters to silence. Luca says, 'Please, don't apologise. I'm sure that, were I in your position, I should be deeply curious.' His voice is warm and calm, and contains no accusation, and Filippo's tense shoulders relax a little. Luca continues. 'Of course *you* know what happened in the court, Filippo. We are so very grateful for your help, as you know.'

'Well . . . I . . . er . . .'

Luca opens his mouth to speak, and then he hesitates. Beckoning to the twins, he smiles as they scramble down and cross to stand in front of him. He takes one of each girl's hands. 'Can you run upstairs for a few moments, girls?' he says quietly. 'I want to talk to Signor and Signora di Laviano about something private. Mamma will call you when you can come back downstairs again.'

They both turn to me. I smile and nod, and, looking at each other with an expression that quite clearly shows their lack of appreciation at being thus removed from a potentially interesting situation, they nevertheless leave the room without comment. Their footsteps sound on the stairs, and then on the ceiling above our heads.

'I don't think that the details of some of the circumstances of these past days are really suitable for their ears,' Luca says to Filippo and Maria, who both nod. Luca says, 'Now. You know that Carlo has been . . . sent away from Napoli.'

Filippo's colour deepens again as he nods. He is looking quite hot and flustered now. Maria looks down at her lap and starts picking at the stuff of her skirt.

Luca pauses and then adds, 'But Maria, I doubt Filippo will have told you the truth about Carlo's case; he is far too discreet. But I'm sure you would prefer to know.' He draws in a breath and then says, 'Carlo was accused of murder. A murder he had quite certainly not committed.'

The silence that follows this is so complete that when Filippo shifts minutely in his chair, I can hear the soft sound of the cloth of his breeches rubbing against the wood.

Luca continues. 'I discovered that Carlo was facing the possibility of summary execution.' He stops. 'And of course, I feared the worst. You know, more that most, Filippo, of the intransigency of the Spanish in situations like this. But then . . . then . . . we had a stroke of luck.' He smiles at me. 'Francesca was able to speak with one of the Spanish, someone she . . . someone she . . . er . . . knows quite well – *Maestre* Vasquez.'

Filippo's colour deepens still further. He cannot meet my eye.

'And she was able,' Luca says, his voice *almost* steady, 'to persuade him to plead for Carlo on our behalf. We were very fortunate. Filippo – you were there – he must have pleaded effectively – for Carlo's sentence although not overturned, was commuted . . . to . . . to one of exile.' There is another pause. Luca's voice cracks now, and I reach across and take his hand as he says, 'My son has left the city. He has left the country, in fact, and is currently travelling, with . . . well, with an acquaintance who captains a small ship. I think they are heading for Africa. I don't . . . know when he'll be in Napoli again.' Another long silence. Then Luca says, 'Gianni's away too.' His voice sounds a little stronger as he adds, 'But he, on the other hand, should not be gone too long.' He manages a smile. 'He's in Roma, taking a break from his studies. He's looking for temporary work, and I expect him to visit in a few months.'

This of course is all true, but Luca's many omissions feel like screaming lies to me.

We all try hard to talk after that, but, as in those dreams where you try to run with leaden legs that grow heavier and less mobile at every step, each word we utter now seems to leave our mouths sluggishly and to be taking too much time to reach the ears of the listeners.

After a moment or two, Luca says to me, 'Shall we bring the girls down now?' and I know he is hoping that their lively and innocent ignorance will freshen the atmosphere in the room. I call up the stairs to them, and within seconds, they have clattered down and burst back into the *sala*, quite obviously hoping to pick up clues as to what they have missed whilst banished to their room. Luca holds out the basket of bread for them to hand to the guests.

It seems, though, that bread in baskets in this room is never very secure . . . in her enthusiastic struggle to be the one to hold the basket, Beata stumbles and knocks most of the pieces out onto the floor; Bella snorts in derision at her sister's incompetence, they both begin to giggle as they pick up what has spilled, and the stifling oppression that Luca's truths have spun between the four adults in the room lifts a little. Well, that's not entirely true: the men begin to talk more freely, but between Maria and me, that day at San Giacomo stands like a great buttressed rampart. I have no idea how to broach the subject, though, in front of Luca and Filippo, without embarrassing Maria.

And then an idea occurs to me.

Reaching out a hand towards Maria, I say, 'Perhaps you would care to come with me to the kitchen – I want to cut up some more bread, seeing as my girls have laid waste to so much of what I had prepared before. I'd be grateful for some help.'

There is another snuffle of laughter from the window ledge where the girls are once more ensconced.

Maria glances at the twins, then smiles and nods. 'I should like that,' she says, shyly.

I pick up the basket, and we leave the *sala* together. The men and the girls watch us go, and I hear the hum of conversation resume as we cross to the kitchen.

Tipping the spoiled bread out into a basket of rubbish, and taking a couple of fresh loaves out of an earthenware crock, I look across at Maria. This has to be done. If we are ever to establish any sort of communication between us, one of us has to say something, and I don't believe she is going to have the courage – I'm not sure how to do it myself, come to that – but I have to try. After a long and difficult pause, I manage to say, 'I had no idea, when we met before, that . . . that you were Filippo's wife.'

Maria's face reddens. She starts twisting the fingers of one hand with those of the other, staring down at them, and avoiding my eye.

I say, 'I'm still so grateful to you, for your kindness that day, outside the church.'

She frowns. 'I couldn't just have walked on and left you in pain on the ground.'

'A fair number of other people managed to do just that, as I'm sure you saw.'

'Perhaps they did, but it seemed unchristian to me.'

'You helped me . . . even though you had realised . . . my profession.'

She blushes scarlet and does not reply.

I hold her gaze and say, 'Maria, I need to tell you . . . I'm no longer what I used to be. That part of my life is over. For ever. And Luca knows my history. He and I have no secrets from each other.'

Maria stares at me for a full minute. She seems to want to speak,

483

but, just as on that first occasion, she opens her mouth several times and closes it before she manages to utter a word. 'You and Filippo seem to know each other quite well. How is that?' she says. 'He hasn't told me.'

Oh, God.

My face feels stiff and the hair on the back of my neck lifts.

I think my silence answers her question very clearly – she bites her lip and stares at me, saying nothing. Then I give her the actual truth. 'I was introduced to him several years ago by a mutual friend, a man called Stefano di Morello. Perhaps you know him.' Put so simply, it sounds innocent. Of course, I don't add that Stefano had been one of my first patrons, and that he had told me that, in his opinion, if Filippo didn't get a fuck within a couple of weeks, he, Stefano, thought that his friend might well explode. But then I don't need to say it. Maria knows all too well. She continues to stare at me, her expression unreadable.

Then she looks down at her fingers and says, 'It's very strange. I had thought before that if I were ever to meet the woman Filippo was seeing, I would hate her. When I sat there in my chamber, week after week, knowing full well what he was doing while he was away from the house, I would often plan that meeting. I would imagine the things I wanted to say to her, things that would make very clear just how much I loathed her.' She meets my eye again. 'But now, face to face with that woman – with you – I find that I can't do it. It would be wrong. After everything you've done for me . . .' Struggling with herself for a moment, she then adds, 'And after everything I know you did for Filippo.'

'He's always loved you. Very much,' I say. 'Never me. It was never like that.'

She regards me steadily for a long moment and then says, 'Yes, I know that now. And I know too, that without you, I might have lost him.' She pauses. 'I want you to know that I did all the things you told me to do that day. And they had the effects that you suggested they might.' She hesitates again and then says, quietly, 'I'm very grateful.'

I put my hands over my face. Her candour and sweet-natured forgiveness after everything I have done are almost unbearable, but within seconds, I feel her fingers on my wrists. She pulls my hands away from my eyes, and puts her arms around me. I hold her, too and for several seconds we stand pressed close to each other, in an unexpected gesture of friendship, mutely acknowledging each other's pain and fallibility.

Then the door to the kitchen opens, and Bella says, 'What on earth are you doing, Mamma? Luca says where's the bread?'

Sixty-one

As December ended its first week, the weather was damp and cold. That morning the sky had been heavily overcast and by mid afternoon it was raining hard. Luca, his teaching over for the day, walked fast, his shoulders hunched against the chilly winter downpour. Dust-laden rivulets were running between the cobbles, merging together at the sides of the road to form grubby little streams and, even though he was taking care to avoid the worst of it, Luca's boots were waterlogged, and his feet were frozen.

He ran the last few yards to the house, fumbled the latch, then stepped gratefully indoors and closed the door behind him. Shaking his dripping hair back from his face, he stripped off his doublet, which now smelled like a wet dog, sat down on the bottom stair and eased off his boots. Then he squelched across the stone flags and up the stairs in his wet hose, carrying both doublet and boots into the kitchen. Two cats slithered out of the room as he came in. The doublet he hung on a hook, then he turned to where a row of six upright sticks, some inches apart, were set into a heavy stand on the floor near the fireplace. Each stick was about two feet high, and each had a carved round wooden ball a couple of inches in diameter at the top. Turning the boots upside down, Luca placed them over two of the sticks, intending them to dry in the warmer air near the fire. One had a worn patch on the sole, he saw now, and he determined to remember to have it repaired. He picked the laces of his breeches undone, stepped out of them and peeled off his hose. He laid all these items over the back of a chair in front of the fire and, clad now only in his shirt, and feeling thoroughly chilled, he stood for a moment with his back to the flames, enjoying the feeling of the heat against his cold buttocks. After a moment or two, he padded across to the stairs and climbed another flight to the bedchamber to find some dry clothes.

His new wife's belongings were evident throughout the house now, Luca thought, smiling to himself as he pulled fresh hose and breeches from a chest by the door and then sat down on his bed to put them on. She was not very tidy. Her combs and hairpins were in a red glass bowl on the window ledge, though some had been left scattered along the ledge and others had fallen onto the floor below. Luca now picked these up and replaced them in the bowl. On a table nearby, a miniature chest of painted drawers held earrings and ribbons and other items of jewellery, many of which had not been put fully away and now protruded and dangled from the part-opened drawers.

Luca crouched down, opened the lid of a large wooden chest that stood against the wall furthest from the door and ran his fingers over the stuff of the dresses and shifts that lay folded within, aware as he did so of a wisp of Francesca's faint scent. He closed his eyes for a second and breathed her in, feeling a giddying rush of love for this extraordinary creature who had so utterly changed his life. Then, pushing his feet into a dry pair of shoes, he picked a soft sleeveless woollen doublet from a hook on the wall near the bed, shrugged it on, and ran down the stairs, intending to prepare something for their evening meal.

He was still not used to Luigi's absence.

It was little more than three weeks since the old man had

succumbed – in a matter of days – to what Luca had at first thought no more than a slight chill. Luca's genuine grief at Luigi's demise – he had, after all, been part of the Rovere family's domestic life for nearly thirty years – had been somewhat tainted by a wash of guilty relief that the whole issue of what to do with the ailing old servant had been thus forcibly sorted. He and Francesca had managed the house between them in the weeks since, with the occasional help of Francesca's enormous and supremely gifted cook, Lorenzo. On the days when Lorenzo came in and prepared their meals, they dined like kings, Luca thought, but he had to admit that he preferred the days when he and Francesca worked side by side in the kitchen, peeling vegetables, chopping meat and coaxing the frequently reluctant fire to a suitable level of ferocity to cook whatever it was they were planning. And the little girls were fast becoming proficient housekeepers in their own right.

He glanced out of the window, trying to assess the time. The light was fading – it was probably some time past five, he thought, wondering how long it would be before Francesca returned home. The house seemed very empty without her.

Maria pulled her hood up over her head, and held her cloak out to one side as she ran, offering cover to one of the twins – she was unsure which one. The child ducked in underneath the makeshift shelter and pressed in against her, little fingers gripping the stuff of Maria's dress, her rain-soaked head at roughly the height of Maria's armpit. 'Better?' Maria gasped. They bumped together as they ran awkwardly.

'It's all gone down the back of my neck!' the girl said breathlessly, her voice quivering somewhere between laughter and tears.

'Quick! In here!' Francesca, hand in hand with her other daughter and with Serafina Parisetto's younger son on one hip, ran past, ducking under a low lintel into a short, vaulted passage. The baby was wailing. 'We can wait in here – come on, Serafina, quick!'

Serafina and the older boy scurried in behind Francesca, and Serafina reached across to take the baby from her. They all seven huddled close, peering out at the teeming water that was now cascading off the roofs and parapets and splattering down onto the cobbles in front of them. Both Benedetto, the baby, and Paolo, the older boy, were now crying, and Serafina clucked and shushed, jiggling the smaller boy in her arms.

'Beata, where's the basket?' Francesca asked.

'Here, Mamma.'

'Quickly, look in it now, and get out a sugar pig for each of you.'

Beata crouched down, reached into the raffia basket she had been carrying, and, pushing her hands down into a jumble of fruit, vegetables, bread and other oddments, pulled out a pair of bright pink lumps of sugar each about the size of her fist and shaped vaguely like a rudimentary pig. A short length of twine protruded from one end of each, like tails. She handed one each to the two little boys. The crying stopped as if plugged tight with a spigot. Two pairs of eyes widened and little hands stretched out to take their treats. Beata went back to the basket, found two more pigs, handed one to her sister and began to lick the last one herself.

'That's better,' Francesca said, smiling at the four children who were now all busy with their treasures. Benedetto had his pig in both hands, he was twiddling the twine tail around one shrimp-like forefinger, and his mouth was stretched so wide in an attempt to fit the head of the pig into it in its entirety, that his face looked quite distorted. Serafina kissed the top of his head.

*

There was a knock at the door. Luca ran downstairs to answer, expecting Francesca, but instead, a young man stood on the door sill, a dirty sack draped around his shoulders to keep off the rain. He reached under the sack and brought out a sealed letter. 'For you, Signore,' he said with a curt jerk of the head.

As soon as Luca had relieved him of the missive, the boy turned on his heel and stumbled off up the street, his outline blurred and indistinct in the wet.

Frowning, Luca climbed the stairs to his study, breaking the seal of the letter and shaking it open as he went. Once in the study, he rummaged under several sheets of paper on his table until he found his spectacles; he stood still in the middle of the room and read for a moment. A wide smile stretched across his face. He returned to the kitchen, his eyes still on his letter; when he had finished rereading it for the third time, he tucked it behind a candlestick on a shelf near the fireplace and put his spectacles in his breeches pocket.

The Angelus had just struck and it was already almost dark. The rain was still heavy and Luca was just beginning to feel anxious. They had been gone too long. He riddled the fire in the kitchen with the poker, startling a cat, who had been sleeping on a nearby stool, wiped his hands on his breeches and put a lid on the large pot of soup he had made. Briefly registering that it smelled more appetizing than his usual attempts, he crossed to the window and peered out into the street below, but, with the room brightly candlelit, he could see nothing but his own reflection, distorted in the flawed glass. He pushed his hands into his breeches pockets and began to pace the kitchen.

Several minutes passed. The fire crackled, the lid of the soup pot sighed and lifted occasionally and little spat-out gobbets hissed as they hit the flames. Luca's shoes scuffed softly on the wooden floor as he crossed back and forth; he told himself he was being foolish, but nonetheless kept pacing.

And then the door downstairs rattled and opened, the sound of voices, breathless with wet and cold and tiredness, filled the hallway, and Luca huffed out his relief, pushing his fingers through his hair. Quickly taking the lid back off the pot, he picked up a long spoon and a handful of parsley, and bent over to inspect his soup, embarrassed now about his anxiety and intending to look happily occupied when they all came upstairs.

'Luca?' Francesca called up the stairs. 'We're back. A trio of drowned rats. Maria and Serafina and the boys have all gone home.'

'I'm in the kitchen. Are you *very* wet?'

'We're *soaking*!' This from one of the girls – more a shriek than an answer. 'Even our shifts are wet!'

'My feet are frozen!'

'Come up and get changed, all of you.'

Noisy feet on the stairs. The slap of sodden skirts on walls and floor. Gasping laughter from the children as they scrambled on up past the kitchen, calling out their greetings on their way up to the next floor. Francesca appeared at the door to the kitchen, holding her arms out sideways and displaying to Luca the extent of her saturation. 'Look! Look at me!' she said, laughing.

Luca looked.

Her hair hung around her face, lank and heavy with rain. Her dress and coat were clinging to her legs, and a dark tide-mark like a meandering coastline stood out around her skirt at about the level of her knees. Coming close, Luca saw that raindrops were glittering in her eyelashes.

'You need to get those wet things off,' he said, tilting her chin with a finger, and kissing her mouth, which was damp and cold against his fire-hot face.

'Want to help me?'

Luca's insides shifted. He grinned, but jerked his head up towards the ceiling. 'I should love to, but we have company.'

'Mmm.' Francesca lifted an eyebrow. 'What a nuisance. I'll have to do it by myself, then.'

Luca picked up the sodden laces of her bodice and pulled the knot undone. 'I'll help you with your dry clothes later on, though. When the "company" has gone to sleep.'

'I'll look forward to that.' Francesca kissed him again, then turned to leave the room. Luca watched her. As she reached the door and pulled it wide, a candle sputtered in the draft and caught his attention; behind the candlestick he saw the letter he had received earlier that evening. 'Oh – before you go . . .' he said.

Her hand on the door jamb, she leaned back into the room. 'What?'

'A letter arrived an hour or so ago.'

'Who from?'

'Gianni.' Luca paused. He smiled. 'He says he thinks he'll be home in time for Christmas.'

Francesca stepped back into the kitchen. 'Oh, Luca – I'm so pleased!'

'He's met a girl, he says.'

'What?'

'The daughter of some well-to-do notary in Roma, apparently.'

'That's wonderful!'

'Well – when I say "met", I'm not entirely sure they've spoken to each other yet. From what he writes, I don't think it's been much more than a case of making doe-eyes at each other so far, with the young lady up in her father's *sala* peering out of the window, and

Gianni sighing in the street below like a lovesick dog. But we'll no doubt hear all about it at Christmas.'

Francesca smiled.

Looking forward to imparting his next piece of news, Luca said, 'But that's not all.'

'Why? What is it?'

'Look.' He held out the letter. 'See for yourself. See who else he met in Roma.'

He watched her read, a frown puckering the skin between her brows. A few drips from her hair fell onto the paper. Then, feeling his own smile stretch, Luca saw Francesca's mouth fall open as she reached the bottom of the page. She looked up at him. 'Oh, Luca. Do you think he'll come too – with Gianni?' she said.

'He might. If he's ready. And if he does . . . he'll be very welcome.'

Francesca crossed the room back to where he stood; Luca put his arms around her and she hugged him fiercely; her dress was cold and wet and smelled of evening air, and her hair lay chill against his cheek. The dampness began to seep through to his skin. Taking her by the shoulders, he kissed her and said, 'Go on, go and get changed. You're making me wet. And then we can all sit down and have something to eat.'

She held tight for another few seconds, and then stood back. 'I'll be down in a moment,' she said.

Acknowledgements

A huge thank you to my lovely editors, Rebecca Saunders and Louise Davies for their tender and expert care of my book – and of me. Also thank you to my ever-wise agent, Judith Murray and to my very special dedicatees, Cathy Mosely and Sahra Gott.

Once again I was amazed by the generosity of the people who offered help, advice and expertise as I was writing *The Courtesan's Lover*. The first five chapters of the book (as they then were) formed my dissertation for the MA in Creative Writing I did at the University of Chichester – heartfelt thanks are due to Karen Stevens, my dissertation tutor. My writing-group friends – Annie Thomson, Chloe White, Mandy Park and Becky Paton – work-shopped sections of the book with great insight and honesty – as ever, I'm very grateful. David Dorning, from the department of Book Conservation at West Dean College, conducted an unprecedented experiment into the burning of vellum-bound books for me. Gordon Frye instructed me in Renaissance military matters with considerable expertise and great humour. Stuart Martell helped with all things seafaring (and hid his astonishment at my initial ignorance with great tact). Lesley Davies, the curator of Tutbury Castle Museum, in Staffordshire, was very helpful in the matter of unravelling the intricacies of sixteenth-century methods of contraception. Barry Stone is an expert on the history of the *castrati* in the Renaissance, and he was extremely generous with his store of fascinating information. Larry Ray, speleologist, told me about the extraordinary underworld network of caverns that lies beneath the city of Naples – the *sottosuolo*. Afifah Hamilton, medical herbalist, kindly advised me on first aid treatments of the period.

A number of books were also invaluable:

Courtesans – Katie Hickman (Harper Perennial 2004)
The Book of the Courtesans – Susan Griffin (Pan 2001)
The Adventures of Captain Alonso de Contreras – trans. Philip Dallas (Paragon House 1989)
Crime, Society and the Law in Renaissance Italy – Ed. Trevor Dean and K. J. P. Lowe (CUP 1994)
The Ship – Björn Landström (Allen and Unwin 1961)
Sex Work – Writings by Women in the Sex Industry – Eds Frederique Delacoste and Priscilla Alexander (Cleis Press 1987)
Daily Life in Renaissance Italy – Elizabeth Cohen and Thomas Cohen (Greenwood Press 2001)
Inside the Renaissance House – Elizabeth Currie (V&A Publications 2006)

If you enjoyed *The Courtesan's Lover*,
read on for an exclusive author interview
and a list of discussion points

Exclusive Q&A with Gabrielle Kimm

What decided you on writing a sequel to *His Last Duchess*?

The Courtesan's Lover isn't really a 'sequel', in that there's no plot progression from one book to the other, but I suppose it could be described as a 'spin off'. Francesca was a secondary character in the first book, but she has taken centre stage here. When I had finished writing *His Last Duchess*, I felt that I had discovered all I needed to know about almost all my characters. I was happy to let them go, and to leave them to their own devices. I say 'almost' . . . Francesca Felizzi just wouldn't go quietly! She kept intruding into my thinking, and demanding to be listened to, and over a number of weeks it began to dawn on me that I was going to have to give her a book of her own. I knew that she had escaped from Ferrara and set off for Napoli, but other than that, I didn't really know too much about her plans at that point.

Was it hard to get into the mind of a courtesan?

In some ways it wasn't at all difficult to get into Francesca's mind – I knew her well before I began even planning *The Courtesan's Lover*, and I was already very familiar with how she thinks and feels about things. But the minutiae of the life of a courtesan and how that would impact upon Francesca's thinking and emotions was something new for me, and it took a fair amount of research.

I began by reading up about the lives of the more famous courtesans: Katie Hickman and Susan Griffin have both written excellent books about the subject, and their accounts were both fascinating and entertaining. The more I read, the more interesting became the possibilities for the ways in which my novel might unfold. What really struck me as extraordinary was the fact that many of these women were basically what amounted to independent entrepreneurs, in a world where women in general had almost no autonomy, either socially, sexually or financially.

Fascinating though this was, it didn't seem quite enough, in terms of truly getting under Francesca's skin, so I also researched into the lives, experiences and opinions of women in the modern sex industry, trying to get my head around the psychology of how these girls survive in such a challenging, dangerous environment. I felt quite humbled by much of what I read.

What were the most interesting factors in your research?
Oh, I have learned SO much over the course of researching this novel. It's strange how these things turn out: in the process of uncovering the motivations of my character Modesto (originally planned as little more than an 'extra'), I found out all about the *castrati* – the appalling tragedy of the thousands and thousands of little boys who were castrated over the course of a couple of centuries, to keep them as lifelong soprano singers. That was gruesomely fascinating and ultimately very revealing about Modesto as a person. Because of what I discovered, Modesto burst out of his original parameters, and became a fundamentally important character in the narrative.

I spent a lovely day at West Dean College, near Chichester, in the book conservation department, with conservator David Dorning. I felt enormously privileged, because, not only did I see some beautiful sixteenth-century books, and learn how they were made, I also saw and handled some *brand-new* sixteenth-century books! David's students were actually making books as they would have been made at that time, so I saw books that looked as they would have looked to my characters – pristine and fresh and unused. David was great – I asked him what would happen to a vellum-bound book if you burned it, and after having expressed surprise ('as someone who conserves books, I've never actually tried deliberately destroying one . . .') he then set about trying it out to see, and recording his findings for me.

Through the wonders of the Internet, I met a lovely man called Gordon Frye, an American who has taught me a great deal about both the Spanish and Italian armies in the sixteenth century – and the depth of his knowledge is exceeded only by the generosity with which he shares it.

And then, possibly most unexpectedly, thanks to an marvellous woman called Lesley Smith, I discovered how women in the sixteenth century tackled the problem of contraception. Erm . . . with citrus fruit.

Is sixteenth-century Italy a particular love of yours?
It is now. *His Last Duchess* was set in Renaissance Italy because of Browning's poem. Browning's monologue, *My Last Duchess*, which inspired my first novel, is narrated by the fifth duke of Ferrara, so, when I decided to tell the back story to that poem, the setting and era of my novel were dictated for me. I was landed in Ferrara, in 1559. As *The Courtesan's Lover* continues that story, I remained in the same era, though the location has shifted a few hundred miles. There is a great vitality and passion about both the country and the era, I've found – an intensity of colours and sounds and tastes and personalities which makes for a most pleasing setting for a novel.

Will you stay with Renaissance Italy in the future?

I may well come back to it, but the new novel I have just started writing is set in Paris, towards the end of the seventeenth century, so I'm in the process of discovering a whole raft of *new* sights and sounds and tastes and smells and social niceties. Lovely! I'm really enjoying it.

What about writing practices? Are you one of those writers who needs a strict routine? So many words a day, come what may?

Absolutely not. Probably the easiest way to explain how I work is just to say that I write in every moment in which I don't have to do anything else. (And quite often I write in many of those moments in which I ought to be doing something else, too.) That might be no more than editing a single paragraph or perfecting a phrase on one day, or writing flat out for six hours and completing a whole chapter on another. But come what may, I write something every day. I am not teaching so much these days – no more than a couple of days a week on the supply lists – so I am able to devote at least three full clear days a week to my writing, which feels like a great privilege.

Reading Group Questions

In an age where women had virtually no rights and no power, the life of a courtesan must have seemed to virtuous women to be in some ways enviable – after all, the courtesans possessed the sort of sexual and social freedom not generally available to women until the 1960s. What are your thoughts on this?

Francesca and Luca each feel they have failed as parents in some ways. Are they right to think this?

Why do you think Francesca is so instantly drawn to Luca?

How far do you think Francesca's abusive childhood experiences led to her choosing a life as a courtesan?

Maria and Francesca's experiences of sex are utterly polarised. But are there any similarities? In what ways do they help each other?

Will Modesto ever come back to Napoli?

Francesca tells Maria to write, as a cathartic exercise to help her to break her out of her self-imposed prison. Have you ever tried writing as a means of escape, and if you have, have you found it helpful?

Will Gianni ever be able to cope with living back at home with his father and Francesca?

What do you think will happen to Carlo? Do you feel sorry for him in any way?

If you had to describe Francesca in three words, what would they be, and why?